DOG DAY

Alicia Giménez-Bartlett

DOG DAY

*Translated from the Spanish
by Nicholas Caistor*

Europa
editions

Europa Editions
116 East 16th Street
12th floor
New York, N.Y. 10003
www.europaeditions.com
info@europaeditions.com

Copyright © 1997 by Alicia Giménez-Bartlett
First Publication 2006 by Europa Editions

Translation by Nicholas Caistor
Original Title: *Día de perros*
Translation copyright © 2006 by Europa Editions

Library of Congress Cataloging in Publication Data is available
ISBN 1-933372-14-1

Giménez-Bartlett, Alicia
Día de perros

Book design by Emanuele Ragnisco
www.mekkanografici.com

Printed in Italy
Arti Grafiche La Moderna – Rome

CONTENTS

DOG DAY

1.

Some days start in a very strange way. You wake up, realize who you are, get out of bed, make yourself a coffee . . . and yet somehow the horizon of the future stretches out in front of you far beyond the day ahead. Without looking ahead, you see. After that, everything begins to take on the same prophetic, quintessential tone. "Something's going to happen," you tell yourself, and you leave home already alert, on guard, open to any possibility; you cast a watchful eye on the reality around you. That morning for example, which seemed perfectly ordinary, I ran into an old lady, a neighbor of mine, on the doorstep. She said hello, then immediately launched into an interminable monologue which ended with her mentioning that my house in Poble Nou had once been a brothel.

After hearing this, I spent some time examining my house with great curiosity. I suppose I was trying to catch some echo of ancient passions played out years earlier within those walls. No such luck: perhaps the alterations I had made were just too drastic: the workmen had probably walled up all the lust, the painters whitewashed any remaining traces of carnal pleasure. It's quite possible that my search for traces of the former house of ill repute was the expression of an unconscious desire for some fresh stimulus in my life. That would not surprise me one bit. For the past two years, work, reading, music and gardening had been my only amusements. I was not too concerned, because after two divorces, boredom can come to seem like peace. And yet, for the first time in two years, discovering the existence of that earlier place had stirred something up inside me, forcing me to ask myself whether I wasn't taking my desire for solitude a little too far.

That mental wake-up call did not have any immediate consequences for my life. Destiny always manages to nullify those impulses which might lead to a personal revolution, and my own destiny suggested I was going to stay on the rails for the foreseeable future. I stopped asking myself awkward questions about long-dead passions. It did not take such a great effort, in fact it was easy, as all my energies were soon taken up by work. Did that mean a lot of files to sort out in the archives? Not at all—that kind of work would not have absorbed my attention any longer than was strictly necessary. No, what happened was that Sergeant Garzón and I found ourselves embarking on another case together. Far more than the existence of the phantom brothel, this explained the strange feeling of that morning. I have to admit it wasn't much of a case at first, but soon it became so complex that in the end it turned into something unprecedented in the annals of modern police history.

I should also say that even though Sergeant Garzón and I had already become good friends, we only ever met in the bar across the street from the police station. Our friendship was on a strictly professional footing, with no dinners or evenings at the movies to help us get to know each other better. Yet we had drunk enough coffees together in that shabby bar to keep a templeful of Buddhist monks wide awake.

Garzón was not particularly thrilled at the kind of case we had been assigned, but he was pleased we would be seeing some action together again. As seemed to be becoming a habit, we were given the case because all our colleagues were up to their eyes in work. We would have to have been very stupid not to clear up something which at first glance looked as if it was "the same old routine." Nor did the way the chief inspector presented things make it seem anything too extraordinary: "It's some guy," he said, "who's taken a real hammering." There was no indication we might need a star detective from Scotland Yard to solve the mystery; but there were at least three questions that needed answering. First: who was the victim? As he wasn't carrying any means of identification on him. Second, why had he been beaten up? And third, who had attacked him?

At first, it seemed we might merely be trying to sort out what had happened in a street brawl, but when the chief inspector added that the man had been sent to the Valle Hebrón hospital, where he was in a coma, we realized that the hammering had been with nails included. This was not a drunken brawl, it was a thorough working-over.

On the way to the hospital, Garzón was still as chirpy as he had been when we were first given the case. He was so happy, it was as if we were about to go on a picnic rather than start an investigation. I realized that until we actually came face-to-face with the man in the coma, Garzón would only see reasons to be cheerful: we were working together once more, and the laurels from the success of our first case were still relatively fresh. I was flattered; it's not every day you get an offer of friendship, even if it's from a paunchy policeman well into his fifties.

The Valle Hebrón hospital is one of those monstrosities built in the sixties by the Social Services. Ugly, huge, threatening, it looks more like a pharaoh's tomb than somewhere for treating ordinary people. We climbed the central staircase and soon found ourselves among the typical hospital population: people from the countryside, limping old folk, women cleaners, and clusters of medical staff. I felt a bit lost in this huge nine-story warren, uncertain of who to ask or where to go to find my way inside the colossus. Fortunately, my colleague Garzón has the soul of a bureaucrat, and this enabled him to see clearly what steps we had to take. He was completely at ease among all those gloomy marble corridors. "We need to see the person in charge of the unit," he said, "and find out who admitted the victim into emergency." I was amazed: it was as though we had some kind of magic charm which opened all the doors to the ogre's lair, without once having to go back because we had taken a wrong turn. Eventually, a tall nurse built like a brick wall led us to our destination.

"You'd better have a look at the poor man while I go and get his file and find out who was on duty that night."

We went into a room with three beds. Our man was in the left-hand one; a tangle of tubes protruded from his inert body. He was silent, pale, and motionless as a corpse. I am so obsessed by recumbent figures, especially sculptures, that it took me some time to focus on his features. Every time I come across one of those flat stone slabs of Charles the Fifth, the lovers of Teruel, or the Duke of Alba, a shudder of awe sends a shiver down my spine. But this prone figure had neither a sense of nobility nor the charisma of a national hero about him. He looked more like a small, mangled bird or a run-over cat. Gaunt, and short in stature, he lay with his misshapen, coarse hands spread out on the bedsheet. His face was swollen from the blows he had received, there was a huge bruise over one eyebrow, and his lips were streaked with flecks of dried blood.

"Quite a sight," I said.

"He's really taken a beating."

"Do you think it was a fight?"

"If it was, it doesn't look as though he defended himself. Besides, a fight creates a fuss—there would have been witnesses."

"What does the police patrol report say?"

"Unidentified male, no papers on him. Found in Calle Llobregós in the Carmelo neighborhood, at three A.M. No witnesses to the attack. No evidence or leads. Immediately transferred to Valle Hebrón, where he was admitted to emergency."

"In other words, nothing."

The man had bright red hair, most probably dyed. It was difficult to make out what he might have looked like under normal circumstances. The nurse came back with the doctor who had been on duty the night he was admitted. He took us into a tiny, ramshackle office. He did not seem particularly impressed that we were from the police.

"I'll read you the admission report," he said, putting on a pair of heavy tortoiseshell glasses that contrasted sharply with his juvenile appearance. "Admitted in the early hours of October 17. Male patient, approximately forty years old. No distinguishing features. On admission, showed multiple traumas to the face and concussion. Not caused by traffic accident. Condition probably the result of having been struck repeatedly with a hard, heavy object. Emergency operation carried out in theater. Currently under observation in a coma. Drip-fed by saline solution. Prognosis: critical."

"Do you think he'll regain consciousness?"

The doctor shrugged.

"You can never tell. He could come around, he could die tomorrow, or he could carry on like this for ages."

"Has anyone asked after him, or been to see him?"

"Not so far."

"If anyone should come . . . "

"We'll inform you."

"And, if possible, keep them here until we arrive."

"Don't raise your hopes too high. Lots of people die in here without anyone ever coming to bear witness to the fact that they've even existed."

"Can you show us the clothes he was wearing?"

He took us to a storeroom that looked like a lost-and-found office. Our man's things were in a plastic bag with a number sewn on it. There weren't many of them: a pair of filthy jeans, an orange shirt with traces of blood on it, a jerkin and a thick chain of solid gold. His shoes—a pair of worn-out trainers—were in a separate bag. There were no socks.

"This flashy piece of jewelry shows he must have been a vulgar type," I said, snobbish as could be.

"And that robbery wasn't the motive for the attack. That piece of junk must be worth a lot of money," Garzón added.

I turned to the woman in charge of the storeroom.

"Wasn't there anything in the pockets—coins or keys?"

This question must have struck her as unfortunate, because she replied bad-temperedly:

"Look here, everything he had on him is right there in front of you. Nobody touches anything in here."

It's something I've seen a thousand times. It's harder not to offend your average Spanish worker than it is to walk past Niagara Falls without getting wet.

As we made for the exit of this crumbling imperial palace, we could already draw our first conclusions. The victim was just a poor devil. Whoever attacked him was not interested in robbing him, but they did want to empty his pockets. Either they didn't want us to identify him or they were looking for something in particular. The victim must have been mixed up in some shady business because otherwise, to judge by his appearance, he could never have had enough money to buy that gold chain.

"Would you like me to solve the case for you, inspector?" Garzón suddenly said.

"Go right ahead, my dear Watson!"

"It's obvious this was an act of revenge, a settling of accounts. And from what we've seen of the guy, it doesn't look as though we're talking about high Mafia finance. No, we have to aim lower than that. I'd be prepared to bet that drugs are involved: that's what it usually is. This poor wretch is a common or garden-variety dealer who got out of line. They decided to teach him a lesson, and lost control. A case like a thousand others."

"There's probably a file on him then," I suggested.

"Either as a pusher or for some minor offense."

"When will we get the fingerprint results?"

"This afternoon."

"Fine, sergeant, so according to you we can start singing 'case closed.'"

"Don't reach for your throat spray just yet. If it's as I said, it'll be up to others to claim success. Another department deals with drug cases, and they don't let anyone else take the credit. They'll have a quick look, and if this guy isn't mixed up in anything really serious, they'll file the whole thing. So what, one pusher less in this jungle?"

I didn't doubt for a moment that he was right. Not because I had developed a blind faith in his skills as a detective, more that his line of reasoning seemed correct. So did his conclusion . . . who would miss a pusher in this world? Daisies were all he was going to push up now, and not a single real drug dealer would pay for it. And perhaps the case would be taken out of our hands that very afternoon.

"What now?"

"Now we need to take a look at El Carmelo, Petra. We can inspect the area, talk to the locals. Then we can call the fingerprint lab from the restaurant while we're having lunch to see if they've identified him and we have to go back and question people. That's all I can think of."

El Carmelo is an odd working-class neighborhood in Barcelona. Clinging to a hilltop, its narrow streets give the impression you're in a small village. Although the houses are very poor, it is somehow more inviting than the wastelands on the city outskirts, with their orderly lines of huge, deathly apartment blocks next to the railway or highway. There were no restaurants as such, but lots of bars where we could have lunch. They were all for workmen, all decorated according to the whim of their lackadaisical proprietors, and all gave off the choking smell of fried oil. I tried to suggest to Garzón that we could make do with a snack standing at a counter somewhere, but he turned on me as if I had offended Honor, God and the Fatherland all in one.

"You know if I don't eat something hot I get a headache."

"I didn't say a word, Fermín, let's eat whatever you want."

"You'll like these bars, they're full of workmen, they're really democratic."

We proved our democratic credentials by going into a bar on Calle Dante called El Barril. The tables Garzón was so keen to sit at were not individual but communal ones. You sat elbow to elbow with a stranger just like in the smartest restaurants of the Quartier Latin.

The customers entered the bar in groups, most of them wearing different-colored overalls according to their line of work. They sat at seats reserved for them by habit, and greeted the two of us as they must always do with people who were not regulars.

Almost at once bowls of soup, bean stews, Russian salads and cauliflowers au gratin made their appearance. The general hubbub indicated that the customers were pretty hungry and pretty content. There was laughter, jokes were swapped between tables, and only occasionally did they glance almost absentmindedly up at a television going uselessly full blast in one corner.

All in all, it was a very pleasant, even enviable place, which gave rise to lots of gastronomic camaraderie. There was only one flaw in this tiny paradise of solidarity. I was the only woman.

Garzón had quickly adapted himself to his surroundings. He was attacking his cauliflower with gusto, sipping his wine, and when the sports news came on the TV and the whole place went quiet, he too sat looking bewitched by the sight of goals being scored or clever passing of the ball. Soon, he was even

exchanging comments with the burly man sitting next to him;
the two of them agreed that one of the trainers was no more
than a "bandit." I felt boundless admiration at Garzón's abili-
ty to blend in so naturally with his surroundings.

We drank a good cup off coffee among the remains of bread
rolls and crumpled-up paper napkins. It was only when his
hunger had been sated that Garzón got up and went round the
bar asking everyone if they knew anything about the attack
that had taken place in the neighborhood. Nothing doing.
Then he called the lab. He returned almost at once, but I
couldn't tell from his expression what the outcome was.

"Damn it!"

"What's wrong?"

"There's no record on the guy."

"You've oversimplified. Besides, why were we so quick to
see him as a crook? For the moment, he's only the victim."

"I'd be really surprised if he wasn't a criminal."

"Perhaps he's one who isn't on file yet."

"Nearly all the little sons of bitches like him have been,
inspector."

We left the bar and headed for number 65 Calle Llobregós.
It was close to here that the body had been found. A first
glance didn't reveal anything particularly interesting: shop
doorways, a shoe-repair place, and further on a wine store
where they sold wine straight from the barrel. Everyone in the
area knew about the macabre incident, but as they had all told
the uniformed branch, nobody knew the man who had been
attacked.

"If he had lived around here someone would have known
him, we all recognise each other in this neighbourhood."

In spite of this we decided to carry out another round of
interviews with the locals. By the time we had knocked on all
the ground floor doors there was no need to go any further:
women opened their front doors, came out into the passages

and even came to us to talk and offer help. Many of them were dressed in housecoats, pinafores or full-length aprons. They were excited and curious, but also indignant that something like this could happen in their peaceful part of town. They were proud of what they were:

"We're working people. There's never any crime here. All we need now is for that riffraff to come and fight in our streets."

It was clear that if anyone had known anything about the victim, they would have willingly told us. Yet, in order to be thorough and miss nothing, we went on combing that blasted street for three more days. With no luck. Nobody knew the guy, nobody saw him that night, nobody heard anything strange early on the morning of October 17. The possibility that he might have been beaten up somewhere else and then brought there seemed increasingly likely. But why to that spot in particular? That was a mystery that didn't bear too much speculation. It was an out-of-the-way and ill-lit place at night, and that could have been reason enough.

It was only at the end of three days that we realised all we had done was waste three days—and precisely the ones usually seen as decisive in solving a case. During what they call the golden hours we also went several times to the Valle Hebrón hospital to see if there was any change in our patient's condition, or if anyone had visited him. Unfortunately, our Sleeping Beauty was still flat out, and all alone. It made me feel sad. It's one thing to have lost all your family with the passing of the years, but it's far worse not to have a single friend to worry about what has happened to you.

We would go to see him in the late afternoon. Even though it was only a few days after the attack, the bruises on his face were fading, and his features appeared more clearly. There was something dissolute about him, perhaps due to his own excesses: a poor man's Dorian Gray. Garzón would stare out of the window, chat to the other old men in the next beds, occasion-

ally go down to the cafeteria. I sat there unable to take my eyes
off our victim, in a state of endless fascination.

"You'll end up attached to him," the sergeant told me one
day.

"Perhaps I'll be the first person who ever was."

He shrugged dismissively.

"Don't go all sentimental on me."

"How can it be that no one realizes he's missing?"

"Lots of people disappear overnight without anyone realizing: old guys the uniformed cops find stinking in their beds two
months after they've died, tramps who kick the bucket in subway entrances, crazy old bats who spend years in a lunatic asy-
lum without a relative ever going near them . . . take your pick!"

"Well, in any case, I feel a bit sorry for him. In the state he's
in he's completely dependent on other people, and that's terrible for anyone. Just look, the nurses haven't bothered to shave
him, and you can see the white roots of his hair beneath the
hair dye."

"But he's not going to notice, is he?"

That was Garzón's abrupt way of putting a stop to our conversation. It was obvious that like everyone else he wasn't particularly bothered about the guy, and certainly didn't feel any
compassion towards him.

Back at the police station, there was a surprise waiting for us.
Sergeant Pinilla said he had something he thought might interest us. People in an apartment block in Ciutat Vella had been
phoning because for the past three days a dog had been barking and howling, apparently left on its own in one of the apartments. The community officers had gone to the building with
a warrant, forced their way in, and found the pooch desperate
for something to eat and drink. The neighbors knew nothing
about who lived there, beyond the fact that he was someone of
average height whom they saw so little of that they would not
even recognize him. The officers had sealed off the apartment

and taken the dog to a municipal depot. If no one claimed it within two days, it would be taken to the dog pound.

Pinilla thought that the apartment might belong to our friend, so he had got in touch with the landlord and had brought him in so we could question him.

"You won't get anything more out of the neighbors, inspector. Even if they'd known him all their lives, they wouldn't say a word. It's a rough neighborhood."

Pinilla knew what he was talking about. Even so, we sent someone to ask them more questions while we concentrated on Sleeping Beauty's presumed domicile.

The owner not only of the apartment but of the whole block was one of the most disagreeable-looking characters I could ever remember seeing. He was wearing a tan leather jacket and had gold rings on almost every finger. He did not bother to smile, and hardly even acknowledged us.

"I already told the community support officers that it's the Urbe agency which looks after my properties."

"Did you never meet your tenant, not even when he signed the contract?"

"No, the agency took care of all that. They found the client, got him to sign the papers, and took his deposit. Afterwards, they sent me a photocopy of the contract and a note saying, Your new tenant is called Ignacio Lucena Pastor. That was all."

"How long ago was that?"

"About three years."

I saw he was wearing a battered pair of shoes.

"Will he pull out of it?"

"We don't know."

"Could you give me details of his relatives?"

"He doesn't have any."

"So who's going to pay the rent while he's in hospital? Can't I at least look for another tenant?"

"No chance. The place is sealed off while we search it."

"Look, I earn next to nothing from the scum living there. I've got Arabs, blacks, you name it; sometimes we have to get rid of people who simply won't pay. Don't get it into your heads that I'm rich, I inherited this crappy block in this crappy neighborhood, but I earn barely enough to eat. I would already have sold it if I could have."

"Did Lucena pay on time?"

"Yes, it was all going too smoothly, I knew something had to happen."

"Do you know if he was mixed up in drugs in any way?"

He grew impatient.

"I've already told you, I don't know anything. I've never seen the guy in my life. It's very simple: one of my tenants has been beaten up, right? O.K., fine, so maybe he was dealing drugs, or perhaps he was a pimp and another pimp settled scores with him . . . it could be anything, who knows, but whatever it was, I knew nothing about it."

So it looked as though the Urbe agency would be the key to telling us if our friend in hospital was Ignacio Lucena Pastor. A young lady informed us that the person who had dealt with the Lucena contract was a secretary who no longer worked there.

"O.K. then, let us have her address. We need her to identify someone," Garzón insisted.

"The thing is, Mari Pili got married a year ago. She left work and went to live in Zaragoza."

"Don't you have her address, or her phone number?"

"No. When she left she said she'd write, that she'd stay in touch, but you know how these things go . . . "

Garzón began to sound desperate:

"And did no one else in the agency talk to this tenant? Nobody went to collect the rent? Nobody ever saw him?"

The girl looked increasingly upset.

"No."

"But at least you must have the name of the bank he used, his account number."

"No, I'm afraid I don't. That gentleman posted us a payment slip on the second of each month, and seeing there was never any problem . . . "

"And of course, the address of the sender was always the apartment," said Garzón, about to explode.

"Yes," the girl said thoughtfully, then hastened to add: "It's all legal and above board."

"Show us the contract."

"I don't know where it is."

"Fine, now I get it. You rent apartments to illegal immigrants or people without any proper identity papers, and you never declare a thing, do you?"

"You'd better talk to my boss."

"Don't worry, I'm going to report this back at the station and they'll send someone to find out what the fuck is going on here."

The girl gave a deep sigh, perhaps because she knew that sooner or later the game would be up.

In the car, Garzón was indignant:

"This is the limit! Don't they always say we're all on file, on hundreds of lists, that the state knows even our innermost thoughts? But it's not true, we can live for a hundred years in the same place and we still won't exist. Nobody will even know our face."

"Calm down, Fermín. Let's go and see if Pinilla has got anything more out of the neighbors."

Sergeant Pinilla was categorical: nothing. Nobody could recognize the victim from the photo taken in hospital. Nobody. His name wasn't in the police database either.

"You could try. Perhaps people get more scared by the police than by us community officers. I doubt it, though. It's so easy to say you don't know someone! Why look for trouble?"

"Where are you keeping the dog you found in the apartment?" I asked.

"In the storeroom."

"Can we see it?"

The two men stared at me in bewilderment.

"I'd like to question him," I joked.

Pinilla laughed as well, and set off down the corridor:

"For all I care, you could give him life! Keeping a dog in a police station is no easy matter, believe me."

He took us down to a big room in the basement. Huge cheap wooden shelving was full of the most bizarre objects. Behind a metal grille in a corner of the room there was a dog. Next to him was a bowl for food and another for water. Seeing us it shot vertically up into the air and started to bark frantically,

"Here's your hound! As you can see, he's still full of beans."

"Christ, he's an ugly bastard!" Garzón exclaimed.

He wasn't wrong. The dog was scrawny, with wispy black hair and drooping ears. His stumpy legs were stuck into a worn-out Teddy bear body. Yet there was something about his steady, trusting gaze that caught my attention. I stuck my hand through the bars and stroked his head. I immediately felt a delicious warmth rising up through my fingers. The animal fixed me with his mournful eyes and eagerly licked my hand.

"He's cute," I declared. "Get him ready, sergeant, we're taking him with us. We need him for our investigation."

Pinilla did not react, but Garzón couldn't believe his ears. He turned to me:

"Listen, inspector, what the hell are we going to do with that animal?"

I pulled rank on him with a look I hadn't used in ages.

"I'll tell you all in good time, Garzón. For now, he's coming with us."

Fortunately Garzón grasped the situation and said nothing.

No need to complicate things still further by showing his surprise in public.

"Could I ask you a favor?" Pinilla said. "Would you mind dropping him off at the pound when you've finished your investigations? I'm sure it's not against the regulations if he's with us one day more or less."

To Pinilla, we were like manna from heaven. Thanks to us, he could get rid of the pooch sooner than expected. He couldn't give a damn what we wanted him for, just so long as we took him off his hands. Garzón was a bit more puzzled. In fact, he was dying to ask me, but the way I had shut him up before meant he would never have allowed himself to query anything. I suppose that when we arrived at the hospital he began to suspect something, but even then he didn't say a word.

The first problem with my plan was how to get the dog to the victim's room without anyone noticing. It was out of the question to ask for formal permission to bring a dog into the hospital. It wasn't so much that I wanted to flout the rules, but I sensed that to try to do anything officially in this gigantic labyrinth would mean filling in hundreds of bits of paper, from insurance policies to photocopies and special permits for black dogs.

So I asked my colleague to take off his ample raincoat. I took the dog out of the car trunk and put him under my arm. Then, trying not to frighten him, I wrapped him in the coat until he was completely invisible. He was no trouble—he even seemed to like it, because I felt a warm, wet tongue on the back of my hand.

The three of us made our entrance into the hospital. I could have sworn that Garzón was protesting *sotto voce*, but it might just have been the dog growling. I was quite calm about it all. It seemed to me this was only a minor infraction of the regulations, nothing that could not be justified as normal procedure. We had no problem with security when we showed them our badges. Nor did we arouse anyone's attention on the way to the mystery man's room. As soon as I opened the door, I realized that the prayers I had been saying between gritted teeth were answered. There were no nurses inside, and the two men in the other beds were asleep. I set my stowaway free from his hiding place and put him on the floor. At first he was confused by the medical smells he could pick up in the air. He sniffed in all directions, panted, wandered about the room. All at once his sensitive nose detected a smell he recognized. He stood stock-still, then, as if the discovery had electrified him, started to leap in the air and then scampered around the bed of our unconscious friend, barking wildly. Finally, he got up on his hind legs, saw that this really was his master, and began to give little yelps of pleasure as he tried to lick the hands lying limply on the sheets.

"Sergeant Garzón . . ." I declared theatrically, ". . . allow me to introduce Ignacio Lucena Pastor."

"Holy shit!" was his only comment. The fact is, he couldn't say much more because all the noise and excitement had woken up the other two old men. One of them was staring at the dog as though it was something out of a nightmare; the other, who had clearly realized that this was no ordinary situation, started to ring his buzzer and shout for a nurse. I stood there for a moment completely blank, without the slightest idea of how to react. All I could do was look on as Garzón scooped up the dog, snatched his coat from me, wrapped it round the animal, and rushed out of the room.

"Let's go, inspector, we shouldn't be here."

We hurried along endless corridors with the poor creature howling, struggling and kicking to escape from Garzón's grasp. Behind us as we approached the exit we left a growing group of astonished faces trying to work out where the noise was coming from. I was desperate not to show any emotion, act as naturally as possible, and to walk as quickly as I could without breaking into a run. We already had the front door of the hospital in sight when one of the security men must have realized that the strange groans and complaints were coming from us.

"Hold on!" he shouted when he had recovered from his bemusement.

"What shall we do?" Garzón asked in a whisper.

"Keep going," I told him.

"Stop right there!" the man shouted again.

"Petra, for heaven's sake!" muttered Garzón.

"Come here, I said!" This time the man's voice was right behind us, and it was when I realized that this was his final warning and that he was about to catch up with us that I reacted automatically. Without turning round or warning Garzón, I took off as fast as my legs could carry me. I ran out of the main entrance, down the steps, and did not stop until I had reached the car park. It was only then that I came to a halt, panting, and turned to look behind me. No one in a white coat or a uniform was following me. The only person in sight was Garzón, who came puffing up red-faced and flailing his arms like a drowning man. He stopped beside me, unable to say a word. I pulled at his coat, and the disheveled, ugly head of our chief witness appeared from among the folds. At least he had realized how dramatic the situation was, and had quietened down. I felt a sudden urge to laugh out loud, and did so. Garzón and the dog stared at me with the same look of amazement.

"Would you care to tell me why the hell you did that, Petra?"

I tried to appear serious.

"I'm sorry, Fermín, I know I should have warned you."

"I just wonder what we'll say the next time we go back there."

"Don't worry, I bet they won't even recognize us!"

"But those old fellows in the room saw the dog!"

"I wouldn't worry too much about them either. Besides, sergeant, what's become of your sense of adventure?"

He stared at me as if he were completely convinced I had

gone mad. I opened the car and dumped the dog in the back. It started howling piteously once again.

"Hurry up, we're going to leave this blasted animal at the dog pound."

Garzón spent the whole journey disguising his reproaches as questions.

"Don't you think we could have found a less ostentatious way of identifying Lucena?"

"Such as?"

"We haven't even been to talk to the other people living in his building."

"We can do that, but it'll be much better now we know who Lucena Pastor was. By the way, don't forget to tell them at the station about all the illegal business that Urbe agency is mixed up in. I hope they throw the book at them."

"Of course I will. But I don't know if using the dog like that . . . "

"Look here, Garzón, have you never heard of the infallible instincts of animals? Do you know what they use in the Barcelona Water Company to test if the water is polluted? I'll tell you: they use fish! And do you know what they turned to in the Tokyo metro to detect the gases a terrorist group had released . . . ? Parakeets in cages! And don't get me started on the long tradition of collaboration between the police and dogs: in customs, in the search for missing people, for drugs . . . "

I glanced out of the corner of my eye to see the effect my words were having: he was thoughtful, but not entirely convinced.

"So why did you run off without telling me?"

"I did that because I've been bored for two years now."

"Well, remind me to buy you a jigsaw puzzle then! I don't think I'd survive another race like that one."

My laughter was cut short by an extraordinary sight. We had reached our destination: an enormous, ancient and run-down building. Hanging there on the heights of Collserola, it looked truly sinister.

"What the devil is this?"

"The city dog pound," said Garzón, driving on up the lonely road toward it. The closer we got, the scarier the place seemed, especially now that the impression was reinforced by the sounds of barking and howling. It was a chorus that made the hairs stand up on the back of my neck.

When we pulled up next to the dilapidated walls the barking grew louder still. When I picked up our miserable specimen again, he clung to me as if aware of his sad fate. A friendly young man came out to greet us. Impressed that we were from the police, he said he usually only had contact with the community support people. We sat down while he filled in a form. The poor dog tried to hide on my lap. Curious, I asked the man:

"Do all the dogs here find new homes?"

"No, unfortunately only those that look like some breed or other."

"Do you think this one looks like any particular breed?"

The young man smiled:

"Some exotic one perhaps."

So he had noticed how ugly the poor thing was as well.

"And what happens if they don't find a home?"

"Everybody asks me the same question. What do you think happens?"

"They're put down."

"After some time. There's no other solution."

"In a gas chamber?" asked Garzón, perhaps getting carried away by images of the Holocaust.

"A lethal injection," the man said. "It's a very civilized way of doing it. They don't suffer or have any death agonies. They fall asleep and don't wake up."

The howling from beyond the office walls underlined his words.

"Would you like me to show you the cages?"

I still have no idea why I accepted his invitation, but I did. The man led us down a long corridor lit only by a few naked light bulbs. Each of the large cages ranged along the walls had three or four dogs in it. As we went past there was an enormous din, and the animals reacted very differently. Some of them tried to push their muzzles through the bars and lick us. Others barked and spun crazily round on themselves. But all these tricks seemed to share a common aim: to catch our attention. It was obvious they knew what a tough game this was: the visitor arrived, walked up and down the corridor, and then one of them, but only one, would be set free. I was horrified. Our guide was giving explanations I could not follow because of the anxiety cramping my stomach. I stopped, and when I looked down at the floor I saw that our grotesque little dog was following me, quaking with fear.

"Hey, Garzón!" I called out.

But my colleague was deep in conversation with the assistant, despite all the noise.

"Hey, wait a minute!" I almost screamed. "Listen, I've changed my mind. I think I'm going to keep the dog."

"What?" the sergeant couldn't believe his ears.

"Yes, just until his owner recovers. In fact, I think we might need him again in our investigation. I can make a bit of room for him in the garden at my place."

The man in charge of the pound looked at me and smiled. He understood, and made no comment. I was thankful for that: all I needed were his congratulations to make me seem like a sentimental old biddy in Garzón's eyes.

For much of the return journey, neither of us said a word. Eventually Garzón fired the first shot.

"With all due respect, Petra, and I know it's none of my business, but going soft on everything you see isn't a good idea for a cop."

"I know."

"As you can imagine, I've seen my fair share of things in this world. I've seen horrors that have churned my stomach: abandoned children, suicides hanging from beams, young prostitutes beaten to a pulp . . . but I've always tried not to let any of it get to me. That's the only way not to end up in a madhouse."

"I couldn't stand the way those dogs were looking at us."

"But they're only dogs."

"Yes, but we're human beings."

"O.K., inspector, don't get angry, you know what I'm trying to say."

"Of course I do, Garzón, and I appreciate your intentions. But all I'm going to do is look after the dog until his owner gets better. And besides, it's true what I said about him helping us in our investigation. We'll use him again."

"Well, if it's like the first time, God help us."

"Why are you always complaining? I'll make a deal: if you take me home, I'll give you a whisky."

When the dog saw his new home, he didn't seem too upset; perhaps he realized he has escaped a much worse fate. He inspected the rooms, went out into the garden, and didn't turn his nose up at the crackers and water we offered him. Garzón and I sipped our whiskies, watching the animal's movements.

"I'll have to think of a name for him," I said.

"Call him Freaky . . . " the sergeant suggested, "he's such an ugly-looking thing."

"That's not a bad idea."

Freaky seemed to like his new name, and flopped at my feet with a sigh. Garzón sighed as well, lit a cigarette, and stared contentedly up at the ceiling. After all the excitement of the day, the three of us made a tranquil picture. I wondered if it was true that as a policeman Garzón had seen so many horrors. It probably was.

2.

We carried out a thorough search of the apartment Ignacio Lucena Pastor had in the old quarter of the city. It was a small, wretched place that he had not done much to improve. The only furniture in the living room was a table, four chairs, a television, and a sofa whose stuffing looked on the point of spilling out. His bedroom was not much more inviting: it contained a single bed, a bookshelf with magazines on it, and a sort of desk with drawers, where we found writing paper and two account books that Garzón removed as evidence. The rest did not seem particularly relevant: there were few personal belongings that might offer clues to his habits or tastes. The magazines offered some insight into his life—weeklies on cars and motorbikes, a few nudie books, and some random parts of three encyclopedias—one on the Second World War, another on dog breeds, a third on photography. The only ornaments in the room were a pair of rough clay doves that Lucena had put on his bedside table.

"If it's true what you said and he was into drug trafficking, shouldn't he have been a bit richer, Garzón?"

"Bah, small-time dealers like him . . . !"

"But they gave him a real beating. Doesn't that seem strange for someone who was so unimportant? I don't get it."

"Do you calculate how hard you're going to swat a mosquito?"

There was a lot of sense to what Garzón said, but there tends to be a certain harmony even to criminal acts, and there was something about his theory that did not fit a well-structured hypothesis. There must have been a powerful motive for such a brutal act of revenge.

The desk drawers were empty. Didn't he keep anything? In that case, why did he need a desk? Wasn't there even a gas bill? Of course, there was the possibility that someone had emptied the apartment after the beating, but if they had, they had been sure to put everything back in place afterwards.

We went to question the neighbors. They weren't exactly pleased to see us. This was the third time they were being asked the same questions: Did you know Lucena? Had you ever seen him? Did he come and go a lot? The replies were always the same: a resounding "no." The photograph we showed them of him in his hospital bed not only did not stir any memories, but was sufficiently disturbing to destroy any possibility of their remembering. Lucena had not existed for any of them. They were frightened, not of something outside themselves and real, something tangible or concrete, but of something floating and insubstantial, of life itself. They were completely and totally steeped in fear. It was probably the only thing they had ever felt as a certainty. Desperate single mothers, lost youngsters, illegal black immigrants, dirt-poor Arab families, out-of-work drinkers, old people with ten thousand pesetas' pension to live on. They knew nobody, and nobody knew them. They did not talk or smile, as though being deprived of human qualities had reduced them to the state of animals. Nothing could have been further from these furtive creatures than the cheerful housewives we had talked to a few days earlier in El Carmelo. Contented women who chattered freely, cleaned their houses with pine-scented products, wore colorful aprons and had a photo of their son doing his military service on their TV sets. A true measure of the distance between the working class and those on the margins of society.

We left the run-down building empty-handed. Ignacio Lucena Pastor was nothing more than a shadow who had lived there and used his lack of substance to float among the living. We were just about to cross the road when someone called to us from the front doorway. It was one of the women we had just talked to. I could vividly recall her: a very young woman, most likely Moroccan, who had come to open her door surrounded by a swarm of children. She motioned to us to come over: there was no way she was going to step out into the street. She spoke very basic Spanish, as soft and guttural as a sigh.

"I saw that man two times in same bar. Me outside, him inside."

"Which bar?"

"Two streets up, on right. Bar Las Fuentes. Many men drinking."

"Was he on his own?"

"Not know. I shopping."

Despite her fear, she was smiling. She had beautiful black, deep set eyes.

"Why didn't you tell the community support people?" Garzón wanted to know.

"My husband open door, not me."

"And your husband doesn't want any trouble, is that it?"

"My husband say not our problem. He is laborer, good worker, but he no want Spanish problems."

"Do you feel the same way?" I asked gently.

"My children now from this country. Go school here. It important not do anything bad, not lie."

"I understand."

"Don't tell I spoke to you."

"I promise no one will know."

She smiled, then disappeared up the stairs. She cannot have been more than twenty-five.

"Well!" exclaimed Garzón. "A responsible citizen at last!"

"Yes, and you can bet your life that this great country of ours will open its arms to her children, will adopt them with great affection and make things easy for them. You can see the welcome it's given them already: did you see the state they live in?"

"They'll be all right, Petra."

"I wouldn't swear an oath on it."

Garzón nodded like the reasonable, patient and fair-minded person he is. My opinions often sound too extreme for his taste.

And of course, the Las Fuentes bar: by now I should have realized that in every Spanish male's life there is a bar, just as every Swede must have wood flooring in his. Whatever their class or beliefs, deep down in all of them there is a neutral, friendly place free of any sense of guilt, a place where they can give free rein to their most authentic side. Just as I had thought, Las Fuentes was situated somewhere in the basement of the social pyramid of Spanish bars. It was as exotic as a baroque church, with a bar for an altar, its stained-glass windows painted with yellow designs for shellfish and paellas. It was also one of the filthiest dens I had ever set foot in. Several bowed-down worshippers were shouting over bottles of beer, while the high priest noisily wiped glasses behind the bar.

We showed our badges to the owner, then showed him the photograph of Lucena. We were rewarded by the usual disdainful replies: he did not know him, had never seen him. Nor had three customers playing cards in a dirty corner.

"We've heard he comes here a lot."

"Then you heard wrong. He's not one of our regulars, otherwise I would have recognized him. He may have come in occasionally . . . We have lots of people dropping in."

That was all we could get out of him. He might even have been telling the truth: the fact that the Arab woman said she had seen Lucena in here a couple of times did not mean he was a regular client.

"Did you notice, Petra, how in detective films they always seem to know who's lying? How on earth do they manage that?"

"What is clear by now, Garzón, is that this case is a load of crap. It's going to cost us an arm and a leg to get anywhere."

"All cases are the same."

"But it's so sordid: a poor guy beaten to a pulp in the street, all those rundown apartments, illegal immigrants, stinking bars . . . the chief inspector's given us a real gem from the annals of criminology, hasn't he!"

"What would you have preferred?" Garzón snorted. "A marquise strangled with a silk stocking in her stately home? A kidnapped Arab sheik?"

"Go get lost!"

I could hear him laughing heartily behind me. But he was right. There's no such thing as an easy case, absolute virtue, or out-and-out evil in this world, so we just had to face up to it. I turned to him:

"Put a man in that bar. Twenty-four hours a day. Undercover, with his ears pricked. For a week at least. And stop making fun of your superiors!"

"Why are you in such a terrible mood? It's not all bad news. We've met a very decent woman—that Moroccan girl."

"Don't remind me, it only makes me feel worse to think of the life she must be leading."

"More of your bleeding-heart stuff?"

I gave him a hard look. He looked so happy and contented, as if we were two schoolkids on recess or two typists on their coffee break. I decided to give as good as I was getting.

"Do you know why I'm like this, Fermín? It's because I haven't had a decent fuck recently."

His reaction was immediate. He looked away, and the smile froze on his lips. I'd hit him right on the chin.

"That's too much, inspector!"

"I'm talking seriously. It's been proved: when you're no longer enjoying an active sexual life, you start to feel sorry for the weak and dispossessed. But if you're having intense sex, you couldn't care less about other people's misfortunes . . . you don't even notice them."

The sergeant was looking anywhere but at me, trying to hide his embarrassment. He was still a shy person. Strange how even a tiny blow to the conventional structures of behavior could bring the walls of relations between the sexes tumbling down like an earthquake.

"Remember, I'm a woman who's twice been divorced, which means I've known the pleasures of conjugal life more or less continuously. Now it's all so hit-and-miss . . . "

All of this was far too much for Garzón, even if he put it down to what he called my "natural originality." He put his coat on and stared up at the sky as intently as a meteorologist.

"So, inspector, do you think it's going to rain? Perhaps we should get back to the station to see what on earth these books we found are."

He was out for the count.

Inspector Patricio Sanguesa of the fraud squad took a look at Lucena's account books for us. To begin with, it did not take him long to discover that they were numbered: books 1 and 2. Then he buried himself in trying to work out what the crude handwriting might mean. He read them forwards and backwards, stroked his chin like a Socratic philosopher. Garzón and I sat in a religious silence smoking cigarette after cigarette, increasingly convinced that our colleague's bafflement was a sign he had discovered something. Finally, he opened his mouth:

"It's very odd. As you may have imagined, this is no official or commercial accounting system. There is no mention of V.A.T., or anything else that might suggest a shop or a trade. It's probably for personal use. But I wonder: what exactly do the accounts cover? The items are odd, and so are the figures. And the lengths of time mentioned are strange too."

"Could you give us an example?"

"Just look at any page! Look: 'Rolly: five months. From 5,000 to 10,000. Sux: four years. 7,000. Jar: one year. 6,000 less costs.'"

"They could be prostitutes," said Garzón.

"So he took on a prostitute for four years? That doesn't make sense. And what are those names?"

"They could be pseudonyms."

"Perhaps. I'll give the books to my men. They'll go through them line by line, and I'll tell you what they come up with. For now, don't rule anything in or out."

I took a taxi home: it was time to see to the dog. As soon as I opened the front door, a yelp made me fear the worst: was I going to find all my furniture torn to shreds? When he saw me, Freaky started whirling round like a dervish in ecstasy. Could he really love me that much? He realized I was his savior and benefactor, and was offering me a sincere tribute of undying affection. If I had only known it was so easy with a dog, I could have saved myself two unhappy marriages. I went to inspect the damage he could have caused while I was out of the house. I soon calmed down: my new lodger had done his business in a corner of the garden, and my carpets and furniture were all still intact. "Good boy," I told him, thinking that was what one did, then stroked his misshapen head. He puffed up with pride, making himself look even uglier than usual.

The crackers I had left him as his only sustenance had all disappeared. I wondered if they were proper food for a dog, and decided they probably were not. I looked in the yellow pages for any pet shop in the neighborhood. I soon found one that sounded ideal: The Dog's Home. Not exactly an original name, but the details sounded perfect: from veterinary consultations to food and grooming items.

"O.K., Freaky . . . " I told him, "I think the time has come for us to take our first non-police walk."

Then because I still had no leash for him, I carried him out in my arms.

The shop was large and welcoming. A smiling, muscular man of approximately my own age greeted me and asked what I was looking for. My mind went blank: I hadn't the first idea of what I needed.

"Well . . . " I said, "for reasons I won't go into, I've inherited this dog here." I pointed to Freaky, sure the man would take pity on me. "So I need everything, everything a dog could need, starting with a vet who could take a look at him."

"I understand," he said in a gruff, manly voice. "I can be your vet. This is my shop, and upstairs I have my surgery, but my assistant is out at the moment, so I can give your pet the once over here if you like."

I agreed. He knelt down beside Freaky.

"What's his name?" he asked from somewhere around my knees.

I hesitated a moment, then confessed:

"Freaky."

He looked up at me with eyes I suddenly noticed were an intense green. When he smiled, he showed a perfect set of teeth.

"Do you know how old he is?"

I shook my head. He opened Freaky's mouth and examined it.

"I reckon he's about five. Do you know who his previous owner was?"

"Yes, a friend."

"I'm only asking because we often have to take into account the habits a dog might have acquired with another owner."

"Aha," I said, nervously.

"He doesn't seem to have any health problems. Did your friend say whether he was vaccinated or not?"

"No, he didn't say, and I can't ask him now . . . he's gone away."

"That's fine, we'll renew his yearly jabs just to be on the safe side." Suddenly he saw something that caught his attention. He took hold of one of Freaky's ears. "Look at this scar! It looks like a bite. It's very deep, it must have been made by a big, fierce dog."

"Is it recent?"

"Not at all. It looks quite old. But the hair will never grow back over it. It's hardly noticeable, though; it doesn't make him look any worse."

I gave a stupid fake cackle.

"Do you think he could look any worse?"

The vet stood up. He was tall and broad-shouldered, with fair hair cut short. He looked at me reprovingly.

"No dogs are ugly, not a single one. They all have something beautiful about them. All you have to do is find it."

"Can you find it in mine?" I asked, completely seriously.

He bent down with his hands on his knees, and contemplated Freaky's charms.

"He has a very noble look in his eyes, and he has long, curly eyelashes."

I bent down as well.

"It's true; I hadn't noticed."

We both realized at the same time how ridiculous we looked, and straightened up more awkwardly than was necessary. After that, things went more quickly. The vet did his job, and vaccinated Freaky. Then he changed roles and began to sell me everything my new companion needed. I realized at once that the poet Antonio Machado, who liked to travel "lightly equipped," could never have had a dog. I acquired a collar and a leash, an anti-parasite shampoo, a wire comb, an automatic drinking bowl, a feeding bowl, a bag of food, a sleeping basket, and some hygienic wipes for his ears and eyes.

By the end it was like a dowry for an oil magnate's daughter. Of course there was no way I could carry it all, so the vet took my details and promised his assistant would bring everything around later that evening. I had to fill in a form. I had no wish to awaken his curiosity or to give any explanations, so in the box for profession I wrote "librarian."

When I got home I poured myself a couple of fingers of whisky and sat down to read the paper. Freaky approved of my behavior so much that he relaxed and went to sleep. Perhaps it was true: his eyelashes were extraordinarily curly. That vet was a curious, sensitive sort. Good-looking too, handsome even, very handsome. He must be married with a wife and five kids, or be homosexual, or his "assistant" would turn out to be a twenty-year-old he was going out with—anything that would make it hard for me to do what I suddenly realized I really wanted to do: go to bed with him. I had been telling Garzón the plain truth: the men I had been with over the past two years had given less than satisfactory results. All in all, they were exactly as expected. I sighed.

An hour later the doorbell rang. I ran to open up, stumbling over Freaky on the way. When I did open the door, I was convinced it must have been God himself who had sent the scurvy animal to me. Standing there was the vet himself, carrying a huge box.

"My assistant had to leave in a hurry, so I decided to deliver this myself. Is it too late?"

I thought over what I was wearing. It wasn't too bad.

"Late? Not a bit of it," I said, laughing, blocking him in the doorway like an idiot.

"Could I put this somewhere?" he asked.

"Oh, I'm sorry, please come in."

If I carried on being so stupid, I'd let this golden opportunity slip through my fingers. I had to act quickly and decisively.

"You can put it down here."

Freaky was jumping round him, sniffing at his trousers.

"I can see he recognizes me! By the way, I forgot to tell you to make sure there's always fresh water in his drinking bowl. This dogfood is dry and needs a lot of liquid alongside it."

I smiled.

"Talking of drinks, can I offer you one?"

He went rigid. He must have thought only desperate forty-year-olds are quite so upfront about it. Well, perhaps I had gone too far in my disregard for the usual niceties. I tried to reassure him.

"I just thought you looked so loaded down . . . or perhaps you've got someone waiting for you?"

"No," he stammered. Then he regained his composure and said easily: "I'd be delighted."

I don't think I had ever been so direct in my approach, but then again, if your quarry just lies there asking for it, what are you to do?

"In fact, it's a loaded invitation: I've got lots of questions I want to ask you about dogs," I said from the kitchen.

"Fire away," he said, offering me a clear shot.

I put some ice in his glass and gave it to him with a hint of seduction I had forgotten I was capable of.

"Tell me everything I need to know to be a dog owner."

He burst out laughing as tunefully as a Mozart arpeggio.

"Well, the first thing you should know is that a dog will always love you, come what may. He will never reproach you for anything, criticize your conduct, or judge your actions. He will always be completely happy when he sees you; he won't have good or bad days. He will never betray you or look for another mistress. It's not all good, though, because together with all this there's the drawback that he'll always depend on you, he'll never become independent the way children do; and it will probably be you who has to decide when to put him to sleep if the illnesses of old age become too much for him."

I felt carried away just listening to him. What he was saying was the most poetic thing I had heard in years.

"And what do I have to do to deserve all this?"

"Not much, really: feed him, look after him a bit, and, if you really want to enjoy his company, observe him. Learn to understand what mood he is in, the way he sighs if he's melancholy, wags his tail if he's happy, see how pure his gaze can be . . . "

"And how innocent," I said, on the verge of heart failure.

"Yes, his innocence," he said, looking me in the eye.

My God, he couldn't be real! Someone so tender, so intelligent, so masculine and yet so open. I would have gladly adopted a boa constrictor just to hear him sing its praises! If I didn't succeed in getting him into bed with me, I would never be able to look at myself putting on mascara again. I glanced at Freaky, who had suddenly acquired the dimensions of a fabulous mythological beast.

"Are you married?" I asked.

"Divorced," he replied, without a moment's hesitation.

The echo of that magic word hung in the air for a second, but it was immediately shot down by the dreadful clatter of the telephone. Freaky raised his hackles; I answered with bad grace.

"Inspector Delicado?"

What could Garzón want at this time of day? Perhaps he had taken seriously the old saying that a policeman is always on duty?

"Bad news, I'm afraid."

Not even then did I manage to concentrate properly.

"What's wrong, Garzón?"

"I'm afraid that our case has just become a murder."

I finally cleared my mind of all erotic thoughts.

"What do you mean?"

"There was a call from the hospital. Ignacio Lucena Pastor has just died."

"What did he die of?"

"Nothing in particular. All of a sudden his vital signs diminished, and by the time they got him to the operating theater he had suffered a massive heart attack. You'd better come. I'll be waiting for you at Valle Hebrón."

"I'm on my way."

"Inspector . . . "

"Yes?"

"Could you please not bring the dog this time?"

I hung up brusquely. This was no time for jokes. I turned to my guest, who had already risen to his feet.

"I'm afraid I've got to go," I said. "Something's come up at work."

"At the library?" he asked with ironic disbelief.

"Yes," I said, without any further explanation. "Stay and finish your drink if you like."

He shook his head. We both headed for the door. His van was parked outside, a new one with a dog's head painted on the side. I shook hands and walked on towards my car. All of a sudden I turned to him:

"Hey, listen! I don't even know your name!"

"Juan."

"Like Juan the Unbedded," I thought, raging with silent frustration. It was more than likely that the magic moment had gone. Maybe the next time I saw him I wouldn't even find him attractive. Ignacio Lucena Pastor! Some people were as annoying as those insects that decide to come and die right in your glass of whisky, and you have to scoop them out with your finger.

And there Lucena was, toast. Garzón and I stared with curiosity at him in his freezing coffin. Death might have done him an ultimate favor, and given his corpse a dignity he never possessed while he has alive. But it hadn't. Lucena looked just like a battered and broken doll. Pathetic. His dyed hair now had the consistency of burlap.

"Has nobody claimed him?"

"No one," the doctor replied.

"What happens in these cases?"

"We'll keep the body three more days. Then, if you lot don't have any other ideas, someone from the hospital will accompany his hearse to the cemetery, and he'll be buried in the common grave."

"Tell us when that's going to happen. We'll get a death notice published in the press, just to see if by any chance someone turns up at the burial."

Things looked complicated, difficult. I had no idea which way to turn. Our man would never open his mouth again. He was taking his secrets with him to the grave, and now we had a murder on our hands. And we had no leads. Before we settled on a strategy we went to see Inspector Sanguesa. He did not have much for us, either. Neither of the two account books had provided them with any intelligible names, phone numbers, or even an address.

"Nothing, I'm afraid, just lists of ridiculous names, those strange periods of time, and the sums of money that don't seem to obey any logic or arithmetical system."

"What about the amounts?"

"Well, in the first book they're very small: five thousand, three thousand, seven thousand, twelve thousand at the most. In the second, they're considerably larger: they go from twenty to sixty thousand. That could mean they're for different things, but we can't be sure. They might be the same, but totaled in a different way."

"And the overall figure?"

"We haven't even been able to work that out, because the time indication in front of each amount creates an enormous variable. What does 'four years, five thousand' mean? That for four years he received or paid out five thousand pesetas—and does that mean every day, or just once, or perhaps even once a year? They're like hieroglyphics, the unreadable ones."

"Don't worry, inspector," Garzón said. "Everything in this case is strange."

"Tell me what you come up with. I'm fascinated."

"We will. Now we've got to see the boys from the press—any message from you?"

"Give them the kiss of death."

We almost had to beg for any of the news agencies to carry the story of Lucena's death. Of course, it wasn't exactly head-line news. There was no sex angle to it, no political or racial implications . . . nothing that would sell newspapers. Who was interested in the fact that a nobody had been beaten to death? In the end, though, I reckoned this lack of interest might work in our favor: at least both the journalists and our bosses would leave us in peace.

In spite of their initial reluctance, the story appeared among the brief news items of several newspapers. That did not help us much, however, as when the moment came for the burial in Collserola cemetery, the only ones present were a priest, a gravedigger, the Social Security employee who officially handed over the body, Garzón, me and Freaky. The sergeant was open-ly hostile to the idea of me taking the dog along. As an excuse, I argued that his presence was essential. I told him I was going to unleash the dog during the ceremony, and that if any of the dead man's friends happened to be there, he would point them out for us. Even to me that sounded like a ridiculous argument, but there was no way I could confess to my colleague that I was doing it because I felt it was the least I could do for the poor wretch Lucena Pastor. I wanted this lonely man to have at least one friend with him when he said his last goodbye.

The ceremony, if that's what it could be called, took place one cold, overcast afternoon. Each time a gust of freezing wind hit our tiny group, everyone seemed to be cursing their bad luck. The wind blew away all the myths surrounding a burial, too. The gravedigger was wearing thick work gloves, the Social

Security man's nose was running while he stared into space, and when the priest muttered, "Lord receive Ignacio into your bosom . . . " Garzón sneezed. The only one who did not appear to be protesting inside was Freaky. He kept close by my legs, standing quietly and looking only vaguely interested in what was going on.

The prayers were said at a speed that took me by surprise. Then the coffin was brought to the edge of the grave. I saw that Freaky had become nervous. All at once he rushed forward and, staring at the simple pine coffin where his master lay, he let out a long, piercing howl. This caused consternation among the mourners. The priest gave me a stern look. I took the dog in my arms but this did not calm him down; instead he gave another, seemingly endless howl.

"It just shows how faithful little animals can be!" the grave-digger philosophized.

The priest was having none of this mystical nonsense. He became extremely agitated, and turning towards me, angrily ordered:

"Get that dog out of here at once!"

I hurried to obey him.

When we got to the car Freaky became calmer, and I managed to soothe his grief by giving him one of the smoker's sweets that Garzón always kept in the glove compartment. He licked it inquisitively, and finally decided it would do. How on earth he succeeded in smelling Lucena through a sealed coffin will always be a mystery to me.

Shortly afterwards, the sergeant appeared, hunched in his raincoat. He was spitting nails.

"For Christ's sake Petra, you should have heard how angry that priest was! I had to put up with a sermon about how a cemetery is a sacred place, about our lack of respect . . . "

"Bah, he deserves it! At least there was someone there to cry over that poor devil's death."

"Poor devil? We've no idea what he got up to!"

"Everyone deserves at least one glorious moment in their life. We gave Ignacio Lucena Pastor his."

"Yes, yes, that's all very fine, but I was the one the priest took it out on . . . What's that? Can I smell eucalyptus?"

"That's Freaky, he really likes your sweets."

"That's all I need! Would you like me to tell you something, inspector? When I was nine I was bitten by a dog, and I've hated them ever since!"

I chuckled.

"Everybody in Spain has been bitten by a dog when they were a child. It must be the collective unconscious, expressing our guilt."

"Expressing my ass!"

"O.K., you know what I'll do to make up for it? Invite you back to my place for dinner."

He changed from pretending to be angry to pretending to be reluctant.

"I'm not sure, inspector, I don't want to put you to any trouble. Perhaps you don't want to start cooking now."

"We could always polish off Freaky's food," I said. "Then you could get your own back for him eating all your sweets."

After the creamed spinach and steaks, we sat in the living room to savor our brandies. It was too soon to lose heart, but we already knew the case was going to be complicated and slow. At first we had not even been able to identify the victim, and now we still did not have the faintest idea of the motive for the crime. We had no sense of what we were looking for.

"My intuition tells me he was a pimp," Garzón said.

"No, let's start from what we've got. We've got no leads and no witnesses. All we have are the two account books and their ridiculous names, plus two specific locations: the bar he was seen in, which could still be promising, and the street where he was found."

"That's nothing more than a street. They could have attacked him somewhere else and simply dumped him there by chance."

I took a lengthy sip of my brandy.

"And we've got Freaky."

"Look here, inspector, don't you think you're exaggerating your bloodhound's abilities a bit? He's no Rin Tin Tin. Besides, every time he gets involved we find ourselves in trouble."

"I'm being completely serious, Fermín. I'm sure that dog went wherever Lucena did, he saw all the people his master met. If we were talking of human beings we'd say he 'knows,' and he probably knows a lot. We have to take him to both of the places we've identified."

"To the bar as well?"

"Yes, there too. Obviously, he's not going to tell us anything, but we can rely on his sense of smell to help recognize people and places. Did you see how he managed to identify his master even in a sealed coffin?"

"If you think about it, it's scary, isn't it?"

"Yes."

We both sat staring at the dog.

"What are you going to do with him?"

"I don't know. For now, he has work to do, and important work at that."

I patted Freaky on the head. He seemed to understand. He lifted his tattered ear and gave me a look of intense gratitude for the starring role I was offering him.

3.

It was not yet nine o'clock when we headed up the steep street until we reached the exact spot where Lucena had been found. Freaky was delighted to be going for a walk: he wagged his tail and sniffed all around him. If Garzón had had a tail, though, it would have been firmly between his legs. He still thought it was absurd to use the dog like this. He had less confidence in the infallibility of animals than in that of the Pope, but he came along. There was nothing else for it.

Freaky did not appear to notice anything special about the place where Lucena was discovered. He walked around, lifted his nose, smelt the air. Then he seemed to choose a direction and set off after something. I was holding his leash loosely, so as not to restrict him. He headed straight up the hill, pausing now and then to sniff at a wall. After a while, he crossed the street and went down a narrower alleyway. He stopped at a tree, lifted his back leg, and peed on it. This bodily necessity enraged Garzón so much he could scarcely contain himself.

When we reached the end of the alley, something seemed to attract Freaky's attention, and he speeded up. I glanced at Garzón expectantly. The dog broke into a trot. I followed him hanging on to the leash, certain we were on to something. The two last big apartment buildings gave way to a vast patch of waste ground. Part of it was blocked off by a wire fence. Inside it we could see several people with dogs.

"What on earth is this?" I could hear Garzón ask as he came puffing up.

"I've no idea. We're going to find out, but don't show your badge until we've got a clearer idea."

As we drew closer I began to understand what was going on. A well-built blonde-haired woman of around fifty was facing a fierce-looking dog. Her left arm was protected by padding; in her right she held a whip. The dog was biting and growling at the padding, while she shouted loud commands. Several men, each of them with a dog, were looking on. We went and joined some other spectators who were standing pressed up against the fence. Freaky was quivering with fear. He hid between my legs, trying to escape from all the growls and the crack of the whip.

Once the woman decided the attack sequence was over, she called to another owner among the group that was obviously waiting his turn. The attack ritual was repeated. The woman shouted orders to the dog in German, occasionally turning to its owner and giving an explanation in Spanish. There was a lot of noise and all in all it provided a colorful, if somewhat savage, spectacle.

"Do you think this has got something to do with what we're looking for?" Garzón whispered to me.

"I've no idea. Keep quiet and watch."

Next to us was a young boy in a tracksuit who had left his bike on the ground to watch what was going on.

"Are they training them?" I asked, as casually as I could.

"Well, it's a training ground."

"Physical training?" I said, trying not to sound too interested. He looked at me as if I were an idiot.

"They're guard dogs, and she is the trainer."

"Ah!" I exclaimed.

"She's a professional," he explained.

"Do you know her?" I insisted, running the risk of arousing his suspicion.

"I see them sometimes, they're always here." He looked down at Freaky and said slyly: "You don't want to train him, do you?"

"Who knows? Maybe; he can be very brave when he wants to be," I said, offended on Freaky's behalf.

The kid turned away, put some tiny headphones in his ears, picked up his bike and cycled off without another word.

Garzón and I stayed where we were until the training had finished. We were the last spectators. The dogs and their owners started to come out of the fenced-off area. The trainer said goodbye to them at the gate, exchanging a few words with each of them. We could not just stand there without attracting attention; either we had to go up to her, or leave. We did not have enough information to allow us to pass up any opportunity for learning more.

"Leave this to me," I whispered to Garzón.

We walked over, and when we were a few paces away, Freaky started to howl like a thing possessed. He tugged on the leash, desperate to escape. The trainer saw us, looked at the dog, and smiled. She said goodbye to the others and came over. Freaky became even more hysterical, wrapping himself round my legs. He may have been small, but he was strong enough to knock me over.

"Still boy, still!" I shouted at him.

The trainer made soothing gestures at me.

"Pick him up," she ordered. I obeyed as best I could. "Now cover his eyes with your hand. That's right!"

Freaky calmed down. The trainer stroked his head, allowed him to sniff at her hand. Freaky relaxed completely.

"You can let him go now."

"I don't understand why he . . . "

"Don't worry, it's always the same. The dogs who see me training get really scared. Because of the way I shout, and the whip."

"I'm not surprised they're frightened," Garzón put in. "You're a fearsome sight out there."

She laughed a hearty laugh.

"Believe me, it's all put on! But dogs can't separate appearance from reality. They're too noble for that. Do you live around here?"

"No," I replied. "We're here on business, but your training caught our eye."

"A lot of people stop to watch. The best spectators are the old-age pensioners, or kids at the weekend."

"Do you teach the dogs to attack?" asked Garzón.

"I teach them to defend their masters, to obey orders and to follow a scent. That's my job."

"Can any dog learn all that, including this one here?" I said, pointing to Freaky.

"In theory . . . but I only work with guard-dog breeds."

"And I guess that these days there's no shortage of clients."

"I can't complain. There are a lot of ordinary people who have guard dogs, and then there are those who need them: shopkeepers who want to train their dogs to guard the store, security guards . . . "

"It sounds fascinating," said the sergeant.

"Do you really think so?"

"Of course! It must be really exciting."

Garzón had not only forgotten my instructions and taken the lead, but was being creative about it. His friendly approach soon got results.

"Listen, I've finished for today. Why don't we have a beer in the bar over there?"

"Great!" trilled Garzón.

I said: "It's getting a bit late for me, I have to get back to the office. Shall I see you there in a couple of hours, Fermín?"

I left them exchanging expressions of mutual delight as they walked to the bar. Garzón had done his job well; if there was anything to discover, he would. His new companion seemed to like to talk.

I took Freaky home and left him there, exhausted from all

his adventures. I went to the vet's. I was attended by the pre-viously mentioned assistant, who turned out to be not a beau-tiful woman but a bored-looking young man. I had to wait for Juan Monturiol to finish seeing his clients. I whiled away the time flicking through magazines, all of them about dogs. It was incredible: for the first time I realized there was a whole uni-verse I had never even dreamt of—vets, dog-food manufactur-ers, dog-sitters, dog trainers. O.K., so it's obvious that not everyone simply reads the newspaper and goes for walks; beneath the homogenizing surface of the city there were all kinds of enthusiasts: oenologists, naturists, mushroom hunters and dog lovers.

Juan finally appeared in his white coat. He was saying a polite goodbye to a lady with a poodle. He saw me and, though perhaps it was only my imagination, I thought I saw his eyes widen a little.

"Is there a problem?" he asked, and I noticed that for some reason or other, the question had a definite ironic ring to it.

"It'll only take a minute," I found myself obliged to say.

He showed me in and sat me down in the seat for clients with dogs. The room smelled of disinfectant. A group of angel-ic puppies stared down at me from a frame on the wall.

"I've come to ask you a technical question that's been both-ering me. I'd like to know if a dog is following a scent and takes you somewhere where there are other dogs . . . " It was hard making such a specific question sound offhand, but I tried my best. He interrupted me.

"You're a policewoman, aren't you?"

"How did you guess, if you don't mind my asking?"

"If someone is told a person has died on the phone and they have to rush out of the house, there are only two possibilities: either that person is a doctor, or a policewoman. As it's a pro-fession so closely allied with mine, if you'd been a doctor you would have said so when I came to see you."

"With powers of deduction like that, you should join the police too."

"If you make me an offer I can't refuse . . . what rank are you?"

"Inspector."

He whistled. Everything he did was typical of someone discovering that you are part of the police force.

"And how can I help the law?"

I tried to stay calm.

"This morning we took my dog to the place where a crime was committed in the hope that he would pick up the scent of something. And he did. He set off, and we followed him. Now, here's my doubt: he took us to a field where there's a training ground with lots of dogs. So, do you think it's significant that's where he led us? Does it mean he knew the way, or was he simply smelling the other dogs in the distance and heading for them?"

Monturiol scratched his shiny blond hair. He looked serious, thoughtful even. He opened his mouth to express an initial doubt. He wasn't attractive, or appealing, or good-looking; he was handsome, deep-down handsome, every last bit of him.

"How far were you from the training ground?"

"Oh, I don't know, about two long streets away, one of them with a corner to it."

"Well, it's very hard to say, because either could be the cause. It might have been the smell of the other dogs that attracted him, but then again . . . I wouldn't like to say for sure, I'm no dog expert."

"But you're a vet!"

"Yes, which means I know their anatomy, their habits, the way they reproduce, as well as everything to do with their illnesses. But there's a lot more to dogs than that. Did you know that in the United States they even have canine psychiatrists? They are complex animals, and because they've been man's best friend throughout history, they've picked up some of our neuroses and manias on the way."

When he smiled, the sight of his fleshy lips and perfect white teeth was almost unbearable.

"Then I'd better ask the dog section we have in the police."

He scratched his head again, and almost drove me crazy.

"I don't know if that's the best answer. I'm sure there they know about training, but not about their behavior. They have too narrow an approach. Besides, they almost always use the same breed: German shepherds."

He got up and went to a filing cabinet. He rummaged inside it. The back of his head was like the most classical of Greek statues.

"What I'll do is give you the address of the best canine expert in Barcelona. There's a whole library just with books about dogs."

He got out a blue card and copied the details on the back of one of his prescriptions.

"It's called Bestiarium, and her name is Angela Chamorro."

"A woman?"

"Are you surprised?" he said, with renewed irony.

"Not at all."

Not at all! What a clever answer, what wit, what verbal cut and thrust! What had happened to the spirit I usually put into my verbal jousts with the opposite sex? It was always the same: just when I thought I was being Diana the Huntress, I had run out of arrows, and found my quiver quite empty.

I thanked him and started to leave. This expert might help our investigation, but I could only see her as an obstacle. Now I would have no excuse to come and see this mouthwatering morsel. Fortunately, there was still Freaky: I would just have to invent some benign but troublesome illness for him, even if it was only a psychological phobia he had caught from some American cousin.

All at once I heard his voice behind my back.

"Petra, how about finishing that drink we never got to have?"

"You're still willing to have a drink with me now you know I'm a policewoman?"

"I like to know who I'm drinking with, and now I do. I close shop at eight this evening."

"I'll come by to pick you up."

So he was a hunter too. Of course he was! Or did I really think it had been a coincidence that he had personally delivered all the things I had bought the other day? A dangerous man: he had been about to have me believe that I was the invincible Diana when in fact I was the lost little hind. And there's nothing in life I detest so much as playing that role. But the hunting party had only just begun, so we would see who bagged their catch first.

Two hours exactly after I had left Garzón at the mercy of that wild-animal tamer, I was back in the police station waiting for him. He was more than half an hour late, which is unusual for him. He eventually turned up beaming and full of himself, and stinking of beer like a Welsh miner.

"You've no idea how fascinating the world of dogs can be, Petra," he declared. "And you can't imagine how good Valentina is at winning them over."

"Valentina?"

"Yes, the trainer. Her name is Valentina Cortés."

"You two seem to have hit it off."

"Well, she's a very open, friendly woman. Of course I was trying to find out what she knew. I don't think there's anything suspicious there—Freaky led us to her by chance."

"We'll have to see if that's the only possibility."

"As you like, but I don't think she has anything to do with the case."

"Come on, Garzón! It looks as though Valentina is as good at bringing policemen to heel as she is with dogs."

He reacted as indignantly as in the days when I was always rubbing him up the wrong way:

"Inspector . . . I don't know what to say to that without being rude."

"Don't get on your high horse, Garzón," I said, giving him a couple of resounding slaps on the shoulder pads. "If you really want a reason to be mad, I'll give you one."

"What do you mean?"

"We won't have time for lunch."

"Why not?"

"I've spoken to our man in Las Fuentes. After a week undercover there, he's reached the conclusion that the regulars drop in just after lunch. At other times it's casual customers. If anyone knew Lucena, he'll be there then; apparently it's always the same group. So we have to go and fetch Freaky from my house and be at the bar no later than a quarter past three."

"Are you still determined that flea-bitten cur should play the detective?"

"'Flea-bitten cur': weren't you just saying what fascinating creatures dogs were?"

He went with me, still complaining. If anything was sacred for Fermín Garzón, apart from fulfilling his duty, it was the need to eat regularly. I clinched the argument by saying he could get a bite to eat in Las Fuentes, and in the car took his mind off his stomach by asking him about the dog trainer.

"Well, she's set up her own business. Her parents were poor farmers. She loves the country, too: she told me that when she retires she hopes to use her savings to buy a small property there. That's her great dream. She has never married, and lives on her own in a small house in Horta."

So his questioning had obviously been mostly about her private life, or perhaps that was what she had preferred to talk about. Garzón could not have asked her too many direct questions anyway without giving the game away.

We picked up Freaky. He was obviously taking his new role as police dog very seriously, and appeared to have forgotten the emotions of the morning. We reached the dingy Las Fuentes just as the wafts of cooking oil were starting to mix with the smell of coffee. Our spy was standing at the bar, and gave us a quick nod of recognition. I felt sorry for him; it must have been terrible to spend a week in such a dive. The owner gave Freaky a dirty look, but he obviously remembered who we were, so did not ask us to leave. We sat at a table and ordered two coffees. Garzón asked for a tortilla with a bread roll. At a nearby table there was a game of dominoes going on. Men on their own kept coming in: some said hello to one another, others did not. Freaky showed no sign of recognizing any of them. I kept my eye on the bar owner: I wanted to see if his face betrayed any sign of warning people. But he looked completely calm, and appeared to be ignoring us altogether. Scowling but methodical, he served coffees and glasses of brandy that smelt of turpentine. Garzón had no luck with his tortilla: the cook had already left. A complete catastrophe. Half an hour went by that seemed an eternity. The sergeant's leg was twitching spasmodically as if to the rhythm of a Dixieland band. Freaky was dozing peacefully on the floor surrounded by cigarette butts, scampi tails and paper napkins. I stroked his head to wake him up. He licked my hand tenderly. Then all of a sudden his ears pricked. His head turned to the door, and he stood up. He started wagging his tail and pulling on his leash. I let him go. He ran straight to a man who had just come in and was standing by the bar. Freaky barked and put one of his paws up on his leg. The guy patted him, smiled and turned to the bar owner:

"What's he doing here?" he asked innocently. As soon as he had said the words, he realized something was going on, and looked around suspiciously. Garzón was already right next to him.

"We're the police," he said. "Do you know this dog?"

"No, no. I don't know whose he is."

"You'd better not say anything now, but come with us to the station."

I cannot remember what incoherent protest the man muttered, but the sergeant snapped at him to be quiet. When we got back to the station, we left Freaky in the car. The suspect was taken to the interview room, while Garzón and I talked over how we would approach the questioning.

"If he's got any sense at all, he won't say a word, however much he knows. I doubt whether we can use the dog as a witness."

"Are you thinking of making him strip like you did with that other suspect?" Garzón asked.

"Not a chance!"

"Why?"

"Because he's as ugly as sin."

He was as pathetic as Lucena. He looked like a vile, scurvy, down-and-out, corrupt, abject little villain. And the clinching detail that he was the absolute dregs of society was the fact that, looking the way he did, he tried to dress up. He was wearing a pair of red trousers and a flowery shirt, with a leather thong and a medallion round his neck, like Buffalo Bill on an off day. He said his name was Salvador Vega, and at first denied even knowing Ignacio Lucena Pastor. He was weak and obviously scared. When Garzón realized this, he immediately adopted his tough-cop routine.

"What do you do in life?"

"I'm a craftsman."

"What kind of crafts?"

"I make plaster doves and other birds. I paint some of them in bright colors to sell to charity shops, I leave others plain and craft shops buy them from me."

"My ass!" said Garzón. "Do you think for one minute, inspector, that anyone can make a living painting doves?"

The little man grew nervous.

"I swear to God that's what I do! If you want, I'll take you to my place and show you the plastic molds and the originals. And I do make a living! I've got enough to live on, to pay the rent and my bills. I've even got a van to deliver my stock! We can go to the workshop right now if you don't believe me."

Garzón leaned over and yanked him up by his lapels until their noses were almost touching.

"Listen, you son of a bitch, I'm not going to believe a word of what you say if you carry on denying that you know Lucena. We have witnesses who say you do!"

"That's a lie!'

"A lie? Here's something you can be sure of: you've got me to deal with now, and I'll make sure things go badly for you, really badly. I'll personally make sure of that. Do you follow?"

I cut in:

"Look, I believe you make doves. And do you know why? Because I saw two of them at Lucena's place, and I'll bet that they're exactly the same as the ones you make."

He was silent for a minute.

"Lots of people buy my doves."

Garzón blew his top. He threw himself on the guy, seizing him by the elbow. Vega was terrified. He cast me an imploring glance:

"Get him off me! He's crazy!"

"No, my colleague isn't crazy, but he loses his patience easily. I'm more patient than he is, but at this rate I'll soon get angry too. A man has been killed, so we've no time for jokers."

"Killed? I didn't know he was dead. In the bar they only said he was in hospital, and that the police were looking for someone—probably the person who had put him there—but I didn't know he was dead."

"So you did know him then?"

His chin dropped on his chest. Then he said in a whisper:

"Yes."

Garzón leaned over again, hauled him out of his seat by the shirt, and cursed him:

"You little asshole, so now you admit you knew him? You're nothing more than scum, you know that? Or rather, you're worse, you're a heap of shit! So you didn't know he was dead? You want us to believe that, you sonofabitch? I bet you were the one who killed him, weren't you? If you don't tell me all you know right now, I'll wipe that smile off your face!"

Even I was impressed by Garzón's ferocity. It must have been the rumbling stomach that had got to him. I put a hand on his shoulder to calm him down. I didn't want him to start punching the suspect.

"Were you friends?" I asked.

"No, not friends. We saw each other occasionally, and had a beer together. I liked him."

"What was Lucena mixed up in?"

"I don't know, I swear I've no idea. I know he lived on his own, with that disgusting dog, but if he was involved in any shady business I swear he never let on. We used to talk about football."

Garzón thumped the table. Vega started back as if afraid the next punch would be to his face.

"About football, you son of a bitch?"

I thought he was going to attack the man. I muttered:

"Take it easy, sergeant, take it easy."

Salvador Vega looked at me desperately.

"Get him off me!" he implored.

"Nobody is going to hurt you, but you have to tell us the truth, and answer all our questions without hiding anything. What did Ignacio Lucena do for a living?"

He slackened the Buffalo Bill thong, and undid the top button of his shirt.

"He dealt in dogs."

Before he could continue, Garzón shouted at him:

"Dogs? Do you think we're stupid? What do you mean, he dealt in dogs?"

"I'm telling the truth! That's all I know—he found dogs for people."

Before my colleague could thrown himself on him again, I restrained him.

"You mean he sold them?"

"Yes, I suppose so."

"Where did he get them from?"

"He never told me. Honestly, he was always very quiet, even when we had drunk a couple of beers he didn't say much. All I remember is he used to say 'This week I have to deliver a couple of dogs.' That was all."

"Do you think they were stolen?"

"That's what I always thought, but I would never have dared ask him, he had a foul temper."

I sat quietly for a while. Garzón sat next to me, panting from all his exertions.

"Did you ever hear him say who he was delivering the dogs to?"

Vega looked at the floor. I tried to sound sympathetic as I went on:

"Think it over carefully. This is a murder inquiry. If you're telling the truth and only shared a few beers with him, you still need to tell us everything you know. If we find out later you've stupidly kept something from us, you could be charged."

He nodded his head as though agreeing.

"He once told me he took the dogs to the clinic for a professor friend of his."

"To the Faculty of Medicine?"

"Yes."

"For experiments?"

"I don't know."

"Is that really all you can tell us?"

"I swear to God! I was always curious that he made a living from dogs, and I used to ask him about it, but he never talked about himself."

Garzón butted in again:

"Of course you thought it was funny: whoever heard of making a living from dogs! You're joking, aren't you?"

For the first time this miserable little wretch of a man summoned up a scrap of courage:

"Everybody has to make ends meet as best they can. I don't know why it seems so strange to you: I make doves, he found people dogs. Not everyone can be an attorney."

Strange indeed that he immediately thought of attorneys. He could have said bankers or industrialists, but for this wretched specimen attorneys were the important people.

"Do you have any idea who might have killed him?"

"None, I swear to you."

"All right," I muttered.

We sent him home with a couple of copo to search his apartment. He said we would not need a warrant, he was keen to prove his innocence. Garzón looked like a Shakespearean actor exhausted and still on a high after playing Othello. His hunger pangs must have made him seem even more threatening.

"Do you believe all this stuff about dogs?" he asked.

"I have to for now. Get them to check if he has a record. Put someone on his tail for a week at least. And keep our man in Las Fuentes, checking who the owner tries to contact. Tomorrow, go there yourself and talk to him. See if he confirms what Vega said about him only talking football with Lucena. If he still refuses to cooperate, tell him we're sure he knew Lucena and that means he's been keeping things from us, so we could bring him in."

"Yes, inspector. I suppose it's too late to go to the Faculty of Medicine tonight."

"We'll go tomorrow."

"So we've finished for today?"

"No, we still have one more visit to make."

"I'm sorry inspector, but it's seven o'clock and the fact is I haven't had a bite to eat since breakfast . . . "

"It's me who's sorry, Fermín, but you don't need me to tell you it's one of the drawbacks of the job . . . just one more visit, then you're free."

Before we got into the car, he went off to a bar and bought a big bag of crisps. Freaky was waiting quietly for us, but as soon as he saw the food he grew frantic.

As I drove through the dense Barcelona evening traffic all I could hear was the whimpering of the dog and the crunch of the crisps in the sergeant's mouth. My nerves were jangling so much that I finally exploded:

"Give me a break, Fermín! Give that poor dog a crisp before I go completely mad!"

Like a stingy, grumpy kid the sergeant reluctantly put a rather small crisp on the back seat for the dog. I remember thinking that never in all my life had I seen anything so ridiculous.

Fortunately, just stepping inside Bestiarium had a soothing effect on all of us. It was a well laid-out and welcoming bookshop, with a pale fitted carpet and gentle jazz music in the background. Angela Chamorro greeted us with a smile. She was around fifty years old, had pretty hazel-colored eyes and was dressed with the same quiet elegance that she had chosen for the look of her store. She had gray streaks in her hair, which was drawn up in a bouncy bun at the back of her head. When I told her it was Juan Monturiol who had sent us, she had nothing but praise for him. When I added that we were from the police, she seemed intrigued. She glanced down at her watch:

"It's almost eight o'clock. I'll close the shop so we can talk more easily. Hardly anyone comes at this time of night anyway."

She showed us into a small storeroom full of boxes of books at the back of the shop. There was a tea set on a camp bed and on the floor an enormous woolly dog lay stoically dozing. I gestured at him with surprise.

"Don't be afraid. That's Nelly, my dog. She's a fine example of a Pyrenean mastiff. She's completely harmless. Take a seat." She stroked the animal's back with a delicate tenderness. Nelly heaved a deep sigh. "What can I do for you? I have to say, though, I might not be able to answer your questions."

"Juan says you're the leading expert on dogs in the entire country."

She smiled, rather embarrassed.

"I hope you didn't believe him."

She had style, and soon showed herself to be intelligent and quick on the uptake too. She immediately understood what we were after when we described how Freaky had behaved up in El Carmelo. She sat thinking about it for a minute, then asked:

"Did your dog look interested when you were taking him along the streets?"

"Interested?"

"Did he have his nose to the ground, did he run along without stopping to sniff at other smells?"

"I'm afraid not. He stopped to smell everything at first, then he started to concentrate a bit more."

"How far were you from the training ground before he started concentrating?"

"I guess it must have been four or five hundred meters away."

"Was there any female dog on heat among those being trained?"

"I'm not sure, there probably was. If necessary, we can find out."

"Well, if your dog went there because he remembered it, that must mean that for some reason or other it brought back pleasant memories. Perhaps his owner took him for walks there, or perhaps they gave him treats. He would never have led you to a place where something bad had happened to him, even if it was only once. On the other hand, if he was following a definite trail, there must have been something really attractive drawing him on: a bitch on heat, for example. Five hundred meters is a long way, it's about as far as a dog can smell. You also have to take the atmospheric conditions into account; they can be decisive. Was it windy that morning?"

Garzón and I stared at each other, both of us caught out by the question.

"Do you remember, sergeant?"

"I've no idea."

"Well, it's not that important. Let's just say that a group of dogs is not in itself enough to attract another dog's attention. Of course, like I said, there could have been a bitch on heat, or perhaps there was some of the food that trainers use to reward dogs that perform well."

"This trainer is named Valentina Cortés."

"She has a very good reputation."

"Do you know her?"

"Not personally, but in the world of dogs everyone ends up knowing everyone else."

"So, to sum up, there needn't be any particular significance in the fact that Freaky led us there. He may never have been there before."

"Find out if there was a bitch on heat, that's important."

Garzón took out his notebook and scribbled something in it.

"There's another question I'd like to ask, Angela, and from what I can see you're the perfect person to answer everything about dogs."

"No, don't say that!" she said, obviously delighted.

"It's about the dogs they use in the Faculty of Medicine. What do they need them for, and where do they get them?"

"Well, I suppose they need them for research. The ideal breed for medical research is the beagle. They're lovely English dogs, not too big and not too small. Genetically, they are hunting dogs. Beagles hunt pheasants, hares . . . but they've even been taught to hunt fish! At some point it was discovered they had genetic material very similar to that of human beings, and ever since then they have been used in medical faculties all over the world. They usually breed their own and have kennels for them."

"So they don't need extra supplies, of stolen dogs for example?"

"I think that the idea of some shady character selling dogs—or dead bodies—is from the distant past, isn't it, although who knows? Private laboratories, cosmetic firms for example, are a different matter. There's lots that isn't clear there. You know how people in general hate vivisection. The result has been that these firms do everything behind closed doors. Nobody knows what dogs they use, where they get them from or how. They never risk any bad publicity, and the animal-protection agencies can never find much out."

She turned her candid eyes away from me.

"Do you think what I've told you might help in your investigation?"

She was delighted to be of some use.

"Of course it will!"

"I should say, though, that when it comes to dogs there is nothing certain or definite. Dogs aren't machines, they're living beings, they can have unexpected reactions, feelings, their own personalities, they even have . . . well, I'm convinced they even have souls."

She stared at us again, carried away by the almost mystical enthusiasm of her words.

"I . . . " for the first time since we had met her, Garzón opened his mouth to speak. She listened intently.

"What is it?"

"I'm sorry, I was just wondering if I could have one of those biscuits." He pointed to the ones on a tray beside an empty tea cup.

Angela did not know what to think, then all at once burst out laughing:

"Oh dear, do excuse me! I completely forgot. I'll prepare some tea for you right away."

Garzón tried to cover his embarrassment with rapid explanations: "We've been working so hard all day I haven't eaten a thing, and I'm being to feel a bit weak . . . "

As she prepared the tea in the adjacent kitchenette, she expressed her sympathy:

"I imagine that spending all day on a case can be very tiring and dangerous."

I shook my head at Garzón as though he were a naughty little boy. He shrugged his shoulders innocently, loving every minute of it. The shaggy dog peered at us.

By the time we left the bookstore it was after ten. We had drunk tea and eaten biscuits; we had learned that Angela was the widow of a vet, that her business was doing fine, and that she adored dogs. Now that he was more relaxed after eating something, Garzón was in a much better mood, and told her all about the curious customs in his distant home village near Salamanca, where dogs were used for the summer changes of pasture. She listened to him with rapt attention, as if those steppenwolves were the most interesting thing anyone had ever talked to her about.

When I finally got home I was exhausted and confused. Freaky threw himself on his food and started eating as if he were starving to death. No doubt about it, that dog was Garzón's alter ego. I threw my coat on to a chair and played back my phone messages:

"Petra, this is Juan Monturiol. I was waiting for you to come and pick me up, but it's already half past eight. I'm going home. I suppose that these things happen if you have a date with a policewoman. I hope that at least you've caught one of those serial killers you see in American films."

"Damn and blast!" I muttered, then increased the intensity of my swearing until it reached pure blasphemy. I had totally forgotten Juan. My work was making a complete fool of me. Who did I think I was, some detective in a novel? What was the hurry to find out who the killer was? He was no less a killer for spending a few more hours at liberty. And I had missed out on a captivating smile, a stevedore's body, an authentic classical Greek ass! And what was worse was that Juan Monturiol was going to think I had stood him up on purpose, determined to show him "who has the upper hand." Which was exactly what I did not want him to think, both because it was true I might do something like that, and second because it meant our relationship was that much more complicated, and it was going to take that much longer to get him into bed. My mood turned blacker than a thunderstorm.

Freaky had finished his meal and came over, wagging his tail.

"Get away from me, you filthy dog!" I shouted, waving my arms to drive him off. He stood there uncomprehending, his tiny black eyes fixed on me. "Oh all right, come here then," I relented, taking pity on his bewildered look. I sat down and he came and lay on my lap, proud and happy. I think that of the two of us, I was the first to fall asleep.

4

We met Don Arturo Castillo, professor of pharmacology at the University of Barcelona, while he was having a coffee laced with brandy in the faculty canteen. He was wearing a white coat with several pens in his top pocket, and a pair of big tortoiseshell glasses. When we went up to him he was laughing fit to burst with one of his colleagues. He reacted as though he had spent his whole life receiving the police and inviting them to have breakfast with him. He immediately offered us a coffee and told us that students, patients of the clinic and people from all branches of the teaching staff met up in this bar. He was a cheerful, extroverted character who probably escaped from the solitude of his research by spending some time in this noisy meeting place. We asked him to take us somewhere quieter, and he led us to his office. He still did not seem particularly curious to know what had brought us to see him. When I asked him directly if he knew Ignacio Lucena Pastor, he gave no hint of recognizing the name.

"Is he a student or something? Has a student committed a crime? I hope it's not murder, although now I come to think of it, any of my students could be a criminal."

He guffawed at his own joke. We showed him Lucena's photograph.

"This is him. We've heard he provided you with dogs for experiments, Doctor Castillo."

"Why, this is Natty Pincho! You're talking about Pincho? Of

course I know him! I never knew what his real name was. He hasn't been here in a long while. A short fellow, odd-looking, who doesn't say much. Why is he in a hospital bed?"

"He isn't in a bed any more; he's dead. He was murdered. He was beaten to death several days ago."

Doctor Castillo's face turned serious.

"Pincho was? My God, I had no idea!"

"Someone told us he was proud of being a friend of yours."

He looked disturbed and confused.

"Well, not exactly a friend . . . each time he brought me a dog we had a bit of a chat, and a beer in the bar. But yes, I suppose he was proud to know me; everything about him suggested he was from a very poor background."

"Did you use the dogs for experiments?"

"Actually, the Faculty breeds its own dogs. But we sometimes used to buy one of his dogs for the interns to do their practicals on. We've stopped that now, but when Pincho was around, it was still quite frequent."

"Did you ever ask him where he got the dogs?"

"No, I never did."

"Could they have been stolen?"

"I shouldn't have thought so! They were all strays, they had no value. There are hundreds of them in the municipal dog pound. We stopped using them because they were in such a bad state: a lot of them were sick, or had worms, and we never knew exactly how old they were. All that made the experiments less reliable."

"Why didn't you just get them from the dog pound, then?"

"It was much more expensive. We would have had to make sure they had all their jabs and their papers in order. Besides, Pincho would bring the dogs here, so it was a great convenience. The poor man needed the money, and he'd been supplying us for such a long time . . . Then suddenly he stopped coming, with no explanation."

"Doctor Castillo, do you think you could remember the names of any of the dogs the Faculty bought? Perhaps they were recorded somewhere?"

"If they had names, I never wanted to know them. It's not very pleasant using dogs for experiments, you know. Come on, let me show you something."

He took us next door to a large laboratory. A few people in white coats were moving around among glass cases, medical equipment and chemical apparatus. Doctor Castillo came to a halt by an examination table. On it lay a medium-sized dog with light-colored fur and brindle patches. It was unconscious, and had all its limbs spread wide. Its trachea had been cut open, and a thick tube led from the bloody incision to some kind of cardiograph. As it breathed, there was a loud rattling noise. The wires attached to different parts of its body were producing lines on a sheet of graph paper. It was a forlorn sight.

"Now do you see why I said it wasn't very pleasant? By the end of the experiment they are no use for anything else. We give them a lethal injection, so that at least they don't suffer. But it takes a strong stomach to look at them when they come in. They try to play with you, they lick your hand . . . then as soon as they come in here, they fall silent, and do nothing: they don't try to run away or escape. If you look them in the eye, you can see they know they are going to die."

"That's awful!" I burst out, shocked.

"That's science for you! That's why I don't want to know the names or anything else about the dogs, until they're under anesthetic here on the operating table. Martin, the man in charge of breeding our own dogs, is the one who looks after them. He feeds them, and then my assistants prepare them for the experiments. It's one of the few privileges of being the boss!"

"Could we speak to Martin?"

"That's a good idea, he might possibly know more about Pincho than I do. He was the one who dealt with him directly—he took the dogs and paid him."

"There's something else you could do for us, Doctor Castillo. Could you see if any of the figures in this book here correspond to payments your department made to . . . Pincho?"

"We can look on the computer. Follow me."

We trooped back to his office. With a wave of triumph, he showed us his computer.

"Take a look at this! The latest word in computing. I had to fight the whole university administration for them to give me the money to buy it, but it's perfect, it does everything you ask of it. It can store scientific information just as easily as it does your shopping bills. And just look, what high definition!"

He leaned over the keyboard and typed: "Up Yours!" Garzón and I shot incredulous glances at each other. A nurse busy filing nearby saw us and smiled. The sergeant took Lucena's second accounts book out of his briefcase and showed it to Castillo.

"Are there no dates?" asked the doctor.

"No."

He glanced at the figures, then exclaimed:

"Fifty thousand, forty thousand . . . " he started to shake his head vigorously. "No, goodness me, that's not possible. We never paid Pincho anything remotely like that for his dogs."

"O.K., let's try these figures instead," said Garzón, handing him the other book.

"Ten thousand, eight thousand five hundred . . . that's much more like it."

He fiddled with the computer, looked in different documents, and soon came up with what we were after. All the figures in the book referred to sums paid to Lucena for dogs they had bought. And they were dated! The last transaction was from two years earlier. We asked the professor to print us off a copy of his list. I saw there was no mention of the strange lengths of time noted in the dead man's book.

"Doctor, have you any idea what these might mean—here, where it says: 'six months, two years' . . . ?"

"Those?" he said offhandedly. "Yes, of course—they're the approximate age of each dog."

Garzón slapped himself on the forehead.

"The dog's age! Of course!"

"Only their approximate age. As I told you, we like to know it to be able to calculate the variables for the results of our experiments. In these cases they were not very exact, though I have to say that Pincho was very good at calculating them. He knew his stuff about dogs. What a way to die!"

He went off with a spring in his step to find the man in charge of the Faculty kennels. The nurse came over and smiled a wry smile.

"Doctor Castillo is an international authority in pharmacological research. He's a recognized expert, and goes to congresses all over the world. But as you probably know, extremely clever men tend to be rather eccentric, don't they?"

We nodded guiltily, feeling we had been caught out by the look we had exchanged. After her little speech, the nurse vanished. Garzón was too excited to be bothered by her remarks.

"You see, inspector, those damned notebooks weren't such a mystery after all! The ridiculous names are of the dogs, the lengths of time their ages, and the figures what he was paid for them."

"But we've only cleared up what's in one of the books; the other's still not resolved. Don't get too confident about it so quickly."

An elderly man in a blue overall came in. He looked unsure of himself. He also identified Lucena as Pincho, and said he had never asked him where he got the dogs from. He was so nervous that Garzón felt he had to reassure him.

"Look, we're just asking questions like we do in any investigation. No one's accusing you of anything."

"It's just that Doctor Castillo told me somebody killed Pincho, and even though I hardly knew him . . . I don't know, but to think he's dead . . . Of course, I've seen a lot of dogs die, but it's different when it's a human being, isn't it?"

"I suppose it is," I said.

"That Pincho can't have been a law-abiding sort. I told the doctor as much, but he's such a saint, he sees only the good in people, and didn't want to deprive him of a few pennies."

"What made you think he wasn't law-abiding?"

"I don't know, perhaps it was just the way he looked. Besides, I was always convinced he must have some deal going with the Community Support people or the ones in the dog pound. It was the only way to explain how he came by so many dogs. He couldn't have caught them all in the street. There used to be a time when we had lots of interns and needed lots of dogs. But if you asked Pincho for seven—that was what he brought! It seemed odd to me that he found it so easy . . . I thought he must be up to something."

"Did you phone him on any particular number?"

"No, he always came here. Besides, it wasn't as if we needed dogs every day . . . "

"When was the last time you saw him?"

"He disappeared a long time ago! We used to comment among the people here: 'Either that guy won the lottery, or he's kicked the bucket.'"

"Did you never think he might have found a proper job?"

"A job? Look, I may be ignorant and know next to nothing, but one thing I can always spot is a layabout. Believe me, Pincho was not someone who believed in jobs."

This unassuming worker with a keen eye had given us our next lead. If Lucena was able to provide them with all the dogs they needed, he must have had some way of getting hold of them. Martin's conclusion was clear: the other man must have had someone he could bribe in the Community Support office or the dog pound. What we had to do was to find out who.

Garzón thought it was more crucial to follow up on the account books, and it was true they were important as well. We knew exactly what the contents of one of them were, and we also knew what time scale was involved. The last sale of a dog to the Faculty was dated two years earlier. It seemed obvious that after that Lucena had not been content just to earn ten thousand pesetas per dog from the Faculty of Medicine. But he was still active: we had the second accounts book, which showed he was still in business. And the sums mentioned there were much higher, which made it hard to work out what they could be for. As Garzón said, they probably referred to dogs, because the names and the dates alongside them were similar to those in the other book . . . the only difference was the sum of money paid.

"Perhaps they paid him more for the same thing somewhere else."

"Supplying dogs for experiments?"

"Exactly. And where is research carried out apart from in the university?"

"In the pharmaceutical industry, as Angela Chamorro told us."

"And would they pay that much more for stray dogs?"

"We don't know what the price of dog meat is on the black market."

I glanced despairingly at the sergeant.

"All this is so macabre and yet so grotesque! Do you realize what an absurd situation we're in?"

"But that absurd situation led to someone's death."

"Someone we don't even know the real identity of."

"Do you remember what you once said, inspector? History cannot tell us who Shakespeare was, and yet we know he wrote plays. Well, we might not know who Lucena Pastor was, but we know he trafficked in dogs."

"Yes, a dog trafficker, for God's sake!"

Garzón suddenly glanced at his watch.

"I have to go, Petra, I have a lunch date."

"A working lunch?"

"No, private business. I'll see you back at the station."

"As soon as you get there, talk to Sergeant Pinilla. Tell him to investigate the Community Officers and the dog pound. We need at all costs to find out who supplied Lucena with the dogs."

"If such a person exists."

I looked at him despondently, and repeated in a glum voice:

"If such a person exists."

The worst thing was to think that perhaps we were setting off in completely the wrong direction. It makes you feel stupid, like a kid playing hide-and-seek who looks in the opposite corner to where his friends are hiding and snickering behind his back. To top it all, this ridiculous case did not arouse any passion in me. it did not stir my emotions. The victim was an insignificant little man, whose death did not even make me want to see justice done as an act of revenge in the way that the raped girls of my previous case had. In fact, neither of us had thought for a minute that Lucena was innocent. From the outset, both of us had been convinced that somehow or other he must have deserved the beating that cost him his life. Looked at closely, it was terrible we should think that way, because our conclusion on was based solely on how he looked—in other words, the signs of his social standing as revealed by his appearance. Would we have condemned him as guilty if he had looked as smart as an executive? Lucena was like one of the dogs he trafficked: no pedigree, no charm, a different name for each master, no one to claim them when they died. The only difference was that the dogs aroused compassion because they were innocent.

But was I right to feel depressed because of the way I had acted so far with regard to this poor little man? Was it fair to criticize myself because I did not feel passionate about finding whoever was responsible for his death? I had already paid him homage by taking his dog to the cemetery—that was much more than any reasonable person would have done. To hell with Lucena! We would do all we could to catch his murderer, we would fulfill our duty and nothing more.

I did not feel hungry, so I decided to fill the lunch break by taking Freaky for a walk. It was not long before our steps took us in the direction of Juan Monturiol's veterinary surgery. Was I starting to follow a set path like animals do, or was it that— like them too—I was simply letting my instincts guide me? We walked in circles round the building: Freaky could not have cared less. Finally at five minutes to two the assistant came out, then at exactly two o'clock Juan did the same. I went over to him. He was wearing a flak jacket that showed him off to good advantage. When he saw me he raised his hands in the air.

"I've got everything in order, inspector, I'm not guilty!"

"It's me who feels guilty. I want to apologise for the other day."

"It's not the first time I've been stood up. Were you on the track of an assassin?"

"Though it might sound like boasting, yes I was."

"I still can't get over the idea that you're a policewoman, I didn't mean to offend you."

I invited him back to my place for lunch, but he said he preferred the restaurant on the corner. I counterattacked by pointing out I had Freaky with me, but he rebuffed me by saying he often took his dog there. How long was this game going to go on? Perhaps I should have given him the option of suggesting his apartment, but it had been my invitation in the first place.

"Why don't you bring your dog with you?" I suggested.

"He was run over a year ago. I didn't want to buy another one; I get so upset when they die."

"Are you worried about suffering?"

"I'm tired of suffering."

"I know what you mean. I suppose that what's most tiring is to get involved in something that doesn't last."

"Are you still talking about dogs?"

He waited for my reply with an ironic gleam in those beautiful big green eyes of his.

"About dogs and love."

I returned his gaze. All of a sudden he looked away.

"I'm afraid I'm an expert in that. I've been divorced twice."

"And I'm afraid you're not the only one. I've also been divorced twice."

Both of us laughed softly. Good, now we're getting somewhere, sweetheart. We're equal in our divorces and in being tired of suffering. To me it was clear that neither of us wanted unnecessary emotional complications. Which meant we had taken a step forward in our surrepetitious negotiations—or, at least, that's how I saw it. I cannot have been that far wrong, because as we were leaving the restaurant, he asked me for a date.

"Shall we have dinner one day?"

"Yes, let's."

"I'll call you."

It was all a matter of patience. Monturiol apparently did not want to take things too quickly, he obviously did not believe in sex at first sight. Did he want to enjoy that very male satisfaction of feeling he was the one taking the lead? All right, the best thing I could do was not to let my pride get in the way, and to accept it. I was ready and willing to be seduced. And besides, I was not so involved in the dog trafficker case to let it get in the way of my personal life.

Garzón turned up at the station after five o'clock, much later than usual. He had been having lunch with Valentina Cortés. The fact that he admitted it so openly was perhaps due

to what he added afterwards: "strictly for work." That did not
fit in with his previous excuse that the lunch was "private business," but I decided not to ask him any more about it. The
important thing was that the trainer had confirmed Angela
Chamorro's supposition: on the day of our visit to the training
ground there had been a bitch in heat—Morgana, Valentina
Cortés's own dog. Garzón was pleased with himself. It simpli-
fied our investigation considerably, because it meant we did
not have to interview all the people who had been to the training session that day.

"Wasn't Valentina surprised at your question?"

"No, I was careful how I put it. Anyway, now we know that
stupid place has nothing to do with our case, I guess I'll be able
to tell her I'm a cop."

"What for? You may never see her again."

"But I might."

With that he buried his face in a file and started rummaging
among the bits of paper. Aha, so had my illustrious friend
Garzón finally picked someone up? And why not? After so
many years a widower, this could be his lucky day. Valentina
Cortés was a good-looking woman. She was attractive and full
of life—just the sort of woman who would appeal to the sergeant. Hopefully our case would leave him enough free time to
proceed to the conquest of that blond mountain, because there
was no way he could combine it with his duties. Anyway, it
seemed as though the evidence was leading us away from the
training ground. Freaky's memory had failed us. The poor animal had been the victim of a passionate attraction, which was
only to be expected given the circumstances.

There was nothing else for it but for us to follow the other
trail: pharmaceutical research. The College of Medicine provided us with the background information we needed. We
were in luck: only six firms carried out research of their own in
Barcelona. The others were either giant multinationals who

operated under license in Spain or were so small they could not stretch to financing their own laboratory. Six seemed a small enough number for the two of us to be able to deal with, without having to call in outside help.

As soon as we began the task, we realized that the pharmaceutical industry is a serious business. Not one of the laboratories would let us inspect their premises without a proper warrant. We thought that getting six warrants just to have a look round was a bit steep, so once again we turned to Doctor Castillo to see if he could help us narrow the number down.

He was delighted to see us again. He rubbed his hands with glee—he obviously enjoyed playing the detective. He looked at the list we gave him, and smiled slyly:

"Do you remember what Don Quixote said: 'We are up against the Church here'? Well, you're taking on one of the most powerful industries in the country. They'll do all they can to obstruct you. Don't expect just to turn up and stroll around their inner sanctuaries."

"But the police don't do industrial spying."

"That doesn't matter; they don't like anyone sniffing round them."

He picked up a pen.

"Let's see . . . I think I can help you cross some of these off your list. For example, these two have merged, so now only the first does research . . . "

He drummed his fingers on the desktop. Garzón and I looked on like idiots.

"You can cross this one off too. They only experiment on cats."

"Are you joking, doctor?" I asked tentatively.

He laughed his little mad scientist's laugh.

"Not a bit of it. Each human organ has an animal that's best suited to it. The pig, for example, has a heart similar to ours, whereas the dog is better for stomach tests . . . and the cat has a nervous system which can be compared to that of human beings. In that laboratory they only produce psychotropic drugs, so I would guess they only use cats."

Garzón whistled.

"Perhaps we were lucky after all, at least it's not pigs we're trying to track down."

Castillo laughed again.

"They might have left you an easier scent to follow."

Both of them were cackling, so I decided to cut in before the male bonding went too far.

"Doctor, you don't think it makes much sense to go on investigating the pharmaceutical industry, do you?"

"I don't know what to say, inspector. I find it hard to imagine such high-powered organizations dealing with someone like Pincho. But it's a possibility. It's very slow and expensive to breed dogs for experiments. Perhaps they do occasionally need an outside supplier, if I can put it that way."

All three of us nodded wearily.

"Anyone else we can ignore, doctor?"

"Yes, you can forget this company too. They get the university to do their experiments. In other words, we work for them from time to time. It's very profitable for the school."

That was all, but it was quite a lot. Six less three meant we had cut the number in half. We only needed three search warrants to get into them. Once we were in, we had to inspect the cages where their animals were kept, make a copy of the accounts for dogs they had bought, and check it against the number of experiments carried out.

"Don't you think it's awful that a pig's heart is similar to ours?" Garzón asked when we were back in our car, but I was in no mood for philosophizing.

"What did Sergeant Pinilla say?"

"We think we're so special . . . "

"Do you mind telling me what Sergeant Pinilla said?"

"Oh, that! He told me they would carry out a thorough investigation, but he was livid."

"Why?"

"He says he would vouch for all his men, that there is no corruption in the Community Police."

"That's all we need, people defending their own."

"The heart! That's almost the same as saying the soul . . . I bet our brain is just the same as a monkey's."

I realized Garzón had fallen into one of his reflective reveries, and said no more.

When I arrived home I was welcomed by the warmth of Freaky's greeting and the blessing of a stiff whisky. I could not have asked for more. At least following our current line of investigation we were getting away from the misery of the illegal housing for immigrants. We were climbing the social ladder right up to the all-powerful pharmaceutical industry. But weren't we climbing too many rungs at once? How had someone like Lucena managed to get up them? There was still a piece missing from our jigsaw. I was thankful, though, not to have to see the animals in the university anymore. Would the private laboratories really make things as difficult for us as Doctor Castillo had said? Perhaps, for once, we would even get to feel like those fictional detectives fighting a lonely battle against powerful financial groups determined to keep their shadowy maneuvers secret. Freaky peered up at me from the floor. I stared back at his ugly face, his tattered ear. It would probably be better if I went back to basic facts: what we had was a man who stole strays, and who had been beaten to death. Forget about multinationals and high finance.

I called the sergeant's boardinghouse because we had not agreed when we would meet the next day. His landlady told me he had gone out to dinner. Obviously his distress about his heart had not deterred him from his amorous advances.

Construction and pharmaceutical companies must be the two most powerful sectors in the Spanish economy. Or at least that was what I thought when we reached the first laboratory. Money and aseptic cleanliness oozed from all sides.

A young doctor with a sharp razor haircut and gold-rimmed glasses took us around all the installations. At first he was tense, but when he learned we were investigating a murder, he relaxed. A murder seemed remote to him, something off the television. He did not ask us any questions, but simply showed us everything we wanted to see, as if we were a school group or a couple of tourists.

We asked him to take us to the kennels, and he did so without hesitating. It was a big room that gave on to a balcony. At least ten dogs shared this clean and tidy space. It was plain they were well-fed and healthy, and led a peaceful existence. The fact that they knew nothing of their cruel fate meant they all seemed contented and quiet. They were all of the same breed.

"Are these all the dogs you use?"

For the first time I noted a gleam of curiosity in our guide's eyes. He had shown us extensive chemistry departments, production lines, computer offices, complex quality-control facilities, and all we were interested in were dogs.

"What do you mean?"

I tried again:

"Do you use other—shall we say less select—dogs for unimportant research?"

Now he really was lost. He smiled with bemused fascination. I felt increasingly ridiculous.

"Unimportant?"

"What I mean is that perhaps you need so many dogs that to use your own sometimes makes it too complicated or expensive."

"Oh, no! We are not always running experiments that require dogs. And besides, if we need one of a particular age or characteristics, we use a commercial kennel."

"But you can only buy puppies from them."

"That depends; they sometimes have older dogs. Anyway, I can assure you that we are only talking of a hypothetical case. Nothing like that has ever happened since I've been working here."

"Do you never use strays in your research?" Garzón asked on the off chance.

Although he had managed to contain himself at the earlier mention of unimportant experiments, Garzón's "strays" was too much for him. He gave a short, sharp snort.

"Does it really look as though we allow any strays in here?" he said once he had recovered his composure.

I cut in icily:

"We are going to need photocopies of all the accounts relating to the kennels and a list with the total number of dogs that have been used in the past two years."

Since he had already decided not to inquire about anything, all he could do now was to nod politely.

"Please take a seat. I'll be back at once."

He left us sitting in a small beige-colored reception room.

"Asshole!" I said as soon he was out of the room. "Did you hear what he said, Garzón? Strays in here? All he needed to add was: 'the only ones are you.'"

"Calm down, inspector. You have to admit, there's not much similarity between this and Ignacio Lucena Pastor's world."

"Even the tallest trees need manure to grow!"

"Why are you so aggressive?"

"And why are you so full of joy? What's up, is life beautiful all of a sudden?"

Mister High and Mighty came back with a sheaf of photocopies and handed them over.

"Would it be betraying your professional secrecy to tell me how the murder you're investigating happened?"

I saw the chance to wreak my revenge.

"It's to do with strays; I don't think it would be of any interest to you."

I could not tell if my sudden blow for social justice had struck home anywhere on this strutting peacock, but at least I left feeling I had done something for the cause of canine equality. Garzón could not understand my outburst, and I would have bet anything that he put it down to nothing more than pre-menstrual tension. But something far less precise was bothering me: I was convinced we were chasing a red herring while our real target was escaping scot-free.

The next day, a visit very similar to the first one only served to depress me still further. We were greeted, shown around, and lectured about the activities of another immaculate establishment. There was nothing to suggest any illegal dealings, or dogs stolen from the municipal pound. They also had all their own dogs, with proper breeds and pedigrees. They were all vaccinated, de-wormed, and they all lived happily until the moment they were disemboweled in the name of science.

As if that were not enough, the model nature of both establishments was only confirmed by the examination Inspector Sanguesa and his team made of their research accounts. Everything checked, and the deaths of each dog was properly recorded. Nothing to port, nothing to starboard, we were becalmed in the midst of a flat, calm sea. I wondered whether it was worth the effort to inspect the third laboratory, or if we were not just simply chasing our own tails and not getting anywhere. But Garzón insisted that my initial hypothesis had been sound, and that we should pursue it to its ultimate conclusion. And yet there was nothing different in our third excursion into the world of pharmaceutics. The truth was, we were on the wrong trail.

I was in such a bad mood I could have bitten someone. But that would have been pointless: the weekend was coming up, and there was nothing more we could do.

During those two days I decided to try to relax. I had let the tension build up inside me in a completely useless way. I took Freaky, put on his collar and leash, and walked him until I was almost collapsing with exhaustion. I ended up sitting on a bench in La Ciudadela Park with my feet so tired they tingled.

I was surprised to see just how many people came out to enjoy the sunshine with their dogs. Youngsters in running gear jogging with their huskies. Families with children, who had been given the responsibility of looking after enormous, fluffy English sheepdogs . . . Above all, though, there were old people, ordinary people with tiny, undistinguished-looking pets, some of them as ugly as Freaky, old women plodding along behind weary animals that looked just like them. Two of them stopped to have a chat near me, and I heard one of them say, "I don't mind that he leaves hairs on the sofa, but my daughter wants to get rid of him, to give him away. And what would become of me without my Boby?" It was sad to see that every mongrel without a pedigree seemed to have an owner with no future.

I got up and wandered round the park. I soon spotted a group of people in the distance. I went over to see what was going on. A crowd of onlookers had gathered round an area fenced off with a wire fence. A banner between two trees announced: XVTH DEMONSTRATION OF GUARD DOGS. ALL PROCEEDS TO CHILDREN'S HOMES. It was impossible to find any room to get a proper view, so I withdrew a little. All around were dogs which must have already taken part in the demonstration and were now enjoying a rest with their owners. All of a sudden, Freaky began to pull nervously on his leash. What seemed to be disturbing him was the presence of an enormous rottweiler. It was a spectacular animal: strong and muscular as a bull, with a compact, round head like a club. He had noticed Freaky and was growling menacingly at him. I was scared, and looked to see who was holding him. Great heavens above, it was none other than Garzón who had control of this ferocious beast! Could it really be Garzón? What on earth was Garzón doing here with a dog like that?

"Sergeant!"

He went as red as a beetroot, looking as if he wished a tornado would come along and providentially sweep him away.

"Hello, Petra, how are you?"

"What do you mean 'how are you'? What are you doing here with that beast?"

He looked down at the dog as if it had suddenly somehow grown on the end of his right arm.

"This beast? Oh, this is Morgana. She belongs to Valentina Cortés! I'm looking after her for a while because Valentina is in the demonstration. She's one of the judges."

We stood staring at each other, neither of us knowing what else to say. The dogs spoke for us. Morgana gave another threatening growl, and Freaky yelped with fear and ran to hide himself behind my legs. He was pulling on his lead for all he was worth. The rottweiler felt even more excited and started to bark.

"Well, Fermín, as you can see, this isn't the moment for a quiet chat. I'll have to be on my way."

"That's a shame, I'd have liked you to say hello to Valentina. By the way, we're going to a Mexican restaurant tonight. Why don't you come with us?"

"I don't know if . . . "

"Go on. I'll call you this afternoon to confirm."

By this time, Valentina Cortés's dog was standing up on its hind legs snarling ferociously. The growls from its hot, wet fangs were deep and threatening. Freaky tugged so hard I could not keep hold of him. He shot off across the park, with me running behind him. I turned back to Garzón and shouted:

"O.K., give me a call around five!"

I only managed to catch Freaky when we were so far away

from the rottweiler that he could not even scent her. I tried to calm him down—his heart was pounding as loud as mine. I could quite understand why: if he had not taken the initiative, it might have been me who had run off from that terrifying beast.

Some time before five I rang Juan Monturiol. I thought he would probably like to meet my work colleague and a fearless near-lion tamer. Perhaps, too, with other people around, he would drop his man-led-up-the-garden-path-by-a-woman attitude, and we might even be able to indulge in a spot of everyday lovemaking. I was half expecting him to make an excuse, but he accepted. And so it was that on a freezing Saturday night we all went to Los Cuates, a lively Mexican restaurant in Gracia.

I think I can say without any fear of contradiction that we formed one of the most unusual groups of all those out on the town in the city that night. Valentina Cortés appeared with her straw-blonde hair combed out in dramatic fashion. She was wearing trousers and a V-neck black jersey that was low enough to show the start of her ample bosom. A leather jacket completed the image of a mature, self-confident woman. I could understand why Garzón was so taken with her: she was a really sexy fifty-year-old. He himself had adopted the nineteenthirties Chicago look, one of those striped classic suits I had often seen him in. His hair was slicked back and his mustache perfectly groomed: it was obvious he was out to seduce. So was I, to tell the truth: I put on a stunning red dress in the hope of impressing Juan Monturiol. I was the one impressed, though: he turned up in a simple ivory-colored turtleneck jersey, and looked even more handsome than before.

When we had all been introduced, we scanned the menu and asked the waiter for the usual explanations of how hot each of the dishes was. Valentina immediately chose the spiciest ones available, and I could see that Garzón was delighted she was so daring.

"I like strong emotions!" she declared, her blue eyes flashing.

"Now I've met your dog, I'm not surprised," I said.

"Morgana? She's one of the noblest creatures you could ever run into!"

"Did you train her yourself?"

"Yes, with my assistants. She's as quick as a flash, and wouldn't let go of her prey even if it was a raging wild boar."

Juan was obviously interested in the topic, and butted in.

"I've always wondered whether dog trainers really know what they're doing. A dog who's trained to attack can cause terrible accidents, bite someone until it kills them."

To contradict him, Valentina waved a piece of spicy suckling pig that she had dipped in an even hotter sauce.

"No, nothing that terrible could happen. We've got things under control; it's only a very remote possibility. In fact, self-defense has become a kind of sport these days."

"Could that dog of yours kill someone?" asked Garzón, all childish admiration.

Valentina heaped more beans on to her plate. Her eyes narrowed as she retorted:

"You could place a bet on it, and probably with a single bite. But like all the dogs we train, Morgana only obeys her master's voice. If I don't give the word, she won't do a thing."

"What if someone tried to attack you?"

"In that case, my friend, I can assure you that the attacker would end up like an angel."

"Like an angel?" We were all taken aback.

"I mean sexless, because Morgana would head straight for the balls."

We all laughed so loudly that people at other tables turned to stare at us. This Valentina was incredible, a real whirlwind; she was at ease in the world as though she had created it herself. She ate the hottest food without even blinking. She laughed, she talked incessantly, swore like a trooper and had a seemingly endless list of anecdotes about dogs. It seemed as though Juan was fascinated by her, and Garzón was levitating higher than a Hindu holy man.

"Which is the easiest breed to train?"

"No doubt about it: the German shepherd. It's so intelligent and sweet it can be used for anything."

"But you chose a rottweiler."

"I did, because of the power in its bite. A German shepherd has a biting power of around ninety kilos. That's pretty good. I find it hard to keep my balance if one of them starts pulling on my arm. But a rottweiler has a hundred and fifty kilos of power in its bite."

Juan exclaimed:

"You couldn't do anything to stop that."

"No, I can't. The fact is, the dog can drag me along and there's nothing I can do about it. But as its movements are clear and direct, there's only a small danger, really."

"But that's an animal which could stand up to a bull!"

"Yes, it could."

"Have you never had problems with any dogs?"

Valentina called the waiter over, ordered another Mexican beer, and for the first time looked serious. She paused mysteriously before she spoke:

"There is one breed I refuse to train," she said, swallowing a large mouthful of guacamole. "The pit bull."

"I have a couple of clients who bring pit bulls to my practice. Just to give them their yearly vaccination I have to muzzle them. They're scary creatures!"

"Really scary. They hardly weigh more than twenty-five kilos. But the power in their jaws? . . . Some of them can pull two hundred and fifty kilos."

"You don't say!" gasped Garzón.

"I can still remember what happened when I was brought

one for training. All the time I was talking to its owner it was calm and quiet. I put on my protective gear and my arm pad, and started to test its defensive instincts by moving around to excite it. As usual in the first sessions, its owner still had tight hold of it. It was still quiet: it didn't growl or bark, but just looked me straight in the eye. I thought to myself: Valentina, take care, this dog is a real bastard. And so it proved: all of a sudden it tore itself free from its owner and, instead of biting the arm pad I was holding out, went straight for my body. I managed to get out of the way, but I'm sure that if it had knocked me down, it would have gone straight for my throat."

Her story left us all aghast.

"Isn't that the kind of dog that can turn against its own master?" asked Juan.

"I suppose you mean the Staffordshire bull terrier. That's an American breed, and the pit bull is related to it. It's the most vicious dog there is."

"And what is its jaw strength?" asked Garzón, who had obviously picked up the terminology.

"Three hundred kilos."

"I don't even want to think about it!" groaned the sergeant.

"You're right not to. It's a truly ferocious animal. It can rip out anyone's jugular. And the thing is that to look at one you'd think it was impossible. It's never more than forty centimeters high and weighs only some seventeen kilos, but it's a killing machine. Only those fuckin' Americans could have dreamt up the idea of breeding a dog like that."

"What is it used for?"

"Only as a guard dog, though as you can imagine, it has to be under strict control."

We all fell silent. I suddenly noticed Garzón had not even touched his enchiladas.

"Congratulations, Valentina," I said. "You've managed to

find a topic so interesting that Fermín has forgotten to eat. It's the first time I've ever seen that."

Garzón shot daggers at me, but Valentina simply laughed out loud and replied:

"Fermín and I get along splendidly. I tell him stories about dogs, and he tells me stories about the police. There's something to say about every profession, isn't there?"

Garzón insisted on paying the bill. He was over the moon, which was understandable. How long had it been since he last went out with friends and had a partner of his own?

"Let's go and have a drink somewhere," Juan Monturiol suggested.

"I'd prefer to go and dance," said Valentina.

"Let's go to the Shutton, then."

The Shutton was an upmarket nightclub for people who liked dancing sambas, rock and roll, and listening to some hot jazz played by a live orchestra. It was true, Valentina wanted to dance: as soon as we had been served our cocktails, she dragged Garzón out onto the dance floor. I soon realized my colleague had more to him than I had ever imagined: he was as multifaceted as a cut diamond. He danced really well, like a modern-day Fred Astaire. He moved gracefully and stylishly, closely following the rhythm, both leading his partner and responding to her. The tight round ball of his body became a bobbing balloon. It was a real sight watching the two of them, free from any inhibitions and pleased with themselves, enjoying every minute of it.

"They're full of life, aren't they?" said Juan.

"I'd love to be able to dance like them."

"We ought to try at least."

He chose a slow smoochy number to lead me out. He put his arms round me and we started to move slowly. I could feel him clasping me that little bit closer when the tune got really romantic. He brought his face closer to mine, brushed it against me.

So he was a classic lover-boy, God help me! The typical attempt at seduction: suggestive music, dimly-lit room, dry cocktail . . . I bet when we left he would suggest I have one last drink at his place and then, when we made love, he'd whisper "darling" in my ear, even though we hardly knew each other. Please! That wasn't my scene at all, so why should I go along with it?

I was right all along the line. Outside the club, after we had said goodbye to Valentina and Garzón, Juan Monturiol whispered huskily:

"How about a drink at my place?"

"No, Juan, I'm really sorry, but I've got such a dreadful headache all of a sudden. All I want is a couple of aspirins and then bed. Shall I give you a call in a day or two?"

That was the last thing he had been expecting. He took the blow and managed to hide his anger, but I could tell how annoyed he was by the way he clenched his teeth.

Too bad, I wanted nothing to do with any traditional sort of seduction! I had too many years' experience, too many divorces, too much of everything to want to end the night whispering "darling, it was wonderful." Not now, even though the candidate was really mouthwatering. Either he changed his approach or he had to let me take charge of things.

The one who benefited most from my early return was Freaky. He was really pleased to see me. We went out for a long walk at two in the morning. The icy streets were completely deserted, and a cruel wind was blowing. I don't know what positive effects the dog got from this unusual nighttime stroll, but the cold and the exercise helped me calm my carnal desires.

5

On Monday morning, my mood was no better. I still had the imprecise but insistent feeling that I had been wasting my time. Our visits to the pharmaceutical labs had yielded nothing. Their accounts were perfect: everything was as it should have been; it all fitted. There was absolutely nothing to suggest they had been dealing in stray dogs. Stray dogs! It was laughable even to think that those aseptic, efficient economic giants would ever have anything to do with a down-and-out like Lucena. You had to be crazy to follow a lead like that.

I picked up Lucena Pastor's accounts books. I opened the second one, and flicked through it: Lili, 40,000; Bony, 60,000 . . . Who could have been paying Lucena so much money? Who on earth was willing to buy non-pedigree dogs at prices like that, and for what? The names must still refer to dogs as they had done in the first book—or perhaps not anymore? I only succeeded in making myself unsure of everything. Like dogs, we had been barking up the wrong tree. At some point we had taken the wrong turn. I was so angry with myself I stupidly threw the book at the wall. The sergeant was astonished.

"What are you doing, Petra? You'll destroy the evidence."

"Do you know how many unsolved murders there are in Spain?"

"No."

"Truckloads, believe me, truckloads! And they're nearly all people like Lucena: people on the margins, prostitutes, beggars, people who have no name or family or friends."

"So?"

"So it bugs me! It bugs me it's always this riffraff that disappears and no one brings them any justice. That was what I thought whenever I read our statistics about it, and now I'm in a position to do something about it . . . "

"Now what?"

"Christ, Garzón, are you an idiot or something? Now I can smell the fact that this case of ours is just going to be another unsolved statistic."

"I don't think so."

"You don't think so! Is that because of the fantastic progress we've made?"

The sergeant's gaze was almost tender. He picked the account book off the floor, and smiled.

"Don't worry, Petra, we will solve the case. Just be patient, Rome wasn't built in a day, nor Barcelona in two."

He opened the book and started peering into it. I laughed.

"Forgive me, Fermín, I'm sorry. That was a stupid thing to do."

He waved his arm in the air as if to dismiss the whole thing, but did not look up from his book. Then he slowly began to speak.

"It seems to me that . . . it seems to me that if we add up all the figures jotted down here, let's say there are forty pages, with two amounts of thirty, fifty or sixty thousand pesetas on each page . . . that makes a total of around three million pesetas."

"What are you getting at?"

"What I'm getting at is, if we say these accounts cover a year, that means Lucena had a large amount of money to spend."

"Yes, he did—remember the expensive chain he was wearing."

"O.K., let's say that chain cost him three or four hundred

thousand pesetas, that's something we could check. The chain was a luxury he allowed himself, but apart from that he led a miserable life. He lived in a filthy apartment and hung out in dives like Las Fuentes. It doesn't seem he was a drug addict, so where is all that money? We can tell from his accounts he was a methodical person, so wasn't he keeping the dough somewhere? There were no signs of robbery in his apartment."

"You mean he had a bank account?"

"What's the matter with your brain today, inspector? A guy who has no papers, who doesn't sign a tenancy agreement, who always uses nicknames . . . can you imagine him opening a fixed-interest account? No, I reckon he had it all hidden somewhere."

A ray of light shone in my head.

"In a safe place."

"In a safe place," Garzón repeated.

"Sergeant, looking for clues is too subtle in this case. What we need is a proper search. You know how these things are organized, so get a team who can do a good job and send them to Lucena's."

Garzón's eyes were shining.

"Whatever you say, boss."

"You had a great idea, Fermín. And if he had his money hidden somewhere, we might also find other things: papers, bills . . . leads, my dear friend, leads! Yes, that was a brilliant idea of yours."

"Don't get your hopes too high, Petra. We could also find that the bastard spent it all on whores."

"I'll keep it in mind."

"What shall we do about the labs?"

"For the moment, we forget them."

As we were leaving the station we were in for a surprise: at that very moment, Angela Chamorro was asking for the sergeant. She came over and spoke to us in her usual friendly way. She asked how I was feeling, and then, to my complete astonishment, inquired how Garzón's hangover was going.

"I think it must have been that drink we had after dinner last night," she said firmly.

Garzón nodded. He didn't know where to put himself. I could never have thought it. This secret lover-boy, this paunchy Bluebeard, was going out with Angela at the same time as Valentina. I gave him a stern look, and he became even more sheepish.

"I was in the neighborhood and suddenly remembered it's my birthday tomorrow. No, don't congratulate me, it's so dreadful I don't even want to think about it! The only way I can accept being that much older is if I'm in pleasant company. Would you like to come to have dinner at my place? That would help me swallow the pill."

Laughing and commiserating, we said yes.

"And of course, if you wish, you can bring someone, Petra."

"Yes, I might bring a friend."

I thought I could ask Monturiol, although it was more than likely he would send me packing for the way I had treated him. Perhaps if I asked him with the right mood music playing in the background . . . our bookshop owner friend said her contented goodbyes. I turned to Garzón.

"What a coincidence Angela was just passing by here, wasn't it, Fermín? But then I don't really believe in coincidences."

"Why not? Sometimes things like that happen, when you're least expecting them."

"Like love at first sight, you mean?"

He pretended not to have heard me.

"Or two loves at first sight?"

A fence post could not have been deafer.

The team they sent to carry out the exhaustive search of Lucena's place did not exactly inspire me. One young fellow with a suitcase and another with no equipment at all. I had been imagining something much more hi-tech. I kept my mouth shut and did not let them my sense of frustration. The sergeant was excited, certain we were going to discover all kinds of treasure. He opened Lucena's front door with all the anticipation of Carter before Tutankhamun's tomb. Everything in the apartment was exactly as we had left it, apart from a further layer of dust.

The expert opened his case and took out a set of small hammers made of different materials: plastic, wood, metal . . . He took off his jacket, chose one of the hammers, and started tapping the floor centimeter by centimeter. Garzón was so enthusiastic he pressed up against him like a commuter in the rush-hour metro. After a while the youngster had had enough, and turned to him: "This could take some time," he said. Sulking, the sergeant left him and came to sit next to me on the battered sofa. We started leafing through Lucena's old magazines. The other man was staring quietly out of the window. He was obviously used to waiting. In the end he sat down in a chair and dozed off.

Several hours went by, each one slower than the one before. As I watched the specialist at work, I realized he was searching for cavities by using different hammers depending on the surface he was examining: walls, the floor, tiles, even the doorframes.

Following his initial enthusiasm, Garzón was getting bored. He tried to make conversation:

"Are you thinking of buying Angela a present for her birthday?"

"I've ordered a bouquet of white roses."

He fell silent, a worried look on his face.

"That's a good idea. I don't know what to give her."

"Buy her a box of chocolates."

"That's very impersonal."

"A book of poems."

"Too personal."

I thought for a moment.

"Why not buy her a toy dog?"

"Oh, come off it, Petra, I was being serious."

"So was I. She'd like it."

"I don't know . . . perhaps . . . but it doesn't seem like much for someone who was kind enough to invite us to her house. What I do know is, I'm fed up with not having a place of my own where I can bring friends. I've almost made up my mind to follow your advice, leave the boardinghouse and rent an apartment."

I sat up, my eyes wide with astonishment.

"Follow my advice! That's a good one! For the past two years I've been going on at you to leave, and now all of a sudden you've decided to follow my advice! Why don't you tell the truth, Fermín, spit it out: what's happened is that you want your own apartment because you've fallen in love."

Alarmed, the sergeant shot a glance at the others to make sure they had not heard anything. Then he tried his best to hide the smug smile that came to his lips, and said in a low voice:

"Yes, it's true, I have fallen in love. The only problem is, I don't know with which one of them."

"Of them?"

"You know exactly who I'm talking about. Angela Chamorro and Valentina Cortés. I've been seeing them practically every day over the past few weeks."

"But that's terrible, Garzón. In such a short space of time!"

"I don't know what makes it so terrible."

The cop in the chair woke up, and told us he was off to the bar on the corner for a drink. We did not say anything more until he had left.

"What's terrible is that people shouldn't fall in love twice at the same time."

"To me it feels like the best thing that's ever happened to me. All I know is that I've fallen in love; later I'll work out with which one. I can tell you that being in love is fantastic, it's a real experience."

"So I've heard."

"I wake up in the middle of the night and I think: I don't want to die now, because tomorrow I'm going to see them again. I count the minutes until the next date, I can't concentrate—why, I'm even eating less!"

"That is serious for you."

"I know you think I'm ridiculous, Petra, and it's true, I am. What is an ugly, old widower cop like me doing getting mixed up in love stories? But I can tell you that nothing like this has ever happened to me before. When I married my wife—may she rest in peace—it was because it seemed like the right thing to do after we had been engaged for so many years. There was never any seduction or passionate declarations . . . well, I don't want to sound even more ridiculous, but you know what I think, Petra? I think that if I feel the way I do it's because, even though it's hard to believe, both of those women really like me! They both like me!"

I couldn't help feeling moved as I looked at his boiled-cod eyes.

"But Fermín, why on earth shouldn't they like you? You're an attractive, generous, funny and honest man. You could make Miss Universe fall for you if you wanted to, and perhaps even if you didn't want to. If any candidate caught sight of you in one of your elegant suits, smoothing down your mustache . . . "

He was laughing like a child, freed from his everyday cares, enjoying this fresh breeze on his weather-beaten face.

"Don't say any more, inspector! If you could only feel the same, you know very well you'd be the first in my . . . "

The expert's voice brought us back with a jolt to a reality we had almost left far behind.

"Come in here, I think I've found something."

He was kneeling on the floor in the kitchen. He had pulled out the grimy refrigerator and was carefully tapping the tiles behind it.

"Hear that? It sounds hollow. It could be an interesting hiding place. Where's Eugenio?" he asked.

"Eugenio?"

"My colleague."

"He's gone for a half," Garzón said.

"A half? Half a dozen more like! He's always doing the same! Just when I need him, he vanishes to guzzle some beer."

The sergeant ran to get him. While he was gone, I looked on fascinated as the expert took a huge felt-tip pen from his case. He marked a couple of tiles and started hammering at them. Then he prized one of them upwards with a screwdriver. Underneath was a hole about five centimeters in diameter. At that moment Garzón and the other cop arrived. They stood staring at the hole without saying a word. The expert took out a long piece of metal wire and poked it inside the empty space.

"Yes . . . " he said, "I think we've found it. There something in there. Over to you, inspector, it's all yours now . . . "

I put on the thin vinyl glove he held out and pushed my hand inside the hole. To do so, I had to conquer my phobias: I was imagining writhing snakes or the rotting skull of a headless man. What I felt, though, was undoubtedly soft plastic. The rubbing sound also suggested the same material. I grabbed hold of whatever it was and tugged. It was a small rubbish bag. I opened it: it was full of money. A pile of five thousand peseta notes. I could hear the little group around me gasp. I dipped my hand in the hole five times, and each time I came up with another bag containing exactly the same. I checked if there was anything else down there, but it was empty. No invoices, or notes or notebooks. Nothing but money.

"Wow! It looks like you're on to something here," the expert said, with a whistle.

"Don't be too sure," I replied. "This only complicates matters."

A few hours later, Inspector Sanguesa told us exactly what was in the haul. Eight million pesetas, all in used notes of different denominations. All of it legal tender, with no sign that any of it was counterfeit. No marks or any other identifying signs on it. All we could say about the eight million pesetas was that they were eight million pesetas. Eight mysterious millions.

"Our friend Lucena could never have salted away so much dough from his stray dogs," Garzón said.

"You can bet your life on that."

"Perhaps we've found the motive for the crime."

"I'm not so sure. If they were after the money, we would have found the place turned upside down. All the furniture ripped open, and holes in the walls."

"Does that mean Lucena's killer didn't know about the money?"

"Even if he did know—even if he was one of his accomplices—he didn't kill him for the money."

"Christ, inspector, so where does that leave us?"

I lit a cigarette and nearly finished it in one deep drag.

"It was your idea that there was money hidden somewhere, and you were right. But according to the second account book, the most we could have expected to find was three million. Where did the rest of it come from? Either Lucena stole it from someone, and that was why he was killed, or the accounts we have don't show everything, and for some reason the other books have gone missing."

"And why did he stash away all that money and not use some of it to improve his life a bit?" Garzón wanted to know.

"Who knows? He may have been a very cautious guy who

didn't want to arouse any suspicion with his spending, or maybe he was just one of those misers who are always being found dead in their hovels with a fortune hidden under their mattress."

"We're in a fine mess, inspector!"

"You said it."

"So now it's back to the dogs?"

"That's right, although perhaps we should put some of this money on the horses instead."

"Or on the cows," said Garzón, with a silly little laugh that only showed how bewildered he was.

In the end, the sergeant took my advice and bought Angela Chamorro a toy dog as a birthday present. He added his own touch, buying a little gold chain with a heart dangling from it, which he had placed around the dog's neck. With a great show of emotion, he showed me what was inside the heart. It opened in the middle to reveal a passport-size photo of the sergeant, perfectly framed. I was horrified, but recovered my wits sufficiently to tell him how pretty it was.

Juan Monturiol, who had accepted the dinner invitation for who knew what reasons of his own, appeared with two magnificent bottles of French champagne. These presents, together with my white roses, led our hostess to receive us with gurgles of gratitude and delight. She put the chain on, pinned a rose in the buttonhole of her silk blouse, and drank a toast in Möet and Chandon.

Angela lived in Las Corts, in a glamorous split-level apartment that she had made warm and pleasant. The living room walls were lined with books, and there was Mozart playing in the background. This welcoming picture was completed by a table laid out exquisitely for us in one corner. Angela's dog Nelly greeted us in her slow, philosophical manner, then ambled off to stand beside her owner. The dog's fur was a beige and white color that went very well with Angela's discreet outfit. The expression, a dog and its master end up looking alike, had never been truer.

She and the vet had not seen each other for ages, so they had lots to talk about, mostly on the theme of dogs. Over drinks they extolled the virtues of our native breeds, and decried the snobbishness that had filled Spain with Nordic breeds which that were completely unsuited to our climate and mentality. Garzón and I sat and listened without contributing much.

The first course, a delicious leek-and-truffle soup, was the occasion for comments on a plan by the Animal Welfare Society to provide pet animals for hospitals. Angela's theory was very interesting. She claimed that if sick and elderly people could have small dogs and cats with them in hospital, it would help them recover a sensitivity many of them had lost a long time ago. Touching the dogs' warm fur and wet noses and feeling their hearts beat must help suffering human bodies regain a sense of vitality. Not only that, but watching the animals, feeding them, laughing at their tricks and the way they reacted must help take the patients' minds off their own problems. They would become aware of the outside world in a way that put their own suffering into perspective.

Both of them kept their most heartfelt theories for the main course, a succulent sea bream cooked in the oven with shallots and potato slices. Not even a lovelorn Garzón could resist it. As we ate, the dog theories reached a mystical level. Both Juan and Angela were convinced that an owner's hidden alter ego found its expression in his dog. All the virtues we hope to possess—kindness, nobility, humility—are present in our pets; but, at the same time, we cast on the dog the most shameful aspects of our character: cruelty, sloth, greed . . . And yet, despite all these parallel qualities, there is also a strange something in a dog that does not come from its owner's interior world. As she spoke about all this, Angela forgot to eat; she was in a trance.

"You can see it in their eyes. It's a sort of universal calm passed down through the centuries, which has nothing to do with the accidents of history, although it is related to events, to accumulated memory. It's like an acceptance that is close to comprehension, a sort of original innocence. I'd even go so far as to say, believe it or not, that the look dogs have is a proof of the harmony of the universe, of the existence of God."

Garzón sat with his fork in midair, staring at her with silent admiration. He was fascinated by how intelligent his possible love match was. It was then that I realized we might never catch Lucena Pastor's murderer, but that this case would definitely be important in our lives. Garzón would come out of it having got in touch with his sensitive side, and I would end up knowing much more about dogs than I could ever have dreamed possible.

"It's obvious that each person has their own view of what the concept 'dog' means. Do you remember the evening we had dinner with Valentina Cortés? For her, dogs mean risk, adventure, something much more physical."

I could see a frown flit across Angela's forehead. Garzón flushed, and looked darkly at me. Apparently the vet had put his foot in it, but what was I supposed to do about it? I could hardly warn him not to mention Valentina, could I? What was this anyway, a cabaret act? I silently cursed my colleague, the cheap little Don Juan.

Fortunately, Angela was too well-educated to allow this to cause anything more than a slight cloud over the conversation. Monturiol was bissfully unaware of his *faux pas*, and did not even notice how the atmosphere had changed. He did, however, seem to be perfectly in tune with the situation between the two of us. We were both on our guard, with the result that when dinner was finished and we were out in the street, he turned to me and asked sarcastically:

"Do you think we could find a neutral spot to have a drink?"

The neutral spot turned out to be Boadas cocktail bar. The tiny premises were packed with a varied display of night owls. It did not seem to me like the ideal kind of place for launching into confessions or emotional outpourings, but Juan was obviously of the opposite opinion, because without warning he suddenly announced:

"Petra, it's clear that between you and me there is some kind of problem that prevents us from getting into a deeper, more satisfying relationship. That much is undeniable, but for the life of me I can't figure out what the problem is."

"You're the diagnostic expert."

"But my patients can't talk. Now that I have the good fortune to be with someone who can, would you mind helping me discover what's wrong?"

I smiled.

"Go ahead."

"Tell me what for you would be the ideal relationship between a man and a woman like us."

"You tell me first."

He ran a long, bony hand through his hair. He sighed.

"It's so simple it sounds ridiculous to have to explain it. It's all about going out together, talking, telling each other a few basic things about ourselves if we want to, having a few drinks, going out dancing . . . and then seeing where that leads, and living it."

"Yes, that sounds very simple, but the consequences of getting to know one another like that can give rise to a lot of misunderstandings, wrong ideas, situations that have different meanings for each of us, lots of unnecessary promises . . . and it ends up just creating more conflicts."

"So what's your answer?"

"It's also something simple. You get to know each other, find each other attractive, don't say a lot, make love, and, if things are going well, you can go on seeing each other from time to time and enjoying yourselves. It's all clear right from the start, and there's no need for pretense or false moves."

"You make it sound like buying something from a catalogue. Practical, economical, and if you don't like what you get you can always send it back."

"You were the one who said you were tired after two divorces, that you were weary and didn't want to suffer. So what are you looking for at this stage in our lives—to play at fiancées?"

He took out his wallet and picked up the bill.

"No, Petra, perhaps we both want the same thing; in other words, very little. It must just be a question of attitude."

"Or pride."

"I'm sorry that's how you see it. Anyway, I hope we can still see each other occasionally."

"Of course, I'll bring you Freaky so you can take care of him!"

We went out into the cold night on the Ramblas and shared a taxi. We didn't say a word to each other in the whole journey. He was humming to himself to lessen the tension. After shaking hands with me in what was meant to be a casual, friendly way, he got out at his place. I said goodbye through the car window with a sphinx's smile.

In the hall, Freaky flung himself on me and left my stockings covered in dribble. On the kitchen table I found a note from the cleaner:

Señora Petra: This dog is so ugly I feel embarrassed taking him for a walk. But if I have to do it every morning, please buy him one of those plaid coats, because the poor thing gets very cold. And maybe that way he might be a bit easier on the eye. I left a plate of lentils in the microwave for you.

Best wishes

AZUCENA

I threw the note into the bin. I was in no mood to think about getting coats for dogs! The telephone rang. I thought it might be Juan Monturiol apologizing, and asking me to come and have a drink to make up.

"Inspector? Garzón here."

"What's the matter?"

"Nothing, except that you could have warned Juan not to mention Valentina in front of Angela."

"It never occurred to me."

"Well, Angela took it really badly. I was going to spend the night at her place, but now I've had to come back to my boardinghouse."

"You're the one who should have told Angela about Valentina. Getting involved with two women at once and building up their hopes is immoral."

I heard a sarcastic laugh at the far end of the line.

"Immoral? I didn't think you were bothered about things like that."

I was furious.

"Don't go too far, sergeant!"

"I wasn't speaking to you as a sergeant."

"In that case I don't see any reason why you should phone me in the early hours of the morning, or why we should continue this conversation."

"You're quite right, Inspector Delicado. Good night."

"Good night."

The sound of him hanging up gave me a stab of pain. Brilliant! In the space of a few hours I'd lost a possible lover and a good friend. I sat on the sofa unable to move or think. As if he could sense my depression, the dog came sidling over.

"Come closer, Freaky . . . " I told him. "Let's see if I can spot the harmony of the universe in your eyes."

I don't know how we expected to make others talk if we

weren't even talking to one another. Garzón seemed determined to stay offended, and I did not feel like making any great effort to bring peace. The wise old saw was about be proved right yet again: it's dangerous to make friends with work colleagues. I tried to tease him a little.

"Haven't we made progress? On the trail of Lucena's killer, we've uncovered a rental agency that deals in illegal contracts, and dog trafficking at the university. The heart of underworld crime!"

"We've been doing our duty to society," Garzón replied in all seriousness.

"Right, now all we need is to catch a gang of floorcloth sellers, a counterfeiter of picture cards, and an international network of fake car-minders."

Garzón could not hide the laugh behind his walrus mustache.

"Yes, and dangerous soft-drink smugglers, and a secret hideout where they play marbles," he said, grinning.

I tried not to laugh: it was too soon to let him off altogether. One of the young Community Support officers poked his head round the door.

"Inspector, Sergeant Pinilla would like to see you in his office. He says he's been looking for you all day like a madman."

I stared him straight in the eye. He cannot have been more than twenty-one.

"I like it when men go mad looking for me."

He blushed, then walked away with a smile on his face, muttering "too much" to himself.

As soon as I appeared, Pinilla got up and came over almost shouting at me.

"See, inspector, see? I told you it couldn't have been one of my men!"

"If you're trying to tell me that particular lead is getting us nowhere, you've picked a rotten moment, Pinilla."

"No, no, what I mean is that we've found the rotten apple. And it wasn't one of my men."

"You've found the dog dealer?"

"It's the kid at the municipal dog pound."

"What kid?"

"The one who looks after the dogs there, the one who feeds them and cleans out the kennels."

"Has he said anything about Lucena's death?"

"Take it easy, inspector! Don't go so fast! What I've discovered is that he was the one who passed the dogs on to Lucena. He was paid something for each one he supplied. He's confessed that much, but I don't know anything more."

"I understand."

"What I do know is what I think of him."

"And what's that?"

"To me he seems like a poor sort who was just trying to earn a bit of extra cash. The fact is, I can't see him killing anyone, and especially for what Lucena paid him."

"Is he scared?"

"No, he's angry."

"How's that?"

"He says he can't believe that we shopped him to you for such a small matter."

"Doesn't he know Lucena is dead?"

"He swears he had no idea. He calls him Susito, not Lucena, but it's the same guy, because he recognized him in the photo. But he also says that the last dog he gave him was two years ago, and that he hasn't seen him since, because he disappeared without a word."

"Do you think he's telling the truth?"

"I don't know, inspector. I would say so, but it's up to you to judge. I've brought him here. He's in Room B up on the second floor, with two guards and two of my men. Not even El Lute was so well guarded!"

"You've done us a real favor, Pinilla."

"All part of the service. And, by the way, inspector, now you can see it wasn't one of my people."

In the same way that a hidalgo's honor depended on that of his daughter's, a policeman's honor depends on his subordinates. I've never understood either situation, but I had to say soothing words to Sergeant Pinilla to smooth his feathers.

What Pinilla had said turned out to be completely accurate: the man did indeed look like a poor sort, and he was very angry. He applied the old saying "better be hanged for a sheep than a lamb" to himself, and based his protests on the equally traditional view that "there are all these criminals on the loose and all you can do is bother honest people."

He told us he got around three thousand pesetas for every dog he supplied Lucena with, and he stuck to the very reasonable line that it was not worth killing anyone for such a small sum.

"But you two might have argued and fought over something. You didn't realize how hard you were hitting him, and killed him. Perhaps you'd both been drinking and didn't know exactly what you were doing."

"I'm not having that. I don't touch alcohol, not a drop, not even beer. Besides, I never had an argument with Susito. How could we, if we never even spoke to each other! We had an agreement: I handed over the dogs, he paid me, and that was that."

"And two years ago, the whole thing finished."

"Yes."

"And did you never see him again, even if not on business?"

"We weren't friends. I don't even know where he lived. He was a strange guy."

"So one fine day he just vanished?"

"No, he told me he wouldn't be coming any more. He said he'd found something better with a hairdresser in San Gervasio."

"What does something better mean?"

"That was all he said."

"Didn't he say anything about this hairdresser?"

"Nothing, and if he mentioned the fact that he was in San Gervasio I guess it was to show that he was on to a good thing."

"Was it something to do with dogs?"

"I've already told you, I have no idea. But if it was dogs, I can tell you they had nothing to do with the pound."

"Could they have been stolen dogs?"

"You can ask a hundred times, but I don't know anything more because he didn't tell me anything more."

"And did he never suggest you join him in the new deal?"

He laughed a sarcastic, dismissive laugh.

"Right! What did he need me for? A new deal! All he gave me was a miserable three thousand! I used to spend it all on the lottery anyway."

"On the lottery?"

"It was the only way the money might be of some use! But now look, all the use it's been is to get me into trouble when it's nothing to do with me. It's not fair that I get done for this crap. To lose my job because of a few stupid flea-bitten dogs that nobody cares about and which are going to be put to death anyway!"

I suppose that from his point of view he was right. We were awash in stuff with little or no value, in strays . . . Lucena himself was another piece of trash that nobody had bothered to claim. But society has its rules, and no one is even supposed to steal what we throw away. Life is beautiful! I thought ironically. Well, at least we had a new lead to follow up. We could forget all the nonsense about medical research. Perhaps the only important thing to come out of it was the fact that we had solved the issue of the first account book, and now we could start on the second one. The sums mentioned there were much higher, so it could be that we were finally getting closer to the reasons that cost Lucena Pastor his life. The ridiculous names and the way the accounts were laid out, as well as what the dog-pound man had told us, showed it was still dogs we were dealing with. The much larger amounts suggested that we were probably looking at a different category: the theft of pedigree dogs. That should make it easier to track Lucena down. And what about this mysterious hairdresser in San Gervasio? I turned to Garzón, who was sitting quietly smoking a cigarette.

"Call Sergeant Pinilla again. Tell him we want a list of all the stolen or missing dogs in Barcelona. Then we can see how many of them were from San Gervasio."

He took note, very seriously and professionally. Then he began on another tack.

"Inspector Delicado, even though lately we have had our differences . . . well, I think that, despite that I am right in saying . . . well, that there is a certain friendship between us."

"Yes, of course there is."

"In the name of that friendship then, I'd like to apologize and to ask you a favor."

"Forget the apology: what's the favor?"

"I have to choose between a couple of apartments for rent. Do you think you could come with me and have a look? You know, a woman's opinion . . . "

"So why all this beating about the bush? Of course I'll go with you. But before we do, find out how many hairdressers there are in San Gervasio."

"Male or female?"

"I don't know. Check on both, then we'll see."

That same afternoon we went to choose Garzón's famous apartment. One was in the Sagrada Familia neighborhood, the other in Gracia. I preferred the second. It was a pleasant old building where they had knocked down some partition walls to create bigger rooms. It had a wide balcony which gave on to several blocks of colorful residential properties, with pigeons and seagulls sunning themselves on their roofs. The apartment was decorated in an eclectic but functional style, with light-colored wood furniture and cream blinds at the windows. It seemed to me the sergeant could be very happy there receiving his little harem, one after the other.

"I think it's perfect for you."

"Do you really?"

"Yes, I do."

"It makes me very nervous!"

"Why? I don't get it."

"Living on my own, having a house to look after . . . I don't know if I'll manage."

"Of course you will! See that freezer over there? All you have to do is fill it with food. Find someone to come and clean and iron once a week. If need be, buy yourself a few more shirts. How is your money situation?"

"I've got quite lot saved—I used to have nothing to spend it on!"

"Well, now you have. It's expensive to run an apartment and a girlfriend. And as for having two . . . !"

"Don't make fun of me."

"But Fermín, you've given me a real shock with all your love tangles. I'd have been much happier if you'd told me you had two friends and not two women you were in love with."

"Yes, I know, but what can I do? I feel they're more than friends."

"Both of them?"

"Yes, both of them. I have fun with Valentina, and Angela makes me feel good. I had never felt that way until now. My wife used to make me feel as gloomy as a Holy Week procession, when she wasn't making me feel like a worm."

"O.K., I suppose they're both old enough to know what

they're doing. The one who ends up with a broken heart will get over it."

"There's another favor I'd like to ask of you, inspector. Would you come with me the first time I go to a supermarket? I did try once before, but when I went in I had the sensation that all those shelves full of colored tins and packets were going to topple over on me. I didn't know where to start. I've no idea what I need; I don't even know what is what. I realize it's taking advantage of you, but for obvious reasons I can't ask Valentina or Angela."

"Count on me. I'm an expert in quick, massive shopping trips."

"I'm truly grateful to you."

"Forget it, that's what female friends are for."

Poor Garzón! The eternal curse of sexual stereotyping had turned him into a hopeless case, someone so completely incapable of organizing even the most basic things in life that he had to ask for help. The golden age had been bad for women, but for men too. Times had changed, and had left lots of them unprepared for what was to come. The joke was on you, poor Garzón! Even these untimely, dazzling but childish love affairs were the result of his lack of experience. He had never even thought of separating from a wife who made him so unhappy. So there he was now, having fun and being made to feel good, seeing what should have been his daily fare as a gift from the gods. Anyway, who was I to talk: despite having two divorces to look back on, I still was not having any fun or being made to feel good. Better not to get involved in all that, not to express an opinion, much less to try to construct complicated theories of the emotions. I would do better to find my own bones to chew on: my jaws were beginning to lose their snap.

When he received Garzón's request for the figures on stolen dogs, Sergeant Pinilla asked to speak to me personally.

He looked at me reproachfully, and repeated the rules and regulations.

"Inspector, surely you know that here in Community Support we don't deal with any reports of stolen or missing dogs."

"No, Pinilla, I didn't know! So who do you have to see if your dog's missing?"

"The autonomous police of Catalonia."

"Right."

"Yes, the Catalans will deal with you. It's not part of our responsibilities."

Thanks, Pinilla! Why is it that every cop, whatever force they belong to, has to be so finicky? Garzón also tried to protest when I sent him on his own to look into the hairdressers in San Gervasio. "But most of them are for women," he protested. I did not listen: it was one thing for me to feel sorry for him as a hopeless bachelor, and quite another for him to think I was an easy touch.

"I'm sure they'll look after you, sergeant. You've already shown you're a ladies' man. While you're doing that, I'll go and talk to the Catalans."

The fact that it was not the Community Support officers who dealt with missing dogs was not the only surprise in store for me. When I talked to Enric Pérez of the Catalan Environmental Services I discovered lots of things I never knew.

The first, as this young and friendly police officer informed me, was that reports about dogs and cats were not really his responsibility, either. The work was shared with something called the Centre de Protecció Animal de la Generalitat. But the basic problem was that, in Spain, the theft of dogs was not considered a crime. Total amazement on my part. No, it is not a crime. At most it is a misdemeanor or, in some cases, a public health hazard, but it is not in the Spanish Penal Code and therefore no one can be sent to prison for it. What would Angela Chamorro make of that when I told her? When she found out that dogs, which she endowed with all kinds of subtle spiritual qualities, were legally considered less than objects. When he realized how shocked I was, Enric went into detail.

"And on top of that, it is a crime to traffic in protected species of wild animals. There are laws against that, but nothing of the sort for pets. The fact is that people only come to us when they've been turfed out of everywhere else. The Community Support people don't want to know, never mind the national police."

"What do you do then?"

"Not a lot. We take the details just to keep them happy and in case we happen to hear something, but we never investigate."

"And what do people think of that?"

"Well, if ever there's a TV program where they say we deal with missing dogs, the next day they're inundated with phone calls from people protesting. How is it that with all the serious offenses being committed, we're wasting our time on such stupid matters? And yet if the same program has an item about poor, innocent dogs stolen by delinquents, hundreds more people phone in to complain we're doing nothing to stop it."

"So our public is always poking its nose in."

"You know what public opinion is like."

"Can you give me any figures for dog thefts?"

"I can give you a printout, but if you want the complete figures, like I said, you'll have to go to the Generalitat."

"What is on your printout?"

"The owner's name and address and the breed of dog. I'll make you a copy now."

He left, leaving me very discouraged. We did not seem to be getting anywhere. Steps and more steps, probably futile ones. It was like learning to dance a new dance. I had the ominous feeling that we were never going to clear up this damned case. Enric came back with several sheets of paper.

"Here you are, all the dogs stolen or missing over the past two years. And I'll write down the address of the Centre in the Generalitat. Oh, and if you want more reliable statistics, you ought to try a private company which specializes in recovering missing dogs."

"There is such a thing?"

"Yes. It's called Rescat Dog. Those who can afford to, use it."

"That's incredible."

My head dropped on my chin. I did not know what to say.

"Is something wrong, inspector?"

"No, I'm just a bit tired."

"If you like I can get you a coffee from the machine."

"Don't bother, it was just a moment's weakness."

I stood up, and took the list of dogs. Enric commiserated:

"This job can be very tiring sometimes, can't it?"

"It's always very tiring." We smiled at each other.

At the Centre de Protecció Animal in the Generalitat they gave me another list almost as long as the one I already had. And then there was still the company of private dog detectives. My God! I went and hid on the hard chair of my office. At four o'clock Garzón arrived. He had just had lunch, so we drank a watery coffee from the machine together, both of us showing signs of existential weariness.

"Did you have any luck with the hairdressers?"

He put his plastic cup down on the desk, and fumbled in his pockets for a cigarette.

"Since we've been on this case I've forgotten what luck is."

I didn't feel as if I had the energy to lift his spirits. I held out my packet of cigarettes as he seemed incapable of finding his own.

"Tell me what you've got, Fermín, I'm in no mood for more complaints."

"There's not much to tell. You can't imagine how many hair-dressers there are, inspector. Some people obviously take this hair thing very seriously."

"How many did you go and visit?"

"Lots of them! One was run by a young couple, another by a gay guy, another by two girls, another . . . "

"Spare me the details. Did you find anything?"

"Nothing. Lucena was Greek to them. When I showed them the photo they all looked horrified. They didn't have the faintest idea what I was talking about: all they knew about dogs was that they bark and have tails. Oh, and I saw something incredible! Would you believe that in one of them they were dyeing a girl's hair green?"

"Today I would believe anything."

"Well, that's all there is. I'll go back tomorrow, although I have to tell you, inspector, that to my mind none of those high-class places have anything to do with Lucena's low-life world. We might be making the same mistake as with the labs."

"You never know, Garzón, palaces and shacks are connected by sewers."

He blew out smoke like a pressure cooker.

"Yes, who knows! Just look at the world we live in!"

A curious world, where buying and selling a living being, or even stealing it, is not a crime. Where people get their hair dyed green. Where other people pay huge sums to a private detective to recover a miserable cat. Where you can beat a poor little guy to death without leaving a trace.

6

We would not have a complete list of stolen dogs until we had the information from Rescat Dog, so that was where we headed next. This strange business was based in the mezzanine of a nondescript building in Ensanche. The walls were full of posters showing lovely floppy-eared puppies gently playing with charming, fluffy cats. Rescat Dog's only employee seemed to be the beautiful young secretary with long blonde hair who received us and the owner himself. In all honesty, the place had the air of only a strictly limited prosperity. The owner was one Agustí Puig, who was ruddy-faced but ugly as sin. He kept bursting out laughing for no obvious reason, as if he were being followed around by a group of buffoons no one else could see. "I've always paid my taxes!" was the first thing he said when he learned we were from the police. He then embarked on a lengthy explanation about how everything the firm did was strictly legal, and swore he had nothing to hide from us.

Puig was proud to tell us that Rescat Dog was the only organization of its kind in Barcelona and perhaps in the whole of Spain. He was also proud of its results: sixty per cent of dogs recovered out of the total they had dealt with. According to him, given the difficulty of the task, this figure was unbeatable. They employed the usual methods to achieve this success: searching the neighborhood, putting up posters, a network of contacts, questions to possible witnesses . . . added together, all these measures were more than a person could manage on his own.

"We often get into a curious situation where stolen dogs are concerned: we find them, but cannot prove they were in fact stolen, so we have to leave them where they are. You must know about the gaps in the law better than I do."

"That particular gap is of benefit to you though, isn't it? If the police took more responsibility for stolen dogs, you'd lose customers."

"I can't complain about the customers I have."

"So you're not in the middle of a crisis?"

This time, his laugh sounded hollow.

"Everyone knows that crises are like summer storms, they come and go."

"Señor Puig, would I be right in thinking that you keep a file on all your clients?"

"Yes, I keep all their details."

"Do you remember having found the dogs belonging to any of these people?"

I held out the official lists of missing dogs, and he glanced at it despondently.

"There are lots of names here, inspector, lots and lots."

"They're from all over Barcelona."

"Exactly! I'd need a bit of time to check."

"We also need you to make a list of all the cases you've solved, and those you haven't."

"That'll take longer still."

"Don't you have computers?"

"We're putting one in next week."

"In that case, why don't you keep a photocopy of these lists and spend a free afternoon looking at them?"

"All right, I suppose I could have it done in two or three days. I have to carry on with all my normal work, inspector, I'm just a poor worker—the only person I employ is my secretary."

He laughed again, as if his business shortcomings were hilarious too. With a weary gesture, I took Lucena's photo out of my bag.

"Before we go, do you know this man?"

He studied it noncommittally.

"No, never seen him."

We left his office with the originals of the lists and our identity photo. We would have liked to have asked his secretary the same questions, but she had vanished. It was obvious that with such dedicated employees he was not going to get very far.

"Does he seem suspicious to you?" Garzón asked, as if he were filling in a form.

"Yes, he does: he was too open, too keen to laugh. And three days to check the photocopies! It's as if, for some reason or other, he was trying to gain time. Besides, wouldn't you be suspicious about someone so ridiculous as a dog detective?"

He looked at me nonplussed.

"I don't know whether I'm coming or going. After all we've seen, if I heard that there are Latin teachers for tortoises, I'd believe it."

So now he was playing the role of the skeptic, the mature man who reluctantly pretends to be older than he is. The wise old bird shaking his head patiently at the oddities of this world. As if he were not just another crew member of this planetary ship of fools. As if being madly in love with two women at his age was another sign of his emotional maturity.

"Where are you going now, sergeant?"

"I have to visit the last of those hairdressers you lined up for me."

"This time, I'll go with you. But tell me, why are you so upset about it?"

"Too many women."

"I thought an excess of women was no problem for you."

"I know you well enough to have a good idea of where you're heading, so you can stop right there."

"O.K., I apologize, but I'd still like to know why you get so on edge at having to go to these hairdressers."

"The fact is, I realize I haven't the faintest idea what we're looking for there."

Garzón was right. What exactly were we looking for? The hairdressers were full of sophisticated assitants attending to their varied clientele: housewives who wanted their scalps massaged for hours to help them relax, female executives in a hurry, reading their reports while getting some highlights done, and the occasional timid male lost amongst all this femininity. What would a human wreck like Lucena be doing in this calm Roman-bath world? The expression on the owners' faces when we showed them the photo of him beaten up said it all. It was like trying to find fish on the moon. A waste of time. By the time we left the last hairdressers I was in a bad mood as well, and thoroughly disheartened.

"You were right, we were completely wasting our time. And although you were also right to remind me Rome wasn't built in a day or whatever, the fact is that the guy who did for Lucena is still going around free, and by now must be thinking he'll never be caught."

"That's good, he'll be over-confident and start making mistakes."

"Perhaps, but we're still so far from catching him he can make all the mistakes he likes."

"It may be we're not so far from him as you think."

I flicked my cigarette butt towards a bin, but missed.

"We'll see. Can I drop you somewhere?"

"If it's not too much trouble . . . I arranged to meet Angela at her shop. We're having dinner together."

"Has she got over the other night?"

"Not completely, she's still a bit strange. She's upset about Valentina."

"That's logical enough, isn't it?"

"Up to a point. But none of us is a child or even an adolescent any more. All there is between the girls and me is friendship and the hope of something more. I'm not making any demands on them. If things were to become more serious, I'd stop this double game at once."

"That's big of you. Doesn't Valentina complain?"

"No."

"Does she know Angela exists?"

"Yes, she knows, but she's not the same. She asks whatever she wants to know about my work or my past straight out. Angela is more reserved, more discreet. And besides, Valentina has her reasons for not being upset. The two girls come from completely different worlds. That's life."

This birdbrain called them "the girls" as if he had all the experience of a Humphrey Bogart who had spent his whole life dishing out favors to a troupe of platinum-blond chorus girls. I gave him a thunderous look out of the corner of my eye. He noticed at once: it was true he was beginning to know me well.

"What about you? How are things with Juan Monturiol?" he asked, cunning as a fox.

"They're not."

"What about your two exes? Any news from them?"

"Spit it out, Garzón. What are you insinuating, that I'm a Mata Hari too? At least I had one at a time, I didn't try them in twos."

He spread his hands in fake indignation.

"Me, insinuate something about you? I'd never do that, inspector. God forbid: who am I to judge anyone? It's all the same to me."

"All right, Fermín, point taken; I promise not to judge you. Is that what you were getting it?"

I caught him smiling to himself beneath his old, nicotine and beer-stained mustache.

"Couldn't you relax a bit, Petra? Is it impossible for us to talk freely and openly, like proper friends? Just to show my good intentions, I'll invite you to a dinner party."

"You're going to give a dinner party?"

"In fact, I'm going to give two. The special guest at the first will be Angela, and at the second, Valentina. But I'd like you and Juan Monturiol to come to both; I don't have very many friends."

"I can't be sure whether Juan still wants to see me, but I'll tell him."

"And what about the supermarket? Will you come there with me?"

"Damn and blast it, Garzón, I've already said I will! What do you think a trip to the supermarket is, an expedition to the Himalayas with sherpas included?"

We reached the bookshop just as Angela was pulling down the shutters. She smiled when she saw me.

"What a nice surprise, inspector. Are you coming to eat with us?"

"I'm afraid I can't."

Nelly was wagging her tail in a friendly way beside her.

"Have a coffee with us, at least," she said, pointing to the bar opposite.

All the waiters knew her, and she moved among the formica chairs like an urbane first lady. She was really charming, with her frank gaze and dressed in an elegant mauve dress.

"How are you, Petra?"

"Not good."

"Because of your famous investigation?"

"That famous investigation is getting on my nerves!"

"And you've visited only one hairdresser. Think how you'd feel if you'd had to traipse around all the ones I've been to," said Garzón, caught between trying to impress and still feeling put out.

"Hairdressers?" Angela asked curiously.

I made a good start on my beer, and spoke to her through the foam.

"Can you believe it, Angela? We've got a good lead in the dogs case that suggests a hairdresser in San Gervasio is involved. But we can't find any sort of connection between all those well-groomed ladies and Lucena's death. It's enough to make you cry!"

"Are you sure it wasn't a hairdresser for dogs?" Angela suggested, at her most angelic.

I could feel the beer I had drunk suddenly catching in my craw. A hot flush spread across my face. I looked across at Garzón, and saw that he too was as red as a beetroot, and as jumpy as a turkey during Christmas week.

"Call me stupid, sergeant, please."

"Stupid? Not a bit of it. You call me a dolt."

"No, Garzón, that's an order."

"All right. Stupid! Now my turn."

"Dolt! Both of us are dolts. We must be dolts and nincompoops, and we deserve . . . "

"To be removed bodily from the force!"

"Body and soul, Garzón, body and soul."

Angela sat watching this impromptu performance with a look of amazement in her lovely hazel eyes.

"Did I say something interesting?" she said delightedly.

Of course there was a canine hairdressing salon in San Gervasio. It was a bright, spacious place with huge posters in the windows and a self-evident neon sign: Bel Can. And there was only one of them: no competition and they did not even dye the dogs green. Garzón seemed to be trying to fit into his new surroundings and was busy tearing his hair out at the thought of all his wasted trips. The explanation for our lack of detective skills could be put down to a joint attack of complete stupidity. You would have to be both positive-minded and charitable to excuse us by saying that, not knowing much about the world of dogs, we had no idea of all the paraphernalia that the consumer society has invented for them. Hairdressing salons, carers, vets, trainers, special foods, grooming products . . . Angela Chamorro told us that although it was still in its infancy, the dog industry was already worth millions in Spain. "It won't stop there . . . " she insisted, "because people are going to have more dogs, and will want them better looked after. It's one of the measures of how developed a country is," she ended, a hint of pride in her voice.

And it must have been true. The canine hairdressing salon looked even more sophisticated than its human equivalents. Lined with light-green decorative tiles, it had several tables where the pooches were attended by young ladies in spotless uniforms. The manager was a Frenchwoman of about thirty. She was smiling and friendly, with a handsome freckled face and shiny black hair. She did not refuse to answer any of our questions, and raised her hands to her mouth in a childlike expression of horror when she heard we were investigating a murder. No, she did not know Lucena, but if we cared to wait, her husband, who was the joint owner of the business, would be back quite soon. In the meantime, she said, she could show us how the establishment worked.

"Here's where the dogs come in . . . " she said, rolling her "r"s in the French way. "Here we give them a good bath, with lots of shampoo," she added, pointing to a tub fit for Cleopatra. "Then we give them a thorough comb to get rid of any remaining parasites, and finally they have their fur cut. I'm the only one who does that. As you know, each breed has its own style, and we also have to take the owner's wishes into account. That makes it quite a skilled job, if you'll forgive my saying so."

"What do you do if a dog objects and tries to bite you?"

She smiled and drew the tips of her fingers across the cheek of an imaginary dog as if challenging it to a duel.

"Dogs know who's in charge," she said.

Later, she showed us the tables where the pretty young girls worked, armed with brushes and powerful hand dryers. On one of them stood a long-haired dwarf pomeranian that looked so tiny it seemed as though every blast of hot air might blow it away. It scowled at us bad-temperedly.

"That's Oscar, who's been coming here for years. And over there is Ludovica, a magnificent English sheepdog."

We guessed at a pair of eyes staring at us from behind Ludovica's thick curtain of fringe.

"What's this one?" asked Garzón, pointing to another dog being groomed up on a table.

"Ah, that's Macrino, a really expensive Afghan hound."

"Good heavens, it looks like the old woman!" Garzón blurted out.

The Frenchwoman found it funny, and they both laughed. Then Garzón asked:

"Do you know the names of all the animals brought in here?"

"That's right, even if they've only been once."

"Incredible!"

"No, really, it's not that important."

"You'd do well in public relations. It's a shame the dogs can't appreciate it."

She laughed again, this time wholeheartedly. It was unbelievable! Was Garzón thinking he could pick her up too, or had he somehow developed irresistible powers of seduction he could no longer control?

"Afterwards we spray them with cologne, and hairspray, and then . . . "

A man had come into the salon. It took him only three strides to reach us. The Frenchwoman broke off from what she was saying to present him:

"My husband, Ernesto."

She spoke to him in French.

"*Écoute, chéri, ces monsieur dame sont des policiers. Ils voudraient bien te poser des questions.*"

I do not know if he tried to avoid it or not, but for a split second his face fell. Almost immediately, though, his expression changed to one of frank distaste. The pleasant part of our tour was over. He showed us into his office without a word. Once inside, he growled:

"What can I do for you?"

"I'm sorry to disturb you like this, señor . . . "

"Ernesto Pavía is the name."

"We're investigating the murder of Ignacio Lucena Pastor and we'd like . . . "

He blew his top.

"A murder? Well, I don't know what on earth you could be looking for here."

"The fact is, there's a statement that links you to the case, señor Pavia, so . . . "

"Me involved in a murder case? Let's be serious for a moment, shall we? I'd like you to explain right away . . . "

"That's fine, señor Pavía, don't be so angry, you didn't even allow me to finish. The case revolves around the theft of pedigree dogs. Someone told us you had dealings with Ignacio Lucena Pastor."

"I've no idea who you're talking about."

"You might have known him by another name: Pincho, Susito, or some other nickname. This is the man."

I showed him the photo. He glanced at it scornfully for a moment, but I could have sworn there was a flash of recognition in his eyes, and he caught his breath.

"I've never seen him in my life."

"Are you sure of that?"

"I know who I know and who I don't. What I'd like you to explain is how it's possible for someone to involve me in a crime when you didn't even know my name."

"You were named as the owner of a dog hairdressing salon in San Gervasio."

"Great! So why didn't you bring this person here for him to identify me personally?"

"He doesn't know you personally, but he says that . . . "

"He doesn't know me personally, but he's accusing me of a murder?"

"He is not accusing you directly of murder, but . . . "

"Even better! Do you have a warrant to interrogate me? Do you have any proof? I think I've been more than patient, but now I'd like you to leave my salon. When you have something that definitely links me to the theft of dogs or anything else, come back and arrest me. Until then, it would be better to stop bothering honest people who have to earn a living."

He stood up and opened the door for us to leave.

"Out!" he muttered.

He was white with fury. His wife came up at once.

"Qu'est ce qu'il arrive, chéri?"

He did not reply. His pointed a shaking finger towards the exit.

"Out!" This time he shouted the word.

The girls grooming the dogs looked around in surprise, and even some of the dogs seemed to be taking an interest. The Afghan hound growled softly. We left without saying goodbye.

"A real gentleman, wasn't he?"

"A really classy sort! Did you see what expensive clothes he was wearing, his fake tan, his Italian shoes?"

"But I can see his point, inspector. We don't really have any convincing evidence. Perhaps it would have been better not to alert him."

"On the contrary! We have to try to make him nervous so that he makes a false move. Get him and his wife watched round the clock."

"You seem convinced he's mixed up in this."

"Whatever this is, he's mixed up in it all right. Now we just have to catch him."

"That won't be easy. He looked like a clever guy to me."

"Clever, but not cool enough. We have to play on his nerves. Get a legal order to find out who his clients are. I think he's going to make a mistake."

"Do you have a hunch about it?"

"What I have is a thumping headache."

"That's a shame, because all the supermarkets are open . . ."

I grabbed him by both lapels.

"O.K., we'll go right now! Have you got money, your credit cards?"

"I wouldn't dream of it, inspector, and you with a headache and everything . . . !"

"I said I'd go with you to this damned supermarket and that's what we'll do, so help me God."

Essentially, Garzón was right. A big supermarket can be a very daunting place. Because of what he had said, this was the first time I had seen it this way, but there was some truth to it. As you pushed your trolley down row upon row of shiny, brand new, lifeless tins and packets, it was impossible not to feel a certain existential anguish. It was something akin to a symbolic view of life itself: you go along dragging a dead weight right from the start, you choose things you think will be good for you, and passing by others that might have been better, you accumulate more and more, and at the end, you have to pay for it all.

"I forgot to tell you that Doctor Castillo phoned this morning."

I was so caught up in my philosophical meanderings that I asked him to repeat what he had said.

"Don't you remember him?"

"Of course I do! What did he want?"

"Nothing, he was just wondering how the case was going. He said he was curious about it."

"The eternal thirst for knowledge!"

I tossed several bags of sugar into the trolley.

"Do you really think that's all? The fact that he called seems suspicious to me. Why are we buying so much sugar?"

"You have to have a proper supply of the basics: sugar, rice, oil, flour . . . you don't buy things like that every week. What motive could a man like Castillo have for killing Lucena?"

"I don't know. Brilliant scientists are often eccentric. What about yeast, inspector? Shall I buy some of that?"

"No! What on earth do you want yeast for?"

"I don't know, to make bread or whatever! What if Lucena knew something about Castillo and threatened to make it public? Look, I need macaroni, don't I?"

"Buy them if you like them. No, it doesn't add up. Besides, if he were guilty, he'd be giving himself away by calling us. Put some of those tins of tomato paste in the trolley."

"To cook with the macaroni?"

"Got it in one! You're learning."

"I personally wouldn't rule him out as a suspect. Hey, inspector, what about some grated cheese for the macaroni?"

"My, Garzón, you amaze me!"

We moved on to the fresh-foods section. I gave him a quick and easy explanation.

"Look, some things you have to freeze. When you freeze them, put a little bit of paper in the bag saying what's in it and the date. If you want vegetables, buy frozen ones; it's much easier and they're good quality."

"O.K., where are the frozen lettuces? I like a bit of salad now and again."

"There's no such thing as frozen lettuces, sergeant, and you can't freeze fresh ones. And don't bother looking for them tinned. If you want to eat lettuce, you have to buy it the same day."

He gave me a crestfallen look.

"I don't think I'll ever get the hang of this, it's too complicated."

"Don't talk drivel. See those beef fillets over there? You
should always have a couple of kilos ready for defrosting. Since
you live alone, you had better wrap them all separately. And
don't tell me that's too complicated for you!"

He was staring at the meat trays as though they were for-
mulas by Einstein.

"Have we got the complete list of dog thefts yet?"

"We still need the one from Rescat Dog."

"I'd forgotten about them. We need to go there this afternoon."

"I've called several times, but there's never any answer. Only
an answering machine."

"Remind me we should stop by. Now we have to see the
household-cleaning section."

"What, cleaning as well?"

"Give me a break, Garzón! You're going to have to put
powder in the washing machine occasionally. And your cleaner is going to need window spray, and bleach, and perhaps
ammonia, too; some cleaners really go for ammonia."

He rubbed his eyes and heaved a deep sigh. I imagined that
it was only the vision of the two beautiful "girls" stepping into
his brand new apartment that prevented him from fleeing *ipso
facto* back to his boardinghouse.

"When are you planning your first dinner party?" I asked,
trying to encourage him.

"I think I'll have the one with Valentina first," he said. "That
could be tomorrow. Will you help me prepare it, or is that too
much to ask?"

"It is, but I'll help you anyway."

"I don't know how I can ever thank you."

"Then don't. I'll think of something far more complicated to get my own back. Can you paint walls, sweep chimneys, or unblock pipes?"

"Of course I can."

"Then some day we'll be quits."

However hard we insisted, no one opened the door at Rescat Dog. We asked the neighbors, and one woman said the office had been closed for a couple of days. Very odd. There were several packages piled on the doorstep and the letter box was filled to overflowing with papers and letters. If they were on holiday, it was a strange way to go about it. We needed a legal warrant to force our way in, so we went off to get one. The whole thing gave me a bad feeling; I was pretty sure that Puig and his secretary must have flown the coop just after our visit. On the other hand, we might be making a mistake and breaking into a perfectly honest and legal business, which would create even more problems. Were our suspicions sufficient to justify smashing down the door of these dog rescuers, or would it be better to wait until they came back from wherever they had disappeared to? I decided there was no point pussyfooting around, and if they made a complaint afterwards, we would have to face the consequences.

Two hours later, armed with all the necessary legal authority and with a couple of men to break the door down, we made a theatrical entry into the premises of Rescat Dog. As soon as we caught a glimpse of the interior, we realized our theory about them taking flight was correct. The filing cabinets had been hastily emptied, there were papers strewn all over the floor, and the general state of disorder was evidence of a rapid evacuation.

"We were the ones who scared them off," I said between gritted teeth.

"I'll check on the guy's personal details and where he lives."

"Stay till we finish the search, Garzón. I don't think there's much point hurrying; our bird must have flown far away by now."

I bent down to look at some of the bits of paper on the floor: bills, publicity shots, business letters . . . If there had been anything suspicious, they would have got rid of it. It was such a shame: we had him in our grasp and did not even realize it. Obviously, whatever it is they call police instinct was not in our genes. Now it would be far more difficult to lay hands on the fugitive. All of a sudden the sound of the telephone ringing made us both start. Garzón and I stayed glued to the spot. At the second ring, the automatic answering machine started up. We could hear the message: "This is Rescat Dog. We are not available at the moment. We will get in touch as soon as possible. Please leave your name and telephone number." After the tone, we heard a man's voice. "Señor Puig, this is Martínez, the blind-maker. I've done the estimate you asked for. Give me a call and we can discuss it. Bye."

I ran to the phone. I pushed the playback button and waved to Garzón to join me. We both held our breath as we listened to the messages. A woman asking if there was any news of her dog. The gas company. A man asking for details of what Rescat Dog did. Garzón himself, giving his name and a number to contact him on. And then, a message that made both of us pay closer attention. The voice of a man who did not identify himself at all. He said, in hurried tones: "Where are you, what's going on? They've been here and I didn't say a word. They don't know a thing, so it's not grave. All right? Don't ring back."

Garzón gave a low wolf whistle. I rewound the tape. We listened again to the ambiguous words.

"Do you have any idea who it is, Fermín?"

"No, he's whispering in such a low voice that at times I wondered if it was in fact a man. Apart from telling us Puig had an accomplice, I don't know where this gets us."

"Unless . . . "

"Don't tell me you think you know who it is!"

"Do you know what a gallicism is, sergeant?"

"A French word."

"Exactly! A word taken from the French, translated directly into another language. A word or an expression, such as *c'est pas grave*. In French it means something like "it's not important," but translated literally into our language it would be "it's not grave." And who might use a gallicism in his vocabulary without realizing it?"

"Someone who speaks French very . . . " He did not finish the phrase, but snapped his fingers in the air. "The dog groomer! Should we go and arrest him?"

"Don't get carried away, Garzón, what proof do we have? The suspicion of him using a gallicism? We'd do better to get a warrant to go through his books. Even if we find nothing, that'll make him nervous. I think we're on the right track."

"What if he escapes as well?"

"You must be joking. His business is too valuable to leave just like that. Besides, I could swear his wife knows nothing about all this."

"You're very inspired, inspector."

"It's not just inspiration that solves crimes."

"Perhaps not, but with inspiration and fluent French . . . "

Agustí Puig was on our files. His real name was Hilario Escorza and he'd been in jail a couple of times for minor offences. Cheap swindles. When he had worked in real estate, he had made off with some deposits, but was found out. Two years later, he had been in public relations for a disco. He hired the place out for private parties without telling the owner. Back in the clink. A cheapskate crook, the kind that fills police records. This time, he had obviously decided to set up on his own and make money out of rescuing dogs.

"That's fine," said Garzón, "but it's not exactly the profile of a murderer."

"I think you have to stop considering Lucena's death as something premeditated. I'm increasingly convinced it was a settling of scores that got out of hand. That makes the case something completely different. We're not looking for a criminal capable of killing, but a nonprofessional who had what you might call an 'accident.'"

"But the money Lucena had stashed away is a lot more than you'd expect for a 'non-professional.'"

"Perhaps they were involved in something bigger than them."

"If you're right, that means we're close to solving the case."

"I think so."

"If you like, we could go and check Ernesto Pavía's accounts right now; I've got the warrant."

"No, there's no hurry. We'll give him the weekend to see what he gets up to. Is he still being watched?"

"Yes, but I'm worried he might give us the slip."

"Don't worry, real businessmen are like ship captains when their vessel goes down."

"So that means we've got the weekend free?"

"Yes, in theory, but we have to stay alert."

"Talking of the weekend . . . I had thought that . . . well, if you agree, I thought we could have dinner with Valentina on Saturday, and with Angela on Sunday."

I smiled ironically.

"That's what I call a housewarming, Fermín. More of a celebration than when they opened the Suez Canal. What about a third candidate for Friday night as well?"

"I'd really like to know how long you're going to make fun of me."

"That's the price you have to pay. If you want me to help prepare the dinners, you'll have to put up with my keen sense of humor."

"I wouldn't like to have to remind you who it was who helped you get free of your two husbands."

"Knights in shining armor don't ask to be paid. And by the way, I demand to be allowed to come to your blasted parties accompanied by Freaky. The poor thing spends all his time alone in my apartment or with my cleaner, and she thinks he's ugly as sin, which must have a terrible effect on him psychologically. I bet that by now his poor doggy ego is lower than a skunk's."

"Petra, you're unbelievable."

"You've told me that before."

That same evening I called Juan Monturiol to tell him about Garzón's strategic double housewarming party. He could not contain his laughter. Good, that broke the ice a bit. He agreed to go with me on both nights. He sounded pleased, happy to come. I was not sure whether his acceptance meant he still felt some interest in me, or simply that he was amused at Garzón and his retarded adolescent flings. There was no point starting a philosophical debate about it, the main thing was that he was coming.

At six on Saturday evening, after finally being able to spend a day resting and enjoying beauty treatment, face masks included, I picked up Freaky, who was also washed and combed, and headed for Garzón's apartment. Ten minutes later, the sergeant and I were both peeling potatoes like new recruits in the army. My colleague was incredibly clumsy with a knife, and there were moments when I feared for the safety of his pudgy fingers. As if he hadn't got enough to do concentrating on this menial task, he launched into a discussion of the case.

"Let's recapitulate, shall we? You know I always like to remind myself where we've got to. So, the dog groomer and the rescuer are in it together. Everything points to the fact that they were involved in some shady business to do with dogs.

Question: what business? Answer: the theft of pedigree dogs. Next question: what role did Lucena play in all this? Answer: he was the perpetrator; in other words, he was the one who stole the dogs."

"You're making me nervous with your interrogation into thin air. Hurry up with your potatoes; I've already finished mine."

"Don't worry, I'm slow but sure. What I'd like to know is: if Lucena stole the dogs, what did Rescat Dog do? As its name suggests, it rescues them. That sounds logical."

"Stick the fork into the potatoes a few times. We're going to soak them."

"Soak them? That's news to me. O.K., so let's start from what we've got. Lucena steals the dogs and Puig receives them. He takes them somewhere safe, then puts on a whole show for the owners, charging them for a fake rescue. But what's the dog groomer got to do with all this?"

I turned to him, my hands dripping with lamb blood and smelling of garlic.

"Have you got any whisky, Fermín?"

"Are you going to put it in the stew?"

"No, but we could get pickled ourselves. That always inspires chefs."

He poured out two glasses with liturgical devotion. Then he was off again on his ramblings, mentally ticking off what he knew.

"I still don't understand where the dog groomer fits into all this."

I abandoned the roast and turned to him.

"He's the key. My first guess is that he does two things: on the one hand he chooses the dogs that could be stolen from among his clients, either because of how rich they are, or how easy it would be to snaffle them. On the other, he recommends that the owners go to Rescat Dog to get them back."

The potato Garzón was holding slipped from his hands and rolled across the floor until Freaky stuck a paw out and started sniffing it.

"You're right! That's exactly how it must have worked!"

"However, there are a number of 'buts' in the argument. For example, it would be too suspicious if all the stolen dogs came from the same neighborhood. That would be too obvious. I suppose that the dog groomer and the dog rescuer must have contacts with other people who supply them with animals as well. It may be, sergeant, that we're dealing with a real criminal network that spreads all over the city."

He lit a cigarette with his hands still covered in potato starch.

"What are you doing smoking? That's strictly forbidden while we're cooking!"

"I thought we'd finished."

"Finished? It's already gone seven and we still have to sort out the vegetables for the salad, make the dressing, chop the fruit for the dessert . . . "

"I still reckon this eating business is far too complicated."

"Cut the lettuce into thin strips."

"I like your theory, Petra, because if we really are up against a network of swindlers throughout the city, that would explain why Lucena had so much money stashed away."

"Yes, he was lining his pockets by stealing dogs! Take the pips from the tomatoes."

"So what was the motive for killing him?"

"Money, no doubt about it. For the moment we don't need to know the exact circumstances. Perhaps Lucena was asking for a bigger cut, and threatened to shop them if he didn't get it. Perhaps he kept money that wasn't his, or wanted to go it alone and was putting the security of the business at risk if he got caught. Or perhaps he simply dipped his hand in the Rescat Dog till when they weren't looking. None of that matters: what they were trying to do was give him a warning or settling scores, and they went too far. If they had intended to kill him they would have shot him, and if they didn't have any firearms, they could have dealt with him with a single blow to the back of the head with a baseball bat."

Garzón was standing there staring at a tomato in his hand like Hamlet and the skull.

"Yes, inspector, yes, you're clever. More than clever, you're intelligent."

"Thanks. I'm like Molière's wise women: with one hand I can bake a sea bass, while with the other I'm writing a sonnet. The only thing I can't do is catch criminals."

"You can laugh, but I know what I'm talking about."

"Come on Garzón, carry on with your culinary tasks. And make sure you pay attention to what we're doing, otherwise you won't learn a thing."

"Not true! Today I learned something very important: the cook has to be sloshed. Do you feel sufficiently inspired? We could have another one just in case the muse deserts us."

I could not help but laugh. There really was no stopping Garzón! He was as happy as a sandboy. At the age of fifty-something he was starting something like a new life: moving into an apartment, enjoying the pleasures of love without attachments, and discovering the possibility of appreciating feminine virtues in general. I sipped the whisky and watched him struggle hopelessly with a slippery radish. Curled up in a corner of the kitchen, Freaky occasionally cast a languid look in our direction, then closed his eyes and sighed. It seemed to me that those deep and weary sighs expressed exactly what he thought of us human beings. He did not envy or pity us, he simply existed alongside us, which is the only possible way to reach any kind of understanding.

"Inspector, I also thought I'd try to find that pretty blonde secretary from Rescat Dog. She might know something. In any case, she is a loose end that it would be good to tie up."

"Fine, do that. But I doubt . . . "

"*Cherchez la femme!* Isn't that what they say?"

"I think you're better at that than I am."

By nine o'clock a splendid salad was waiting in the fridge and the warm smell of roasting meat filled the whole apartment. Garzón and I were on our fourth whisky, so our gastronomic inspiration had reached Byronic heights. The sergeant was so euphoric he was suggesting imaginative variations for the fruit salad, such as adding dried herbs or bits of crackers. Thanks to my iron hand, none of his suggestions were accepted.

"I'm feeling a bit nervous, inspector. This is the official start of a new way of life, and we're about to solve our case . . . I've never had so many reasons to be excited all at once."

"Don't get ahead of yourself, Fermín, one step at a time. We're going to need lots of evidence if we're really going to wrap this case up."

"We'll get it."

"We'll have to find the dog-rescuer, get the dog groomer to talk . . . "

"We'll do it."

"And before any of that, we have to make sure our theories are correct."

"Are you still worried about that? I'm convinced of it: this time we can't be mistaken."

Garzón was suffering from an attack of omnipotence typical of someone who feels free after a long time in a cage; although, of course, his euphoric state also owed something to our intense bout of alcoholic inspiration.

We set the table carefully. As we went along, I drew up a list of everything Garzón still needed to purchase: a salt cellar, a bread basket, sharp steak knives, glasses for sparkling wine . . . The sergeant watched the list growing and growing without a word of protest. He was ready to make every sacrifice if it meant setting up house properly.

Juan Monturiol arrived at a quarter past nine. While it was true that when I did not see him I hardly even thought of him, having him there in front of me rekindled my desire for some kind of adventure. He looked tremendous, just like a wild pirate tamed by civilization. And he smiled at me openly and in a friendly way, leading me to think he wasn't upset any more. So there was light shining on the horizon, but I would not let it dazzle me. I would accept whatever cruel fate threw my way, and, if it proved impossible to bed him because of our different approaches, I would do nothing to try to change things. If we ended up friends, at least he might give me a reduction in the fees he charged for seeing my dog.

Freaky ran to meet him and leapt up to lick him all over. Monturiol calmed him down expertly.

"How is your case going?" he asked Garzón.

"We're making progress. If everything goes according to plan, there could soon be cause for another celebration."

"Will that be a double one too?"

"Please be discreet when you're talking to the girls, Juan."

My colleague served Juan a stiff drink and put on his most angelical expression to ask him to be careful about his amorous dalliances. I did not like these two men agreeing to a pact of silence right under my nose. I felt a sense of solidarity towards the girls, which was still there when Valentina appeared. To my surprise and to Freaky's consternation, she had brought the ferocious Morgana with her. As soon as my poor little dog caught a glimpse of the rottweiler, he shot across the room and hid under the furniture. The fearsome beast growled a couple of times and considered attacking. Before its mind was made up, its mistress gave an abrupt order in German which it immediately obeyed. It collapsed on the floor and lay there watching, with ill-concealed contempt, Freaky's muzzle poking fearfully out from beneath the sofa.

Valentina looked stunning. For the first time since I had met her, I could appreciate her in full feminine gear rather than dressed as an Amazon. She was wearing an apple-green chiffon dress that left her muscular back almost completely bare. High-heeled green shoes. Around her neck she wore a heart-shaped locket, and a pair of big imitation emerald earrings dangled from her ears, completing the chlorophyll picture of a sylvan nymph. As he showed her round the apartment, the sergeant could not take his eyes off her. I managed to draw him aside for a moment to ask him if Valentina's little heart opened in the middle too. "I'm afraid I don't have much imagination when it comes to presents," he whispered back. I could have killed him. What on earth was he thinking of, duplicating this supposed love token as well? The truth is, I had no idea what Monturiol and I were doing there on this saccharine love-date. Later, over dinner, I decided the explanation must be that Garzón felt so happy he needed others to witness his pleasure.

Wine flowed in our glasses like the Nile in flood. Garzón had the unbelievable nerve to launch into a detailed description of how he had prepared each of the courses. The cheeky devil was displaying his domestic know-how to his beloved. It seemed to me this was the wrong strategy, or at least a waste of breath: Valentine did not seem in the least bit interested in his newfound prowess. She ate with great gusto, listened with half an ear to what the sergeant was saying, and showed all the confidence of a mature woman used to living on her own and fending for herself. She steered the conversation with Juan to dogs, and gave us a long list of Morgana's talents. She could do just about everything: she kept strictly to heel when she walked alongside her owner, waited for Valentina in the street outside shops, could follow a scent in open country no matter what the weather, and given an explicit command, would attack. In short, she was far more capable than I was on a Monday morning. I glanced over at Freaky. The poor thing was still hiding under the sofa, perhaps in dismay at hearing of so many canine virtues. Even Garzón joined in the praise for the rottweiler, who pretended to take no notice and sat there as serene and stiff as a greyhound on an Egyptian hieroglyph.

By the time we reached dessert, we had downed several bottles of wine, and Garzón went in search of some sparkling white. His fridge was well-stocked with alcohol—that was the one thing for which he had needed no advice. The result was we were all merry, and Garzón and I a little more than that. Juan Monturiol proposed a toast: "To the new life that a new home always brings." I saw Garzón dedicate a profound, misty gaze to Valentina, but could have sworn she did not return it. Juan's toast seemed instead to have conjured up dreams of her own. She raised her glass level with her heavily made-up eyes and said: "Let's drink to that." She finally came out of her deep reverie and explained:

"Some day I'll have a new home too. It'll be in the countryside, surrounded by trees and grass. At the back of the garden I'll keep dogs. I'm going to be a breeder, probably of rottweilers. I'm not talking about a commercial kennel where they churn out puppies like *churros*. I'll only have a few litters, it'll be a mark of distinction, something only those in the know will frequent. I'll perfect the breed, and people will come from all over to try to buy one of my creations."

I could have sworn that to her this was something more than a mere pipe dream.

"And when is this marvel going to happen?" I asked.

She came out of her dream and shook her golden locks, spreading wafts of a heady jasmine perfume.

"Oh, at the moment I'm just saving up for it! I don't want the place to be too far from Barcelona, which makes it very expensive. Besides, I need a big house and proper facilities."

"That means you're going to have to train lots of dogs, Valentina."

She gave me a sad look, then a smile gradually chased away the worry on her face.

"Savings can work miracles! And it's important, too, to believe you can get what you want."

"And I believe this woman will get whatever she wants," Garzón burst out. Valentina protested unctuously.

"Oh, Fermín, don't be so flattering. Don't you have any music in this den? We could dance!"

Garzón was not sufficiently well-installed to have foreseen such a request, but he found a temporary solution by bringing in a transistor radio from his bedroom. I guessed he must have had it in his boardinghouse to listen to football matches on lonely Sunday afternoons. The sound quality was dreadful, but that did not seem to matter a bit to him or Valentina. They threw their arms around each other and started leaping round the room like a pair of demented grasshoppers. Monturiol watched with pure delight on his face, cheering the mad couple on. In order not to miss anything, Freaky stuck his head a little further out from under the sofa. Only Morgana remained unmoved by the spectacle, showing that her square Teutonic mind would not allow itself to be affected. I was not sure how to react to all this pandemonium either, and could only raise a smile. When the dance had finished, overcome by alcohol and love, Garzón did his party piece. Pretending to be a huge, angry dog, he started to growl and leap around Valentina. She immediately joined in, picking up a napkin to use as a whip and flicking it at him while she shouted confused commands in German: "Aughf! Sine grumpen!" The sergeant had completely lost his head and was barking like a thing possessed. It was probably just my prejudice and the fact that I was used to regarding him as a somewhat old-fashioned representative of the law, but it seemed to me there was something vulgar about the whole thing. As if the noise they were making was not enough, Morgana joined the general air of excitement and started to bark. I thought the neighbors must be delighted with the new tenant. Eventually Valentina shouted at her dog to be quiet.

"Silly dog! It won't let us be. Why don't we leave her at my place and then go on and dance somewhere?"

Garzón didn't have to be asked twice. "Dance, did I hear you say dance?" he said over and over, as he put on his jacket to go out.

"I don't think I'll go," I said.

"Nor me," Monturiol added.

"Oh, go on, why not?"

"We'll catch up with you later, I promise."

They were just about to leave when Garzón realized something and came back, concerned.

"We can't go with the table in such a mess."

"You two go on. I'll clear things away this once, Garzón, but remember, that's something else you owe me."

"I swear I'll pay you back everything."

"We'll be in the Shutton, I really like that place!" Valentina exclaimed, putting on a bottle-green shawl.

They rushed out arm in arm, talking at cross purposes like a music-hall act. Juan was still laughing.

"Were you serious when you said you'd join them later?" he asked.

"Of course not! And I didn't mean it when I said I'd clear everything away either. I think making dinner for him was quite enough. I'll just get rid of the leftovers."

"I'll help."

"No, you go home and sleep. Remember, we've got to go through all this again tomorrow."

"I hope that with Angela it'll be a bit quieter."

He carried out dirty plates after me. The kitchen looked as though a bomb had hit it. There was no room at all to leave the things, but I managed to make some room to put the dirty glasses down. As I turned around, I bumped into Juan.

"Sorry, the place is such a mess."

He did not step out of the way, but stood where he was, preventing me edging past him. He had a faint scent of cologne, mixed with the body smell on his clothes. We were both breathing heavily. He closed his eyes and kissed me, first on the nose and then on the mouth. He was still balancing several plates in each hand, like a circus acrobat.

"God, what shall we do with these?"

He bent down and laid them on the floor. We started kissing again.

"Where shall we go?" he groaned.

"To the bedroom."

"Here?"

"It's neutral territory."

"But they might come back."

"Not for a long while."

Freaky was standing in the doorway, observing us. I gave him a lamb bone to chew on so he would leave us in peace.

Garzón's bed was king-sized and had been carefully made—not for us, of course. But what did that matter? Was my friendship with the sergeant so weak it could not withstand such a small transgression? Anyway, I soon stopped worrying about what Garzón might think. I could feel Juan's naked body next to me. That body I had seen so often without ever touching it had now become real, something I could stroke, something warm and solid. I realized how much I had been wanting this, how much I wanted to be able to feel his naked body, perhaps any man's naked body.

I woke up the next morning in my own bed. I was alone and relaxed, my mind full of mixed feelings, but my body clear and glowing. I felt good, pleased I had been able to discover a tiny Switzerland where Juan and I could sign an armistice. In the end, it had been simple. I only hoped we would not have to use Garzón's apartment each time we felt pangs of desire. Then all of a sudden I saw it from a different perspective, and remembered what a dreadful state we had left the battleground in. The mess in the kitchen was one thing, but how we had left the bed! It was not only unmade, but was stained with the traces of our love-making . . . we had gone too far. Garzón would be horrified when he went into his room. He might even lose all respect for me as a superior officer. How on earth could I explain to him the special political and diplomatic circumstances which had led to us making use of his bed? That would be even worse. No, we had to let him jump to the most obvious conclusion: that Juan and I had been so overcome by our passion we had been unable to wait. I felt as though I would die of shame when I saw him again. My only hope was that he was too much of a gentleman to say anything remotely connected to the subject, or that when he had got back that night he had been too drunk to notice a thing.

I had breakfast and went to the police station. Not many people there on a Sunday, thank heavens. On my desk were two reports from the people we had watching the dogs' beauty parlor and Rescat Dog. Nothing from either team. I also had the information we had asked for on missing dogs. It looked very complete. They had made a single alphabetical list out of all the different ones I had given them. It looked clear and easy to consult. They had also added a map of the whole of Barcelona, with all the addresses where a dog had gone missing from marked with a little red bone. I loved that idea: it showed a touch of humor that was unusual for any police department. Casting a quick glance over the map, it seemed as though the dogs had disappeared from all over the city. There were more of them in the richer neighborhoods, which was not surprising because those were pedigree animals. I looked more closely at San Gervasio, in the area around Bel Can. Yes, perhaps there were more bones there, but it did not seem as though there were many more than in other parts of the city. It seemed logical to suppose that there was a whole network involved. The nerve centre must have been Rescat Dog, but Bel Can could not have been the only place that identified dogs to be stolen: that would be too suspicious and not profitable enough. If all the missing dogs had come from that one salon, even their owners would have noticed. No, it must have been a much larger organization, one involving so much money that a man could be killed if something went wrong. And Lucena probably was not the only dog thief on their books. There must have been others. So it was a big organization, and its most obvious ringleader had fled. I was hopeful that the arrest warrant we had put out for Puig would soon bring results. I had reason to believe he had not gone very far. The setup was too lucrative for him not to have stayed close by, watching to see what was going on, or trying to settle accounts with his associates as quietly as possible . . . however profitable the business had been until now, it could not have provided him with enough to set him up for life in Brazil. He was here, close by, waiting for things to blow over in some safe hiding place. We had to make him come out into the open, like a mushroom after rain. Either he would make a mistake himself or we would have to bring things to a head. And we had to make sure we had proof of everything, to make the pieces fit. I looked again at the amusing map. Elegant neighborhoods peppered with little red bones. The same old story: thieves, swindlers, conmen . . . all of them just waiting to discover rich people's weaknesses: their love of designer jewelry, signed paintings, pedigree dogs. They knew how attached the well-off were to their beloved pets. Probably each and every one of those dogs whose rescue was paid for had known more love than Lucena. Did the thought ever occur to him? Was it in his mind when he hid all that money under the floor in his kitchen? Did that help compensate him for all the wretchedness in his life? Had Lucena ever really thought or felt these things? Yes, his dog showed he had. Freaky was a sensitive, even thoughtful animal, and must have taken after his master. Lucena must at some point have felt sad and alone, robbed of his family, his name, his pedigree. He must have seen himself as a piece of trash thrown aside by the consumer society around him. But he was not the only one: there would always be leftovers, unwanted bits, remains, like the piles of debris left after any building job. There was nothing I could do to change that, but it was my responsibility to discover who had killed him, if only to show that human waste is more valuable than a heap of lime or sand. After all these weighty deliberations, I decided to go home and make myself a snack.

In the early evening I got out the car. I drove past Juan Monturiol's veterinary surgery. We had spent a wonderful night together. Everything was working out fine: perhaps at last I could find someone to fuck and be friends with at the same time. In the hope that things would continue in a similar vein, I went on to my second and last cookery class. As I drove, disturbing memories of the bed we had made love in flashed through my mind. The sergeant's reaction when he saw me would be crucial to my mood for the rest of the evening. Fortunately, there was no problem: Garzón opened the door then rushed off back inside his apartment without hardly even saying hello. "I've got something on the stove," was his only greeting. Intrigued, Freaky trotted after him. I preferred to take advantage of his confusion to have a quick look round the apartment. Everything was spick and span—Garzón had cleaned it thoroughly. Although it was rather childish of me, I glanced surreptitiously in at the bedroom. The bed looked immaculate; there was no trace of our unauthorized occupation of it.

Relieved, I went off to find out what was happening in the kitchen. Freaky was sitting on the floor, stretching his neck to follow every detail of the chaos the sergeant was creating. A brownish mixture composed almost entirely of thick lumps was cooking or, rather, congealing on the stove. All around the pan were trails of flour and spilt milk.

"To judge by the evidence of the disaster, you were trying to make a béchamel sauce."

"Christ, Petra, don't talk about it! You can't imagine the stew I've got myself into!"

His hair was all over the place, his face was bright red, and he was pouring sweat.

"I wanted to surprise you, so this morning I went out and bought some ready-cooked cannelloni. It said that all you had to do was add the bechamel, so I went to a bookshop to buy a recipe book. Then I carefully followed the instructions, and yet look at the mess I'm in. I'll never believe you again when you say how easy it is to do all this domestic stuff!"

"Let me do it! First, help me throw all this away!"

Between the two of us we reorganized the work. I put the pan back on the heat, and added a generous lump of butter.

"Didn't the recipe book tell you to heat the milk first?"

"How on earth should I know? That damned book uses more complicated language than any lawyer. I glanced at it, and didn't understand a word: *bain-marie*, brown, beat until stiff, fry lightly, season . . . why can't they use ordinary words?"

I shook my head several times as I sifted the flour.

"No, it's not the words that are to blame, Fermín; the problem is that unconsciously you think you'll never be able to learn any of this. And deep down what you really believe is that it's unworthy of a man and that there's no reason for you to make any great effort as long as there are women who are good at it."

"That's all I needed right now, a feminist harangue!"

"Think about what I'm saying, think about it."

He started muttering curses under his breath, still trying to recover from all the stress his culinary adventures had caused him.

"Don't take it out on me, Fermín, I only came to help. Oh, by the way, I've brought you something you'll enjoy."

"Another recipe book?"

"No, the computer printout of the missing dogs and a map. I left them in the living room."

"I'll have a quick look at them."

"No chance! You're going to stay here and watch how I make the béchamel."

"You really like giving orders, don't you?"

I burst out laughing. I took the pan off the stove so that I could look Garzón in the face.

"Do you really think I like giving orders?"

"No, no inspector, I didn't mean that . . . "

"Don't be polite, Fermín: tell me the truth. Do you think I like to give orders?"

"Yes," he admitted.

"It's odd," I said, "you may be right, and yet it's not something I'm aware of."

"Watch out, the béchamel is going lumpy again."

"Don't worry, we'll give it a good stir. Come on, you try." I stood behind him and explained how he should stir the mixture. After floundering at first, he soon got the hang of the simple procedure, and even began to enjoy himself.

"You're doing just fine."

"Well, in the end . . . "

Within an hour we had finished preparing the fateful meal. As we sat with a glass of whisky in our hand, we glanced at the computer printout of the missing dogs. I awaited his verdict.

"What do you think?"

"I don't know what to think. There are dogs stolen all over the city. San Gervasio doesn't look especially different. Those people must have spread everywhere."

"That was my conclusion, too."

"That would explain all the money Lucena had hidden in his apartment."

"The only thing I find strange is that he didn't have it all written down in any of his account books."

"Maybe if such a book existed, they took it from him when they beat him up."

"That's what we always say when we reach this point."

"If that's so, it must be because we're right."

I lit a cigarette and nodded, but I wasn't convinced.

"I think we've given Pavía time enough. First thing on Monday morning I want a search warrant for Bel Can. We'll take away all their accounts and get our experts to pore over them."

"Perfect, inspector. Damn it!"

"What's wrong?"

"It's twenty to nine, and Angela is arriving at nine. I'm going to change and shave again."

"You're fine as you are."

"No . . . for Valentina perhaps, but not for Angela . . . everything has to be just so for her."

I did not know what to make of that. Did it mean Angela was ahead in the race to win my colleague's heart, or was Valentina the favorite? Was it a positive sign that the sergeant felt our bookshop owner was so demanding, or did he prefer Valentina's more casual approach—did that make him feel freer? Ah, love and all its questions. I would not have wanted to be in Garzón's shoes for all the world. Love: choices, decisions, uncertainty, insecurity, guilty feelings, suffering . . . Thank God I had left all that behind me! I raised my glass in a toast to my troubled emotional past and to my untroubled erotic present.

"Here's to you, Freaky, my heart's one faithful companion."

Freaky did not seem impressed by my grandiloquent gestures. He yawned and did not show the slightest interest. I drank my whisky. From the bathroom I could hear the sound of Garzón's electric razor. If it had not been for the insistent doubts and queries raised by the case of the missing dogs, this could have been a moment of utter calm.

At nine on the dot Angela appeared with her dog, Nelly. The bulky creature shuffled over to Freaky, and the two of them sniffed and investigated each other. Then they both started to wag their tails: thankfully there seemed to be little risk of a quarrel. Angela was not merely pretty, she was beautiful. A simple black dress with a wide neck perfectly framed her calm face. Her hair was gathered back and showed gray streaks at the sides. The disgusting pendant Garzón had given her and Valentina hung round her neck. I hated him for that. I glanced over at the dogs.

"Freaky gets on very well with your dog, he's not scared of her like he is of . . . "—I caught myself in time—" . . . of other big dogs."

Is it possible to make a fool of yourself precisely when that's the last thing you want to do? Angela looked at me sourly and said:

"Guard dogs are very scary, especially in a small apartment like this."

Oh God, she knew: she knew Valentina had been here with her rottweiler, or she suspected as much! I only hoped that at least that animal Garzón had not told her himself, and then thought nothing of it. I felt such a renewed sense of solidarity with the dog expert that when the sergeant came back into the room, freshly washed and brushed like a schoolboy at tea-time, I could have smashed my whisky glass on his head.

"About time too, Garzón! Angela has been here for ages!"

He looked at me in bewilderment, then went over to his guest and in the best old-fashioned way took her hand and raised it to his lips. She smiled and seemed to relax.

Two minutes later, Juan Monturiol arrived. The sergeant

slapped him on the back like an old friend and joked about how good it was to have another man around. I did not take kindly to that, either, but luckily the ravishing sight of my handsome vet restored my good mood. How could he show off such astounding green eyes and still pretend to be no more than a normal being? I was filled with a sense of pride at being at least the fleeting repository of all that beauty.

It was a pleasant evening. The conversation flowed freely and easily, as it always did when Angela was with us, and yet, in spite of the agreeable appearances, under the surface there was a certain tension. Every so often the bookshop owner launched a veiled attack on the sergeant by referring to the uncertain future, loneliness, or how men were incapable of understanding women's hearts. Whenever she did, Juan looked down, feeling himself a target too; I thought vengeful thoughts about Garzón, and Angela turned sad. The only one who stayed cheerful all the time was Garzón, who took the blows apparently without even noticing them. So this was what a provincial policeman was like! I don't know why I had not realized earlier what a satrap, what a heartbreaker, what a Casanova he was! He was showing the excessive tendencies typical of people who have been deprived of something for too long. People who are used to fasting and then suddenly succumb to bulimia, puritans who switch completely and become inhabitants of Sodom and Gomorrah. Too bad for him; too bad for all of us.

After our dessert, when we sat on the sofa to have a brandy, the elusive sense of unease that had been present during the entire meal led to an awkward clearing of throats. Angela decided to break the silence.

"How is the case with the dogs going?"

"We've got to the bottom of it!" Garzón chortled.

I gave him a skeptical look and explained.

"Let's just say we're getting somewhere. I've just been given the complete statistics for missing dogs, and a computer map showing where they all disappeared from."

"How odd! Do you think I could have a look?"

Garzón brought her the map, and she stared at it with great curiosity.

"It seems as though dogs have become the centre of a lot of shady business," she said.

"Like everything that can be bought and sold."

Garzón had got up again, and a minute later came back carrying his radio. I prayed to God he was not thinking of dancing again. God must have heard me, because instead Garzón chose some gentle background music and then sat down again. He cast a dreamy glance towards Angela, who was still absorbed in the map. All at once she looked up and spoke to Juan Monturiol.

"Did you notice how odd it is? Look at the breeds involved: giant schnauzers, German shepherds, briards, rottweilers, boxers, dobermans . . . "

"Yes, they're all guard dogs."

"They're the ones that figure most in the list. There are lots more of them than hunting or lapdogs."

"How do you interpret that, Angela?"

She shook her head from side to side, slightly flustered.

"I don't know, it just struck me, I wasn't trying to interpret it."

"Would a guard dog be more expensive, easier to sell?"

The two dog experts looked at each other quizzically.

"They could be; they've become fashionable."

"Does it seem significant to you?" I asked her again.

She became as confused as a little girl asked to explain too much after something has happened.

"I was simply commenting on what I saw!"

"I know, but after your brilliant suggestion about the dogs' beauty parlor . . . "

Flattered, Angela laughed and smiled coquettishly at Garzón. He did not seem the least bit interested in the dogs case; when he was with one of his "girls" he could not care less about work. I could tell that he was probably abandoning all sense of responsibility, but there was very little I could do about it: this was obviously not the moment for detective work. Perhaps I was the one who carried my sense of duty too far into my private life; I had not even realized that the evening was coming to an end, and that Monturiol was looking inquiringly at me. Yes, it was time for us to beat a retreat: Angela and Garzón were already in their own lovey-dovey world. They said goodbye at the apartment door, thanking us for coming and promising we would meet again soon.

Juan and I walked down the dark street to the car. Freaky lolloped along behind.

"It's all quite strange, isn't it?" I said. Monturiol looked at me as if he did not understand what I was talking about. "I mean, my relationship with the sergeant, his affairs with Angela and Valentina, our own fling."

When he heard that, he started.

"Don't you like the word 'fling'? We can call it what you like: liaison, flirtation, adventure . . ."

"I'd prefer not to call it anything."

I realized we ran the risk of falling back into our earlier problems. I took his arm and shook him a little.

"You're right, words can destroy everything. Your place or mine?"

"You decide."

"I don't mind."

He smiled. I smiled. Another battle avoided. In the end it is good to leave the suit of armor at home from time to time.

7

Garzón and I met up at the station first thing on Monday morning. We both had rings under our eyes worthy of Ivan the Terrible. Too many celebrations, too much lovemaking. I swore to myself that, apart from the lovemaking, I was not going to indulge in any more serious socializing. This was not the moment. We were as slow as the Church in our investigation, and yet, instead of getting on with it or at least getting some proper rest, we had embarked on an entire round of festivities. Before we left for the dog beauty parlor, we had a couple of coffees as crammed to overflowing as a train in India with caffeine. Garzón clung to his cup as if it were a life-buoy. I tested to see how far I could count on him.

"Are you in any shape to work?"

"I'm fresh as a daisy," he said. Looking at him, I could not help seeing one of those faded flowers pressed for years between the pages of a book.

"Do we have the search warrant?"

He felt inside his jacket pocket and tapped it reassuringly.

"With specific permission to inspect their accounts."

"I think we should devote all our efforts to the case, Garzón."

"I agree."

"Things are looking good, and with a bit of luck we'll be able to wrap it up brilliantly."

"I agree to that too."

"So you'll keep your mind on the job?"

"Absolutely," he said, pleased with himself.

What more could I say to stir his professional conscience? Nothing: I had to give him credit for being sufficiently grown up. Yet as we were driving along in the car, my heart sank when out of the blue he said:

"Angela is a wonderful woman. Wonderful."

I said nothing, so he asked:

"And how are you getting on with your vet?"

I did not like this amorous chumminess one little bit. I grew tense and answered curtly:

"I'd appreciate it if we changed topics."

"Of course!"

He had not even noticed my sharpness. He was so euphoric nothing could bring him down. Fortunately, his attitude changed once we reached the canine beauty parlor. His face took on a serious expression, and his eyebrows changed in an instant from darting bluebirds to threatening black lines.

Ernesto Pavía was on the premises, together with his enchanting wife. He did not seem surprised to see us, and received us coldly and calmly. We were shown into his office. The girl assistants looked far more interested in us than in the fur of any of the dogs they were meant to be combing. We sat down in a civilized manner.

"Señor Pavía, we have an official warrant to search Bel Can and to go through your books."

He opted for a cynical smile.

"Fine, I have no intention of standing in the way of justice."

The Frenchwoman butted in.

"I would never have dreamed we could be treated this way."

"It's nothing personal, señora."

Pavía patted her to reassure her. She fell quiet.

"Look, señor Pavía, I think all this would be a lot less unpleasant if you were to cooperate with us."

"I've already told you I have no objection to you going through whatever you like."

"That's not the point. The point is we are going to accuse you of robbery and fraud, and they are serious charges. All the more serious because together with that charge there is another one of murder, in which you could be involved either as an accomplice or even as the main perpetrator."

He was immediately on his guard, sitting forward in the executive's chair and spreading his hands in front of him.

"Just a moment please: you're going to have to explain all this to me."

"We're going to charge you with being the accomplice of someone called Agustí Puig in a series of swindles, and also of involvement in the murder of Ignacio Lucena Pastor."

"Not that again! I've no idea what you're talking about."

"We have proof, Pavía, so don't play the innocent."

"You have proof? Proof of what?"

"We have the recording from Puig's answering machine. The one with your voice warning him that we are snooping around. That was your fatal mistake—so amateurish. You didn't think Puig would scarper."

I was trying to stay calm and to speak as slowly as possible so that I could observe even the smallest sign of a reaction. Apart from a logical nervousness, he did not react in the slightest. It was obvious he had been expecting all this and was ready to deny everything.

"I still say I haven't the faintest idea what you're talking about."

"You don't know Agustí Puig?"

"No."

I did not hold out much hope that we could provoke him and make him lose his temper, but I started to rummage in my huge shoulder bag. I took out a small recorder, placed it on the desk, and pressed play. The voice of the stranger, which sounded so like Pavía's, reeled off the whole message we had heard at Rescat Dog. While it was playing, I was keeping a close watch on the Frenchwoman. I wanted to find out if she knew what was going on. She blinked once, perhaps a sign that she found it harder to control herself than her husband did. But yes, she knew all right. Perfect, that was another opportunity for us to apply pressure. After he had heard the recording, Pavía smiled. I guessed this was because he had not remembered exactly what he had said, and was relieved he had not given even more away. He flashed his set of perfect teeth in a smug smile.

"So that's meant to be me?"

"That's what we think."

"Oh please, inspector, be serious for once! That could be anybody's voice."

"But it's yours."

"You're trying to get me to believe that you're going to use that nonsense as evidence to accuse me of murder? That's quite enough: even little kids know recordings aren't admissible as evidence in any court of law!"

His wife butted in again. This time she was angry.

"This is an insult and an abuse. There is no way that voice was my husband's. We are honest businesspeople who work hard and give employment to others, but you come in here and accuse us of consorting with swindlers, and even of murders! I'm going to consider asking my consulate for protection."

This time, Pavía made no effort to calm her down. I put the recorder away.

"Could we take a quick look around?"

"Go right ahead. Perhaps you'll find a body or two."

"We also need photocopies of all your accounts for the past two years."

"Of course: I've got nothing to hide! I recently had a visit from a tax inspector, so I don't suppose you're going to be more demanding than him."

He was firmly on his high horse. I looked over at Garzón,

and nodded at him to make a start. He began with the shelves in the office and the desk drawers. Then he went out into the salon and flicked through the appointments book. All this was a waste of time of course, and I realized from the casual way he was doing it that Garzón knew as much. We were not going to find anything incriminating there, but it was something we had to do to put psychological pressure on our suspect. Not that he seemed in any way affected by it. He himself gave us a computer printout with all the accounts for the period we were interested in.

"I don't want to seem mistrustful, but since you have everything on computer I think it would be a good idea for our experts to come and have a look at all the information *in situ.*"

"Oh, of course, we'll make them feel right at home! We'll give them a snack, and, if any of them would like to spend the night here, we've got lots of dog blankets."

"No, thank you, a few hours should be enough."

There was no way I was going to start swapping sarcastic comments with him. Back in the car I said to Garzón:

"This is going to be tougher than we hoped. There's no chance of that bastard cracking. Make sure his phones are tapped."

"I'll take care of it."

"We'll have to think of some way of putting him under psychological pressure."

"We'll find something, and perhaps in the meantime our boys will lay their hands on Puig."

"We can't count on that. Did you get a list of the salon's customers? We need to find someone who lost a dog and then recovered it thanks to Rescat Dog. Then we can question them."

"I'll see to that too. I'll take someone along to help."

"O.K., do that. I'm going to give all these accounts to

Inspector Sanguesa. I'll ask him to send two men to Bel Can; I don't expect they'll find anything, but that way we'll keep the pressure up."

"Our visit was a good start."

"Do you really think so? Well, then, you have to admit those two are good at resisting it."

"No one can resist forever, inspector."

"Or insist forever either; it might be us who give in first."

"Never!"

"Don't be so sure. I'll see you back at the station later."

I couldn't help but wonder why Garzón could feel so sure of himself. I could not see any reason for it. We were staggering from one sordid business to another without being able to find Lucena's murderer, and yet the sergeant seemed to feel we were on top of the world! Not to mention the blasted love triangle he found himself in! But Garzón was imperturbable, he was strolling naked through Paradise, delighted to be the only Adam in sight.

At my desk I looked through Pavía's account book before handing it to our fiscal team. Not even a coffee and a cigarette helped me make head or tail of it. What exactly was I searching for? Something that linked them to Lucena's second book? Was his cut so generous he had made all that money in the space of a year? How many dogs could a poor wretch like him have stolen? Someone knocked, then a cop stuck his head round the door.

"Inspector Delicado, there's a woman outside asking to see you."

"A woman?"

"She says her name is Angela Chamorro, and that you know her."

"Show her in."

It was bound to happen! The dog expert was going to ask me to put in a word with my colleague, or complain woman to woman about his behavior, or any of the other things that a woman in love does when she feels threatened. Damn and blast Garzón! He would have to pay me back for this. If there had been a window handy, I would have skipped out of it. But when I saw that Angela was her usual calm self, I felt reassured.

"Angela! Have you abandoned your bookshop?"

"I've left my assistant in charge for a while. I'll only be a moment: I know you have lots to do."

She sat down opposite me, gathering up her green check skirt. I thought she looked rather thin.

"Can I get you a coffee?"

"I don't want to put you to any trouble."

I left the office to get a couple of coffees and to prepare myself for what was to come. When I came back, Angela received me with a sad smile. We stirred our cups in a somewhat strained atmosphere, and then finally she made up her mind to speak.

"The fact is that yesterday after we met at Fermín's place I felt bad."

My heart sank, but I tried to appear natural and to have no idea what she was talking about.

"Why was that?"

"I couldn't stop thinking about the huge number of guard dogs that there were on your list. It bears no proportion to the size of those breeds in Barcelona. Do you understand what I'm trying to say?"

I did understand. Not only that, but I was mightily relieved that our case was the reason for her visit.

"I kept thinking and thinking about it, until I remembered something a friend of mine called Josep Arnau told me. Arnau runs rottweiler kennels close to Manresa. It's way out in the country, like most kennels of that type. He told me there have been thefts of his dogs at night for some time now. Good adult specimens that he keeps for breeding. The poor man is fed up with it; they're very valuable dogs."

"Do you think it has something to do with our case?"

"I have no idea, Petra, but my friend said that several of his breeder friends were complaining of the same thing. And they all breed guard dogs! And seeing that you are investigating dog thefts, I thought . . . "

"Yes, but what we're really looking into is the death of Lucena, and I don't see what link there could be between the dog breeders and that."

Angela looked slightly disappointed. She nodded:

"I suppose you're right. You know about these things. It was stupid of me to come."

"Not in the least! What's more, if you give me your friend's address, I'll go and have a chat with him. The fact that guard dogs are involved is a curious coincidence, and however remote the possibility, we need to investigate it."

She lowered her eyes gratefully.

"Oh well, you know what's best!"

"You gave us important information by concentrating on the breed of dog rather than where they were taken from, Angela, and we need to follow that up. Have you got your friend's address with you, or will you give it to Fermín?"

"I wasn't sure whether I was going to see Fermín today, so I brought it with me." She searched in her bag and pulled out a small piece of paper. "By the way, Petra, about Fermín . . . "

My worst fears were confirmed. Now we were getting to the real reason for her visit.

"Yes?"

"Well, you know he's also going out with another woman, don't you?"

"Well, I . . . "

"Don't be afraid of giving anything away. I already know about it: Fermín himself explained the situation."

I got up to light a cigarette without even realizing the last one was still burning down in the ahstray.

"The last thing I want is to create any kind of problem for you, but you know Fermín well: you've been working together for some time now."

"We're only work colleagues."

"Perhaps that's enough to help you explain why Fermín is doing something like this. I don't get it: he behaves as if he's really in love with me. He calls me, demands to see me, says the tenderest things to me . . . and yet at the same time he is going out with that Valentina woman and doesn't even bother to hide the fact from me. He doesn't seem to feel any remorse and appears to think it's the most natural thing in the world."

"Yes, I've noticed his attitude."

"How can he be so flippant about love? Ever since the death of my husband . . . well, until now I have never fallen in love since then, Petra. Fermín seems like a straightforward, good and funny man. He's full of vitality, but I can't work out what he wants from me, or get used to being treated this way."

"I understand you perfectly, Angela. But I'd also like you to understand that Fermín is not playing with your affections. He's old enough to be mature, and the fact is that he does behave maturely in many instances, but not when it comes to love. He spent much of his life with a woman he did not love and has never asked himself exactly what love means. And now, when he was least expecting it, two wonderful women appear in his life at the same time. He doesn't even think much about it except that it is tremendous. He is discovering what it means to be in love, but doesn't yet know what it really implies. He'll probably find out soon enough, but at the moment he is incapable of listening to anything beyond his own emotions."

Angela had listened to me with rapt attention. She nodded her head sagely.

"Yes, I understand."

"But if you like, I could at least tell him that . . . "

She jumped back and thrust her arms out towards me.

"No, please, don't do that, I beg you. Don't even mention that we've spoken."

"All right."

She stood up, shook hands, and walked towards the door.

"Angela!"

She turned to face me.

"Thank you for coming. The information about your friend is very useful. I'll make sure I talk to him."

She smiled a melancholy smile.

"Ah, and believe me: Fermín is not a bad man."

"I know," she said in a low voice, and disappeared, leaving a faint trail of expensive French perfume in her wake.

No, Garzón was not a bad man, he was the most disgusting son of a bitch I had ever had the misfortune to meet, and if he had been there then I would have proved it by giving him a sharp kick in the balls. To think of what I had to put up with for his sake! Dragging his love affairs into a police station! Of course, I deserved it for allowing him to get me involved in his childish nonsense. Then again, what on earth could I have done to stay out of it? He had met both his sweethearts during our goddamn investigation. Well, what was done was done, but on the first appropriate occasion I had to make it clear to Garzón there was no way I wanted to carry on being part of his twisted love life. I glanced again at the incomprehensible lists of figures in front of me and could feel gloom of epic proportions descending on me. If only to get out of my mousetrap of an office, I decided to find out if there was any news in the search for Puig.

We spent the next few days waiting for the results of the police inspection of the Bel Can accounts. One of Sanguesa's men would arrive at the dog beauty salon every morning and spend the whole day sniffing around. A combination of investigation and psychological pressure. It was obvious that the presence of the police expert, plus our occasional visits, bothered the Pavías; but the slight signs of displeasure they showed were far from leading us to think we could expect an imminent confession.

Garzón had begun interviewing the Bel Can clients. Most of them had never recovered their lost dog, but from the third day on there were some who said they had used the services of Rescat Dog successfully. None of them felt there was anything suspicious about the way the firm had dealt with them; everything had seemed completely normal. They paid around a hundred thousand pesetas for the recovery, which did not seem expensive to them. They were so pleased to have their beloved pets with them once again, they would even have paid more. How had they "lost" their animals? Most of them did not have any very clear idea: they had let them off the leash for a moment in a park, or left them in the car while they went into the supermarket . . . How had they heard about Rescat Dog? Those who remembered said they had found advertising about the firm in their mailboxes. One lady though said she was recommended them by her dog groomer, señor Pavía. Garzón had carefully transcribed all their statements, and was pleased with the fruits of his investigations. I warned him not to rejoice too much because of that: it would be hard to prove anything with those clients, they would probably not help us establish any firm connections between Puig and Pavía. I still put more faith in the psychological pressure we were putting him under, which did not seem to be having much effect.

Then, one afternoon as the two of us were sitting in my office, I said to Garzón: "Let's take a little trip out into the country." When he looked at me inquisitively, I had to give him a brief account of Angela's visit, her suspicions about the thefts of guard dogs, and her breeder friend. Garzón was flabbergasted. He was amazed that Angela should have come to see me without saying anything to him, but he managed to conceal his reaction beneath a veneer of professionalism. "I think it's ridiculous to get that kennel owner mixed up in our case," he said, and I knew that whatever else he was hiding, he really thought so. He was completely against opening up fresh lines of investigation when we had not exhausted the ones we already had.

"What have we got to lose?" I argued. "Besides, I'm fed up with waiting for Pavía to get nervous. I'm the one who's growing hysterical! And Sanguesa and his men are slower than snails! There hasn't been a word from them in more than a week about those damned accounts, which I have my doubts about anyway."

"So you're not happy about anything we're doing at the moment?"

"Not completely."

"But you're happy to follow one of Angela's hunches?"

"It's more than a hunch, it's a suspicion."

"Hasn't it occurred to you that Angela's suspicions might not be entirely innocent?"

"What do you mean by that?"

"Well, I guess that Angela would like us to realize how clever she is, how interested she is in our work."

"What you're trying to say is that she wants you to have a high opinion of her."

"More or less."

"The fact is that had never even crossed my mind, just as I had never imagined there could be anyone so vain, fatuous and heartless to think in those terms."

"Inspector!"

"Don't you 'inspector' me! You got me mixed up in your private life, so I've every right to say what I think. And you know what, Garzón? I think that the way you're playing the god of love saying 'suffer the little girls to come unto me' is ridiculous in someone your age. It's pathetic! Why can't you realize for once in your life that the people around you have feelings and suffer?"

"Did she say something when she was here?"

"However unbelievable it may sound, she didn't even mention you. All she did was express her concern as a good citizen."

Garzón chewed his lip. I tried to calm down, then went to the coat stand for my jacket.

"Are you coming, or do you prefer to stay here?"

He followed me, sulking like a little boy. In the car he was not so much angry as thoughtful. I asked him to give me the cigarettes from my bag. The pack was unopened and he opened it for me. He took one out, handed it to me, then lit it, trying not to get in the way of me seeing out of the window while I was driving.

"I'm sorry I shouted at you, Fermín. Forgive me, I had no right to. I got carried away."

"No, you were right. What you said was right, completely right."

We drove on in silence. The sergeant's gloomy thoughts floated out from his head and hung in the air. I stared out at the countryside. Winter was over and fresh green was appearing everywhere. If we had not been cops working on a case, the whole scene would have been idyllic. But that was what we were, and the case could not have been more sordid. What was I doing chasing after dog thieves and clumsy murderers, while outside the spring grass was growing? I switched the radio on. I did not want to hear any classical music that would make our harsh reality seem even worse with its beauty, so I tuned in to a sports station. Ranting voices were protesting about how unfair referees are. That was much closer to our own situation. We spent the whole journey to Santpedor in the company of this barrage of stupidities.

Josep Arnau's kennels were made up of a big fenced-in rectangular area in the middle of the countryside. Inside the fence there was a garden, with kennels lined all around it. There were about fifty dogs in them. As soon as we stepped inside, they started such a racket that we had to cover our ears. I was impressed by how fierce the animals looked. Fifty rottweilers together, all of them black, all of them baring their teeth behind the wires: it was a spectacular sight. On first impression, it seemed unlikely that anyone would dare break in and steal any of those wild beasts.

Arnau knew we were coming and came out to greet us. He was a small, skinny, nervous-looking man. You wondered straightaway how anyone like that could possibly control all those ferocious animals. He signaled for us to follow him to his tiny office. He cupped his hands and shouted: "They'll calm down in a couple of minutes!" The three of us sat down to wait in silence. I made use of the time to glance at the walls, which were covered in photographs of dogs and diplomas from dog shows. After two minutes exactly, the deafening barking outside came to an end. Arnau finally said hello and started to talk nonstop. He complained about the thefts, which seemed to him very odd. They were never very numerous, but always precise. Usually a single dog, always a male, almost always a youngster or an adult. They were particularly valuable specimens which he had set aside for breeding purposes because of the calm temperament they had shown since they were small. Arnau was surprised both that it was always one dog that was stolen and that it was never a puppy. There had always been puppies from several litters when the robberies took place, so why had they not touched them if they wanted to sell them afterwards? A puppy is always easier to find a home for. He looked at us as though hoping we could resolve these mysteries for him.

"Yes, it is strange, señor Arnau, but what seems stranger still to me is that anyone could succeed in stealing any of those fierce dogs."

"Whoever got in knew what they were dealing with, and someone in the know could find a way."

"Don't you have any security systems?"

"I leave a dog loose in the garden all night. It's a specially trained guard dog."

"Are there any alarms?"

"Because it's all in the open air, any alarm system would be very complicated and expensive. Besides, we're so out of the way here I'm not sure how much use it would be. I prefer to lose a dog occasionally."

"Do the thieves cause any damage when they get in?"

"None, they're perfect gentlemen."

"Have they left any marks or traces or . . . ?"

"Nothing. Not at my colleagues' places either."

"Your colleagues' places?"

"I don't know whether Angela told you or not, but other kennels in the province have also had dogs stolen, in the same way as I have. You must be aware that we all know each other in this business."

Garzón smoothed his mustache with his little finger before he spoke.

"Look here, Arnau, I still don't understand how, however smart the thieves are, they can come in here and do what they like with your guard dog. Could they have drugged it?"

"No, I took it to the vet's to see if there were any traces of drugs in its blood, but the results were always negative."

"So how on earth do they do it, then? As I understand it, if you give a dog like that the proper command, it will attack without thinking twice."

It was obvious that the sergeant had learnt a lot about dogs. Arnau stood up and began to pace nervously around the room.

"I've often asked myself exactly that same question, and I've come to the conclusion that there are only two possible ways of doing it. Either the thieves come here and bring a bitch in heat with them. Then all training goes out of the window. It's hard to imagine, but it's a possibility. Or the guy, or rather the guys, who climbed over the fence kept the guard dog on the alert but gave it no reason to attack."

"How could that be?"

"By moving slowly, cautiously, with no sudden movements. So one of the thieves would keep the guard dog barking at him without actually attacking, while the other headed for the cages and stole the dog they were after. To do that of course, begging your pardon, inspector, you need real balls."

"There's no way I would do it," said Garzón.

"Nor me!" Arnau quickly added, in order not to make it look as if it were just the sergeant who was not man enough.

"It's a big risk, and all to steal a single dog. Why don't they just shoot your guard dog?"

"They probably don't have any firearms, and don't want to. If they used a gun, the police would be more interested and they'd risk losing the whole business."

"Have you ever reported the thefts? I asked.

"At first, but I might just as well have saved my breath . . . are you going to look into them?"

"We're investigating the murder of this man, señor Arnau. Do you know him by any chance?"

He stared wide-eyed at the photo of Lucena.

"No. Who is he?"

"A dog thief who was beaten to death."

"Christ, I didn't think things were that bad."

"Well, as you see . . . "

We got up to leave.

"Hang on a minute! We have to say goodbye in here. As soon as we step outside, we won't be able to hear a word."

On the drive back, Garzón could not conceal his bad temper.

"We've identified two prime suspects and all you can think of is to go and visit kennels in the country. Sometimes I really don't understand you, inspector: are you trying to solve a few other little things along the way?"

I smiled wryly. I felt tired and in no mood for an argument.

"Perhaps you're right, and I'm just not up to the big challenges."

"That wasn't what I meant to say!"

"I know, Garzón, I know. Shall we have a drink when we get back to Barcelona?"

He shifted uncomfortably in his seat.

"I'm sorry, but I'm meeting someone for dinner."

"Ever since you've turned into a Casanova there's no way we can meet socially."

"Don't tease me, Petra, please," he said, like a guilty little boy, then started to stare out of the window at the already darkening landscape.

When Inspector Sanguesa gave us the results of their examination of the Bel Can accounts, we became even more disheartened. If there had been large sums of money entering or leaving the business irregularly, there was no trace of it. Everything indicated that they had thoroughly laundered everything. What we did find, however, were some unjustified amounts of money that in fact coincided with the figures on Lucena's books. But that did not lead us very far. I do not know what Garzón had been hoping for, but it was obviously more than me, because when he realized that not even the accounts could help us out, he was livid. He could not contain his indignation.

"So tell me: how on earth are we going to accuse anyone of murder on the basis of the crap evidence we have so far?"

"We'll try to put pressure on Pavía with whatever is floating around."

"You know perfectly well it's all rubbish, inspector."

"The accumulation of evidence that in itself isn't very convincing has trapped more than one suspect in the past, or at least has been useful to force a confession out of them."

"That bastard Pavía couldn't give a damn about psychological pressure. We've been turning up at Bel Can day after day, questioning him, asking for documents, squeezing his balls in whatever way we can, and what have we achieved? Nothing, he's still fresh as a daisy."

"You were the one who said the affair was ripe!"

"And I don't think I was wrong. It's just that he needs a different kind of pressure."

"What do you mean, roughing him up?"

"It's a thought."

"Don't be stupid Garzón, that wouldn't get us anywhere, either."

He muttered darkly for a while. I tried to ignore him, but there was no doubt he was right. The chances that either Pavía or his wife would crack were growing less by the day. On the contrary, they would feel increasingly confident that we could not prove their guilt. Besides which, it was still not clear what we thought they were guilty of. Who had killed Lucena? Puig, Pavía, or both of them? Or perhaps neither of them? And what about the millions Lucena had been hoarding? That money still stood out like an unharmonious brushstroke in the almost complete picture. But we could not allow ourselves the luxury of adding fresh unknowns to our mix. We had to work with what we had, so I made one final attempt at intimidation and called Pavía into my office.

We tend to think of airline pilots or poker players as people with nerves of steel. After Pavía's questioning, dog groomers will have to be added to the list. There was no way we could shake him. He did not flinch. He did not flinch when we asked him about the small amounts of money that were unaccounted for, or when I told him several of his clients said he had rec-ommended Rescat Dog to them.

"Well," he said, "why does that surprise you? I've got their name and address on my board. I also have theater groups, graduation-party organizers—anyone who asks me to put up a free ad. Did you not see them?"

He was full of suppressed delight and insolence. He felt he had got away with it. He was convinced we knew nothing and could not charge him properly. He turned the screw a bit further.

"Are you still determined to accuse me of murder?"

"Of course, just as we are going to accuse you of being involved in a network that specialized in kidnapping dogs."

He burst out laughing. His body was shaken with fake con-vulsions. I stared at him without comment. I could feel Garzón shifting nervously beside me.

"I'm sorry, inspector, it's just so funny! And after we've kid-napped the dogs, what are we supposed to do? Do we send the owners a lock of their hair or photograph them next to a news-paper to prove they're still alive and well? No, better still: we call their owners and make the dogs bark into the mouthpiece so they can hear them."

He was still laughing like a man possessed. All of a sudden, Garzón got up and went for him like a ponderous buffalo.

"Listen, asshole, I swear that when I get you on my own you're never going to feel like laughing again. Ever!"

I had just enough time to leap up and hold him back. If I had not done so, I am sure he would have smashed his hairy paw into Pavía's nose. The dog groomer turned white, but quickly recovered his composure.

"Inspector, I'm no country bumpkin, and I won't stand for any abuse of authority. I'll make an official complaint. Can I go now?"

"Yes, you can go, señor Pavía, but rest assured we'll be in touch."

After he had left, Garzón was still furious. He looked at me and snarled:

"How could you allow that jerk, that son of a bitch dog shearer, to laugh in our faces? Why didn't you let me have a go at him?"

"Have a go at him? Don't you realize what you're saying, Garzón? That dog shearer, as you call him has got a lawyer advising him. He knows we don't have enough proof to charge him. And you want to get us into more trouble by 'having a go' at him?"

He slammed his fist into the back of the chair where Pavía had been sitting.

"Shit! You can't imagine how much I'd love to!"

"You have to control yourself."

"We're stuck, inspector, though you don't seem to realize it. If that bastard doesn't confess, the whole case collapses."

"Just calm down! We'll think of something."

He went over to the coat stand and seized his shabby coat.

"Let's go for a drink. I've had it up to here with all this."

"Sorry, Fermín, today I'm the one with a date."

"A date?"

"Yes, I can have a date too, can't It?"

He left, still irate. What with his crumpled overcoat and his knotted brow, he looked like a parcel that had been in a postman's sack for a thousand kilometers. Garzón's fits of anger were something to behold! If he was equally passionate in love, I could understand why he had so much success with women. I picked up the papers from my desk and left. That was enough for now, and I did not want to be late.

Monturiol was waiting for me outside my house. He was in his van decorated with ads, just like a true tradesman. Framed by his economic reality, he seemed somehow less attractive. Opening the front door, I could see my cleaner had left everything neat and tidy. I felt a rush of adoration for her. Freaky, too, would have passed a Russian Army inspection with flying colors, and the dinner was sparkling in the microwave like a medieval jewel. All I had to do was to be at my seductive, enchanting best towards my handsome guest, so I set to it and served us drinks to get things going. I smiled, with a slow, sensual fluttering of my eyelids I had learned in my youth. Monturiol smiled back at me, but then to my complete amazement launched into a speech:

"You must be wondering about my love life before we met."

"No," I said, desperately hoping to put a stop to the topic once and for all. I hoped his question had been a rhetorical one.

"It's kind of you to say that, but I know it's not true."

Useless: any effort I made was bound to fail. Juan Monturiol was determined to make the fatal mistake of flinging himself down the slippery slope of telling me his secrets. A mistake comparable only to a woman deciding to appear before her lover in her first communion dress. There is nothing guaranteed to destroy desire as quickly as the roll call of disastrous marriages the man we lust after has been through. But I sat and listened to him: what choice did I have? I listened to him over our drinks, over dinner, and was still listening to him when I served the coffee. I heard about his first marriage to a truly beautiful schoolteacher who became interested in strange Oriental positions. All the expected elements were in the story: how the two of them grew apart, how they found it impossible to communicate, how what they wanted from life was increasingly different . . . Then the dramatic dénouement: his ex-wife had walked out on him with some kind of Buddhist who was not hot on personal hygiene. After the disaster, the huge, humiliating question: how can she be happier selling trinkets on the Ramblas with a guy like that than enjoying the peace and calm of a happy home with me?

With his second wife it had been love at first sight. A

divorced woman with a young daughter aged three. Love at first sight, and her desperate urge to marry. It was all perfect: a daughter, dogs, breakfast in bed at the weekend . . . just like a Christmas card. Until the second year of their marriage. Everything seemed to have been going along swimmingly, when she turned up in floods of tears to tell him she was thinking of going back to her husband. Astonishment, indignation, but above all, curiosity: why go back to someone you have been shouting at over the phone for the past four years with the most ridiculous excuses? Reply to make your hair stand on end: she realized that not everything was lost, and that it was best for the girl to have a normal family once more.

"Can you understand it?" Juan pleaded. "Can you understand why women end up running away from me?"

By now I was clinging to the life raft of my fifth whisky, and was tempted to give him a truthful response, but a final glimmer of common sense led me to reply what he was expecting to hear.

"You shouldn't torture yourself over that, Juan," I cooed rather incoherently, to which he replied with the cliché of clichés:

"I try not to, but in the end I always find myself wondering if I'm the one to blame."

Every love story since William Shakespeare put down his pen is exactly the same, so whenever I feel like bathing in the lakes of love, I read one of his tragedies and quickly get over it. But that is something men can never understand: they have to reinvent the wheel a hundred times, to feel they are the first to have been there and done that, like Amundsen in his polar suit.

"Shall we go to bed?" I asked him, as the only sensible way out.

He agreed, but things did not go particularly well: he was still caught up in his past misfortunes, and my head with spinning with both alcohol and all his confessions. On top of everything else, at seven the next morning the phone rang. I awoke with a start.

"Inspector?" I could hear Garzón's wide-awake voice like birdsong at the far end of the line.

"Garzón! What on earth . . . "

"I've got some good news for you, inspector. Pavía's confessed."

"What!"

"Yes, that's right! I've made him confess."

"What have you made him do? What happened? What the devil did you do to him?"

"Take it easy, I didn't touch him, I didn't even go near him. I simply used psychological methods, the way you like it."

"I want to know where he is and what happened."

"Don't be angry, Petra. I'm at the station, and everything is fine."

"Has he confessed to killing Lucena?"

"No, he hasn't confessed that. In fact, he swears it wasn't him."

"Well then?"

"You'd better come right away, inspector. Pavía is ready to give his statement. I'll explain everything to you."

I thought Juan was still asleep, but as I put down the phone he seized me in his arms, and I could feel him kissing me all down my spine.

"I'm sorry, Juan, but I have to go."

"Right now?"

"It looks as if we've caught Lucena's murderer."

"If you've caught him, he's not going anywhere, is he? So stay a little longer."

I jumped out of bed. I was annoyed at the frivolous way he was taking the news. I finished dressing in the kitchen and made myself a quick cup of coffee. As I drove to the police station I felt uneasy both because of my hangover and my doubts about Garzón. Psychological methods! What on earth did he mean by that? I felt convinced I would find the dog groomer flayed alive like some poor victim of the Inquisition.

And yet Pavía was fine, just as the sergeant had promised. Physically fine, I mean, because his nerves were shot to pieces. After I had heard what my colleague had to say, I realized that what he meant by "psychological methods" were nothing less than all-out mental torture. Garzón, the brute, had waited for Pavía until Bel Can had closed. As he was leaving, the sergeant went up to him and asked him to get into his car. Then he made him get in and drove him to an empty waste lot. And how had the sergeant succeeded in persuading someone so obviously sure of himself and who was probably advised by a lawyer—someone who was no fool, in other words—to trot along behind him in what by all accounts was a very irregular procedure? Easy: Garzón was not alone. Growling menacingly on a short lead beside him was Morgana, Valentina Cortes' dog.

"For Christ's sake!" I shouted.

"Let me finish, Petra, don't be so hasty. I know how to handle Morgana. Valentina has taught me. There was no risk of the dog getting out of control."

I had to clench my teeth, my fists, and every other muscle in my body in order to allow him to finish.

"At first, to show Pavía this was no joke, I gave Morgana a few commands, which she obeyed at once. 'You see, Pavía . . .' I told him, 'if I give the word, this monster will leap on you and rip out your jugular. Just like that, clean as a whistle. Then who is going to know who set her on to you?' Even so, he still refused to answer my questions: he was nervous, but would not budge. So I shouted to Morgana: *Gib laut!* which means 'Bark.' She advanced towards him with a deep, threatening growl. Pavía began to look scared. That was when I shouted at the top of my voice: *Voran*, which means 'Go for him!' You should have seen Morgana! She flew at him, and it was all I could do to keep control. She snarled, foamed at the mouth, snapped at the air close by him. And the suspect caved in completely, begging me to get the dog off him. He was ready to talk."

"The suspect! Don't call him that: martyr or victim more like. How on earth did it occur to you to try something like that? Don't you know that confessions extorted under pressure have no legal validity?"

"That's not true! Pavía has been thinking it over and says he wants to make a clean breast of it. He says that what he did wasn't serious enough to warrant being put away for life. It was when he saw how far I was prepared to go that he realized just how much trouble he was in. Morgana helped him see the reality of his situation. Anyway, I called, *Aus*, meaning 'enough,' to Morgana, and she automatically stopped."

"Stop shouting at me in German like a crazy Nazi! So he's been thinking about it, has he? As soon as he has his lawyer with him he's going to make a complaint that could well mean you're suspended. Can't you see that?"

"It won't happen! His lawyer will see we've found out his client is guilty and that things could get worse if we accuse him of being involved in a murder."

I sat down and buried my face in my hands.

"It was a mistake, Garzón. A foolish mistake."

"I was pissed off with that smart-ass thinking he could lord it over us! He's not laughing any more, I can tell you."

"We'll see who has the last laugh."

"Don't you even want to know what Pavía told me?"

I nodded despairingly, trying to put a brave face on it.

"Just listen, Petra: all our suspicions were correct. Puig and Pavía are accomplices. They used Lucena: every so often they paid him thirty to fifty thousand pesetas to steal dogs that the dog groomer pointed out to him. Those were the amounts in

the second account book, weren't they? Pavía says he wasn't
the only one who tipped off Rescat Dog. Puig had other
informers in strategic places. And the two of them were
involved in another swindle, something to do with money-
laundering."

"What about Lucena's death?"

"He swears it was nothing to do with him. And he says it
wasn't Puig. According to him, they had not seen Lucena in a
year. It was Lucena himself who dropped out: he said his face
was too well-known and that could be dangerous. He moved
on to something else."

"Like what?"

"Pavía doesn't know."

"Of course he doesn't."

"I don't think he was lying, inspector. It might be true that
they stopped seeing Lucena—we've heard that before. The
guy was so scared I think he meant what he was saying."

"Of course he meant it. Wouldn't you if you had a sixty-kilo
wild beast showing you its bloody fangs . . . I bet he would
have confessed to killing Kennedy just to get the thing off
him!"

"Exactly! So why did he refuse to admit at all that he had
killed Lucena?"

"You mean you were still setting the dog on him after he had
confessed?"

"He hadn't confessed to the main thing!"

"You're another Nero; Nero and Caligula all rolled into
one."

"I can be whoever you like, but thanks to me we'll be able
to unravel the case."

"Yes, provided they don't throw you off the force, which
I'm beginning to think wouldn't be a bad idea."

I questioned Pavía myself. He was still white as a sheet. He
repeated word for word what he had said to my colleague. He

strenuously denied having killed Lucena, whom he and Puig knew by the nickname Retaco. They had not seen him for a year. As for his accomplice, Puig, he said he knew he was mixed up in all kinds of shady business that he himself had nothing to do with. He also had no idea what Lucena could have been doing during what turned out to be the last year of his life.

It looked as if history was repeating itself: if they had nothing to do with Lucena's death, what did we have? Nothing more than yet another sordid story of swindlers and dog thieves. Unless of course Pavía's confession was incomplete, and he was refusing to admit that he had killed Lucena even with a mad dog threatening him. We had not made as much progress as Garzón seemed to believe. There was only one way we could prove more or less conclusively that Pavía was telling the truth, but it would be difficult to achieve and there could be no guarantee of the outcome. Even so, I explained the idea to the sergeant, and he agreed. We did not have many other options.

Two days later, we offered Pavía's lawyer a deal. It was a simple one: if Pavía agreed to make a phone call to Puig (we were convinced he knew where he was hiding), his client would not face any charges until the other man had been arrested. That would mean he would not have to spend all the intervening days in jail. If Pavía really were innocent, Puig's testimony would help us get at the truth, and the dog groomer would not be charged with murder. The second part of the plan was even simpler: Pavía would suggest to Puig they settle their affairs, he would make an arrangement to meet him in some out-of-the way spot, and we would nab him. After that we could question him and make sure his version of events corresponded to what his accomplice had already told us. We calculated that Puig would accept such a meeting, because, as a fugitive, money would be too important for him to refuse.

The lawyer agreed. He did not have much room for maneuver and the main thing for him was that his client would not be accused of murder. All we needed to find out was whether Pavía had the number of Puig's hideout. He did, of course. The fact that according to his tapped telephone line there had been no calls from his accomplice was proof of that. Of course, the possibility that the two of them had spoken together at some point also meant that Puig's testimony had less validity. They could have agreed to stick to the same story. But, even so, both Garzón and I thought it was essential to question Puig.

We laid the trap. Our quarry had to fall into it. I swore to the sergeant that if the Lucena case went up in smoke yet again, I'd join the order of Barefoot Carmelites. He agreed, and said he would become a Benedictine monk. We were relying on our priors to allow us out to partake of some digestive liqueur every once in a while.

8.

Pavía arranged to meet Puig at a bar in Casteldefells at ten in the morning of the following Wednesday. Two plainclothes men put on blue workers' overalls and went inside. Because Puig knew what we looked like, Garzón and I waited in the car a few blocks away. At twenty-three minutes past ten we saw our men coming towards us, with a handcuffed Puig in between them. He was not nervous or angry. He even said hello as if he had run into us by accident. Our prey seemed to have walked willingly into the trap.

Back at the station, we questioned him for three hours. Unfortunately for us, he corroborated every word of what Pavía had told us. Lucena had stopped collaborating with them a year earlier, because he thought it was dangerous and because he was thinking of doing something else. What might that be? Puig hadn't the faintest idea: Retaco never said much. At no point did this strange little swindler point an accusing finger at his accomplice for the death of the dog thief. I guessed that if they had really been mixed up in that, they would have tried to shift the blame on to each other. Even more so given the logical desire for revenge that Puig must feel at that moment, after being caught thanks to Pavía. But we could get nothing more out of him. We threatened to charge him on his own for the murder of Lucena. That scared him, but he did not change his declaration. Everything seemed to suggest he was not lying. We decided not to bring the two of them face to face for the moment, although there was still the possibility they had agreed all this together on the phone. That was unlikely; after discovering Pavía's betrayal, Puig's mistrust and loathing of him would have destroyed any prior agreement they had made.

I displayed endless patience asking him about what might have happened to Lucena after he gave up kidnapping dogs. Garzón looked on skeptically: if it had been up to him, he would have unleashed an entire pack of rottweilers on the suspect rather than give him the chance to explain. Eventually I saw Puig was becoming intrigued by my insistence on what had become of Lucena. He sensed we might not bother too much about him, and his attitude changed drastically. He started to make a real effort to remember something that might be of use to us. And in the end he came up with something that could be relevant.

"When I said goodbye to Retaco . . . " he said, "I wished him good luck and rich pickings. He did not tell me what he was planning to do, and I wasn't interested in finding out, but I remember he commented: 'You can never tell what the pickings may be, but at least I'll be leading a healthier life, because I'll be in the country . . . '"

"Is that all?"

"I swear it is! I never saw him again. I didn't even know he was dead."

"What happened to your secretary?" Garzón wanted to know.

"When you tracked me down I sacked her, but she doesn't know anything."

"Where does she live?"

"I've no idea."

"Do you have her phone number?"

"She never gave it me."

There was little more we could do. We handed him over to the prosecution people so that they could draw up the proper legal charges against him and continue with the investigation into possible money-laundering. Garzón was climbing the walls.

"This is impossible, inspector! We can't be back at square one all over again! It's like a nightmare: have you never had one where you're being chased by a bull and however hard you run, you always seem to be rooted to the same spot?"

I didn't feel at all like doing so, but it was my turn to look on the bright side of things.

"We're not in the same spot, Garzón, we've been following the lead of the account books."

"But now we've run out of leads, Petra, and we've run out of account books. We've discovered what was in the first one and in the second, but we still have no idea where Lucena got so much money from. We've come to a dead end and we still don't know who in the name of God finished off that poor devil."

"We've managed to recreate two years of his life; all we need now is to do the same with the third and last one."

"That's easier said than done! There are no more trails for us to follow, inspector. If those bastards were telling the truth, we're done for. We might as well start packing for the convent."

"Sergeant, have you got Valentina's phone number on you?"

"What's that?"

"I want you to call her and ask her to come down here. I think her knowledge might help us."

This took him by surprise, but the mere mention of one of his girls embarrassed him so much he did not dare ask me why I wanted it.

Valentina Cortés was as she always was: impressive, beautiful, full of life. She did not seem to be suffering too much from the love triangle she found herself in. She listened to me with her big blue eyes wide open, turning them away only occasionally to shoot tender glances at Garzón. The little gold heart rose and fell round her neck.

"Guard-dog breeders? Yes, they're all in the countryside. Of course I know them—the ones around Barcelona, at least. I've done business with them from time to time. I mean, they've brought me dogs to train. There are some I don't know personally, but I have all their addresses and phone numbers. For my work."

"What do you think Lucena could have been doing in that world?"

She flung her head back.

"The fact is, I can't see what. A miserable little guy like that, nothing more than a dog thief . . . those breeders are people who earn a good living. Every dog they sell is valuable, and as soon as a kennel gets a good reputation, clients come to it from all over. Why would any of them want to use a cheap crook like Lucena?"

Her reasoning was faultless.

"Perhaps he stole dogs in the city and sold them to the breeders."

"But Petra, the breeders only deal in puppies or very young adults! I can't imagine what they would do with a stolen dog they didn't even know the age of."

"Don't forget our hypothesis is that we're dealing with a pretty unscrupulous breeder."

"No, I don't see it. They're all real professionals. They're not the sort of people who buy a couple of dogs and leave them out in their garden. These professional breeders manage to create a name for themselves—like when a wine is certified as being from a certain origin. It's only after a lot of crossing, care, and purifying the breed that they can do that. So their reputation is all-important to them. Do you think they'd put that at risk by selling stolen dogs?"

"Perhaps what he did was steal dogs from the breeders and then sell them elsewhere."

Valentina scratched her powerful head and looked dubious.

"I can't see that, either. I don't know what Lucena could be doing with breeders. Why is that the direction you're looking in?"

"One witness says that Lucena had got involved in something to do with the countryside," Garzón replied.

She shrugged her shoulders like a little girl.

"Valentina, could you supply us with a list of all the guard-dog breeders in the province?"

"I think so."

Garzón cast me a suspicious glance.

"You're not thinking we should visit them all, are you, inspector?"

"That's exactly what I'm thinking."

"Just because someone told us Lucena had something to do with the countryside?"

"Do you think it's ridiculous to even try?"

"I don't know."

"That was the direction we were going in even before we heard about Lucena, so we'll carry on along it. We'll find out how many breeders have had dogs stolen, and search for any leads there might be. When could you have the list for us, Valentina?"

"By tomorrow. But what happens if I forget someone?"

"Don't worry, we'll ask the Canine Society to check your list and fill in any gaps. They must have information like that."

So far, our problems in solving Lucena's murder had at least allowed us to clear up a few minor offenses. That was something. We had set off to hunt wild boars, and come back with our bags full of snails. But we weren't going completely empty-handed to our bosses. If they assigned us another couple of murders, we might be able to rid Barcelona of all its petty criminals. Would they promote us on the strength of that or throw us off the murder squad? It would not be true to say I was someone who found it easy to accept feeling frustrated; it was more that I had gotten used to plodding along without ever reaching my goal. We had spent so long bogged down in this rotten case that trying to follow Lucena Pastor's trail had become our daily routine, just as if we were sitting down at our desks in an insurance company every morning. Yet, in what were barren months for us as detectives, Garzón had encountered love not once but twice; I was having a fling with a vet and had entered the dog owners' club. What more could we ask for? We were like one big happy family, with Lucena as the dead grandfather ever present in our memories, binding his earthly descendants together from the Great Beyond. We could carry on like this forever, especially as it all had such a transient feel to it that there was no reason for us to grow anxious: Garzón could not make his mind up about which "girl" to choose, I did not know what exactly my fling meant, our case had still not been solved, and even Freaky was only on loan to me. Absolutely no cause for despair.

Valentina sent us the list we had asked for the next day. It contained one more person than the list the Canine Society had given us. Garzón and I sat down to assess the information. He was not in the least convinced by the line of investigation we were embarking on. It was useless for me to show him how I thought the clues came together and made sense: statistics indicating the large number of guard dogs that had been stolen, guard-dog breeders complaining of thefts, kennels in the countryside, Lucena's last venture in the countryside. Lots of money all of a sudden. To me it seemed a watertight syllogism. All men are mortal, Socrates is a man, therefore Socrates is mortal. Of course, there were variations on the theme. All dogs are mortal, Socrates is mortal, therefore Socrates is a dog. I decided not to inform Garzón of these philosophical niceties, especially as he could not see the connections. I emphasized how Lucena had gone up in the world professionally. He had been a big success:

first he had stolen stray dogs, then pedigree ones. So by natural progression he would then concentrate on one type of dog: guard dogs. Our little man must have made a contact in this world, and by taking greater risks had earned greater rewards. At this point the sergeant went off on a tangent.

"How could someone with no driving license get out into the countryside?"

"Maybe he went on a moped."

"Right! And he made the dogs he stole ride pillion."

"Remember what Angela's breeder friend told us: it takes two people to carry out this kind of robbery."

"All right, inspector, all right, let's assume Lucena was mixed up in something like this; but tell me, how do we get to grips with it, what proof do we have?"

"You've gotten into bad habits! The police are supposed not only to follow trails, they're meant to discover them. And that's exactly what we're going to do, discover them."

He grunted.

"If the idea doesn't appeal to you, Fermín, I can ask them to replace you. I promise I won't be upset."

"Don't be funny, Petra. O.K., where do we start?"

"By reading the famous list."

"Go right ahead."

"Let's look at the breeds involved: boxers, Belgian shepherds, German shepherds, dobermans, rottweilers, giant schnauzers, German bulldogs, briards, bouviers, pit bulls and Staffordshire bull terriers."

"My God! People breed all of them round Barcelona?"

"Yes, but don't worry: it's the same person who breeds the briards and the bouviers. The same for the boxers and the Belgian shepherds."

"They sound like dishes in a French restaurant."

"Well, then, look on this as a kind of picnic, sergeant. Have you got a pair of walking boots?"

"Yes, and a water canteen!"

"We've got all we need to set off then."

As recommended in *Guidelines for Police Officers*, I tried to appear pleased and full of enthusiasm, but deep down inside I felt the exact opposite. The sergeant was completely right: we were following a very faint trail. It was only my conviction that Lucena had not left the canine world that led me to go on searching for his hypothetical "specialization." If there was one thing I was convinced of, it was that Lucena had a special gift for dogs. Life is full of surprises like that: you may be born poor, ugly, with little intelligence and less luck, and yet discover you have a natural gift for humming music, doing mental arithmetic, or scaling walls. Lucena had used his talent in the world of crime, which was a pity. He might have made a good vet or an outstanding dog trainer; instead, he stole dogs, and by doing so had amassed a not inconsiderable amount of money. And I was determined, if it was the last thing I ever did, to discover what doggy misdemeanor had led to the death of this insignificant little man on the margins of society.

One Tuesday morning in the first hot days of June, we visited a breeder of dobermans named Juan Moliner. For the occasion, Garzón was sporting a bright pistachio-colored shirt I never thought he would dream of wearing.

"It's a present from Valentina," he told me.

"What does Angela give you?"

"Books. She's bought me the complete works of Pablo Neruda, two American novels, and a guide to dogs."

"No thrillers?"

"She says they are rubbish. Angela is a very cultured, classy woman."

"Which means you're growing bored with her?"

"Not at all. I simply wonder if I'm good enough for her."

"I wouldn't worry about that."

"No, the fact is I don't worry that much."

It was hard to find out more about his emotional conflict, so I did not ask him anything else. We were already standing in front of Juan Moliner, who seemed like an honest, pleasant sort. He had been a farmer before he turned to dog breeding, and while he showed us around, he sang the praises of the animals he dealt with.

"We have to put up with a lot of ignorance from people," he said. "Dobermans have got a dreadful reputation, and that is stoked up from time to time in the newspapers. We suffer the consequences."

"Mad dogs," said Garzón.

"Dreadful things have been written about them. That their brains are disproportionately big, that they come from a cross, which means they are genetically prone to madness; all sorts of things."

"It's true, though, that there can be serious accidents with them, isn't it?"

"No more than with other guard-dog breeds. It's just that dobermans appeal to journalists' morbid side. Look at this."

He rolled up his shirtsleeve to show us a huge scar that ran the length of his forearm.

"See that? It was a German bulldog who gave me that, and I was his friend and knew him very well. I've been working with dobermans for twenty years now, and none of them has so much as threatened to bite me."

Garzón and I were still staring apprehensively at his wound.

"Did it hurt?" I asked.

He raised his eyes with an old soldier's pride.

"Have you ever been bitten by a dog?"

I shook my head, hypnotized by his face.

"A dog bite produces a very special, extraordinary kind of pain. It reaches right deep down inside you."

I immediately thought of the labor pains I had never known.

Then I looked over anxiously at the preening dobermans pacing in their cages.

"Why don't you tell us something about the thefts you've had, señor Moliner?"

The information he gave us was not very different from the story we had already heard. The targets were always young males, never more than two at a time. The thief must have been someone who knew about dogs. There were no tracks or clues. The only thing that was clear was that whoever it was had climbed over the wire fence, because it was left sagging at one end.

"What do you think they wanted your dogs for?"

"That's what I've been asking myself. If they wanted to sell them it would make more sense to steal puppies, or even a bitch for breeding purposes."

"Perhaps the robbers had a client lined up and were stealing to order?"

"It's a possibility."

"How do you think they managed to get them out over the fence?"

"Carrying them to the top, then dropping them. The fence isn't high enough for them to hurt themselves."

"Do you think two people would be enough to do everything?"

"Possibly. Perhaps it's kids looking for excitement, just some adolescents."

"How do you explain, then, that some of your colleagues have also had dogs stolen?"

"It must be a fashion."

"Despite the fact that your dogs are not specifically trained to do so, could they attack people?"

"No, I don't think so. Not unless someone tried to take one of their puppies or something of the sort."

He put his hand in between the bars and patted one of the dogs on the head.

"Touch him yourself, inspector! You'll see he's not at all fierce."

I stretched out my hand and stroked the animal between the ears. It opened its mouth and licked me in a friendly way. I smiled, then pulled the photo of Lucena out of my bag and showed it to the dog breeder.

"Do you know this man?"

"No. What happened to him?"

"He was attacked, but not by a dog."

"If it had been a dog, he would look even worse."

"His name is Ignacio Lucena Pastor. Are you sure he never did any business with you?"

"I don't think so, but I can look in my records. Wait here a moment."

He went off towards his office. Garzón smiled mischievously at me.

"I bet you don't dare stroke that dog now its owner isn't here."

Garzón could be just like an adolescent gang member too, a real troublemaker. I stuck my whole arm into the cage and stroked the doberman again. It wagged its tail with delight.

"Happy now?"

We heard Moliner's voice behind our backs.

"I'll let you have him for a good price! The perfect protection for a policewoman."

"Thanks, I already have a dog."

"Does he protect you?"

"It's more a case of him needing protection. I prefer it that way."

"It takes all sorts . . . "

When I got home that night the phone was ringing. It was Juan Monturiol. He wanted to talk. I held the phone under my chin and while we were talking started to undress. I urgently needed a bath.

"Petra, there's a question I'd like to ask you. Is everything fine with you about the way things are now between us?"

"I don't understand."

"I'm talking about our friendship, relationship, or whatever else you want to call it."

He must have had a bad day.

"Well, if you're not talking about anything specific . . . yes, I think things are fine."

"Petra, we see each other occasionally, we go to your colleague's soirees, sometimes we make love . . . yes, it's all fine on the surface. But that isn't how things should be."

Some dog must have bitten him.

"What things?"

"People, normal people, talk to each other; they explain how they're feeling, they call each other on the phone, chat about what's going on in their lives."

"I'm sorry, but the fact is, my work . . . "

"I know your work is difficult, but it's easy to pick up a phone."

"I didn't have anything in particular to say to you."

"That's the problem."

I began to grow impatient.

"Juan, we've already talked about this, and I thought we agreed. Marriage is a bad scene that . . . "

"There are lots of possibilities in between a white wedding in a cathedral and an occasional fuck. Hadn't you thought of that?"

"Which one do you want?"

"None of them, you're right. It's a waste of breath trying to talk to someone who refuses to understand."

He put the phone down. I stood there dumbstruck, naked and ridiculous with my clothes strewn all round me. What was all that about? Had it been so many days since I had called him? Had we agreed to phone each other a certain number of

times a week? Was it really that important? I decided the problem was that he could not face going on with a relationship he
could not categorize. What a shame: we would probably never
go out again or make love any more. I would miss his beauty.
A shame, but not the end of the world. All right, I had never
told him what I was feeling, but how was I supposed to
describe it? Men hate being told you love their beauty, they
don't know how to take it. And then there was the case I was
involved in. It may be that a vet does not get too involved with
his animals. But a police case is a different matter. Too bad, to
hell with him. Problems of the heart can wait, my bath could
not. I was too tired to think.

Early the next morning Garzón was waiting for me in the car
outside my house. We were off on another of our country
excursions; the only thing missing was the picnic basket. We
hadn't been together two minutes before he realized something was wrong.

"Are you still annoyed with me?"

"Annoyed with you?"

"Yes, for being a Don Juan and all that other stuff you called
me."

"I promised I wouldn't stick my nose in your affairs any
more."

"Don't worry, I promise I'm going to solve the problem
quite soon."

It seemed I could not get away from affairs of the heart. They
were lying in wait all around me. I pretended not to have heard.

"Where are we off to today?"

"We're heading for Rubí, to see a man who breeds
Staffordshire bull terriers."

"Aren't they the murderous dogs Valentina was telling us
about?"

"That's right! The owner is called Augusto Ribas Solé. Let's
see if anyone has had the balls to steal one of his vicious lot."

So that Garzón would not start up again with his love-life problems, I pretended to be asleep. I had enough of my own. My make-believe was so real that a few moments later I was fast asleep. I woke up only when the car came to a halt. I saw we were in an isolated spot with a large fenced-off area. A sliding door was the only way in or out. A sign said: *Beware of the dog. Ring here.* A small red arrow pointed to a bell.

"Ready for the moment of truth, inspector ?"

Garzón was up to his tricks again; he was increasingly skeptical about anything to do with this line of investigation. We rang the bell. To our surprise, we were not answered by the usual chorus of barking. Nobody came to open up. We rang again, with no success.

"Are you sure that this kennel is still open to the public?"

"It's on the list."

"There doesn't seem to be anyone here. Ring again."

Garzón kept his hand firmly on the bell. No response.

"And after we came all this way!" he grumbled.

I got hold of the gate handle and pulled. It slid back, leaving just enough room to slip through.

"Shall we go in?" I asked.

"Let's call first," he said.

We stepped inside. In front of us was a wide patio planted with several mulberry bushes.

"Is there anybody there?" shouted Garzón.

As if responding to the sergeant's call, a mysterious dog suddenly appeared out of nowhere, and stood staring at us. It did not bark or move. It was small, tough, solid as rubble. A fearsome Staffordshire bull terrier. Its eyes were gleaming with a hypnotic intensity. I could hear Garzón whispering to me:

"Have you got your service revolver on you?"

"In my bag," I croaked.

"Don't even think of reaching for it."

"Where's yours?"

"In my jacket, and my jacket's in the car."

"Damn and blast!"

Just by raising my voice to curse, I set the dog off growling. It was a deep, low growl that seemed to come straight from its iron breast.

"Fermín, I'm scared."

"Don't worry. Don't make any sudden movement, don't move, don't say anything too loud."

"Is it one of those killer dogs?"

"It's a Staffordshire, yes. But I hope that this one in particular hasn't killed anyone."

The dog came towards us, scratching the patio tiles with its claws.

"Sergeant . . . "

"Don't worry."

"You're supposed to have learned all about dogs."

"I've just forgotten everything I knew."

"What shall we do?"

"Start backing out toward the exit. Slowly, very slowly, and don't turn your back on him."

He took hold of my arm. I could feel him squeezing it.

"Let's go."

We started to edge a little way toward the gate. We hardly moved, but the dog sensed it and started growling more loudly.

"Fermín!"

"Don't pay any attention, he's just trying to intimidate us. Keep edging backwards, a bit to your left. Come on."

My legs were trembling so much I was not sure whether I was actually moving or not.

"Say something to him in German."

"This is no time for showing off my languages. Keep moving."

Our movement only disturbed the animal still further. It shifted position, and began a long, menacing growl. I could see a thick stream of saliva dripping from its jaws. It seemed to be staring straight at me, and I could hardly breathe. Then it started to bark fiercely, like a soul out of hell, and I could not stop myself gasping with fear. This only made the dog even more ferocious. Enraged, it barked furiously, and squatted back on its haunches as if about to launch itself at me. I was groping desperately for my gun when all of a sudden I heard a loud, precise order being shouted behind our backs.

"*Aus!*" Then again, less aggressively: "*Aus!*" Like a lion in a Roman circus faced by Christians in a state of divine grace, the dog lowered its gaze and looked all around, shifting nervously as though trying to hide the terrible intentions it had harbored only seconds before.

"Who on earth are you?"

A tall, strong-looking man of around fifty, with a weather-beaten complexion, was standing looking at us, hands on hips.

"We're police officers," Garzón managed to say in a quavering voice.

"And how the devil . . . ?"

"Leave the devil in peace and get that dog out of here," I ordered him as soon as I had got my voice back.

Augusto Ribas Solé confirmed we had been in serious danger. We should never have gone into the compound. He had gone out for five minutes, never imagining anyone would come to visit in mid-morning. But it seemed pointless trying to apportion blame: we were safe now, and the dog breeder offered us a stiff drink in the back of his premises. He had set up a very pleasant terrace there. I think that was the first time in my life I have downed a big glass of whisky straight off at eleven in the morning.

"Nice place you've got here," Garzón said.

"I like to be able to greet people properly when they come to see me."

"If they survive the dog torture."

He laughed out loud.

"Can't you just see the newspaper headlines: 'Police torn to pieces by killer dog.' They would probably have made a film of it! That's the kind of thing people love."

"Why on earth do you breed killer dogs?"

"Oh come on, inspector! There's no such thing. It's human beings who create killer dogs by training them for that purpose."

"So we weren't in mortal danger?"

"I'm afraid you were: all dogs defend their territory. I suppose if I hadn't shown up . . . Yes, I think I saved your lives."

"That's the least you could do, seeing these are your dogs."

He laughed again.

"Aren't you interested in why we're here?"

"I already know that. You've got the whole profession in a stir. My colleagues can't wait for you to visit them so they can tell you about all the dogs they've had stolen."

"And what do you have to tell us about that?"

"Not a lot. I've lost a couple of dogs, and I told the police about it. Of course, they didn't do a thing."

"Did the thieves leave any clues?"

"No, they're professionals."

"What makes you say that?"

"What else could they be? They come, steal the dogs and disappear without leaving a trace. And they always take strong, healthy specimens, the best."

"Were the ones you lost young males too?"

"Yes, and I don't know why the other breeders are so amazed at that. They must sell them to people who don't know much about dogs, telling them they are already trained and are ferocious. They're thieves and swindlers at the same time."

"Why do they take only one or two each time?"

"They take what they need. Why would they want to have to look after more dogs than necessary? Where would they keep them without rousing suspicion? And besides, it's so easy for them to steal more . . . "

"It sounds as though you're all resigned to the fact."

"I agree, and that's what I've said a hundred times to the others! I've got a very clear idea of what we need to do. If the police won't do anything, we have to sort this out ourselves. We should meet, set up a vigilante group, and the first guy that we catch trying to steal our dogs: bang! One shot and problem solved. Then we toss the body on to a rubbish dump and we'll see if anyone else thinks they're smart enough to steal more dogs."

"Well, señor Ribas, we might have to intervene at that point."

"Not at all, inspector, not at all. There's a gap in the legislation where dogs are concerned, so we have to make our own laws. A couple of dogs here and there might not amount to much, but it's a nuisance all the same. We're hard-working people, it takes a lot of effort to make money, so why should we have to put up with these villains?"

I took another sip of my whisky, shaking my head vigorously.

"Anyway," he went on, "You needn't worry, not many of the others backed me. So we'll just have to go on putting up with the thefts."

"I see. What about this man, do you know him?"

He looked at Lucena's photo with disgust.

"No, I don't. Is he a dog thief?"

"We think so."

"Well, then, he deserved what he got."

A real vigilante. A vigilante who said goodbye at the gate after assuring me that it was only thanks to Garzón's cool head we had not been eaten alive by his dog. Great, another wasted day and more useless putting ourselves at risk. Garzón was impressed by señor Solé.

"That guy knows what he's talking about," the sergeant said in the car. "It all sounded logical to me. Of course the people to blame are thieves and swindlers, and we've got two thieves and swindlers banged up. Why look any further? I'm sure that Pavía and Puig are guilty of this too."

"They never tried to get any ransom for these dogs."

"But, inspector, that means they simply stole them and then sold them on. Crooks commit all kinds of crimes at the same time; it's not like they specialize in one particular thing. They steal what they can get their hands on."

"I'm not convinced."

"You may not be convinced, but just you wait and see how those two confess to the prosecuting attorney to killing Lucena. And to stealing dogs from these kennels. Everything will come out."

"So you think we're wasting our time?"

"I think you're stubborn as a mule, that we've already wrapped up the case."

"And I think you don't take things seriously enough."

"There you go again!"

"What do you mean?"

"You say that because you don't think I take love seriously enough, don't you?"

"Forget what I said, Fermín."

"Perhaps you'll change your mind if I tell you I've already made a decision."

I turned to get a better look at his face.

"A decision?"

"Yes, inspector. What just happened to us was an eye-opener for me. When we were there with those dogs that could have killed us, I could see clearly how I felt. I know whom I am in love with, and whom I have to say a fond farewell to."

"Who?"

"Angela."

"Angela what—she's the one you're in love with or she's the one who goes?"

"She goes, Petra; I say goodbye to her with a heavy heart. Angela is charming, but I'm in love with Valentina. She was the one I would have liked to see one last time if I were about to be eaten alive by a killer dog."

"Perhaps it was just an unconscious wish for her to be there and give an order in German."

"Don't joke about it, inspector, I'm sure of what I'm saying."

"I'm sorry. Are you completely sure?"

"Yes, Angela is too well-educated, too refined, she's from a different class to me. She would end up thinking I'm a clod-hopper. But Valentina is always happy; she brightens up my life."

We sat for a moment in silence.

"Well, Fermín, you know that Valentina was not my choice, but . . . in any case, I glad you've made the decision."

"You were right; I can't go on playing the field."

"When are you going to tell Angela?"

"Tonight."

"Not an easy thing to do, is it?"

"No. I hope I can be gentle about it."

"So do I. Angela is an extraordinary woman."

"I know that."

I could just imagine Angela's reaction. Seeing another hope gone, at her age, perhaps the last opportunity she would have. But I could understand Garzón's choice. He wanted to enjoy the life he was only now starting to discover. A widow in love with an emotional adolescent. All of this only convinced me still further of how everything to do with love was bad news. A cross the human race has to bear century after century, even though it undermines all its coherence and capabilities.

I spent the afternoon shut in my office, trying hard to forget all that and concentrate on the case. I glanced at the information on the kennels. Was that where the last year of Lucena's life was hidden? Young males, dog experts who left no traces.

Carefully chosen targets. Two people to carry out the robberies. No clues. A paradoxical world: the act of stealing leaves
no traces, but the act of love does. There I went again: I could
not keep my mind solely on the case. I decided to go home.

Sitting in an armchair, newspaper in hand, things were not
much better. Questions kept going through my mind: how
would Angela feel? What would she think about life from now
on? I put on some Mozart; I had noticed that was Freaky's
favorite music. Whenever he heard it, he stretched out his
back in a very special way and relaxed. I opened the patio
door and let the warm evening air into the house. I relaxed as
well. I put on a soft, old nightdress. That was better. I was not
responsible for the world's heartaches. There was not much I
could do for Angela or anyone else. All I could do was make
sure I myself did not suffer. I gave a sigh of relief. Freaky
sighed with me.

A couple of hours after I had achieved this state of peaceful
bliss, the phone rang. The clock said it was one in the morning.

"Petra."

This was not said in an inquiring tone, but with lugubrious
certainty.

"Sergeant?"

"I need to see you."

"Is something wrong?"

"It's strictly personal."

"I understand. Why don't you come to my place? I'm still
awake."

"No, it has to be in a bar."

"In a bar?"

"I'm sorry, inspector. This is the last thing I'll ever ask of
you, I promise."

"It all right, Garzón. I think there's a cocktail bar open near
here: do you remember it?"

"I'll be there as soon as I can."

I felt far too tired to dress properly, so I just put a mac on over my nightdress. I put Freaky on his leash and went out into the deserted street. After spending ten minutes walking up and down outside the bar, I saw Garzón's car arrive. Freaky was immediately pleased to see him, but Garzón made no attempt to stroke him. He didn't even seem to realize he was there. He wouldn't have noticed even if I had brought along a giraffe. He looked wild and woolly; his face was pale and he seemed to have fresh rings round his eyes. We sat at the tables that were left outside because of the good weather. He demanded a whisky and, as soon as the waiter brought it, downed half his glass in one.

"Christ, sergeant, you're in a good mood!"

"Call me Fermín tonight, if you don't mind. And I should warn you, I intend to get drunk. Fair warning."

"Is that why we had to meet in a bar?"

"Because of that and because I don't want to keep myself under control, Petra. If we met at your place I'd have to behave myself, to watch the time. It's easier here. When you've had enough of me, you can just get up and go."

He ordered another whisky, a double this time.

"It was hard," he said eventually. "I would never have thought it was so hard saying goodbye to someone. As I was approaching Angela's place I still thought it was going to be easy. I had rehearsed all my lines. But as soon as I got there I realized how much more difficult it was going to be." He took another mouthful of whisky and stared at the ground. "I've been a fool all along, right up to the end. You were right, Petra."

"Look, I . . . "

"Don't try to pretend. I didn't take it seriously enough, I'm a complete idiot."

"Did Angela get angry with you?"

"No, she didn't get angry. She said she understood, and that no one can fight the dictates of the heart. She was crying the whole time."

At that, he fell silent. Then he asked for another drink. I decided to join him.

"Don't feel too guilty about it, Fermín. You were simply unaware of the pain you were causing."

"I never dreamed that leaving her could cost me so much. On the one hand, I knew I had to end the relationship, but on the other I still felt I loved her."

"It's always a complicated mess, believe me. Love is frustrating and painful; it burns and it destroys . . . well, and why do you think I've pensioned myself off from all that?"

The waiter came out.

"I'm sorry, we're about to close. But you don't have to leave: you can sit out here all night if you like."

"What about the glasses?"

"Just put them on the doorstep when you go."

"Bring me another double before you leave," Garzón asked him, searching for money in his pocket.

A short while later all the waiters left. They pulled down the metal shutter and walked off, casting sideways glances at us. The sergeant had not opened his mouth again. Freaky was asleep. I began to feel ridiculous, sitting there in my old night-dress under my mac.

"Not knowing love is bad, but knowing it means learning how to suffer," I said, hoping this might be enough of a summing-up for me to be able to go. But Garzón did not even seem to hear me. He was lost in thought, or full of remorse or regrets or God knows what, slumped there in that absurd aluminum chair. There was no way I could abandon him: being a friend means staying with a drowning man, even if you have no idea how to pull him out.

An endless hour crawled by in silence. At first, Garzón took occasional sips from his drink, then sighed. After a while he just sat there, staring into space glassy-eyed. In the final five minutes he closed his eyes, and his head dropped on to his chest. I thought the time had come to declare the wake at an end.

"Fermín, don't you think we should go?"

He gave no sign of life.

"Fermín, please, get up."

It was useless: he didn't move a muscle. I tried to jolt him back to reality by subterfuge:

"Sergeant, this is an order: get up!"

It worked. He raised his eyelids half an inch and said in a whisper:

"I can't; I've taken a tranquilizer."

"Where on earth did you get that from?"

He replied so softly I had to lean across to hear him.

"My old landlady gave them me. The poor woman used to see a psychiatrist for her nerves."

That was all he said. He sat there all of a heap, like a boulder at the foot of a slope. I was furious.

"You should have told me! How am I going to move you from here, with what you weigh?"

I realized complaining would do me no good, and, besides, when he heard me raise my voice, Freaky started to howl. I looked for some change in the fallen one's pockets and went to the nearest phone booth. What was wrong with calling Juan Monturiol in an emergency? After all, he was a neighbor.

He did not show up in pajamas as he should have if this had been a Hollywood movie, but his hair was tousled. He immediately sized up the situation and used those magnificently strong arms of his to lift Garzón and throw him over his shoulder. I supported the left-hand side as best I could, muttering excuses mixed with curses at no one in particular. We pushed him into Juan's car. The vet was sweating, looking attractive and manly in a simple white shirt.

214 · ALICIA GIMÉNEZ-BARTLETT

"What's got him into such a state?"

"The pangs of love."

"It could have been even worse, then."

We took him home; it was a heroic undertaking to carry him up to his apartment. I searched his pockets until I found the key, and we finally deposited him on his bed so he could sleep it off.

"We can't do anything more for him," Monturiol said.

"You've done more than enough already. I'm really sorry to have made you come like this."

"It was a pleasure to see you again."

"I feel the same, although I wish I looked a bit more presentable."

I opened my mac like a classic flasher and showed him my awful nightdress. He burst out laughing. Was my action an entirely innocent one? I still have no idea, but the fact is, it brought dramatic results.

Juan came up to me, grabbed me round the waist, and started kissing me. We devoured each other with kisses for several minutes, then sank to the floor and made love. It was all very strange: the circumstances, the place, the fact that Garzón was snoring like a hippopotamus next door; and yet I have no hesitation in saying that it was wonderful, something very special. It had all the attraction of urgency and rawness, somewhere between the sweetness of a reencounter and the sadness of a goodbye. When it was over, I laid my head on Juan's chest and rested.

"So your colleague is feeling the pangs of love."

"He's pushed Angela out of the triangle."

"I see."

"He's an innocent where feelings are concerned; that's how he can cause so much damage without meaning to."

"He can hurt himself, too."

"Of course. Love stains everything."

He sat up, forcing me to move off him. He lit a cigarette and stared at me.

"You're a real radical against love, aren't you?"

"It's not a theoretical position."

"How do you explain how intense what we've just done was?"

"I guess Garzón's apartment encourages fucking."

He smiled sadly, then laughed equally sadly.

"Ah, the terrible Petra: to fuck or not to fuck, that is the question."

I had not the slightest intention of starting an argument at that moment. I stood up, wrapped my mac around my naked body, swept up the nightdress and put it in my bag.

"Let's go, Juan; it would be dreadful if the sergeant woke up and found us here. He would feel awful if he had to try to explain what had happened."

"That's very thoughtful of you."

I accepted his irony without comment. On the drive back to my house we did not say a word. Our goodbyes were strained. "Adios," he said, imperceptibly suggesting this time it was for good. "Adios," I replied, as casually as possible. I went in tired and in a foul mood. That's enough! I thought to myself, enough mystification and lies, enough of trying to bring the sublime down to daily reality. What Monturiol is feeling is nothing more than typical wounded male narcissism. Adios? O.K., then, Adios muchacho, I can play tough too, forget that we met by chance in a trench while the bombs were falling all around us. I refuse to pretend this is some kind of romantic novel: enjoy what's on offer or get out of here. Freaky was gazing at me affectionately. I think that as well as Mozart, he likes Bogart films, too.

The next day, Garzón was at the station on time, but with eyes ringed with mourning black. He got a cup of coffee from the machine and took a couple of aspirins. I sat going through my papers and did not look up.

"Inspector," he said at last. "How did you manage to get me home?"

"I called Juan Monturiol; he carried you."

"I'm really sorry you two had to do that for me."

"Forget it, we would have done the same for any idiot."

He smiled.

"Well, I'm glad you did, but I still feel bad, it was unforgivable of me."

"I'm going to get my own back by sending you to another kennel on your own. It's near Badalona; here are the details. I'm going to stay here to sort out all these statements."

I watched him leave, looking happy and at ease. I admired the male propensity to switch from executioner to victim just by feeling sorry for themselves. For him the tragedy was over, but for Angela it must just be starting, on the fateful morning after. I forced myself to go back to the statements the breeders had made. There was something that did not fit somewhere. Dog thieves who risked their lives for one or two animals that they sold on the cheap. Had any of the kennel owners lied? And if so, why? What sense did it make to lie about the thefts of their own animals? It was a mess, an unholy string of messes that had begun months ago. We were stuck and time was passing. Was Lucena's body clamoring for justice? Not a bit of it: his was the most silent body I had ever had to deal with. If we did not succeed in finding his murderer, it would just be one more injustice in this world, as annoying as the pangs of love. Big deal!

9.

The last dog breeder on our list had been visited, questioned, registered, checked. This latest statement matched the others. All of them obsessively the same, dramatically identical. Lucena was unknown in Catalan pedigree-dog kennels. The effects of the sun from what Garzón called "the natural environment" were visible on my face. His skin was even more tanned: he looked brown and healthy. He probably added the occasional weekend picnic with Valentina to our excursions. They spent as much time together as possible. She was all Garzón could talk about. I had the feeling he could not care less about our case. By now he had decided it was a lost cause. And he was probably right: any time soon we would get instructions from our bosses to file the whole thing. We were paid out of the public purse and had been given more than enough opportunity to solve the murder. But Garzón was waiting quite patiently for this final resolution; in the meantime, he carried out my orders in a routine way. It seemed as though his happy love life shielded him from feeling any great sense of frustration. He went to question the dog breeders almost as if he were mushroom hunting. To him, Ignacio Lucena Pastor was no more than a reference from the distant past, a sort of tiny black mark on his police record, something to be recalled only in a fit of drunken melancholy.

"I'll type up the report on this last visit tomorrow," he said that afternoon. "And if you don't need me for anything else,

I'll be off, inspector. Valentina is coming to dinner and I have to prepare everything."

"You feel confident enough to make it all on your own?"

"Salad and beef fajitas."

"You've come along a lot."

"The fajitas are frozen."

"Even so . . . "

He smiled proudly in a rather childish way and departed. I was left alone, alone in the office, in the investigation, alone with the ghost of Lucena, if Lucena had ever really existed. At least there was Freaky, the only witness to his master's reality. When I got home, I studied him again. The image of the murderer was stored somewhere in that dog's brain, but there was no way he could communicate it to me. Strange relationship: he could communicate to me his affection, but not the whole truth. That must be why a dog is man's best friend. I went out to the patio. The air was warm and restoring. The best thing would be to go to bed, after a couple of whiskies to help ward off the absurd sadness that was beginning to envelop me. I poured out a large glass and seconds later was fast asleep.

In my dreams, in deep, clinging dreams I heard the insistent ring of the phone. I did not answer. Some indefinite length of time later, which seemed like minutes to me but must have been longer, the ringing started again. This time I made a huge effort to rouse myself from my catatonic state and picked up the phone. Garzón's voice sounded as if it was coming from another galaxy.

"Inspector? Inspector Delicado?"

"Speaking."

"Christ, inspector, thank heavens you answered! They've been ringing you from the station for ages. We know that if you're not at home you leave the answering machine on, so we were worried something must have happened to you. In the end, they got through to me."

"And where are you?"

"I'm at home, with Valentina—like I told you."

"Sorry, Garzón, I'm still half asleep. What's all this about?"

"Inspector, we've had a tip-off from an informer. A woman called the station saying that if we wanted to find out something about the dog robberies we should go at once to Sector A of Calle F in the Free Trade Zone. Shall I see you there?"

"I've left my car at the office. I'll call a taxi."

"No, I'll come and pick you up, it'll be quicker that way. But, please, don't keep me waiting."

It took me another five minutes to work out what was going on. A tip-off. A woman's voice. The Free Trade Zone, the Free Trade Zone: that's an industrial estate full of warehouses. It was one in the morning. I still did not understand very much.

Garzón had checked on a street map before leaving, so he knew exactly where he was driving.

"Tell me more," I said when I was in the car.

"There's nothing more to tell. A woman called the station and asked for you."

"She knew my name?"

"Yes. When she was told that naturally you were not there at that time of night, she left the message I gave you, then hung up without giving her name."

"Did they trace the call?"

"No, they didn't even try. Later, when they couldn't get through to you, they called me. And I can tell you that after we had been ringing you for ages, Valentina and I were really worried."

"We've lost a lot of time. Did you alert a patrol car?"

"Yes, don't worry. They'll have been on the spot for some time already."

In fact, the patrol car had got there ten minutes before us, but it had been too late even for them. The place the woman had identified was a big warehouse where heavy machinery was stored. The front door had been forced. They had not found anyone inside, but there was something that had caught the uniformed cops' attention. In one corner of the huge factory a space was cordoned off with portable wooden barriers. It measured about five meters by five and there was straw spread all over the floor inside.

"What the devil is this?"

"We've no idea, inspector, but they've gone to fetch the warehouse owner so he can explain."

"Good."

The patrolman went off in search of more clues. Garzón and I were left standing by this strange square.

"Do you think it's part of the warehouse?" I wondered.

"I haven't the faintest," he said, pulling out a cigarette.

I stopped him with a gesture.

"Wait, Garzón, don't light up, the smoke will hide the smell."

"What smell?"

"It smells of dog in here, can't you tell? There's a smell of sweat and of tobacco, but, above all, of dog."

He sniffed at the air as though he were a real bloodhound.

"You may be right."

I stepped inside the barriers, picked up a handful of straw and lifted it to my nostrils.

"Yes, I'm sure of it. Dogs have been here, and recently."

"What can they have been here for?"

"Just a moment, sergeant, let me think. Perhaps they were some of the stolen dogs, perhaps they were showing them to potential customers . . . "

"That fits. They were in the middle of showing them when we arrived and upset their plans."

"Someone must have warned them we were coming. The smell is still fresh."

"Could it have been the same woman who phoned the station?"

"The same woman? That's absurd: why would she have done that?"

"Perhaps she changed her mind at the last minute."

I nodded, though I wasn't convinced.

They had finally found the warehouse owner sleeping peacefully in his own bed. He came over to us, surprised and not in the least pleased. He had never seen anything like this on his property before. We asked him to have a good look round and tell us if anything was missing or had been touched. His report was categorical: everything was just as he had left it, apart from this monstrosity. Nothing had been stolen or damaged. We would need to question him more closely, although at first sight it did not seem he was involved in any way. The cops would make a thorough search of the warehouse looking for more clues.

Garzón was still thinking out loud:

"Dogs in a warehouse? Why break into a warehouse just to keep dogs there?"

"Maybe it's safer. They don't have a place of their own, or, if they do, perhaps they don't want to raise suspicions. So they do the deals somewhere else. When they leave, all the evidence goes with them."

"But that's risky, too."

"If it had not been for that informer, I doubt whether we would have found them in the early hours in the Free Trade Zone."

Garzón sat down.

"The informer. A female informer. Who could it be? Perhaps it was Puig's secretary. We haven't heard any more about her, and there are no other women in the whole case."

"Don't keep insisting on Puig. I think we're on a different track now."

"What about the warning? Who could have warned them here? Just our luck that there's a tip-off and nothing comes of it."

"It wasn't even useful."

"You can't be sure of that!"

"What do you mean?"

He looked all around him.

"Inspector, I think the bar in the food market opens about now. Let's go and have a coffee; I've got something to tell you."

He was right, the bar was open. Truck drivers drinking coffee were starting to bring the place to life. We asked for two cups as well. I was nervous: Garzón always put the wind up me when he wanted to talk about his private affairs. And this wasn't exactly the moment! The waiter soon brought us our breakfasts. I took a bite from the still warm croissant and cleared my throat. I was nervous about what was coming next.

"What's on your mind?" I plucked up my courage to begin.

He smiled vaguely, stroked his mustache to build up the suspense, then finally said:

"Inspector, I know that professionally we're in a real mess and that we've got lots to do. But it'll only take me five minutes to tell you something I think you should hear."

"Go right ahead," I said, by now completely panic-stricken.

"Inspector, tonight when they called me from the station, I had just asked Valentina to marry me."

In order to buy time, I took another quick bite of my croissant. He was staring at me expectantly, while I sat chewing like a ruminating cow.

"Haven't you got anything to say to me?"

I wiped my lips at least ten times on the paper napkin.

"Jesus, Fermín, what could I say?"

"Congratulations, for one."

"Of course, yes, congratulations! By all means!"

"I could swear you don't think it's a good idea!"

"It's not that. It's just that I was wondering whether you and Valentina know each other well enough. You've only just met her, you know."

"Don't be like that, Petra! What do you want, a ten-year courtship? I never thought you were that old-fashioned!"

"I was simply thinking of how hard it is to adapt when you're not so young anymore."

"Yes, it may be more difficult, but it's precisely because we're not so young anymore that there's no time to lose."

"Fermín, you're right. I don't know what I'm doing sitting here preaching at you. I wish you all the happiness in the world; you deserve it."

"Thanks, but first we'll have to see if Valentina accepts or not."

"Hasn't she said yes already?"

"I think I took her by surprise. She asked me for a couple of days to think it over."

"I thought things like that only happened in films."

"Well, the truth is, there's a slight complication."

"What's that?"

He tried to attract the waiter's attention, then cleared his throat and said:

"Would you like another coffee?"

"I'm fine, thanks."

"Another croissant?"

"No, thanks."

"I'm sure another coffee would do you good, we got up very early."

"All right, then."

He gave the waiter our order, then did not say another word until the cups were on the table. He stared across at me.

"Well, Petra, it's like this. When I first met Valentina, she was in a relationship with a married man."

I was infinitely glad to have a cup of coffee in front of me so that I could disguise my astonishment. I poured in lots of sugar and stirred it as thoroughly as if I were conducting a scientific experiment.

"You don't say," I spluttered.

"At first neither of us made any serious plans . . . and she has been seeing less and less of him. I never said anything to her, but she has told me several times she wanted to end what had become a very unsatisfactory relationship."

"When did you get to hear about it?"

"She was the one who told me, as soon as we realized how much we meant to each other. Everything was very open and aboveboard."

"Do you know who the man is?"

"She didn't tell me, and I didn't ask. All I know is that it's not someone I might have met."

"Has Valentina not told you what she's thinking of doing now?"

"No, but I know what she's like. I'm sure she needs a couple of days to say goodbye to him. It's been a long-term relationship. But to show you how convinced I am that Valentina is going to marry me, I've already told my son to come from the United States."

"Do you think that was wise?"

"Of course, I have to introduce them to each other."

I was worried that Garzón was getting himself into real trouble, but there was no way I could tell him that. How was I to know what was for the best? Perhaps the sergeant was heading for his lifelong dream, perhaps he would be happy ever after. I had no intention of spoiling things in the name of some abstract idea of being cautious.

"Well, Fermín, I hope you'll keep me informed of developments."

"Of course I will. And now, Inspector Delicado, to return to our work, there's a favor I'd like to ask of you."

"You're being very mysterious this morning."

"No, it's simply that I wanted to ask you not to rule Puig's secretary out completely. And to ask your permission to go on trying to track her down and ask her what she knows about all this. As you can see, I can't get it out of my head that Puig and Pavía are involved in our case in some way. I'd also like to have someone tail Pavía's wife."

"You think one of them was the woman on the phone?"

"Both of them could be implicated in this, and we haven't investigated them properly. We can't afford not to."

"Go right ahead, Garzón. I'll take care of the search in the warehouse. I suppose we'll have the results of the fingerprint tests this afternoon."

"Will I see you tomorrow?"

"You'll see me."

Maybe I was being too stubborn in thinking that the Puig-Pavía duo had nothing more to do with our case. It was even possible that we had our culprits in jail already. That sort of thing happens sometimes. Crimes are plants with tendrils that cling where you least expect them. It could be that Puig's secretary was still in touch with some of her boss's accomplices, or she could be trying to wriggle out of it without being caught. That was a good enough reason to turn informer. And yet I was still not convinced. Why would two villains like Puig and Pavía be covering up for accomplices who had not been caught? Unless, that is, their associates were keeping the business going until the day that our two prisoners were released and everything could carry on as before? And what about the Frenchwoman? Perhaps she was in some way acting on her own behalf? Nothing could be ruled out: that was precisely the problem. I had to let Garzón *cherchez la femme*, especially seeing how successful he was with women in general. Although, poor Garzón, perhaps marriage was already bringing his career as a Casanova to an end. It had been a short but intense one; at least now he would not die feeling he had never put his talents as a demon lover to the test.

I went back to the warehouse. In the short time I had been

away, the Free Trade Zone had become a hive of activity. There were trucks and workmen in overalls everywhere. Word had obviously got out that the police were in the neighborhood, because there were several curious onlookers peering into the warehouse or staring at the patrol car. The officer in charge of the search told me they had not found anything significant. The only discovery of note were the marks of cigarettes on the floor, which meant they had had the time to clear away the butts and leave everything clean. They were very careful. I stood looking at the small wooden enclosure that they had not managed to dismantle. It was like a small stable. Somewhere to keep dogs so they could sell them to selected clients. A really smooth operation. Was there no other way for them to do it? It was difficult to speculate without any more precise information. I told the officer to take samples of the straw and send them to the lab for analysis. Then I left. The warehouse was to stay cordoned off until I returned.

I should probably have made the visit I was planning to make now much earlier, but that's life: hectic and unjust. I felt like an intruder when I stepped across the bookshop threshold, and then increasingly nervous when Angela came toward me, arms wide open.

"Petra, how nice to see you!"

The worst thing was that her greeting seemed sincere.

"How are you, Angela?"

She lowered her gaze for a moment, and when she lifted her head again, there was no hiding the veil of sadness in her eyes.

"As you can see, doing my duty."

I struggled to say something, to find some new formula to express my sympathy, my regret, my understanding.

"Angela, I . . . "

She took me by the arm, trying to give the impression everything was as normal.

"Let's go into the back, I'll make you a coffee."

I stayed silent while she prepared it. I realized I should explain the reason for my visit before she got the wrong idea. I described the strange pen we had found in the warehouse and asked her to come with me to have a look at it. She accepted at once, but then seemed to hesitate. I thought perhaps this was not a very good moment.

"We can leave it till this afternoon if you prefer."

"No, it's not that . . . it's just that . . . well, I wouldn't like to meet anyone, it's too soon for that."

"Don't worry, he won't be there."

She put on a jacket which, as ever, combined perfectly with her smart dress. I noticed she was still wearing Garzón's locket around her neck. She saw me looking at it.

"I've never been one to deny the past; I'll go on wearing it," she said, and smiled with fake bravura. I responded with a twitch of my lips. Damn and blast Garzón, that cheap Casanova, that incurable idiot. Some day I would stick a knife in his back.

Angela's reaction when I showed her the wooden barriers was bewildering. She did not move or speak. She did not walk around it to look from a different angle. She just stood there, hypnotized, lost in thought. I let her be, and made no attempt to interrupt her thoughts. All of a sudden, she turned to me and said with unusual firmness:

"I know what you're looking for, Petra. I know what this is."

She fell silent, and started to stare at the space again, but this time I could not bear to wait a moment longer. I took her by the forearms and made her look at me:

"What are we looking for? Go on, tell me!"

She gave a weary sigh and said:

"Dog fights."

"What?"

"What you heard. Secret fights, between dogs. Just like in Roman times or in the Middle Ages."

I struggled to make sense of what she was telling me.

"Dog fights as entertainment?"

"Dog fights for people to bet on, Petra. There's a lot of money at stake."

"How does it work?"

"I don't know the details, but I've heard about it and not long ago I read a ghastly article about it in a magazine. I think I've still got it at home."

"For the love of God! Dog fights?"

"You should go to the Catalan police right away, Petra. I'm sure they'll have information to give you. Meanwhile, I'll get my copy of the magazine."

"I imagine you're sure of what you're saying."

"Completely! What I'm upset about is not having thought of it earlier, before I saw this ring."

"A ring! Of course, that's what they have made here. I didn't see it either! O.K., let's go. And you try to find me that magazine."

The Catalan police remembered me well.

"Hallo, inspector! Still chasing stray dogs?"

I nodded. Very funny.

"Listen, Mateu, I need information about illegal dog fighting."

"Now we're getting somewhere, that's serious business!"

"But you didn't mention it last time."

"You didn't ask!"

He led me to his computer and put on a pair of thick glasses that made him look less youthful.

"Let's see . . . sometime around '94 there was a case in Deltebre, in Tarragona province. Someone reported strange noises in an abandoned farmhouse, but by the time we got there the villains had left. Through the different statements we managed to put together a good picture of what had gone on, but we were never able to confirm it. The alleged ringleader was a guy who had come to the town saying he was a dog train-er. We later deduced that it was he who was responsible for thefts of guard dogs in the region. He would set up these fights from time to time with some assistants, and people bet on them. We even found some half-dead dogs wandering around the countryside. I guess he must have been pretty much an amateur, but now we think there may be better organized net-works here in Barcelona. What we don't have is any solid proof, so we can't lay our hands on them."

"What would happen if you did catch them?"

"They'd be fined, from a quarter of a million to a million pesetas."

"I'd jail them all for life."

"You women are always so radical," he said.

I called Garzón and told him the news. He could not get over it. The third time he repeated to himself: "Fights between dogs?" I decided not to talk about it to anyone else; no one would believe me.

"So, shall I drop what I'm doing, inspector?"

"Keep on trying to find the girl, but if nothing happens soon, drop it."

"Inspector, how on earth did you get the idea of dog fighting?"

"Someone put me on to it."

"Angela?"

"Yes."

"I knew it."

"Why?"

"I don't know, I just did."

"Fine, Garzón, but now forget about your personal affairs and concentrate on our investigation."

"Whatever you say."

The cheap Don Juan! Stabbed in the back, lynched, black magic pins stuck in him, it did not matter which, so long as he died a horrible death.

Shortly afterwards, Angela got through to me. She had found the magazine. It was *Reportaje*, a sensationalist current affairs weekly. I asked her to accompany me again, this time to their editorial offices, because her professional skills might come in useful yet again. Unfortunately, I could not worry too much over whether or not it was painful for her to be so involved in Garzón's line of work.

We met in the *Reportaje* reception. Angela still looked upset. The person who had written the article was someone called Gonzalo Casasús. We asked to see him, and I spent the time he took to come out flicking through his piece. The photos horrified me. Close-ups of the heads of two dogs with their jaws locked together, staring wide-eyed into empty space. Dogs leaping on other dogs, fierce expressions on their faces, blood dripping from their mouths.

"Who on earth would do something like this?" I asked to no one in particular.

"People just like you or me," Casasús replied, coming over smiling.

"I hope not," I said.

"Money arouses our worst instincts. So you two are from the police. What do you want to know?"

He must have been around thirty, with close-cropped hair and a silver stud in his right earlobe.

"Everything."

"About dog fighting?"

"Yes. Where did you get these photos—did you go to some of the bouts?"

"I suppose you've heard about protecting one's sources."

"And I suppose you've heard that you can be charged for concealing information."

"Yes, I've heard something like that. Look, we're starting off on the wrong foot here. Why don't we begin again?"

"Fine, you first."

"Can I publish what's said between us?"

"Not yet, but if you help, I promise that you'll be the first to hear when we solve the case."

"That's a start. I have to tell you anyway, I don't know much. I've never been to one of those fights, but I know how they work and that they take place in Barcelona."

"How do you know?"

"A little bird told me."

"Who?"

"You're asking about names again?"

"Who?"

"Bah, an insignificant little fellow, I don't think he was very high up in the organization."

I took out Lucena's photo and showed it him.

"This little fellow?"

"Christ, yes! What happened to him?"

"He's been dead for some time now; he was beaten up."

"That's interesting. Who beat him up?"

"That's what we're trying to find out. Did you get in touch with anyone else?"

"No, just him. We talked in a bar. He made me pay for the information, then left without even telling me his name."

"Who mentioned him to you?"

"I don't know, one of the creeps who pass us information about the underworld."

"So how does the organization operate?"

"The article explains it more or less. It seems they've copied it from the Russian mafia. There are lots of dogfights in Moscow."

"So what happens?"

"Well, there's a guy who has several dogs trained to fight. He gets someone to steal specimens from dangerous breeds. Sometimes they use them just for sparring, others go straight into fights after a bit of training."

"I get it."

"Then they look for different venues, which never belong to anyone in the gang. That's so no one can ever give information that might compromise them. They put on several fights each time, and the spectators place bets. And apparently they are for big money. The people who go to watch are always interested in something new and exciting."

"How can anyone enjoy such a revolting spectacle?" Angela burst out.

"Well, they do enjoy it. And believe me, they are normal people, guys with lots of money who are tired of the usual stuff: executives, businessmen . . . "

"I can't believe they're normal."

"At the moment I'm working on an article about pedophiles, and I can assure you that compared to them, this lot are boy scouts."

Angela's eyes opened wider still. I continued:

"Where did you get the photos?"

"We bought them from an agency. I haven't the faintest idea where they were taken; not in Spain, that's for sure. They're from France-Presse."

"That's an easy way to write an article."

"You use Interpol, don't you?"

"You've seen too many films."

He looked at me, amused.

"Would you like me to show you more photos? I've got quite a few the editor thought were too shocking to publish."

He left, leaving a smell of American tobacco in his wake.

"I'm amazed how well you deal with young people like him," Angela said.

I smiled.

"What do you think he is like?"

"I don't know . . . so up-front."

"He's no more than a little squirt."

He came back carrying a bunch of photos and handed them to me.

"Take a look at these, you'll like them."

I looked at them one by one, and passed them on to Angela without a word. They were truly disgusting. Fangs sinking into flesh, thick streams of saliva, blood spurting or dried on fur . . . Angela covered her eyes and dropped them on the table.

"It's terrible that so much cruelty could exist in human beings."

The journalist looked at her scornfully.

"Don't be too horrified: all over the world every day there are kids dying of hunger, wars, people who get their stomachs ripped out in brawls. At least these are only dogs."

Angela turned on him:

"But the cruelty is the same in both cases, isn't it?"

He glanced at me in surprise.

"She's not a cop, is she?"

"No, you're right, she isn't. We cops and journalists have thicker skins, don't we?"

He shrugged.

"I didn't make the world."

As we left the magazine office, I noticed how pale Angela looked.

"I think we should have a stiff drink, it would do you good."

We dived into the first bar we came across. I ordered two brandies. Angela drank as if she needed it.

"I'm sorry I made you come, it wasn't a good idea."

"You must think I'm an old fusspot who has nothing better to do than get emotional over dogs."

"No, this sickens me too."

"I guess I'm not at my best at the moment anyway," she said. "You know about Fermín, don't you, Petra?"

"Yes, I do."

"Did he also tell you he's thinking of getting married to that woman?"

"Yes, but how did you find out?"

"He called to tell me. Even though he had finished with me, he didn't want me to hear from someone else. Deep down, he's a gentleman."

"Look, I don't know if he's a gentleman or a son of a bitch, but whichever it is, he's an idiot: people don't get married just because they feel like it."

"He's afraid of being lonely. He's someone who's felt lonely all his life."

"But marrying her will be a disaster. By the time you're our age, living with someone is almost impossible."

"But by the time you're our age, you appreciate company."

I looked down at my drink. I stared into the brandy, then downed it in one gulp. Angela's beautiful eyes were moist with tears, but she soon recovered her composure.

"Well, after all I've been through, I reckon I ought to ask for a deputy's badge!"

She laughed more forcefully than normal, and said goodbye with another joking remark. Wonderful, I thought. Long live love, laughter, jokes, long live life. A heap of shit, all of it.

I went back to the station. Sat at my desk. Made out a report. "We have received information that Ignacio Lucena Pastor was involved in illegal dogfights," I wrote. It all seemed so ludicrous. The front desk rang. There was a man on the phone who wanted to speak to me. Put him through.

"Inspector Delicado, this is Arturo Castillo. Do you remember me?"

"Hello, Doctor Castillo. Of course I remember you. What can I do for you?"

"I was wondering if you had solved that case about the dogs. From time to time I feel curious about it, but I've seen nothing in the papers . . . "

"But Doctor Castillo, don't you realize that if you keep calling you're going to become a suspect yourself?"

"What? I trust you're joking!"

"No, I'm not. It happens sometimes: suspects who think they have a cast-iron alibi, but can't bear the uncertainty about whether the long arm of the law is stretching out in their direction."

"The things you say, inspector!"

"Are you sure you have nothing to hide? Perhaps you hated Lucena for some reason or another."

"Inspector, I'll come and testify whenever you like!"

"I'll think about it, Doctor Castillo, I'll think about it."

I hung up. My sense of indifference had turned into state of fury. The whole world was full of injustice, dogs tearing each other to pieces set up by human greed, love always ending up with heartbreak and yet, in spite of everything, we had to go on being polite to one another. To hell with that! I slammed my desk drawers shut as loudly as I could. I got my jacket and charged out without saying goodbye to any of the colleagues I met in the corridor. I was going to have dinner on my own, in some squalid little restaurant, and was going to have macaroni in tomato sauce with a huge blood sausage to follow. My laughable revolt against good manners.

The next morning was not quite so bad. As soon as I returned to the office I had quit so violently the evening before, I saw the lab report on my desk. I opened it eagerly, and after a couple of seconds I was reading it with real optimism. No doubt about it, there were traces of canine blood and hairs on the sample of straw we had sent them. Angela had hit bull's-eye. I left a note for Garzón explaining things and rushed off to the lab. The man in charge confirmed all the findings and gave me a tiny airtight bag containing several short, stiff hairs whose colors varied from brindle to ivory. The only thing he was sure of was that they were from dogs. If I wanted any further precision, he said, I would have to ask a vet. I did not dare ask him if we had any forensic vets on the force, but decided to turn to one I knew close at hand.

I turned up at Juan Monturiol's surgery without even phoning ahead. I waited my turn among old ladies cradling their Yorkshire terriers on their laps and men carrying cuddly puppies to be vaccinated. I could see once again that there was a special kind of kinship between dog owners. Nobody was embarrassed if they were suddenly sniffed, or felt offended if they somehow set off some unfriendly barking.

Juan's reaction when he came to the door to say goodbye to a client was not exactly encouraging, but I put his grim face down to the surroundings. I was as patient as a saint. I sat there reading the most unlikely magazines all about dogs and cats, and when the last patient had finally gone, the vet came and offered me his hand. Keeping his distance; probably no more than I deserved. I tried to be natural and friendly in my personal remarks, serious and slightly mysterious in my professional comments. He caught on at once, and asked to see the hairs. I took them out of the bag with all the devotion of someone handling a holy relic. We went into his lab and he put the hairs on a slide.

"Looking at them through a microscope wouldn't help, so we are simply going to magnify them a lot."

He peered at them through a magnifying glass, and studied them for some time. I had forgotten how beautiful he was. Those strong, slender hands of his with their delicate fingers. His thick, blond hair. His perfect nose and cheekbones. He raised his big green eyes to me.

"What do you want to know?"

"What breed of dog are they from?"

He hesitated a moment.

"There are some that are almost golden; others are off-white. They could have come from two or more dogs, but they could also come from the same dog which had different coloring on its back and stomach, or from one that had patches. What I can say for certain is that they come from animals with very short hair, and, from their texture and good condition, I would think they must come from young dogs."

"Doesn't the blood tell us which breed they are?"

"No, not at all."

"We know they were guard dogs and we can see what color they were. Do you think that the hairs are enough to tell us which breed they might or might not be?"

"That would take a long while."

"I can come back tomorrow."

"No, stay. I'll go and get something to eat."

"I'll go."

I went out and looked for a bar. I found myself asking them to put extra cheese in one of the rolls. I was looking after Juan; it was not such a bad feeling after all. My unhappy lover had been kind to me yet again. Although he had been working long hours in his surgery, he still found the time to help. But I had not been very kind to him. I had not been serious. Perhaps it was not that terrible to put your trust in someone. At least he was company, as Angela said.

It was a long and intense evening. Monturiol consulted all his books and photographs, then gave his verdict.

"Write this down, Petra. These hairs could belong to the following breeds: boxer, Staffordshire bull, short-haired German shepherd, bulldog, or Canary Island hound. I suppose that's too many to be of any use to you?"

"If these crooks operate in the way that a journalist told me they do, one of the dogs was stolen, so knowing what breed it was does not get us very far. But the other belonged to the organizer, and must have been one of those breeds. That's why it's important to know which."

"Are you thinking of dog breeders?"

"Possibly."

"I can't help you any further."

"You've already helped a lot. What can I do in return?"

"Drop me at my place. I didn't bring the car."

And I took him. Perhaps it wasn't so bad to show some affection now and then.

The next morning Garzón and I held an emergency meeting in my office. He reported the progress he had made in his *cherchez la femme*, which I did not listen to, and I told him how far I had got. We had to concentrate on the kennel owners who raised the breeds Monturiol had mentioned.

"But we've investigated all of them!" my colleague argued.

"Then we'll just have to do it all again."

"I still think we're getting off track."

"We have to work with the evidence we've got. We now know that Lucena was mixed up with illegal dogfights, and we also know that in his new line of work 'he spent his time in the country.' What do you think he went to the country for, picnics?"

"But the 'country' could mean the garden of any house sufficiently secluded."

"O.K., but who could keep killer dogs like that in a house? And where could they do the training for fights with stolen dogs without arousing suspicion? No, Garzón, the 'country' might mean a lot of things, but before we start looking for a needle in a haystack, let's try a pincushion."

"Have you seen how long Monturiol's list is?"

"Well, at least there are no breeders of Canary Island hounds near Barcelona."

"Even so . . . "

"We'll split them. You visit the breeder of Staffordshire bull terriers and the bulldog kennels. I'll take the German shep-

herds and the boxers. You'll have to go and get the search warrants, though. This time we're going to search all the premises,
and thoroughly. We will also need to inspect the dogs, to see if
any of them have got marks or scars that show they have been
fighting."

"In that case we need to take an expert with us. I'll ask
Valentina to go with me."

"Good idea. I'll ask Juan or Angela."

"Inspector, if I happened to run into Angela . . . "

"Don't worry, I'll make sure there are no awkward encoun-
ters."

"Thanks. I see you understand."

"You can't imagine how much I understand."

He chose not to risk any more of my ironic barbs and but
almost ran out of the office. He was probably delighted he
could share his tasks with such a perfect expert.

By four o'clock that afternoon I had all the relevant search
warrants on my desk. Garzón the Magnificent had fulfilled all
his duties; in spite of his amorous affairs, he was as efficient as
a Swiss watch. I arranged for Juan Monturiol to accompany me
to the German shepherd kennel. It was a relaxed occasion,
almost a pleasure trip. We chatted, commented about things,
and then when we arrived at the kennel I could see how excited Juan was to take part in a police search. The breeder was a
calm, elderly man who completely gave the lie to the saying that
owners and their dogs end up looking alike. He was very different from his fierce German shepherds. He took our visit so
philosophically that he even asked after Sergeant Garzón,
whom he remembered from the previous time. If he was the
guilty one, he had developed a remarkable capacity to hide it.
Nor did his premises raise our suspicions in any way: we
opened doors, peered behind kennels, poked our noses in every
corner. There were no hidden rooms or anything that looked
like a fighting ring. There were no dogs kept on their own or

treated differently. Juan went from kennel to kennel, inspecting the dogs' front legs and necks carefully . . . he had told me that these were the parts that other dogs usually went for in fights: biting the front legs prevented the rival from moving, a bite in the neck could be instantly fatal. He had brought a long pole with him, and he sometimes thrust it through the wire to get the dogs to change position so that he could examine them more easily. None of this was any use, because the final verdict was that none of them showed any signs of having been in a fight.

In order to make the search seem more thorough, I cast a suspicious rather than an expert eye over the account books. There was nothing obviously amiss. The kennel owner watched us doing all this resignedly, and, although he was curious, he did not ask a thing. It was only at the very end that he shrugged off his diffidence and said that never again would he inform the police that a dog of his had been stolen. Juan made the mistake of asking him why, to which he replied: "The police always end up treating you as if you were guilty of something." This phrase impressed my veterinary friend, but I told him later on that it was something we heard all the time, although that did not make it any the less true.

On our way back, things were even more relaxed and warm between us. Acting as though he were really on the case, Juan dismissed all possibility that the German shepherd breeder could be guilty. He constructed hypotheses, then himself put the theories to the test. I smiled at him.

"I reckon we could make a good policeman out of you."

"But as I told you, peace and tranquility are what I value most in life."

"But you could play at being a detective now and again, couldn't you?"

"That means you need me again tomorrow."

"I'm afraid I do. Could you arrange it? We have another couple of kennels to visit."

"I'll arrange it."

"What about now: could you arrange it to have dinner with me?"

He looked at me questioningly.

"An unhurried dinner?"

"Yes."

"It's already arranged."

So we had dinner at his place, and then made love in a gentle, affectionate way. It may be that there are relationships that need to be broken off and begun again several times, I thought as I dressed again, being careful not to wake him. Perhaps one of those beginnings will show us the right way to make it last.

I reached home at three in the morning. I played back the messages on my answering machine. Nothing. My cleaner had prepared vegetables for me to eat. They lay cold as corpses on the kitchen table. Freaky was busy chewing on one of those pretend bones made of cartilage. He was so taken with his synthetic prey he did not even come over to say hello. I had a bath, plucked a few hairs from my eyebrows and chose a book, with every intention of falling asleep indulging in a cultural pursuit. But a few moments later, the phone rang. It must be Juan, I thought, with one of his typical romantic touches: "That was wonderful, I'm missing you already." But no, it was Garzón, at three in the morning.

"Inspector? There's something very important I have to tell you."

I felt a stab of anxiety.

"The Staffordshire bull terrier man!" I almost shouted.

"No, it's not about that. Look, I'd prefer to come to your house and tell you myself. I didn't even want to leave a message on your machine. I've been calling you all night."

What else could I do but tell him to come? He must have a piece of information about the investigation that was so important he couldn't even tell me it by phone. I put some clothes on and looked to see if I had any whisky left. Then I sat and waited for the sergeant. As soon as I opened the door I realized my worries about not having any whisky were unfounded: Garzón was triumphantly waving a bottle of French champagne.

"Find a couple of glasses, inspector, and forgive the intrusion, but I wanted you to be the first to know."

I stared at him like a dummy. Finally he burst out:

"Valentina has said yes!"

He had caught me so unawares that I almost asked him, Yes to what? But then I suddenly remembered he had proposed to her. All I could think of to say was:

"That's wonderful, Fermín!"

He slid into the living room and went to fetch the glasses himself. He patted Freaky on the head and opened the champagne like a seasoned *sommelier*. We drank a toast.

"To your happiness!" I exclaimed, not entirely sure it was the right thing to say. He lifted the glass high, then drained the contents without a moment's hesitation. We sat down and he started to confide in me.

"Apparently it wasn't easy for her. That guy, her lover, didn't want her to leave just like that. He's been putting an awful lot of pressure on her these last two days. He even told his wife about Valentina, and then said he was leaving her. Of course that was just to blackmail Valentina. The bastard has kept her as his secret lover for years, and now he is offering to leave his wife and marry her as soon as the divorce comes through. Valentina didn't want to know. 'It's too late,' she told him. 'You've upset your wife unnecessarily.' What do you think of that?"

"Good for her."

"In the end, it seems the guy realized there was nothing he could do, so he's going to leave her in peace. What do you reckon, Petra?"

"Well, it's all very exciting."

"And now for the really big news. In fact, that's why I took the liberty of coming to see you so late at night."

"Spit it out, Fermín, before I have a heart attack!"

"As soon as we're married, I'm going to leave the force."

"Leave the police?"

"Early retirement."

I was left speechless.

"Are you sure about this, Fermín?"

"Look, if we pool Valentina's and my savings, we'll have enough to buy a plot of land and build a house and kennels like she's always wanted. Isn't that incredible? That's the advantage of being a married couple. The two of us can spend our time quietly raising dogs and living in the heart of nature. Can you see me as a dog farmer, inspector?"

"I don't know, Fermín; have you thought this through? Leaving the police and changing your job at your time of life . . . it may be Valentina's lifelong dream, but is it yours?"

His face fell and he stared at me.

"I'm tired, Petra, really tired. You joined the police because you wanted a change; you were a lawyer, so you could have done anything. But I joined the force as a young man simply because I had to earn a living. I've spent my whole life on the street, and tell me: what's a man my age doing chasing dog thieves?"

"I suppose you have every right to choose."

"This is the first time in my life I've ever made a real choice. And it's not one, but two choices: a wife and a job. I feel like a king."

"I wish you every happiness. Your bachelor pad didn't last long, did it?"

"But it was important while it did. It gave me freedom and intimacy. And it's you I have to thank for it."

"You can pay me back with another glass of champagne!"

We drank and laughed for quite a while. I had never seen

anyone so happy. There was no doubt I would miss Sergeant Garzón. I would miss his loyalty, his wolfish hunger, his merry, round stomach. I had underestimated him: perhaps he was not as immature as I had thought; after all, he had managed to get what he wanted. He left flushed and happy, as gay as a lord. Would he spare a thought for Angela? Of course not. Being happy in love vaccinates you against painful memories. The pleasure of company. I sat down again and stroked Freaky's head. He had fallen asleep curled up with his fake bone. I picked up the phone and called Juan. I didn't care about waking him up. He sounded frightened.

"Petra! What's wrong?"

"Nothing; I just wanted to know how you are."

It took him a moment to get his voice back, but when he spoke it was gently.

"I'm fine, my love, fine."

I hoped he would see my call as the symptom of a welcome change in my character.

My sleep that night—or, rather, what little was left of it— was so deep that even though it was only a few hours, in the morning I felt like new. I woke up feeling on top of the world, and went to have a shower. As I was drying myself afterward, I heard the phone ringing in the living room. It would have been worse five minutes earlier, I thought. I ran to get it: such an early call must mean it was from the station. And so it proved. I immediately recognized the Galician accent of Julio Domínguez, a young cop who had recently been posted to Barcelona.

"Inspector Delicado, I'm calling you on behalf of Inspector Sánchez."

"I'm listening."

"The body of a woman has been found."

"So?"

"Well, the thing is that Inspector Sánchez told me the

woman, the dead woman, was wearing a locket or something round her neck, with a photo of Sergeant Garzón in it."

"Blonde or brunette?"

"I beg your pardon?"

"Is the woman a blonde or a brunette?"

"I don't know inspector, I only know what I told you."

"Where did they find her?"

"On her house patio."

"And where is her house, for Christ's sake?"

"I don't know that either. It wasn't me who took the message. If you wait a moment, inspector, I'll go and find out who talked to Inspector Sánchez, and get back to you."

"Goddam it! I'll come to the station straightaway, it'll be quicker."

I put on the first things that came to hand in my wardrobe. I fumbled with the zips and could not do the buttons up. I forgot to comb my hair or to stroke Freaky. As I started my car, I could feel the adrenaline coursing through my body.

10

Sánchez was shocked. He was a man with a lot of experience, a man who had been around, but even he said: "In all my years on the force, I've never seen anything like this." I had a lot fewer years' experience, but perhaps I would never see anything like it again either. On the floor, torn and ripped like an old dishcloth, lay the body of Valentina Cortés. The visible parts of her body were covered in purple wounds. Her face was covered in blood; her eyes were creased in a look of terror that now was eternal. I knelt down beside her. Her beautiful blonde hair was streaked and matted from the coagulated blood. Sánchez squatted down next to me.

"She's a friend of Garzón's, isn't she?"

"Yes."

"I thought she must be as soon as I saw that medallion . . . I thought it was better to call you so that you could come and have a look."

"What are all those wounds?"

"Bites. Apparently she was attacked by her own dog. It's over there, holed up in its kennel. If we try to go near, it snarls. I don't think it will come out, but I've got a man with a gun standing by just in case. You can't be too careful with a beast like that."

"Have you spoken to the forensic people?"

"Yes, and to the coroner so he can issue a death certificate. We've done an initial search inside the house, but there's nothing unusual there. It looks as though it attacked her out here close to the kennel, because it's tied up."

"Did the neighbors hear anything?"

"They say they didn't."

"That's strange, isn't it?"

"That depends on what time it was; besides, seeing it was her own dog, it probably took her by surprise and she didn't have time to shout."

"By surprise, with all those bites on her body?"

"What we don't know is if it killed her with one bite and then went on attacking her."

I stood up. My head was throbbing.

"Were she and Garzón close friends?"

"Yes, very close."

"Shit! How are you going to tell him?"

"Why does it have to be me?"

"He works with you, doesn't he?"

I called the sergeant on the phone. There was no other choice, and, besides, it was my duty. At least there were more people around at the scene of the crime and I would find somebody to help me soften the blow.

"Sergeant Garzón?"

"Yes, inspector? I'm sorry I'm a bit late, I was just leaving for the station."

"Garzón, something terrible has happened. I want you to listen to me and to stay calm."

"Jesus, inspector, don't scare me like that."

"Valentina has been found dead in her home, Fermín. They think it was Morgana who attacked her again and again until she was killed."

Nothing but silence at the far end of the line.

"You understood what I said, didn't you?"

"Yes."

"Do you feel all right?"

"Yes."

"Will you come here?"

"Yes."

The forensic expert arrived, then the coroner's man, and finally, tieless and with the flaps of his jacket blowing in the breeze, Garzón appeared. I avoided looking him in the face. I avoided talking to him. From a distance, I watched as he went over to where the body lay and lifted a corner of the blanket covering her. Sánchez was giving him all sorts of explanation. He listened very quietly to everything. At that point I walked over to him and put my hand on his shoulder. He turned and looked at me. His face was ashen, his eyes completely lacking in expression.

"Fermín," I said.

"Hello there, inspector," he replied, in a deadened voice.

"The forensic expert says she died around two in the morning, and confirmed that those are dog bites. They're going to take her away now to perform the autopsy," Sánchez said.

"It wasn't her dog that killed her," Garzón insisted in a low voice. "Inspector Sánchez, I think this was a murder. Can you carry out a thorough search?"

Sánchez looked at him doubtfully for a second, then answered:

"Of course. I'll tell them right away to check everything again, to look for prints and take samples of the carpets and curtains. We'll dispose of the dog and I'll have its teeth inspected for any traces of blood."

"You don't have to dispose of it, I'll get it out of the kennel."

"But that's impossible, Fermín."

Garzón did not reply. Instead, he went over to the kennel. When it saw him approaching, the dog started to growl, but Garzón kept on going. All the rest of us stood looking on, horrified. The sergeant bent down by the small opening, stuck his open hand inside, and said evenly:

"Come on out, Morgana."

The dog almost crawled out of her hiding place, and sought refuge between my colleague's legs. He stroked her silently. Neither of them moved, and none of us dared interrupt them. I went over.

"Fermín, they have to take the dog away: they need to do tests on her teeth."

"Tell them not to put her down, we'll find someone to look after her."

"All right, don't worry, I'll tell them."

He took the dog by the collar and untied her. She followed him tamely to the van. They injected her with a sedative and took her away. Garzón stood in the road staring after the disappearing vehicle. I had to get him away from there, if only for a few minutes. He must not see them take the body out.

"Let's go and have a coffee, sergeant."

"A coffee?" he asked blankly, as if he had forgotten the meaning of the word.

"Yes, just for a while, come on."

"What about the search?"

"Inspector Sánchez is taking care of that. Don't worry, you've heard how thorough it will be."

I pushed him gently but firmly away from the house. We went into a run-down bar full of noisy workmen having their breakfast.

"Do you want it with milk, Fermín?"

He nodded absentmindedly.

We drank our coffees in silence. I listened to the workmen joking with each other, the muttering of the radio news adding to the hubbub, in a corner the sound the high-pitched clicks of a slot machine inviting more customers to play. All the happy sounds of a normal, routine morning. I have never been very good at the heroic or the emotional. Condolences or pep talks are not my style. When people are suffering, there's nothing to say; it may be that everything in life sorts itself out, but there is something immoral about reminding a person in trouble of that. All I could think of was to suggest to Garzón:

"Would you like something stronger?"

He said yes, and when he had the glass in his hand he downed it at a gulp. Then he said:

"It was Valentina's lover who killed her."

"What do you know about him, Fermín?"

"Nothing, that's the problem, absolutely nothing. I never felt like asking and she never said anything." He sat there for a moment lost in his thoughts, then added: "Let's go, I want to see how the search is getting on."

Insisting on the professional course of things seemed like a good way to face reality. When we got back to the house I saw with relief they had taken the body away. Sánchez came up to us.

"We found something in the dog's kennel," he said. "Figueredo, let me see that piece of evidence!"

"We've already put it in the car, inspector."

"Who told you to do that? Bring it here, for Christ's sake!" As the cop was walking off, Sánchez turned to me and said loudly:

"Soon we'll have to be asking them 'please.'"

When Figueredo came back, he was carrying a small note-book. Garzón snatched it from him and began to flick through it nervously. His mouth twitched painfully as he handed it to me. It was Lucena's third account book. There was no doubt about it: it was his handwriting and his figures. And this time, they were for sums large enough to fit in with the amount of money he had hidden in his apartment.

"Where was it?"

"Stuffed into a deep crack in the inside wall of the kennel. It was a good hiding place: nobody would have had the nerve to stick their hand in there. Does the book make sense to you?"

"Yes, Sánchez. I'm afraid we're going to have to tell the commander that we're taking over the investigation. I think it's part of the case we're already on."

"You can't imagine how pleased I am: this looks like a dirty business."

Garzón was as gloomy as a gravedigger. After we got into my car, there was a lengthy silence. Finally, his voice exploded next to me:

"All right Petra, say it, you can spit it out right now! Valentina was in cahoots with Lucena's killers, perhaps she was the one who killed him. That's why she made friends with me right from the start. She wanted to get information, to know what we were finding out and pass it on to her accomplices. Why don't you say so? Tell me what an imbecile I am!"

He was screeching at the top of his voice.

"Take it easy, Garzon, and don't be so hasty. If you want, we can talk this over calmly in my office."

"I'm sorry, all this is like a nightmare."

"Calm down, there's no use feeling sorry for yourself. We need to investigate and find out what really happened."

Back in my office, I sat behind my desk and Garzón sank into a chair opposite. I looked through the book again. No doubt about it, it was Lucena's third account book. I picked up the phone and called Juan Monturiol.

"Juan? I've got another favor to ask. Not a very nice one: I'd like you to go to an autopsy. I want you to look at some dog bites. Yes, later today. I'll call you."

I was gripped by a strange kind of energy. The end was in sight. I did not know what it might be, but I could sense it was there, within reach at last. I looked over at Garzón.

"Let's go through this together, sergeant. It's obvious that from the moment we discovered her in her training ground— and I'm inclined to think that Freaky did know where she was going—Valentina deliberately cultivated a friendship with you.

That friendship allowed her to pass on information to her associates about how far we had got with our investigation, and to reassure them. But there are two things you can be sure of: first, Valentina did not murder Lucena, and second, she was going to marry you."

"How can you be so sure of that?"

"Just think about it, and don't be so despondent or angry that it affects you. The fact that Valentina had that account book points the finger at her: she must have been involved in whatever Lucena was up to. But at the same time it exonerates her. Why do you think she kept the book in such a safe place?"

"Because it was evidence against her."

"If that were so, it would have been much safer still to destroy it. No, Valentina got hold of the book when Lucena died, and she was obviously using it to threaten someone else. It's most likely that her accomplice was that other person and that therefore he is responsible for Lucena's death."

He stayed silent for a while, turning this over in his mind. I went on with my explanation, which seemed to grow more and more convincing to me as I laid it out it forcefully to him.

"It may even have been that account book which cost Valentina her life. Probably, when she decided to marry you, and this is the proof that she really had taken that decision, she said she wanted nothing more to do with the others, but they would have none of it. They were scared she might give them away, might tell her secrets to her husband: just imagine, she was about to become a policeman's wife! So they threatened her. She counterattacked by reminding them of the notebook, they demanded she hand it over, she refused because it was her future guarantee . . . then in the end they set a trained dog on her and it killed her. They searched for the notebook but couldn't find it, and afterwards they straightened up the house and tried to make it look as though Morgana had killed her by accident."

"My God, you've got quite a theory there!"

"It's just logical. Do you have any idea whether Valentina's lover could be one of her accomplices? Did she ever tell you he had something to do with dogs as well?"

"I've already said, I know nothing about him. I'm beginning to wonder whether he ever really existed."

"Did Valentina have any family?"

"She always told me she was alone in the world."

"Friends?"

"No idea."

"Well, find out at once."

"I'd like you to give me something more important to do."

"You'll do as you're ordered, Garzón, and don't bring your personal feelings into this or I'm going to have to ask the commander to transfer you off this case."

"Whatever you say," he said, and walked out of the office frowning and muttering to himself. I felt relieved: it was the first sign in hours that things were getting back to normal.

Going to the autopsy must have been a real trial for Juan Monturiol, but he was so caught up in the mysteries of our case that he put his doubts to one side and showed great strength of character. Naturally enough, I waited for the results in the corridor. No one could have made me go into the room. My muscles relaxed when I sat down, but my back still ached. It all seemed like complete madness. The closer we got to solving the case, the further off we still seemed to be. Freaky had given us the key, or at least part of it, from the very first moment. It was clear now. His tattered ear. I recalled the way he had reacted when he first saw Valentina, but she had been quick and intelligent enough to make the right move. After that, we were operating right in front of her eyes, so she knew if we were getting close to the nub of the affair or were still a safe distance away. The sergeant was an easy victim, the little Don Juan, the hunter hunted. Beyond that, there was an avalanche of questions, particularly with regard to their love story. Had Valentina ever at any point really been in love with my colleague? Was she really going to marry him? He was offering her the chance to quickly fulfill her dream of a house in the country; she had probably also discovered what a good sort he was, and was seduced by it. I had to think this was the right hypothesis, both for the sake of the case and to help Garzón get over her death. I thought he must be asking himself the same kind of questions, with an added sense of painful uncertainty.

When Monturiol and the forensic surgeon came out, I was no longer thinking about the case. It was the terrible reality of Valentina's death that was churning my stomach. Seeing Juan's face did nothing to calm it down. He was white as a sheet, with a desperate look in his eyes and clenched teeth. So there still is some difference between seeing animals and human beings with their insides ripped out. Or perhaps it was simply a question of getting use to it: the forensic surgeon was beaming.

"A clear-cut case," he said. "She did die at around two o'clock in the morning. I have counted at least twenty-five dog bites on her body. One of them severed her jugular. It seems likely the attack took place in the house and not on the patio, because when she fell she banged against the edge of something, possibly a table: there is a cut on her side. I suppose they dragged her outside and left her there. Was the front door unlocked?"

"Yes, and the victim was not wearing a nightdress. She must have been expecting a visitor."

"That sort of thing has nothing to do with me. Nor are the zoological deductions—that is up to our good friend here. You didn't enjoy it much in there, did you?" he said, laughing as he clapped Juan on the back. "I have to be off, I've got another autopsy. I'll send you the written report this afternoon, Petra."

He left, leaving behind him a distinct smell of disinfectant.

"I threw up," Monturiol confessed when we were on our own.

"I'm sorry, Juan, really."

"I felt like a little kid."

"Were you able to reach any conclusions?"

"That would have been too much to expect. I took some notes. I've got the size of the bites and I made sketches. Now I'll have to work on them back at my surgery."

"We could leave it till tomorrow."

"No, I feel better now."

"Are you sure?"

"I'll tell you when we get out of this sinister place."

He was extremely good with the computer—yet another virtue. For several hours, we worked up his scribbled sketches into exact drawings of the bites on the screen. Then he used them to work out the shape of the jaw that produced them. I sat waiting flat-out in a chair. I was so tired I eventually fell fast asleep. When he woke me up, I had no idea what time it was.

"I think I can see it clearly now."

I woke with a start and went over to the computer.

"Of course it was not Morgana who attacked her. It must have been a smaller dog than a rottweiler, but one with even more strength in the jaw, because the bites are deep and precise. There is no tearing, they are a single stab. It was a dog trained to attack. It did not get tired; the force of the assault was even all the time. All the bite marks are similar."

"Could it be one of the breeds we chose from the hairs the other day?"

"That's precisely what we're going to see now."

He sat opposite me and got out some paper and a pencil.

"Let's see. It cannot have been a boxer. Its mouth is marked by what we call inferior prognathism. That means its lower jaw sticks out further than the top one, which produces a

characteristic kind of bite—and Valentina's are not like that."
He crossed boxer off his list. "It can't have been a German
bulldog, either. It's got a huge mouth, so the bites would have
been a lot bigger. So all we are left with are the German shepherd or the Staffordshire bull terrier. It's impossible to tell
their bites apart."

"That's fantastic, Juan! This is a really important step forward. I must tell Garzón."

At the police station they told me Garzón had already left,
so, rather worried, I called him at home. He was there, as
faded as a burnt-out bulb. When I told him what Juan had
deduced, he answered in monosyllables. When I had finished
he didn't ask for details or make any comment.

"Are you all right, Fermín?"

"Yes."

"I hope you're not drinking whisky like a drain, I need you
to be on the ball tomorrow. We've got lots of work to do."

"Don't worry, I'm not drinking."

"Do you need anything?"

"No, Petra, thanks anyway."

"Good night, then."

"Good night."

Juan came up behind me and put his arms round me. I
turned round and we kissed.

"I think that as a reward for all my detective work I deserve
you to invite me to dinner and then . . . "

"I'm sorry, Juan. I'm worried about Garzón. I'm going to
call in on him."

"I thought I heard him say he was fine."

"You never can tell. He's taken a real blow, and he's all on
his own. I'll call you tomorrow."

He lowered his eyes, then smiled.

"Do your duty, inspector."

I kissed him lightly and drove off to the sergeant's apartment. When he opened the door, it was as if he did not recognize me.

"I came to check you weren't drinking."

"I told you I wasn't."

"In that case, maybe you should be, but with company. Do you have any whisky?"

He let me in. He went off like a robot to find the bottle, and served the whisky into two glasses.

"What do you think of Juan Monturiol's conclusions? Incredible, aren't they? Do you remember who the breeders of those two sorts were? We were nearly killed at the Staffordshire bull terrier place, so perhaps . . . "

"Here's the thing, inspector: I don't feel like talking."

"Let's watch TV, then."

We put on a football match. I didn't understand a thing. We sat and watched in silence, occasionally sipping our whisky. Fortunately, the players fought amongst themselves and argued with the referee. I could understand that, and it kept me sufficiently entertained to almost reach the end of the game. I could see Garzón nodding off, so I got up and whispered to him:

"I'll be off, Fermín. I'll see you tomorrow at the station."

He grunted agreement but did not stir. At least he had found a position he could relax and fall asleep in.

All my life I had wanted things to happen to me like they do to detectives in the movies. That night when I got home my dream finally came true, but paradoxically, I didn't like it one bit. I found the front door broken on its hinges. The living room was in an incredible mess: they had tipped all the books from their shelves, thrown all the cushions on the floor, opened all the drawers. I ran into the bedroom. The same sight awaited me. The few jewels I possess had disappeared from my bedside table. I flung my bag on to the bed. I made the air blue with my curses. All of a sudden, I remembered Freaky, and my heart was in my mouth. I started desperately calling out to him and looked for him everywhere, but there was no reply. I ran to the kitchen and tried to push open the door, but there was something blocking it. There he was behind it, rolled up in a ball, lifeless. I knelt down beside him and hardly dared touch him. Eventually I put my hand out carefully, almost affectionately. He was stiff and cold. There was blood on his head from where they had hit him. I went to find a cushion, put Freaky on it, and carried him into the living room. I sat down in front of his dead body. I felt sad and weary. Now the last traces of Ignacio Lucena Pastor really have vanished from the planet, I thought. The poor devil and his ugly dog. A sad story.

"Of course they weren't burglars," I told Garzón, who looked calmer the next morning. "They only stole my four almost worthless rings to conceal what they were really after."

"Lucena's notebook?"

"They would have to be rank amateurs to imagine we keep the evidence stashed in our wardrobes!"

"So their real aim was to get rid of Freaky. They were scared he might be a silent witness again. They've seen the cops guarding Valentina's apartment and realize we haven't fallen for the story that it was Morgana who attacked her. And while they were dealing with Freaky, they looked to see if they could find anything in your place."

"That's possible."

"Now they no longer have Valentina to tip them off, they have to try to get rid of any evidence against them."

"This is nerve-wracking, sergeant. We're in the final straight. We've got all the cards in our hands, so let's play them properly for once and for all. It's absurd we've been stuck with this ridiculous case for so long."

"With Valentina spying on us, we never got anywhere."

"Don't blame her too much; she was only partly responsible. After all, she gave her life for you."

"Are you sure of that?"

"Of course. She even started to take our side. It was she who informed the police, even though she changed her mind and said the opposite later."

Garzón wagged a finger in the air.

"Just a second, inspector! You're only saying that to comfort me, and that's not right."

"What do you mean?"

"Don't you see? Valentina could not have been the informer, because at the time they took the call at the station, she was at home with me. And of course she found out exactly what was going on. I told her myself. As soon as I left, she must have phoned her accomplices and told them we were on our way. That explains why they had vanished by the time we got there. She was the one who made the second call."

"Have you checked the times?"

"Of course I have."

I scratched my fringe despairingly.

"So, Fermín, who on earth was the woman who made the first call?"

"You can be sure it wasn't Valentina."

"What about your investigations into the people around her? Is there any sign of her family, friends, or this supposed lover?"

"Nothing. Valentina had no one around her, she was a lonely soul. And the diary she kept in her bag hasn't turned up either. Perhaps she lost it before she died."

"How is it possible for a woman to have a lover for years and for him to leave no trace in her life?"

"If what she told me was true, they must have been very discreet about it, because he was married."

"O.K., but she wasn't, so why didn't she have anything of

his at home—a present, a piece of jewelry with his name on it, a photograph . . . don't you remember ever having seen anything?"

"I suppose that when I went there she hid anything she might have had of his. So as not to upset me. Unless . . . "

"Unless whoever killed her made sure he got rid of anything that could have given him away, including her diary. He had the time to do it."

"Which means that the lover and the accomplice are the same person, if she didn't make up the whole thing."

"I can't imagine why she should want to make up a lover."

"To keep me at a distance."

"But she didn't keep you at a distance, she was all over you!"

"That's true."

"Do we have someone monitoring her phone line?"

"Yes. No one has called."

"That's further proof. Her lover would have tried to see her, unless he already knew she was dead."

"Still supposing there was a lover."

"I'm sorry, sergeant, I know it must be painful for you to admit it, but I'm afraid the lover does exist. I'm sure of it. I'm a woman too."

He lowered his gaze, defeated. He was a man, and to admit that his rival had won affected him badly. He left my office with his head sunk on his shoulders. He had aged years in the previous couple of days. There is no justice in this world, and it is no longer possible to pretend there is. I wondered if at his age he would be able to get over this. But whether or not he did, he would go on living. Everybody goes on living despite the scars, the bruises, the marks of endless blows.

I phoned Sánchez. The report on the search at Valentina's apartment was ready. Tiny drops of blood had been found on the furniture. Some larger ones had been almost entirely cleaned away with soap and water. Which meant we could make out a crime sheet for the murder of Valentina Cortés and formally accuse someone of causing her death. Our prime suspects were the two dog breeders. There was a knock at my door. The laid-back Galician came in to tell me that there was a man to see me. A man? It could be a confession, or a witness. My mind was still racing with the prospect of finally bringing our case to a conclusion, and so I found it impossible to place the young man now looking at me round-eyed. He had dark hair, was a bit on the short side, and was putting on weight.

"So you are Inspector Delicado."

"That's right: and you?"

"My father often talks of you."

"Your father?"

"I'm Alfonso Garzón. I've just arrived from New York."

I am sure my jaw dropped a little. I looked him over hungrily, checking out all his features. That skeptical look about the eyes . . . and the sitting Buddha earlobes, weren't they the ears of Sergeant Garzón? He coughed, uneasy at my inspection.

"Of course, how silly of me! Your father left the station some time ago."

"That's what they told me, and that's why I'm here. He's not at home, either."

"Yes, that's right. I'll get us a coffee."

It was true, Garzón had reproduced himself, there was someone going around the world who was the issue of my colleague's unlikely genes. His eyelashes were identical too: stiff and slanting downwards like roof tiles.

"I suppose you can imagine why I came. By the way, do you know when the ceremony is?"

"What ceremony?"

"My father's wedding. I flew over especially to meet his fiancée. Didn't he tell you? I told him I was coming a week ago."

I tried hard to swallow my coffee. Why did I get all the dead bodies?

"Well, Alfonso, a lot has happened in the past two days, things that were so serious that perhaps your father forgot you were coming. I would have preferred him to tell you, but the fact is that your father's fiancée has been murdered."

His voice acquired a strong American accent as he almost shouted:

"What do you mean, murdered?"

"Yes, brutally murdered."

"But that's impossible! My father said she had nothing to do with the cops!"

"She doesn't, but she was involved in a case. I'd better let your father explain all that to you."

"Why did nobody tell me?"

"Well, logically enough, your father is tremendously upset."

"But I came all the way from America. I took days off from the hospital just when I had a lot of work building up. I canceled two important lectures at the university . . . "

"All the same, I'm pleased you came. Your being here will help cheer your father up. He's been hit very hard."

"Yes, of course, there is that."

He was confused, as if someone had stolen a taxi from him on a rainy day, or he had found a cockroach in a luxury hotel room.

"Here's what we'll do. I'll get someone to take you to your father's apartment, and in the meantime I'll find out where he is and tell him to meet you there."

"O.K.," he said, as if he had just won the consolation prize.

I was relieved to see him go. It wasn't hard to track down Garzón. "My son?" he asked, as if I was talking to him about some strange kind of African ant. "I'd completely forgotten about him!" So that was that. In a way, Alfonso Garzón's arrival helped my plans for the case. I was sure it would be easier to keep the sergeant out of the investigation at a time when what we needed most of all were patience and guile, two qualities that grief and the personal way he took the case had robbed my colleague of.

This time I intended to interview the suspects at the police station. Both breeders would be fetched in police cars from their homes, not their workplaces. We would try to ensure everything was done as loudly and as obviously as possible. We would intimidate them as much as we could and hold them until the last minute, which would probably be when their lawyer arrived.

I questioned Pedro Costa, who had the German shepherd kennel, without Garzón this time. He might have been Valentina Cortés's associate, but I could not see him as her lover. His skinny, almost ascetic body did not seem to offer enough room for such a magnificent performer, although of course nobody knows the secrets of women's hearts and some of them do choose lovers out of maternal instinct. But his attitude during the interrogation did not suggest he was a man ruled by passion, either. In spite of the fact that I pressured him and spoke to him in the crudest possible terms, his monkish demeanor never once slipped. He was resigned to suffering abuse from us and had no inclination to rebel. His behavior could mean either that he was completely innocent or that he knew he had a cast-iron alibi. Where was he the night that Valentina was killed? At home, sleeping with his wife. She confirmed his story. I let him go. We had no conclusive evidence against him, and I wanted him to leave feeling he was a free man. So I apologized, I said I was truly sorry, this time he could be sure we would not bother him again, it had all been a momentary confusion, a bad mistake.

As I suspected, when I told him what had happened, it was hard to get Garzón to understand this attitude. His questions quickly turned to protests. Did I really think there was no chance the man was guilty? No, I could not yet say that for sure. So why had I let him go and apologized so profusely? He was angry and despairing that we could treat any possible murderer of Valentina with such kid gloves. His reaction was exactly as I had feared, but it made it completely impossible for me to keep him out of the second interrogation, which obviously only complicated matters still further.

The patrol car picked up Augusto Ribas Solé at his house before work. He was much less philosophical than our other suspect and started protesting as soon as he was brought in front of us. As an early indication of how things were going to be, Garzón shrieked at him to shut up. I stepped in at once.

"It may be that the way you were brought here was a little brusque, but that's the way those cops are."

"Well, it's high time they changed, inspector."

"I agree, and in time they will."

He gave me the same impression as he had on the day he saved us from his fearsome dogs. He was arrogant, self-assured, likeable and friendly. I tried to make my voice sound as calm as possible:

"Where were you when Valentina Cortés was killed?"

"I hardly knew Valentina. We had only met once or twice for work reasons. I learned about her death from the news items in the paper, so I don't know exactly when she died. That's normal, isn't it?"

Garzón nearly flung himself at him.

"We'll decide what's normal, right?"

Horrified, Ribas looked at me.

"What is this? Why is he talking to me like that? Tell him to behave, inspector. You know perfectly well I can't answer anything until my lawyer is present, so if you carry on in that tone, I'll get up and go. I'm only here to try to help you."

I looked daggers at Garzón.

"You're right, señor Ribas, I'm sorry. I'll tell you what you want to know. Valentina died last Tuesday, at two in the morning."

"Two o'clock in the morning of a Tuesday? Well, I suppose I was at home in bed as usual."

"Is there anyone who can corroborate that?"

"My wife, of course!"

"May I ring her to confirm that? Is your wife at home?"

"Yes, call her, please, and try to calm her down. She got the shock of her life when your men burst in this morning."

I picked up the phone and spoke to her briefly, then turned back to Ribas and smiled.

"She says she got back late that night, señor Ribas. Apparently on Tuesdays she has dinner with her female friends."

"It's true, I'd forgotten that. But she must have told you what time she got back, and that she found me fast asleep in bed, didn't she?"

"That's what she told me, yes."

"What I'd like to know is if you have any evidence for apparently accusing me of the murder of a woman I've only seen a couple of times in my life?"

Again, Garzón was about to fling himself across the table, but I restrained him.

"None at all, really, señor Ribas. This may all have been a mistake, but we had to be completely sure of where you were that night. Now we are. You can go."

His face showed he did not understand much of any of this, but he said goodbye calmly and swaggered out of the room. Before the smell of his good male perfume had faded, Garzón turned to me indignantly.

"Would you like to tell me what you're playing at, inspector? Why did you let him go?"

"Because we don't have enough evidence."

"If you carry on like that, we never will. Why didn't you put pressure on him over the dog fights? Why didn't you put pressure on him at all?"

"What did you want me to do, beat him up?"

"Yes!"

I brought my face close to his, clenched my fists, and spat at him through gritted teeth:

"Be careful, Garzón, be very careful. I'm not going to let you bring your personal problems in here. Even if we have someone with a signed confession you are not going to touch a hair of his head, get it?"

He relaxed, and looked down.

"All right," he said. "What do we do now?"

"We wait."

"Wait for what?"

"I don't know, sergeant, but something is bound to happen. If nothing does, we'll try a different tack. What we're not going to do at this stage in the proceedings is grow desperate and do something stupid."

"That's easy for you to say."

"Perhaps."

And so we waited, trying to stay calm. I used the time to sort out my papers and to tie up some loose ends. At least that stopped me thinking obsessively about the case. Every day in the late afternoon, Garzón and I met in my office. We discussed various topics, avoiding any mention of what was in fact uppermost in our minds. I asked after his son. He told me he had decided to stay on a few days in Barcelona to see the tourist sights. He had already taken him to the Sagrada Familia and up to Montjuic. The boy liked to remember his past in the city. One day the three of us arranged to meet for lunch in Los Caracoles. The two men arrived more than half an hour late.

"It's because of this crazy traffic," said Alfonso Garzón.

"How do you ever manage to work? I guess no one is ever on time."

"Are things different in America?"

"Of course! Over there everything is more . . . organized. Nobody would dream of being at the mercy of traffic jams; if there are likely to be problems, you take the subway."

"I see. What would you like to eat? I've seen lots of nice things on the menu."

We started to choose. I could not get over my fascination at seeing the sergeant next to his offspring. I secretly watched the way they moved and talked, to see if I could spot the similarities.

"What about some tripe?" Garzón suggested.

"But Dad, that's pure cholesterol!"

"It's only this once . . . " said Garzón.

The son turned to me.

"Only once! You can't imagine: yesterday he ate paella, the day before it was shoulder of lamb. And at night he usually has eggs and coffee. Ah, and don't get the impression that for breakfast he has fruit or yogurt. No, it's always hot dogs or bacon! How many years do you think someone can go on eating like that before they have a heart attack?"

"Well, your father's been doing it for a good few years now!"

"Exactly, so now is the time for him to start to look after himself."

"You're right."

"My son is always right," Garzón chipped in, trying a good bottle of Rioja.

"When mum was alive things were different. She was a very sensible, thoughtful woman. We ate lots of greens, vegetable soup, things like that . . . "

"And cod on Fridays," the sergeant said with a hint of malice.

"Yes, she was a very religious woman. But, as everyone knows, there are reasons for religious scruples. It's been shown that all of them aim to prolong life. They are against possibly dangerous foods, and promiscuity . . . "

"Yes, yes, we know that," Garzón said, tucking into his tripe. I had risked ordering asparagus tips, in the hope that they were not prohibited by any religion.

"You're not married, Alfonso?"

"No, I haven't had time so far."

I burst out laughing.

"You mean you've had no free time?"

"Don't laugh, inspector, I was telling the truth. Life in America is very tough, there's a lot of competition, especially if you want to be the best. I've had to redo all my medical courses, because they're much harder over there. I chose a specialization and got a post in a hospital. Now I'm a lead surgeon: do you think that was easy, especially since I wasn't born there?"

"I'm sure it wasn't."

"Fortunately, it's a world full of opportunities for anyone who is willing to work."

"A world where anyone can get to be President?"

"From here that might sound like a cliché, but it's true."

"I might have a try to see how far I get," said Garzón, his annoyance showing through his attempt at a joke.

"You wouldn't get anywhere, dad, and do you know why? Because you don't really believe in man's capabilities. You're too fatalistic, like all Spaniards."

"In case you hadn't noticed, fate exists, son. So do not having any luck, failure and the lack of equal opportunities and conditioning since you were born. Don't talk to me about becoming President . . . "

"But dad . . . "

To avoid the argument going any further, I raised my glass.

"Let's drink to fate, or whatever it was that brought us together here today."

That was not my last toast during the lunch, partly because I had to intervene on several occasions to prevent the father-son arguments from getting out of hand and partly because I needed to cheer myself up at this somewhat uncomfortable reunion. By the time we reached the coffee stage, both Garzón and I had drunk a lot. Faithful to his medical prudence, the son had stopped at the third glass.

We said goodbye to Alfonso Garzón in the door of the restaurant. He wanted to visit the Catalan National Museum, and was of the opinion that the late lunches we had in Spain were ridiculously impractical. Garzón and I returned to the police station. I invited him to have a last coffee in my office before he went back to his own.

"A little more sugar?" I said.

"Do you think it's wise for a decrepit old man like me? Would my son approve?"

"Oh come on, sergeant, you should be pleased. Your son is worried about you."

"My son is an asshole, inspector."

"Fermín!"

"I know what I'm saying. A complete ninny! I've had it up to here with him. It's been two weeks of him constantly giving me advice, telling me all the time how perfect the United States is, remembering how sensible his mother was, what a saint she was. I'm sick and tired of hearing him say that life is beautiful, that man can reach as far as he wants to, that work is a way to redeem ourselves, and that anyone can be happy if they really try."

"Your son's only trying to cheer you up."

"Well, he's failed! What does he know about life, real life? What does he know about how his father broke his back in a tough job like this just to give him the chance to study? What does he know about how impossible his mother was for me? Has he seen even a tenth of what I've seen: drug addicts,

down-and-out whores, human dregs, anonymous corpses?
President . . . !"

"You're being unreasonable, Garzón. You've always fought
so that he could have a different view on life."

"O.K., but he needs to see that life is full of a lot of different things: wretched, messed-up people, people who have
never found a way out of their misery! And above all, why
can't he let me be; why shouldn't I eat all the tripe I feel like
eating, and blood sausage too, and fried eggs in gallons of oil!"

I burst out laughing. Garzón looked at me, astonished.

"What's wrong?"

I could not stop laughing. Eventually I managed to blurt
out:

"With a double ration of sausage on Fridays?"

"Christ, Petra, you're impossible. You make fun of everything," he grumbled, but I saw that he too had smiled, and that
underneath his droopy mustache he was just managing to sti-
fle a grin. I felt relieved.

Just as Garzón was leaving, he bumped into the Galician
desk officer in the doorway. If Julio Domínguez was in such a
hurry, it must be something really urgent.

"Quick, inspector, pick up the phone. It could be important."

Garzón dodged back into the room. I grabbed the phone.
The desk man out front was already speaking to someone
whose voice sounded very odd, as if it were imitating a cartoon
character. The person was asking for me.

"Yes, this is Inspector Delicado, who's that?"

Nobody answered. I was afraid I had made a mistake by
talking. I repeated my question. Eventually, and with the same
ridiculous intonation, the voice said:

"Go to number twenty-five in calle Portal Nou. Second
floor A. Ask for Marzal. He knows."

The person hung up. I had scribbled the address down.
Garzón and the cop stared at me, transfixed.

"What's up?"

"Come on sergeant, we need to hurry. Get a patrol car outside right away."

Garzón did as he was told without asking anything more. He hurried out of the room and I followed him. We ran into the desk man.

"Did you write down the address, inspector?"

"Yes."

"So did I, just in case."

"Was it you who took the call from the informer about the Free Trade Zone?"

"Yes, it was."

"Was it the same woman?"

"Did you hear how she was talking? It's impossible to say. But I'm sure that even that time it was a woman."

Garzón came back towards us.

"Everything's set, inspector. There's a patrol car outside. Will three men be enough?"

"I hope so. Give them this address. We'll follow them in your car."

We raced off. The patrol car put its lights and siren on. I told them to pull up some distance away from the building so as not to alert Marzal.

"Who on earth is Marzal?"

"I don't know."

"Did you recognize anything in the voice?"

"It was a woman, but she was disguising her pronunciation."

"With a handkerchief?"

"No, more like Donald Duck or Tweety; you know what I mean."

"The informer last time spoke normally. That means either it's the same woman trying to put us off the scent or another woman whose voice we might recognize."

"There's no point guessing now; let's wait and see what this Marzal fellow knows."

"My heart's beating fit to burst, inspector."

"Try to calm down. I've already told you, I don't want you to do anything wild."

"Are we going to ring the bell?"

"If there's any delay, we break the door down."

"What if he's not there?"

"We'll wait inside for him to come back."

"And if he doesn't?"

"Christ, Garzón, you're making me nervous now! Just be quiet, will you?"

"Petra! We forgot the search warrant!"

"Sergeant, either you shut up at once or I throw you out of the car!"

He fell silent, and I cursed myself for not having had the nerve to stop him coming with me. This was going to be a lesson that ought to be preserved on tablets of stone: a policeman who is personally involved in a case only gets in the way. Things could turn nasty. I had to keep a close eye on Garzón.

The building at number twenty-five had nothing special about it: an old house that was completely run-down. The patrolmen got out of their car and took the lead. There was no elevator. When we reached the front door, I gave a signal and Garzón rang the bell. There was a long pause. He rang again. This time we heard steps approaching and the sound of a sleepy voice.

"Who's there?"

"Police, open up!" I was surprised at the tone of stern authority in my voice.

"What on earth . . . ? Listen, you won't find anything here, you've got the wrong address."

"Are you Marzal?"

There was another long silence.

"Open up, will you?"

There was no sign of anyone complying. The sergeant took the initiative.

"Open up, you asshole, or I'll break the door down! There's a busload of cops out here, so open the door!"

He pushed one of the uniformed men in front of the spyhole and a few seconds later the door opened. The cops rushed in, pinned the man down, searched him. We switched the light on in the dark hallway and could finally get a look at him. He was a small, skinny-looking man of around forty, with pale skin, unkempt curls, and horribly sunken cheeks. He was wearing an undershirt and crumpled jeans.

"Listen, I haven't done anything, there must be some mistake."

"Fine, show us your papers then."

"They're in the bedroom. I was asleep. I worked late and . . ."

"Go and get them."

He went off, with a cop following him. The apartment was tiny and miserable. I ordered the others to start a search. Marzal came back with his papers.

"Enrique Marzal. Scrap merchant. Is that what you do for a living?"

"Yes. I trade in metals."

"Fine. Get dressed. You're coming down to the station, we can talk more easily there."

"Hang on a minute! What have I said or done; why do I have to go with you?"

I went out on to the landing, then down to the front doorway. I needed some fresh air: I could not stand the stink of stale food and old cigarette butts, the subtle smell of poverty, that had built up inside. I was angry, upset. This was the worst part of the job. You had to put up with looking at men like him in their underclothes, and be polite to them. If I had had a bottle at hand, I would have drunk to the indignity of it all.

Back at the station, Garzón was impatient to interrogate the guy. I could see the glint of a passion to get to the bottom of things in his eyes. A passion like any other. I explained to him my tactics for getting the suspect to confess. He was scared, and he was probably not a hardened criminal because we had no fingerprint records for him. My colleague began the interview.

"So you pick up scrap?"

"Yes."

"What do you do with it?"

"I sell it, get paid, and everyone's happy."

"What about dogs?"

I caught a glimpse of a furtive gleam in his eye.

"What about them?"

"Let's try again. Do you know Ignacio Lucena Pastor?"

"No."

"Take a look at this photo. Do you recognize him?"

"No, I've no idea who he is. What happened to him? Why is he in that state?"

"He's not in any state any more he was killed."

Marzal's ghastly face flushed with color. I took up the questioning.

"And Valentina Cortés? Do you know someone called Valentina Cortés?"

"No."

"Let me explain. She was a blonde, very attractive. She trained dogs. I said 'she was' because she's dead as well. She was ripped apart by a specially trained dog. Murdered. Are you following me?"

"Listen, where's all this leading? I haven't the faintest idea what you're talking about."

"Yes, you do. Someone told us so. We know you're mixed up in the dog business, and the person who told us that is already in jail. That person gave us your name and address, and, what's more interesting still, swore to a judge that you were the one who killed those two people you say you've never heard of."

"The bastard!" exclaimed Marzal. My pulse started to race: we were getting somewhere. Garzón backed off, leaving it all to me.

"We're talking about two murders here, my boy, so you can see you're in serious trouble."

He started to sweat and his chin began to tremble.

"Listen, I wouldn't hurt a fly, believe me. I'll tell you . . . I'll tell you the whole truth, everything I know, I swear to God. I'm no killer! Stealing dogs is not the same. We didn't even mistreat them, I swear, and I even spent my own money to feed them when sometimes I had to keep them at my place for a couple of days. I made friends with them; it's true, I swear it."

He was in such a hurry he could hardly get the words out. He was coughing and spluttering. I should have known it from the moment I first set eyes on him: the dregs of a human being like him could be only Ignacio Lucena's assistant and then his replacement.

"How did you steal them?"

"We would go . . . "

"Who is 'we'?"

"Lucena and me."

"So you knew him."

"Yes, but I heard he was no longer in the business. I swear I had no idea he was dead."

"Go on."

"We would arrive at the kennels at night. We would climb the fence and he would look after any guard dog. He was expert at that. He didn't even touch them. He stayed close to them, moving around slowly so that the dogs barked but never went for him. He used to say it was because they could tell he wasn't frightened of them. While he was doing that I would put a dog in the cage we brought with us, then we'd climb back over the fence. That's all there was to it."

"Who went with you when Lucena stopped coming?"

"My brother-in-law. We never hurt them, I swear. I really like dogs."

"You didn't like them so much that it stopped you handing them over for fights."

He seemed paralyzed for a moment.

"Fights? I swear to God I don't know what you're talking about. I used to see that guy, give him the dog and he'd pay me, and that was that. He never even wanted to tell me his name, and I've no idea where he lived. But he knew all about me all right, and now I know what he wanted the information for, the son of a bitch! Listen, I swear to you . . . "

If he really did not know the other man's name that could complicate things.

"Don't talk so much. Listen to me and think about what you're saying. As you can tell, this is no laughing matter."

"O.K., but you believe me, don't you?" By now it was not just his chin that was quivering, his whole body looked as if it was on the verge of a fit.

"I'm starting to believe you, so calm down. Who else did you see during the handovers?"

"Nobody, I swear to God!" He hesitated for a moment. "Well, once I also saw the blonde you mentioned, but I never spoke to her. I didn't even know she was dead. I swear to God I didn't!"

"Didn't you read about it in the papers or see it on TV?"

"I swear I didn't! I keep to myself. If I had known, I'd have got out of my house and never seen that guy again! I don't want to get mixed up in anything nasty, I'm no criminal."

"Fine, all right, you can stop swearing on oath, I believe you. So you usually saw only that one man."

"Yes. Sometimes he came with a woman, but she never said a word to me."

"You mean with his wife?"

"Yes."

I was so tense that the blood started throbbing at my temples and the bottom of my back started to ache.

"Fine, fine. What car did they use?"

"I never saw it. We used to meet in a street in La Sagrera at night. They always came on foot. They must have parked the car some distance away so I would not see it. I told you, they didn't trust me, they wanted to keep me out of the loop, that's why I know nothing, I swear."

My ruse to find out which car it was had failed, so I had to take the risk, to take the fifty-per cent chance.

"Did he ever come with another man? A tall man, getting on a bit, with long, very white hair?"

He stared at me for a moment without replying. I held my breath. Were we coming to the climax, or would he see through my bluff, and make us start all over again?

"No," he said. "I never saw any other man. It was just him, always."

I took a deep breath.

"So you only ever met Augusto Ribas."

"I already told you, I don't know his name."

"And you're also trying to tell me you had no idea that a guy who refused to tell you who he was could be up to no good? Why did you trust him: just because he looked the part, was tall, middle-aged, a bit of a paunch, nice haircut, well-dressed, easy smile?"

"Yes! Because of all that and because he paid me, right? How could I know someone like that was a murderer?"

Mission accomplished. Garzón stood up so suddenly his chair toppled over. He ran out of the office. I rushed after him and caught him in the corridor.

"Where the hell are you going?"

"To arrest him."

"Take it easy, Garzón. Don't ruin things, you can see we're getting there. Let's do this calmly. Let the cops bring in him and his wife. Make sure they separate them immediately in two different cars, and don't let them see each other in the station. Get the arrest warrants. Ask that villain in there the name and address of his brother-in-law. Bring him in, too. And give Marzal something to eat and a pack of cigarettes. Keep him locked up until he's identified our man, then have him charged. I want everything legal and according to the rules. I don't want to throw everything away now because of some irregularity or other." I looked him straight in the eye. "That means no violence, got it? How are you feeling, Fermín?"

He gave a deep sigh, then smiled and relaxed.

"You were fantastic, Petra. I thought I was going to have a heart attack. If it had been the other dog breeder, that runt would have realized we were only bluffing."

"But now you've calmed down, haven't you?"

"Yes, I'm calm."

He walked off down the corridor. He might have been calm, but I was still trembling.

carcely an hour later, we arrested Augusto Ribas at his kennels. He came quietly. Marzal identified him through a two-way mirror. Two hours later, when she finally got back from a shopping trip, we picked up his wife. She did not seem surprised and did not protest. From then on, I stopped eating, apart from an occasional sandwich that I took the odd bite from and hardly digested, a brioche and coffee. My mind forgot my body. All I could do was crazily sift through strategies, construct theories, elaborate ways of interrogating them. Garzón was the same, except that he did not lose his appetite, and all his intellectual effort went into asking me questions. He tormented me: his constant fidgeting and dreadful anxiety prevented me from thinking with a modicum of calm. Who are we going to question first? How are we going to go about it? Are you going to put Ribas and his wife together? Are we going to have to bring Marzal in? I had to give him another stern talking-to.

"That's enough, sergeant! If you don't get a grip on yourself right now, I'll have you dropped from the case."

He fell silent, then raised his cow-like eyes at me and made one last plea.

"All right, but promise me you'll let me have a go at Ribas. Just let me get at him once, inspector; it'll make me feel better. I promise I won't fly off the handle, I'll wait until you say it's the right moment. Hitting him just once isn't too much to ask."

"Are you out of your mind, Garzón? Don't you see this is the most crucial moment? This guy could still slip through our grasp. I've already told you, there'll be no violence in the inquiry, and I mean it. At the slightest sign of it, I'll be down on you like a ton of bricks."

That was all I needed: to have to fight against Garzón over his vigilante instincts. I should have sent him home then and there, but I didn't have the nerve. Too bad for me. A person in charge should never be ruled by compassion, not even for friends, and if its a police officer he shouldn't even have friends.

We questioned Ribas's wife first. Her name was Pilar, and she was worlds apart physically from her husband. She was small, pale-faced and with straw-colored dyed-blond hair that looked a mess. She seemed as helpless and twitchy as a schoolkid's pet. Her hands were shaking, and to disguise it she held them together on her lap with fake determination. This impression of helplessness vanished as soon as she began to speak. Her voice was strong, firm and lively.

"Señora Ribas, do you know why we brought you here?"

"No," she said, twisting her mouth.

"But you do know why your husband is here, don't you?"

She hesitated for a moment, twisted her mouth again, then imperceptibly clenched her fists on her skirt.

"Yes."

I nodded several times. I tried to look her straight in the eye, but she avoided me.

"Well, that's somewhere we can start from. Your husband organizes illegal dogfights, doesn't he?"

"Yes."

"And you were the one who made the anonymous phone call that took us to one of those fights in the Free Trade Zone, weren't you?"

"Yes."

"And again, more recently you passed on information about your husband's organization, didn't you?"

"Yes."

"And in that second phone call you disguised your voice?"

"Yes."

"Why couldn't you come and tell me in person?"

"Why would I do that?"

She was beginning to show signs of impatience.

"What kind of a question is that? I didn't want my husband to know it was me, and I didn't want the police to get me mixed up in his affairs."

"But you knew all about those affairs."

"He never tried to hide them from me. I had a general idea of what was going on, but I never got involved."

"Are you sure, señora Ribas?"

"Don't call me that! My name is Pilar!"

"All right, Pilar. Tell me something, did you know your husband had killed a man?"

She stared at me, a look of panic on her face. Her hands shot from her lap to grip the arms of her chair.

"No!" she said categorically.

"Did you ever meet Ignacio Lucena Pastor?"

"I've no idea who he is."

"But you knew Enrique Marzal, the man who took over from him, well enough to tip us off."

"I knew that Marzal fellow had been working with my husband for several months now, but I did not know what they were up to. I found his address in Augusto's diary and passed it on to you, that's all."

I took Lucena's photo out of a drawer and showed it her.

"Do you know this man?"

She looked at me, a puzzled expression on her face.

"Yes, that's Lolo. I've seen him at home occasionally. I've hardly spoken to him. He stopped coming some time ago."

"Didn't that seem strange to you?"

"Why should it? My husband deals with lots of people.

From time to time they come home, I say hello and goodbye to them. I prefer not to know what they're up to."

"Well, Lolo was beaten to death. We have reason to believe it was your husband who did it, and we think we may have to accuse you of being an accomplice."

She stiffened. Her dull eyes suddenly came alive.

"Do you think that someone who phones you not once but twice to give a tip-off could be guilty of anything? Why would I point an accusing finger at myself?"

"I don't know. So why did you give your husband away, Pilar?"

She said nothing. Then eventually she stammered:

"That woman . . . "

Garzón shot upright as though he had a bedspring in his spine.

"Which woman?"

She looked at him fearfully, then back at me. I tried to smile.

"Which woman do you mean?" I said, with as much tact as I could muster.

"That woman. The one he had been seeing for years. I never complained, I just put up with it. But she was a cheap whore: she knew he was married but they still went on seeing each other. The business was just an excuse."

"Are you talking about Valentina Cortés?"

"Yes."

"Is that why you called us?"

"Yes, I wanted you to catch them."

"But why now, Pilar? You've just said it had been going on for years."

"For some time Augusto has been more on edge than usual. I was sure it wasn't just because you were on his trail. I caught him phoning her several times from the house. He hung up as soon as he saw me, but I knew it was her he was talking to. So I decided to tell you about their business. It was a way to put a stop to everything. But you didn't manage to arrest them. Time went by, then one evening Augusto came home completely distraught. He said he was leaving me, that he was truly sorry, but that he was going to lose Valentina and could not bear the thought."

A desperate, anxious Garzón interrupted her.

"Was she going to marry someone else?"

"How should I know? Do you think I wanted to know his reasons? He said he was leaving, and it was the first time he had ever said anything like that. All those years he had gone on seeing her, but he'd never threatened to leave. Never! I was always his wife."

The sergeant pulled back like an animal in wait.

"What else, Pilar, what else happened?"

"He was such a bundle of nerves he could not stay still. There was a dog fight that night, so he left the house at about eleven. I thought he would probably see her there, and then come home and tell me he was abandoning me then and there, that he was packing his suitcases and . . . "

She fell silent, and stared down at the floor.

"What happened then?"

"I was anxious, so I went out for a drive. I did not want to have to see him again that night. When I got back he was already in bed."

"What did he say?"

"Nothing. He said something had gone wrong so they had postponed the fight."

I lit a cigarette and thought about it.

"So then the next morning you heard that Valentina Cortés had been killed, and suspected your husband had done it."

"Yes, and a few days later I called you again. It seemed as though you hadn't uncovered anything. You came to question him, but then let him go at once. So I searched for his diary, then gave you the name of the fellow who worked for him. It was my way of putting you on the right track."

"But why, Pilar, why? By then the danger Valentina represented had been removed. You had your husband to yourself again."

"He wanted to leave me, and I knew nothing would ever be the same again. Besides, I knew he was a murderer. He did it, and he has to pay."

I looked at her suspiciously.

"I see. Of course, there could be another explanation . . . it could be that it was your husband who would accuse you of killing Valentina. I mean, trying to say you were the guilty one. If you think about it, going out on your own that night gave him the perfect opportunity. Tell me something, Pilar, do you have a dog at home?"

She had flushed, and looked at me inquiringly.

"Of course we do."

"What breed?"

"The breed my husband raises. A Staffordshire bull terrier called Pompey."

"Did you take Pompey with you that night?"

"I always take him with me when I go out at night! It makes me feel safer."

"I suppose you feel safer because your dog is trained to defend you?"

"Of course he is! What are you trying to imply? As I told you before: if I were guilty of anything, I wouldn't have called you."

"But just look, Pilar. There are two ways of considering all this. Either your husband could be trying to make you the guilty one, or you could be trying to do the same with him, and that's why you called. So tell me, has he tried to make out you murdered Valentina?"

She shifted nervously in her seat.

"Yes, he has. I'm still amazed at his gall. When the police came to question him the first time, he threatened to tell them it was me who'd killed her. He became obsessed with the idea and carried on saying it day after day. I think he's gone mad, he's capable of anything. I want it to be clear I am innocent of everything."

I scrutinized her.

"It will be clear, I promise you. If you are innocent, people will know. And they'll know if you're not, as well."

She left the room escorted by a cop. Her small cat-like face looked old and creased. Garzón leapt at me.

"Do you think she did it?"

"I don't know. It could be either of the two of them. We need to check whom he was with when the fight fell through, before he went home."

"I bet he has no alibi. I'd be surprised if it was his wife who killed Valentina."

"Doesn't that simply mean you want to get at him?"

"I promised there would be no violence, and I'll stick to my promise."

"Good, Garzón. Let's get him in here."

Augusto Ribas Solé knew what a tight spot he was in. He had been informed that his wife had been brought in as well, but nothing more. We gave him time to think this over. As soon as he came into my office I realized he wouldn't put up much of a fight. More than anxious, he looked at the end of his tether. His impressive appearance was ruined. He sat next to the sergeant, across the desk from me. I had decided to question him step by step.

"Señor Ribas," I said, "I'll try to be as clear as possible with you. We know a lot about you, including a few things you yourself are unaware of. So I am not going to try to get you to contradict yourself, or to lay traps for you. I don't think there is any need for that. On your side, I want you to make an effort not to deny things that are obvious. Let's be adult about this, then we can get it over with as quickly as possible."

He listened quietly, his eyes fixed on my face.

"Someone has decided to crucify you, señor Ribas. You've been betrayed. Do you want to know who it was? I'll tell you: it was your wife. She was the one who gave you away."

His big eyes gave only the slightest hint of surprise. He drilled them into me.

"Of course. She said that to try to save herself. She killed Valentina Cortés."

I got up, walked around the room, stood next to him.

"I'm not talking about Valentina."

"Who are you talking about then?"

"Do you remember the tip-off we got when you were holding a fight in the Free Trade Zone?"

"I don't know what you're talking about."

"You know very well what I'm talking about. It was your wife who tipped us off. She's just confessed as much."

Ribas' face fell. He could no longer look me in the eye.

"And yesterday she gave us another tip. That's why you're here now. She told us where to find Enrique Marzal, and Enrique Marzal told us all about what you get up to. So you see, Ribas, it's two against one. There's no way you can wriggle out of it."

"Shit," he growled.

"Why did you kill Valentina?"

"I didn't kill her!"

"Because she was going to leave you for someone else, or because she had all that evidence against you?"

"Evidence? What are you talking about?"

"Who killed Ignacio Lucena Pastor? Was that you too?"

"I don't know who he is."

All at once, Garzón leapt up and slammed his fist on the desk.

"Yes, you do. Goddamn it!"

Ribas started back in his chair. He blinked furiously, and did

not know what to say. Garzón was still shrieking. The color
drained from Ribas' face.

"Who was it? Who killed Lucena, you absolute bastard?"

"Her, it was her!" squealed Ribas.

"Her, who?"

"Valentina!"

"You're lying, you asshole!"

Garzón flung himself on the other man. He picked him up
by the lapels and shook him like a rag doll. I ran behind him,
grabbed him by both elbows, tried to restrain him.

"Calm down sergeant, calm down!"

He regained control of himself. He looked at me and bit his
lips. He was panting. We were all panting. I got him to sit
down again. I started the questioning again.

"It wasn't Valentina. At her house we found one of Lucena's
account books. If she had killed him, she would never have
kept something like that."

Ribas lowered his eyes, then dropped his head on his chin.
None of us said a word for some time. The stale atmosphere of
the room was punctuated by heavy breathing from all three of us.

"Where did you find the notebook?" Ribas eventually
asked.

"In Morgana's kennel."

He nodded reluctantly and covered his eyes with his hand.

"You ransacked my house to try to find it, didn't you? It was
serious evidence against you, wasn't it? And you killed Valentina because she wouldn't give it to you as a leaving present.
She wanted to keep some sort of control over you, because she
never trusted you. And she wanted to make sure you wouldn't
spoil the new life she was making for herself."

"No," he said, but without much conviction.

"Stop playing games, Ribas, you're done for."

His hands started to shake. He gave a deep sigh, then his
body seemed to relax.

"When I hit Lucena I had no intention of killing him. I was just settling scores. Perhaps I overdid it, but I did not intend to kill him. I learned later that he was in hospital, and then that he had died, but I never intended to kill him. If I had wanted to, I would have shot him. I have a gun license, I've been a hunter."

"Why didn't you go to the police?"

"I got scared. And I thought that, after all, Lucena was a poor wretch who had no family. My telling the truth would not change anything. It had been an accident and it was all in the past. It would only have complicated my life unnecessarily."

"And brought your business out into the open."

"My business is my kennels."

"And illegal dogfights, which must have brought in a nice bit of extra cash. Why did you kill him?"

"I didn't mean to kill him."

"O.K., why did you beat him up?"

"He had been siphoning off money for ages. He pocketed our earnings, he used my name to do business on the side. He even gave details about the fights to a journalist so he could make more dough. He was asking for it, and I warned him. He paid no attention, so I wanted to give him another warning. I hit him a bit too hard and he couldn't take it."

"Some warning."

"He was a weak sort."

"So you got Valentina to look for the money in Lucena's apartment."

"Yes."

"But she didn't find it. What she did discover were the account books, and she took the one that might implicate you. She was worried when she saw the lengths you were prepared to go to. She was trying to cover her back. It didn't even occur to her to keep the other two books as well. That was a stupid mistake, which shows she wasn't a real criminal."

"She said my name was in the book she had."

"It isn't."

"I always suspected as much."

"But even though that's what you suspected, you killed her."

"I swear I didn't do it! I've already confessed. I've told you the truth. I hit Lucena and killed him by accident. And yes, I organize dogfights. But I did not kill Valentina. I always loved her."

Steaming like a freshly baked loaf of bread, Garzón was struggling to control himself.

"Tell me what happened the night Valentina was attacked."

"She arrived that evening at the kennels. She said she was finished with me forever. After watching and deceiving your fat friend here for so long, she had fallen for him. They were going to get married "

He looked scornfully across at Garzón. I also cast a sideways glance in his direction. His face had relaxed all of a sudden. He had probably just heard what was most important to him.

"So you got angry with her."

"No. I begged her to stay, not to leave me."

"And threatened her."

"No. I promised I would leave my wife for her."

"And did you?"

"Yes, as soon as I saw Pilar I told her I was leaving. She'd always known Valentina was my lover, but it had not bothered her. But when she realized I was walking out on her . . . "

"She reacted badly?"

"No, she did what she always does, she burst into tears. But that was how we left it: I had a fight on, so I couldn't stay any longer."

"So what happened then?"

"Not all the gamblers showed up, so we postponed the fight. I went to the kennels, left the dogs we were going to use, and when I got home she was no longer there. By the time she came back I was already asleep. She told me she had gone out for a drive because she was so agitated."

"What time was that?"

"In the early hours, I don't know exactly."

"Didn't that seem strange to you?"

"I didn't give it much thought. But when I heard that Valentina had been killed that same night . . . "

"You thought of your wife."

"Yes."

"Of course, it might also have occurred to you how convenient it was she had gone out for a drive. That gave you the perfect excuse to accuse her."

"I swear to you that I did not kill Valentina. I'm not even saying for sure that it was Pilar; she is my wife, after all."

"And you're the perfect Spanish gentleman," Garzón shouted, his blood boiling again.

"I don't want to talk to you."

I feared the worst.

"This isn't a hotel, you know, you'll talk to whoever we say you should."

"Not to you."

"Was it you who searched my house?" I said.

"No, it wasn't me. I don't know what you're talking about."

"My house was searched and Lucena's dog was killed. They must have been looking for his account book. Didn't you know any of that?"

"No."

"It cannot have been your wife. She probably didn't even know the notebook existed."

"That's not true. I told her about it."

"You told her your lover had evidence that could be used against you?"

"Yes. It was a way to keep her quiet after she asked me to leave Valentina."

I could feel the tension building up in the air again, so I decided to call in a guard to take the suspect out. That was enough for now. Garzón was hissing like a pressure cooker.

"You've no idea how much I regret being a policeman," he said.

"Why's that?"

"Because if I weren't, I'd beat the living daylights out of that guy until . . . "

I paid no attention, and started gathering up my things.

"Where are you going?" he asked.

"Home. Do you know what time it is?"

"O.K., it's late, but we need to press home our advantage . . . our suspects are tired, so perhaps their defenses will be down."

"I'm the one whose defenses are down. We've just heard someone confess to a murder, Garzón. My head is spinning, I'm not sure what to think. I need to go over everything I've heard, to have a shower, get something to eat . . . and so do you."

"No, I'm fine."

"Well, you'll be better still in the morning. Go and have dinner with your son."

"My son? He left a week ago. I didn't even get the chance to say goodbye. He left a note for me on the fridge."

"You didn't have much to do with him, did you?"

"I had other things to worry about."

It was strange going home and not finding Freaky there. Perhaps I had gotten used to the pleasure of company, even of such a small animal. I slumped into my chair. I did not even have the strength to pour myself a whisky. A crime of passion and a beating that had gone too far. Not exactly sophisticated stuff. Love and money. Brutality and despair. Too vulgar for words. The list of reasons for murder is a short one, it's been the same since Shakespeare, since Cain and Abel. The rest is repetition. Life is almost as stupid as death, and much harder to bear. I was sleepy, my back ached, and yet what I most felt was an odd sense of missing something. What could it be? Perhaps I missed Freaky's misshapen head, or how easy it was to get my feelings across to him without having to say a word. One or other of the Ribas couple had killed Valentina. Now Garzón would never get to live in the country. How absurd! My eyes hurt along with all the rest. It's unhealthy to fill your mind for weeks with the same unedifying thoughts, they end up dirtying the receptacle, they might even make it rot. You have to know how to break free. I picked up the phone and called Juan Monturiol. I told him everything that had happened.

"So as you see, your contribution to the case was decisive."

"Professional skill, nothing more. How is Garzón?"

"Dreadful."

"What will you do if neither of the Ribases confesses?"

"I can't think of that now. Why don't you come over so we can have a drink together?"

"I don't think that's a good idea, Petra."

"Why not?"

There was a pause. I could hear him clearing his throat.

"I sincerely think we shouldn't go on with our relationship. Do you understand?"

"No."

"I'll never get used to it, Petra. Even if there isn't the slightest commitment between us, I like the woman I sleep with to see me as a priority, to call me, to keep me informed about what she is doing . . . and so on. I can't cope with the friendsbed sort of relationship. I'm very sorry about this, because I'm really attracted to you. Now do you understand what I'm trying to say?"

"Yes."

"This doesn't mean I'm angry with you. We can meet when you bring Freaky to my surgery."

"Freaky is dead. They killed him when they were searching my house."

"I'm sorry. Well, then, we'll meet in the neighborhood, we can have a coffee together sometimes."

"Yes, of course."

"I'd really like you to understand my point of view."

"I do understand it, and have no quarrel with it."

"That's good. Will you tell me how things end up with the Ribases?"

"I will."

I hung up. Jilted at my age! I'd deserved it. Who did I think I was, Miss Universe? A skittish fifteen-year-old, getting someone to fall in love with me at first sight? A femme fatale? Have a coffee together! How on earth was I going to settle for a coffee with Juan Monturiol sitting next to me? To see those strong hands of his unwrapping a sugar cube, his lips touching the rim of his cup, those huge green eyes staring at me. To hell with coffee! I was going to go to bed straightaway and forget about the shower or my dinner, forget about all this pile of trash that love affairs are. I missed Freaky more than I could say.

It is difficult preparing to bring two suspects face to face. Any strategy can fail because of the inertia the meeting provokes. And the closer the relationship between the two of them, the sooner that inertia sets in. So it was bound to rear its ugly head quite soon between a husband and wife. But apart from listening, drawing conclusions and, where necessary, directing things, there was little else we could do.

When his wife came in, Ribas stood up. I tried to analyze the furtive look they exchanged. It seemed to me as if it was one of mutual embarrassment. They made a perfect couple. He was strong, powerful, attractive. She looked fragile, lifeless and childish. Ribas was the first to speak. He sounded hurt, and spoke the words like a lament.

"How could you . . . ?"

She did not respond. All she did was frown and grit her teeth. She was determined not to give in. She stared down, crossing her legs with a strained bravado. Then she looked at me.

"Will I have to be here long?"

It was obvious a struggle was going on inside her. She was not used to being challenging or impolite.

"Pilar, we want you to confirm to your husband that it was you who called the police twice so that we would catch him in the midst of his illegal activities."

She kept her eyes on me as she replied:

"Yes, it was me."

"Could you tell us why?"

She said nothing.

"Reply, please."

She tried to appear cynical, but was not very convincing.

"I'm a responsible citizen."

"You have a charge of murder hanging over you: do you think this is the moment to try to be funny?"

Ribas interrupted us.

"She rang because she was consumed with jealousy."

She stiffened, but did not look in his direction, and said casually:

"Yes, that must be why I put up with you seeing that woman for five years."

"I should have left you ages ago. You don't have blood in your veins, you don't react to anything."

For the first time, she shot a glance at her husband. Her weak child's hands suddenly became a pair of claws.

"You've always been a louse, Augusto. You've never looked after me. You were always so sure you were superior; I was supposed to be so grateful for having you that you always treated me like a piece of dirt." Ribas was stunned; his eyes opened wide. "You were the best thing that could ever have happened to me, weren't you? The king! You felt you'd done enough by agreeing to marry me. I feel sorry for you!"

Ribas finally reacted:

"Shut up!"

His wife's tiny face turned a bright crimson.

"I won't!" she shouted. We were witnessing a revolution, probably one that had been brewing for some time. "I've been quiet for too long. Now it's my turn to speak! You're nothing but a failure, Augusto. Where are all the delights you promised, where's the big house in the country, the travels we were going to do? You were going to be on top of the world, and in the end you had to employ wretched dog thieves to make a few extra pennies."

Her husband was squirming. He appealed to me.

"Tell her to shut up."

I spread my hands as though I could do nothing about it.

"We're here to talk."

"Thanks to you, we didn't even have children! All you ever did was chase other women, and the more vulgar the better."

"That's what you couldn't stand, wasn't it? That's why you killed her."

"You were the one who killed her! You were the one who got into a fury when she said she was leaving you for the policeman! Leaving a god like you for a fat old policeman! I suppose deep down that was what got to you most: a woman's affection means nothing to you. All you have ever wanted in your life is to be important, to be the center of things. Why did you have to get mixed up in all that shady business: didn't we have enough money already?"

Ribas started up threateningly. Garzón threw himself at him a little too eagerly.

"That's enough, all of you! If you don't stay calm, we'll have to suspend this interview."

I cast a worried glance at Garzón. He let go of Ribas's arm and sat down. Ribas undid the top button of his shirt and snorted like a horse. When he spoke, it was in more measured tones.

"Don't go on lying, Pilar. You were the one who killed her. You've punished me enough. Tell them why you went out that night."

"Because I was frightened of seeing you, of having to watch you leave. I've been frightened of you far too often, Augusto. That's not normal between man and wife."

"Nonsense! You took Pompey and went to her house. You couldn't bear the thought of me leaving you. You set the dog on her and kept ordering him to attack until he killed her. Then you thought you could make it look as though I had done it. Or perhaps that was what you'd planned right from the start!"

"No! You killed her because you couldn't persuade her to leave the policeman!"

We were headed up a blind alley. The knot in my stomach had mysteriously converted into a ringing in my head.

"That's quite enough! I think it would be better to suspend this session until tomorrow."

I had them taken out. I studied Garzón's face. There was a smear of blood on his mouth where he had bitten his bottom lip. I gave him a tissue. He wiped his mouth. We sat there looking at each other. We did not know what to say. I could not bear his eyes any longer, and looked down at my watch to see what time it was.

"What do you make of it all?" he asked finally.

"I don't know. What about you?"

"I think he did it."

"Why?"

"He had more to lose. Remember the account book."

"People don't always calculate before they kill."

"But he sent Marzal to your house."

"I'm amazed that someone with so much criminal experience could be so stupid."

It was clear that Garzón was betting on Ribas being the guilty one. I wondered how much this was an unconscious wish that might help ease his own pain. His anger at a rival for Valentina's affections was leading him to see him as a monster. A proof of that was the fact that he saw the account book as the reason for the murder, forgetting the emotional element.

The way things stood, I felt sure it would be our suspects who would provide us with the answers. And so it proved. The next day, as soon as I entered the station, a desk man told me Ribas wanted to talk to me in private. I immediately took this to mean that he did not want Garzón present. Yes, that was probably the only way we could make any progress

Ribas looked grim, and wanted to talk. He said he had not been able to sleep at all. The time spent in one of our cells had enabled him to get a clearer notion of who the guilty person must be; he continued, of course, to insist it was not him. He was well aware that the charge he was facing for killing someone more or less by accident was very different from one of murdering someone in cold blood. He asked if he could see his wife alone. I said I could not allow that; I could not permit any attempt by him to influence her outside my control.

"All right. At least let me talk to her with just you in the room. I mean without your colleague."

"Do you really think you have so much influence over her she'll tell the truth?"

"I'm sure of it."

"It didn't look like that yesterday. Perhaps her attitude towards you has changed."

"I know what I'm talking about."

"All right."

"One more thing. I don't want anything of what I say to be used against me. Remember, I'm only trying to get her to tell the truth."

"We'll see."

"What about that sergeant?"

"Don't worry, he won't be there."

I was expecting a violent reaction from Garzón when I told him this, but instead all I got was a look confirming my treachery. *Et tu, Brute?* it said. Yes, me, too, there was a murder at stake here, I had no time to dwell on hurt feelings. He agreed reluctantly and went back to his office, where I suppose he spent some of the worst hours of his life. I set up the fresh confrontation between our two suspects, trying hard not to reach any foregone conclusions. I was surprised at how calm I was. I was determined to behave like the three Chinese monkeys: to see, hear, and say nothing.

Pilar came into the room before her husband. I was able to verify a simple but terrifying truth: a single night under arrest can undermine the character of anyone who is not used to it. She looked pale and haggard, but above all lost, as if her dignity had collapsed. When Ribas appeared, she looked at him as if he were a stranger. She didn't even look at me. We sat in silence for more than a minute, which to me seemed like an anxious eternity. Finally, it was Ribas who spoke first.

"Are you tired?" he asked his wife.

She frowned, and put a hand on her back as she straightened up.

"I want to go home," she said.

"Don't worry, you will."

There was a strange warmth to Ribas's voice. He went over to Pilar and took her by the hand. She did not resist. Nor did she protest when he gave her a few comforting taps on the shoulder.

"You'll soon be home."

He was in complete control of the situation. She slumped in her chair.

She started talking without looking at him. I had ceased to exist for both of them.

"Why did you have to leave with that woman?"

"But as you saw, I didn't leave. I came to sleep beside you, as always."

"Because she threw you out!"

"I came to sleep in our house, and I would never have left, you know."

"You've hurt me a lot, Augusto. This time you really did."

"And you hurt me, my love, you hurt me. That's why we're here, because you told the police."

"I wanted to punish you. I wanted it all to finish, I wanted everything to finish between you and that woman."

She began to cry gently. He consoled her by clicking his tongue, as if she were a baby. They were both whispering. Watching them, I felt anguished at her wounded, defenseless pathos.

"But you'll soon be going home."

"What about you?"

"I can't go, Pilar. You told them about me, don't you remember? I'll have to go to jail. I'll go for you, too, I'll tell them it was me who killed Valentina. I'll be guilty for both of us. You go home and wait for me. I'll be back some day."

This was the crucial moment. I had lowered my eyes out of a sense of shame, but now I raised them and looked straight at her. I could see her struggling with her tears, pain, and bewilderment.

"No," she said at last. "I don't want you to do that. I killed her, I'll go to jail for as long as you. I killed her and I'm not sorry. Now she no longer exists."

"She had already ceased to exist for me. For me there is only you."

There were tears in her eyes. Ribas looked up at me. I spoke for the first time, and my voice sounded strange in the midst of theirs.

"Did you kill her, Pilar?"

She nodded her head several times.

"And it was you who came to my house to look for the notebook?"

She nodded again.

"I wanted to get rid of it. I wanted to get rid of everything that could stand in the way of my husband and me. I wanted to find the notebook he was so scared of, then wave it in front of his face and say: 'See? There's nothing left of all that, the notebook's gone, the woman is gone . . . now you and I can start all over again . . . '"

"But it was you who called the police! How could you do both things at the same time?"

"I don't know. I must have been crazy. I don't know!"

"Can you describe my house?"

She wiped her tears away with her hand. Ribas was still standing next to her. He stroked her head. She tried to concentrate. When she spoke it was with an innocent little girl's voice.

"Yes, more or less. Your house is in Poble Nou. In the hallway there's a long oblong picture, and there's a small garden at the back. In the living room there's a beige sofa. There are lots of books on a bookshelf, and in the drawers you keep a whole lot of table linen, all of it green."

That detail would have been enough in itself. For some absurd reason, I had bought all the green table linen in a sale. But she went on to describe my bedroom with surprising accuracy. Apart from looking for the notebook, she must have been curious as well.

"What about the dog?" I asked.

For the first time, she raised her eyes to me. I could see the fear and horror in them. As she spoke, her chin started to quiver.

"At first he was quiet and even wagged his tail. Then all of a sudden he began to bark. He went on and on, getting louder and louder. I was afraid someone would hear him. So I hit him. I hit him on the head with the chopping board you have in your kitchen. It was dreadful, I . . . the blood came pouring out . . . I didn't mean to . . . "

She began to cry hysterically, hiccupping, twitching, gasping for breath.

"But that can't have affected you so much, Pilar. After all, you had already killed Valentina."

She looked up, her face still contorted by tears.

"I didn't even have to touch her. It was Pompey who did that, I didn't even get my hands dirty, it was like a . . . "

She broke off, so I finished the sentence for her.

"Like a game, wasn't it? Or like one of your husband's training sessions. A dummy that the dog attacks and bites. Only this time, the dummy was real. That was how it was, wasn't it? You were hardly aware that you were killing her."

She stopped hiccupping for a moment, and looked at me with a faint gleam of lucidity.

"Yes, that's right."

"That's very understandable, Pilar, but don't deceive yourself: you killed her and you meant to. She probably opened the door because you said you wanted to talk to her, then you set your dog on her and killed her. You killed her in a savage fashion. And you got rid of all the evidence and dragged her out into the garden. All that was deliberate, premeditated. It's the work of someone determined to kill. It's no game."

She leaned forward in her chair, wracked by violent sobs. Ribas bent over her, straightened her up, took her shaking head in his arms.

"Leave her, leave her now. She's confessed, is there any need to torture her any more?"

It seemed to me this was not an act, but that he really was trying to protect her. They made a strange picture. He stood there, tall, strong-looking still, holding against him the seated body of the frail woman who was his wife. In some odd way, they were consoling each other. I left the office without saying a word. I was not sure whether I felt moved or revolted.

When I entered Garzón's office, he controlled himself sufficiently to let me speak without asking any questions. Before I said anything, I lit myself a cigarette with trembling hands.

"O.K., sergeant, we have our murderer."

Wild-eyed, he interrogated the air.

"Ribas's wife killed Valentina."

"Are you sure?"

"Yes, you can take it for a fact."

He stood up and ran out of the room. I ran after him, my heart in my mouth.

"Sergeant, where are you going?"

I saw him go up to Pilar. He made the two policemen escorting her come to a halt in the corridor. I heard what he said to her.

"Was it that dog called Pompey you took with you?"

"Yes, I've already said that."

"So he killed Valentina?"

"Yes. Can't you leave me in peace?"

"Where is the dog now?"

"At the kennels."

"Which part?"

"He's the only dog loose in the garden. Now leave me alone, will you?"

I was worried Garzón might slap her or something, but all he did was turn on his heel, pick up his raincoat, and rush out. I followed him. At the entrance to the station I found Ribas with two guards. He was on his way to be charged. When he saw me, he burst into tears, his defenses finally breached.

"However strange this might sound, inspector, I beg you to treat her well. Pilar is weak, and maybe I behaved badly towards

her, but she's still my wife. I don't know if you understand what
I'm trying to say."

"I understand," I said, but in fact I did not understand a
thing. All I wanted to do was to get out of there; Garzón had
vanished and I might not be able to find him. But I caught up
with him just as he was getting into his car.

"Where are you going, Fermín?"

"For a drive."

"Can I come with you?"

"Suit yourself," he said, giving a terse shrug of his shoulders.

We left the city. Neither of us spoke. Garzón had put the car
radio on so loud there was no possibility of us talking. It was
growing dark outside. The radio program was an interview. One
of the hundreds of psychiatrists who write books was holding
forth. The devaluation of the self. "In an increasingly materialist
world, social success is all that counts for the individual." What
the devil was he talking about? Lucena, the dregs, miserable dog
thieves and multifarious swindlers, ageing, lonely lovers, married
couples who love and destroy each other. None of them would
ever lie on a psychiatrist's couch. The individual, the self, social
success, rubbish, waste, human waste. And love.

The car came to a halt. We were outside Ribas's kennels. It
looked as dark and impenetrable as a castle. Garzón got out and
I did the same. He went to the entry gate. A huge chorus of barking started up and then immediately Pompey appeared. He
looked as fierce and challenging as ever. He thrust his nose
through the wire, baring his teeth. The noise he made was not so
much a loud, warning bark as a deep growl, a hot, threatening
exhalation of breath. Garzón stared intently at him through the
gloom. He was quite calm: his expression did not change, his eyes
were unblinking. I felt cold and, without knowing why, afraid.

"What are you doing, Fermín?"

He did not reply.

"Come on, let's go!"

He did not move a muscle. Night had fallen and there was a satanic chorus of dogs barking incessantly . . . what was he hoping to discover in that animal, the remains of Valentina's soul, its transmigration?

"Sergeant, let's just get out of here."

Garzón put his hand under his jacket and pulled out his revolver. He took aim.

"Don't do it, Fermín. Let it be. The dog isn't to blame, is it?"

He was still pointing the gun at the dog, staring down the barrel. He was breathing slowly.

"You'll feel bad afterwards! Why kill it? He's innocent. Let him be!"

He raised his arm. The dog knew it was going to die. It fell silent, raised its head like a brave prisoner in front of a firing-squad. Garzón fired. All the other dogs stopped barking too. Pompey fell to the ground and lay there, a small, compact bundle. Then one solitary dog began to bark again, and after that another one, and another. Soon all of them were howling. With my heart in my mouth, I went up to the sergeant. He was sobbing quietly. Tears and mucus ran down his limp mustache. I put my hand on his arm.

"Let's go, Fermín. It's very late."

We left as stealthily as we had arrived. I felt as though I had witnessed the execution of the Tsar of Russia, but it was only the death of a dog. One more death. A heart no longer beating. One more death. Men and dogs; women and dogs. All defenseless creatures in the night.

EPILOGUE

I invited Angela and Juan Monturiol home for lunch. I owed them that, at least. They had the right to know what had happened. I prepared three different salads, a good quantity of salmon, and a huge cake decorated with a chocolate dog. Ridiculous, really, nobody was in the mood for jokes. My guests were taken aback at the way things had worked out.

"What a crafty woman!" Angela said of Pilar. "She controlled everything from the shadows."

"I felt sorry for her."

"Do you think she was unbalanced in some way?"

"Even if she wasn't permanently disturbed, she must have had some sort of breakdown. She wasn't really the murdering type."

"And who is the murdering type?" Juan said, making it sound as much an affirmation as a question.

"Well, as a policewoman I've studied different sorts."

"What good are studies compared to the complexities of human beings!" he exclaimed, philosophically.

"What surprises me is so much passion among people who are no longer young," Angela said, with a touch of disgust in her voice.

"And what about that married couple?" I added. "They loved each other, hated each other, attacked each other, helped one another . . . "

"Isn't that how it always is?" Monturiol declared, with another of his rhetorical questions.

"I hope not!" I said, with too much emphasis.

"Does that mean you're hoping to get married again?" the vet said immediately.

"I was talking in general."

"Above all, it was a tragedy," the Angela concluded.

"What surprises me is that it never occurred to Ribas that his wife could betray him," said Juan.

"He thought he had her under his thumb. He despised her; that's why he never took any precautions."

"But she grew tired of it. Sometimes we women can show some common sense."

We both looked at poor Juan Monturiol, who squirmed instinctively in his seat.

"It really was tragic," my fellow-accuser said.

"And damned complicated! Who would have thought it involved dog fights!"

"We haven't made much progress since the days of the Romans," said Monturiol.

"By the way, Petra, what happened to Valentina's dog?"

"Once the case is closed, I suppose it will be put down."

"That's terrible! Couldn't I adopt it?" asked Angela.

"Would you do that?"

"It's only a poor animal who has lost its mistress."

"I don't know. I can make some enquiries."

"I'd like that."

Juan glanced at his watch.

"Ladies, I'm afraid I have to open my surgery. I'll leave you."

He kissed Angela on both cheeks. I went out into the hallway with him. I held out my hand and he took it.

"Thank you for all your help. You're my favorite vet."

"My pleasure."

"I'd like to know if it really was a pleasure."

He stared me straight in the eye, then smiled.

"Rest assured, it has been a pleasure."

I smiled back at him. He turned and headed off to his van. I watched sadly as the dog painted on the back disappeared round the street corner. I sighed.

Back in the dining room, Angela looked melancholy too.

"More coffee?" I suggested.

She pushed her empty cup toward me.

"Petra, now we're on our own, there's something I'd like to ask you. Was Valentina really thinking of marrying Fermín? It seems to me she might have been playing a game: perhaps she just told her lover she was getting married so that he would finally leave his wife."

"We'll never know. It's a secret she's taken with her to the grave."

"Do you think Fermín feels that doubt too?"

"He doesn't seem like a man who likes to deceive himself."

"Then he must have suffered twice as much, and to be suffering still."

"Have you thought of calling him and talking to him? Perhaps you could . . ."

She shook her head, and turned very serious.

"No, Petra, that's out of the question. I know when things are over once and for all."

I studied her pleasant, friendly face. I tapped her gently on the back of her hand.

"He'll never know what a woman he lost."

She made an effort to smile.

"I'd like you to do me a favor. Give him back this."

She pulled the little gold locket with Garzón's photo inside it out of her pocket. She laid it on the table.

"Do you think that's necessary?"

"I think it's best. There is no denying the past, but it's not good to carry around reminders or fetishes."

"You could be right."

She stood up with all the dramatic impetus of a fictional heroine. She put on her jacket, and we embraced. I shut the door behind me. I had promised I would go and see her from time to time, to have tea together. It was not very likely I would ever need her expertise about dogs again, but at least in her company I could enjoy the gentle glow that comes from true kindness.

When I got to my office I started thinking everything over. The first phrase that came to mind was: case closed. Case closed. Ignacio Lucena Pastor seemed like something from the distant past, lost and buried in time, like a dream or a forgotten article from some Sunday magazine. Of course, as a result of that shadow, that hardly seemed to exist in this world, a woman had been killed and my colleague had a broken heart. Occupational hazards, I told myself, trying to use this banal phrase to help me return to my daily routine.

The next thing I did was to look at my diary. I knew perfectly well whom I should phone. I hummed as I picked up the phone and dialed:

"Doctor Castillo, is that you?"

The scientist who was so curious about police matters was so taken aback that at first he could not say a word. He could not believe it was me, or understand the reason for my call.

"I hope you've read the conclusion of the case in the papers."

"Yes, I was very relieved."

"Relieved?"

"Well, I felt as though I'd been saved from the electric chair or something. I saw "The Wrong Man" again on TV the other day, and I broke out in a cold sweat."

I could not help laughing out loud.

"You can laugh, but you really unnerved me."

"I think I owe you an apology, and that's why I called. But

you did phone when I was under a lot of stress. Besides, why were you so interested in the case?"

"Well, I haven't the faintest idea! I always liked thrillers. And it wasn't just that, it was . . . are you single, inspector?"

"Divorced, why?"

"You'll think I'm stupid, but I was wondering . . . I was wondering if you'd come out for a drink with me, so we could have a chat. I was divorced not so long ago as well. But then, when it seemed as though you were about to accuse me of the crime, I changed my mind. I thought it would be safer to stay out of your clutches."

"I'm not surprised. But I can think of a way out of your predicament."

"Such as?"

"We could finally have that drink."

"I'd be delighted! And following the drink, it might be a good idea to have dinner in a restaurant. I mean tonight, if you're free."

"Count on me."

"Good! I'll pick you up at eight at your office."

"No, I'm taking the afternoon off. I'll go and find you at the Faculty."

"If you don't remember me, you'll be able to identify me by my murderer's look."

I laughed again. It had never occurred to me that the professor might like to go out with me. Fine, he had a good sense of humor, so it could be a memorable evening. We had things in common: both of us undertook research in our different fields. He tried to alleviate human suffering and I wallowed in it. A small but significant difference. How sterile police work was! I thought to myself, turning over in my mind all that had taken place recently. There was no chance of changing the future, of avoiding what had already happened. I remembered my short-lived companion Freaky, with his ear probably bitten by one of the fighting dogs. How blind I had been not to see it! I couldn't even protect him, help from him from his dreadful fate. I got up and went into Garzón's office.

The sergeant was sitting morosely at his desk. He looked up at me without a great deal of interest.

"How are things, inspector?"

I could see he had been doodling on a bit of paper. I collapsed into the nearest chair without asking.

"What the hell are you doing?"

"As you can see, not a lot."

"We'll have to make a start on the written report."

"I don't feel like it."

"Nor do I."

"There's plenty of time."

"Yes."

I crossed my legs and stared at the bare walls.

"Why don't you hang a picture or two in here? There's no personal touch in this lair of yours."

"Bah!"

I knew this was not the best moment to carry out my errand, but it would only be worse if I left it. I might not even have the courage to do it. I took Angela's locket out of my bag and handed it to Garzón.

"Fermín, I was asked to give you this."

He looked at it wearily. Picked it up. Rummaged in his pocket and pulled out another, identical heart. It must have been removed from Valentina's dead body. He showed me them both in the rather rough, time-worn palm of his hand.

"Life gives me back my presents," he said.

"Life never gives anything back."

"Then I'm being punished for being such a complete asshole."

"There's no such thing as punishment, either."

"What is there then?"

"I don't know, not much: music, the sun, friendship . . . "

"And the faithfulness of dogs."

"Yes, that too."

We exchanged sad and weary glances. I had to take a deep breath before I could go on.

"And there's drink as well. What about going across the street and having a quick one?"

"I don't know if I feel like it."

"Oh, come on Fermín. Stop this *Dame aux Camélias* act! I'm offering you some spiritual medicine!"

"O.K., let's go. Anything rather than having to sit here and listen to your insults."

We left the police station. The guard on the door saluted us. We went into the Jarra de Oro and ordered a couple of whiskies.

"I bet you can't guess who I'm having dinner with tonight?"

"Juan Monturiol."

"No chance! That's water under the bridge. I have a date with Doctor Castillo, remember him?"

"Are you really going out on a date?"

"Of course, and, if he doesn't watch out, I'm going to seduce him. I don't have any crazy scientists in my femme fatale files."

Garzón laughed the scandalized laugh he always came out with whenever I began to talk dirty.

"Petra, you're incredible!"

"I am, aren't I?"

"You certainly are."

At that point our whiskies arrived. The waiter slid them on to the bar with a practiced gesture. We clinked glasses discreetly and proposed a toast to ourselves. At that moment we could not think of anyone else who deserved it more.

Barcelona, December 4 1996

ACKNOWLEDGEMENTS

The background information needed to write
this novel was provided thanks to the close collaboration of Antonio Arasa, an expert in canine behaviour. He supervised the book and con-
tributed a large amount of information to help
make the plot convincing.

I should also like to thank Carlos Esteller
(veterinary surgeon), and the Enivornmental
Department of the Mossos d'Esquadra de la
Generalitat de Catalunya y Guardia Urbana of
Barcelona for their kind help.

ABOUT THE AUTHOR

Alicia Giménez-Bartlett was born in Almansa, Spain, in 1951 and has lived in Barcelona since 1975. After the enormous success of her first novels, she decided to leave her work as a teacher of Spanish literature and to dedicate herself full-time to writing. In 1997, she was awarded the Feminino Lumen prize for the best female writer in Spain. She subsequently launched her Petra Delicado series, whose success rapidly made her one of Spain's most popular and best-loved crime writers.

AVAILABLE NOW from EUROPA EDITIONS

The Days of Abandonment
by Elena Ferrante
translated by Ann Goldstein

"Stunning . . . The raging, torrential voice of the author is something rare." —Janet Maslin, *The New York Times*

"I could not put this novel down. Elena Ferrante will blow you away." —Alice Sebold, author of *The Lovely Bones*

Cooking with Fernet Branca
by James Hamilton-Paterson

Gerald Samper, an effete English snob, has his own private hilltop in Tuscany where he wiles away his time working as a ghostwriter for celebrities and inventing wholly original culinary concoctions—including ice-cream made with garlic and the bitter, herb-based liqueur of the book's title. Gerald's idyll is shattered by the arrival of Marta, on the run from a crime-riddled former soviet republic. A series of hilarious misunderstands brings this odd couple into ever closer and more disastrous proximity. "A work of comic genius." —*The Independent*

Minotaur

by Benjamin Tammuz

translated by Kim Parfitt and Mildred Budny

An Israeli secret agent falls hopelessly in love with
a young English girl. Using his network of shady contacts
and his professional expertise, he takes control of her life without
ever revealing his identity. Minotaur, named "Book of the Year"
by Graham Greene, is a complex and utterly original story about
a solitary man driven from one side of Europe to the other
by his obsession. "A novel about the expectations and compromises
that humans create for themschres... very much in the manner of
William Faulkner and Lawrence Durrel" –*The New York Times*

The Big Question

by Wolf Erlbruch

translated by Michael Reynolds

Best Book at the 2004 Children's Book Fair in Bologna.
A stunningly beautiful and poetic illustrated book for children
that poses the biggest of all big questions: why am I here?
A chorus of voices—including the cat's, the baker's, the pilot's
and the soldier's—offers us some answers. But nothing is certain,
except that as we grow each one of us will pose the question
differently and be privy to different answers.

Total Chaos

by Jean-Claude Izzo

translated by Howard Curtis

"Jean-Claude Izzo's [...] growing literary renown and huge sales are leading to a recognizable new trend in continental fiction: the rise of the sophisticated Mediterranean thriller . . . Caught between pride and crime, racism and fraternity, tragedy and light, messy urbanization and generous beauty, the city for [detective Fabio Montale] is a Utopia, an ultimate port of call for exiles. There, he is torn between fatalism and revolt, despair and sensualism." —*The Economist*
This first installment in the legendary Marseilles Trilogy sees Fabio Montale turning his back on a police force marred by corruption and racism and taking the fight against the mafia into his own hands.

Hangover Square

by Patrick Hamilton

Adrift in the grimy pubs of London at the outbreak of World War II, George Harvey Bone is hopelessly infatuated with Netta, a cold, contemptuous, small-time actress. George also suffers from occasional blackouts. During these moments one thing is horribly clear: he mission is to murder Netta. "Hamilton [...] is a sort of urban Thomas Hardy: [...] always a pleasure to read, and as a social historian he is unparalleled." —Nick Hornby

I Loved You For Your Voice
by Sélim Nassib
translated by Alison Anderson

Love, desire, and song set against the colorful backdrop
of modern Egypt. The story of the Arab world's greatest
and most popular singer, Umm Kalthum, told through
the eyes of the poet Ahmad Rami, who wrote her lyrics
and loved her in vain all his life. Spanning over five decades
in the history of modern Egypt, this passionate tale of love
and longing provides a key to understanding the soul,
the aspirations and the disappointments of the Arab world.
"A total immersion into the Arab world's magic and charm."
—*Avvenimenti*

Love Burns
by Edna Mazya
translated by Dalya Bilu

Ilan, a middle-aged professor of astrophysics, discovers
that his young wife is having an affair. Terrified of losing her,
he decides to confront her lover instead. Their meeting ends
in the latter's murder—the unlikely murder weapon being
Ilan's pipe—and in desperation, Ilan disposes of the body
in the fresh grave of his kindergarten teacher.
But when the body is discovered… "Starts out
as a psychological drama and becomes a strange, funny,
unexpected hybrid: a farce thriller. A great book." —*Ma'ariv*

Departure Lounge
by Chad Taylor

Two young women mysteriously disappear. The lives of those
they have left behind—lovers, acquaintances, and strangers
intrigued by their disappearance—intersect to form a captivating
latticework of odd coincidences and surprising twists of fate.
Urban noir at its stylish and intelligent best. "Entropy noir . . .
The hypnotic pull lies in the zigzag dance of its forlorn characters,
casting a murky, uneasy sense of doom." —*The Guardian*

The Jasmine Isle
by Ioanna Karystiani
translated by Michael Eleftheriou

A modern love story with the force of an ancient Greek tragedy.
Set on the spectacular Cycladic island of Andros, The Jasmine Isle,
one of the finest literary achievements in contemporary
Greek literature, recounts the story of the old sea wolf,
Spyros Maltambès, and the beautiful Orsa Saltaferos,
sentenced to marry a man she doesn't love and to watch
while the man she does love is wed to another.